Siblings

By:

Julie C. Lombard

Contributing proof-editors: Mary Lombard, Rebecca Fox & Mary Huckstep.

Cover Design by: Jessie Vaughan

ISBN 10::0997177128
ISBN- 13:978-0997177121

Just to be as clear and factual as possible in a work of fiction; INTERPOL itself has no agents who are able to make arrests. Instead, it is an international organization that functions as a network of criminal law enforcement agencies from different countries. Therefore, characters referred to as INTERPOL in this book are simply done so for simplification purposes and would, in reality, be part of their country's national police force. The below is extracted directly from the INTERPOL website as of October 1st 2017.
https://www.interpol.int/en

INTERPOL enables police in our 192 member countries to work together to fight international crime. We provide a range of policing expertise and capabilities, supporting three main crime programs: Counter-terrorism, Cybercrime, and Organized crime.

At the heart of every INTERPOL member country is a National Central Bureau (NCB), linking national police with our global network. It is typically a division of the national police agency or investigation service and serves as the contact point for all INTERPOL activities in the field.

Staffed by highly trained police officers, NCBs are the lifeblood of INTERPOL, contributing to our criminal databases and cooperating together on cross-border investigations, operations and arrests.

INTERPOL cooperates closely with a number of partners in the public sector, and maintains representative offices at the African Union, the European Union and the United Nations.

Other public-sector partners include the World Customs Organization, CEMAC (Economic Community of Central African States) and numerous government agencies.

We also work with select partners from the private sector, encompassing both for-profit entities and non-profit bodies, such as non-governmental organizations and foundations.

The organization's official name is "ICPO-INTERPOL" The official abbreviation "ICPO" stands for 'International Criminal Police Organization'. In French this is "O.I.P.C.", which stands for "Organization internationale de police criminelle".

The word "INTERPOL" is a contraction of "international police", and was chosen in 1946 as the telegraphic address.

Special thanks to my mother,
I never would have finished this
without your support!

Chapter One

North of Geneva: Dec. 2015

Magdeline watched as each flake fell, no two alike she thought, as she twisted an auburn lock around her finger. Each flake's pattern was like its own DNA. It really was awesome to consider. Trillions of little white flakes with their own intricate design, floating through the air only to land and melt into one another.

Her reverie ended at a knock on the door.

"Come in," she called.

Soren entered and shut the door behind him. She turned in her wheelchair, as he held out a thin folder to her.

"To be honest, I've never seen anything like it. We ran the sequencing three times at two different labs, all with the same results. Are you going to tell me what this is?" he asked.

"You know I can't. I have to maintain doctor patient confidentiality."

"Will you at least have dinner with me Maggie?"

"I'm afraid I have other plans tonight."

"Oh?"

"But I could do lunch?"

"Okay then. Cafeteria at...?"

"1:00 O'clock."

"1:00 O'clock it is."

Magdeline opened the folder alongside another with her own name as the patient. Somewhere in these results had to lie the answer.

Seattle: Dec. 2018

Alice scanned through the photos she'd taken the night before and stored her camera bag. Who was he? She had no doubt that he worked for her parents, yet he seemed to be keeping, rather than divulging her secrets. He had popped up randomly in photos ever since she had turned eighteen. From what she could see, he appeared handsome, with a tall steady frame, and neatly cropped blond hair the color of maize. She had thought to simply confront him, but she frequently didn't even know he had been there until she went back through the photos. She had usually felt his presence though, and that was when she would pull out her Nikon. If she hadn't been so sure that he worked for her parents, she might have been scared.

Her parents, Edgar and Suzanna Morgan had started their company, "Morgan Acquisitions", nearly fifty years ago, and Alice had worked there from age sixteen, after she had attained her MBA from the university of Washington. She attended parties and meetings with company owners and managers from around the world, and although she had never traveled aside from a few meetings she attended with her father in New York, she spoke French, Spanish, Russian, Chinese and Japanese fluently and could hold her own in Latin, German and Greek as well.

Alice's parents had been in their late forties when she was born and had been highly protective of her, but while Alice had always believed they loved her, she never really felt it the way she thought she should. She thought back to the photos and wondered what her watcher thought, then laughed when she remembered how she had eluded him the night before and made it onto the ferry to Bremerton. She had spotted him a few minutes later from the upper deck, as he rode another ferry bound for Bainbridge Island.

Her parents also tried to fix her up with what they deemed suitable young men, but Alice had always felt bored by them. Maybe that was why, to a degree, she was more intrigued than annoyed by the stranger in the photos.

Today Alice Morgan found herself being sent on her first solo business trip to New York. At seventy-nine, Edgar Morgan had decided to start turning over a little more control to his daughter. He also had another motive in Alice going to New York, namely Albert Starling. At thirty-five, this young man had the tenacity Edgar admired, and if Albert could take care of Alice as well as he did business, then his bed would be made as the next CEO of Morgan Acquisitions. Suzanna Morgan was also anxious that Alice make, what she considered an appropriate and logical business match. What Edgar and Suzanna had failed to notice or really even consider, was that Alice couldn't stand the man!

Alice was also dreading sitting in the stuffy boardrooms and wearing stuffy suits every day with shoes that made her feel like a stilt walker.

Kicking off her three-inch heels, Alice leaned back in her first-class seat, as the plane began to pull away from the gate. She was watching the first flakes of falling snow, mixed with typical Seattle rain, as it fell from the gray December 5th sky. It was the beep of a text that broke her reverie. It was Albert. It read, "Just wanted to let you know that I will be at JFK personally to pick you up. I also made reservations for dinner at *Le' Miracles* for six. Albert xxx."

Alice hit delete and turned off her phone for the flight.

As the plane descended into JFK, Alice thumbed through the Skylines magazine. She knew there would be no time to enjoy the sights. What time wasn't spent in the offices, Albert was sure to consume.

Alice had to figure out a way to lose him for a few hours, to stroll through Central Park, visit The Met, and take a subway. The last would be unheard of. She knew there would be a company car and driver or Albert there with her at every move. It was suffocating. Why hadn't she been able to find some reason, any excuse, not to come?

She turned the page and saw a photo of a wedding on a tropical island. Other photos showed couples and families frolicking on the beach. They all looked so happy. She closed the magazine and stuffed it back into the seat pocket.

Alice longed for freedom. It seemed that day in and day out, throughout her life, she always felt as though there had been somebody watching her and not just the man in her photos. There never seemed to be any day when her parents didn't want to know her every move. One of them called her every morning, and every day when she got off work, they would call again to make sure she was home safe and ask what her plans were for the evening. She always hated to lie, so she had needed to become creative in her answers. Weekends were no different. They always had something scheduled that they expected her to attend or some man they wanted her to meet. Alice knew that her seemingly close relationship with her parents was something many envied, but the truth was, it wasn't as close as it seemed. They never discussed anything personal, and every time Alice made an attempt at expressing her feelings, the subject was somehow changed. Yet, they wanted to know as many facts about what she was doing when not in their actual presence as they could dig up. What was she eating? Was she taking her vitamins? What was she wearing, watching, reading...? It was either the most impersonal personal relationship or the most personal impersonal relationship a family could possibly have. Alice couldn't decide which, and she was certain that it would be no different here in

New York with Albert. In fact, it would likely be worse. At least at home she had learned how to carve out a few moments of time for herself. In New York she was on a tight schedule, and all of her time not in the actual office would be taken up dining with clients and Albert.

When the plane arrived at the gate in New York, and the other passengers reached into the overhead bins to retrieve their luggage, Alice, in no hurry, decided to wait as long as possible.

The last people off before her were a young couple holding hands. Alice watched them go, as her phone beeped with another message from Albert. Why hadn't she just left it off? Alice ignored it, as she slipped her shoes back on, grabbed her bag, and headed toward the exit.

"Thank you for flying with us. We hope you enjoy your stay in New York," chirped a perky blond stewardess with a wide smile.

"Thank you," Alice replied half-heartedly, as she stepped off the plane.

Albert was waiting by the baggage claim. He was an attractive man at six feet tall, with black hair, and a chiseled jaw, wearing a well-tailored suit. Albert could have been a model for GQ, and he knew it.

He ran his fingers through his hair, as he scanned the area for Alice. He also made sure to flash his flawless smile at several passing women, some of whom glanced back at him with returning smiles.

This is the image Alice watched as she approached. She rolled her eyes and muttered, "They can have him." Oh, how she was dreading this week with him. Maybe she should just turn around, perhaps sneak onto another plane or at least into the ladies room for a few more minutes reprieve. It was too late for that though. Albert had already spotted her.

"Alice!" Albert declared in a loud voice through the crowd. "Over here!" he called.

As Alice made her way toward him, she could feel the scrutiny of the other women in the crowd, and she longed to dash away. Instead, she stopped, as Albert moved toward her. He immediately put an all too familiar arm around her and kissed her cheek. His cologne was enough to asphyxiate Alice, who had a very acute sense of smell.

"My bags," Alice said, as she spotted them coming around the carousel and managed to detach Albert.

"Wait, wait," he called, as he came up behind her. "I'll get those. What kind of gentleman would I be if I didn't carry your luggage?"

"Gentleman my foot! Octopus would be more accurate," thought Alice. Albert reached his left arm around Alice, as he pulled her bags from the carousel with his right.

"There we go. Now off to settle you in and on to Le' Miracles," Albert said, as he let go of Alice in order to carry both cases.

"You know, I'm really sleepy Albert. I think I'll just skip dinner and go to my hotel."

"Nonsense. You must be starving," Albert countered.

"No, really, I would just like to get to my hotel," she tried again.

"Don't you feel well?" Albert asked, an air of almost genuine concern in his voice.

"I'm just tired Albert. Really, I mean, you wouldn't want me to fall asleep in the clam sauce, would you?"

"It's only five O'clock though, two O'clock your time. Are you sure you're not ill?"

"Positive. I'm sorry you made reservations, but can we please skip dinner tonight?" Alice persisted.

"As long as you're sure you're alright. Your wish is my command," he said, relenting.

"I'm fine. I just didn't have time to sleep last night. I was finishing some last-minute touches on tomorrow morning's presentation," she explained. Alice hated lying even to Albert, but a few hours without him more than justified it in her mind.

"Very well," Albert said, as they walked outside, and he handed a ticket to the valet.

At that moment, Albert's phone rang, and Alice was blessed with a moment of peace while he answered it. A minute later they were in a black Mercedes and on the way to the "Alexandria Place," a guesthouse in Manhattan, where Morgan Acquisitions kept a leased suite.

On the way there Alice feigned sleep, and on arrival insisted on letting the porters, rather than Albert, help take her bags up. "Maybe you can find someone else to take for dinner," she suggested. "It's still early. Why don't you give Shelly a call? I believe her apartment is on the way, and it would be a shame to waste the reservation."

"Shelly?" Albert questioned, with an annoyed expression.

"Just a thought," Alice replied.

"You must be tired," Albert answered, ego in full view. "Sleep well."

Before Alice could sidestep him, Albert kissed her cheek. "I guess I could call Stan," he said. "Maybe we could meet for some pre-meeting planning."

"Good idea," Alice answered, as she followed the porters up the front steps.

"See you in the morning! A car will be here at seven!" Albert called after her.

As soon as they reached her room, Alice tipped the porter, kicked off her shoes, and wriggled her toes in the plush forest green carpet. She then moved her bags into the bedroom and flung herself onto the king-sized four-poster bed. Honestly, she wasn't the least bit tired. She had slept most of her flight. She was really hungry though, and a smile crossed her face as she realized she had done it! If only for this evening, she was free! Hmmm, where to go?

Alice jumped off the bed and went into the living area. The suite at Alexandria Place was well appointed, with a large sitting room, business center, entertainment center, wet bar, and even a separate guest bath.

Alice looked around and spotted a guidebook on the entertainment center. Then, slipping into a pair of slippers provided by the door, she took the book out onto the balcony. It was cold, but Alice loved the view. Though the sky was dark already, she gazed out into the city lights. To her right, just a block away, she could see Central Park. She flipped through the guidebook to the restaurant section. "Turkish Delight Café," she read, "Journey to another world of tantalizing taste sensations from Asia and the Far East. Join us in traditional dance with our live band, sample multiple flavors from our Hookah bar, and don't forget for dessert, to sample our specialty, "Turkish Delight."

A few minutes later, changed into jeans, sweater, and tennis shoes, Alice grabbed her wool coat and started to make her way down the bustling New York streets toward Central Park. A light snow had started to fall, and she breathed in deeply of the brisk winter air, as the sounds of "Holly Jolly Christmas" floated in the light breeze from the ice rink, where she stopped to watch a group of skaters. One of the men was particularly good, not to mention handsome. He had a full head of dark brown hair, cut just to the top of the black turtleneck he wore under a brown windbreaker, and Alice found it hard to tear her eyes away. In a few minutes though he skated away from the rest. He looked at Alice as he left and even gave her a wave and a smile. Alice smiled, feeling as though she had entered a dream. She felt a freedom, like a bird who had been set free, if only for an evening. She looked on at the other skaters a minute more before her stomach growled, reminding her of her plight, dinner. Dinner in Turkey!

Alice looked at the guidebook she had taken from her room and headed toward the subway. Her adrenaline was pumping, as she purchased her pass and followed along with the flow of humanity. Alice couldn't help grinning. This was the most fun she had had in years! She only wished her traveling companions looked half as happy.

Alice gazed around the car, where if not turned down, most of the mouths were straight or talking. One man appeared to be on two cell phones at once. In another seat two women were complaining about the inequality in their workplace, while across from her a man spent the whole ride staring down, apparently examining his fingernails.

When Alice reached her stop, she felt like a giddy teenager, making her way through the throngs of people, down the street, and toward the Turkish Delight Café.

On arrival, she chose a cozy table in a corner next to the window so that she could watch and soak up as much of the city as possible.

When the waiter, whose name according to the badge attached to his vibrant blue shirt, was Sammy, came over she ordered a combination meze plate and a glass of rose wine.

"Will the gentleman be joining you again tonight?" inquired Sammy.

"Excuse me?" asked Alice.

"Will you have company coming?" he inquired again.

"No. Just me. Thank you," Alice replied.

Alice wondered if all Turkish men were as forward as this waiter, who seemed, somehow to assume that she must have a man joining her. Granted, she was the only single person in the café, but that was exactly the way Alice wanted it tonight.

She knew that this was some place that Albert would never dream of coming to, and she smiled to herself as the soft, yet spirited mix of Mediterranean, Asian, and Middle Eastern melodies flowed from the live band behind her.

Alice gazed at the people hurrying home, as the light snow began to increase, and the wind picked up, causing leaves to dance around their feet. As she watched through the window one of the people caught her eye. It was the skater from Central Park. She was sure of it. A minute later, he saw her too and hurried inside.

"Here you are Sophie. I thought you wanted to try the Cuban restaurant on the next block tonight. Where did you get the new coat? I like it," he said.

Alice stared at him, stunned, as Sammy brought her glass of wine.

"Ah! So, you did come back tonight. I am so pleased!" Sammy exclaimed, shaking the man's hand.

Alice finally found her voice to ask, "I'm sorry, but who are you?"

"Sophie?" the man laughed, and Alice found herself wishing that she were in fact Sophie.

"And who is Sophie?" she asked, as the waiter, keeping one eye on them, went to wait on the next table over.

"Sophie?" He looked at her more closely. "Oh my! You really aren't Sophie."

"No, I'm Alice."

"And I am Jack," he stammered, "Jack Wilson, possibly the most embarrassed man in the city. I am so sorry. It's just that you look so much like my cousin Sophie. It's really beyond words. I only noticed the difference when I saw you didn't have the scars, and well, your accent is different of course, but

Sophie has always been good with accents," he continued, setting down the sports duffle he carried by the table.

"Scars?" Alice asked.

"Yes, well..." Jack stood with his eyes fixated on Alice as he spoke. "I really must call Sophie. Excuse me," Jack finished, and abruptly turned away from Alice going outside to make the call.

Jack felt at a loss, as he stood under the awning outside. Occasionally he would glance back to Alice through the window, feeling as though he had entered the twilight zone.

Inside, a waiter arrived with the meze Alice had ordered.

"So, is everything alright?" enquired the waiter.

"Fine. Thank you," Alice answered more dismissively than she meant, while she watched Jack pace back and forth on his phone.

As Jack completed his call and came back inside, he stopped to say a brief word to the waiter, before returning to Alice's table.

"May I?" Jack asked, indicating another chair at the table.

She nodded her consent.

"So, Alice," he started.

"Yes?" She couldn't help but smile at him. He had the sort of boyish good looks that charmed her, and his subdued awkwardness over the situation only made him more appealing. His eyes were brown and fringed with thick, dark lashes, she noticed, meeting them with her own inquisitive emerald gaze.

"So, tell me Alice, do you live around here?" Jack asked with a serious set of his face, that almost made Alice giggle.

"No. Do you Jack?" she countered, and he smiled.

"No."

"You know, they say everyone has a twin. Perhaps your cousin is mine," Alice said.

"Just wait until you see her," he replied. "She's on her way over."

"So, where are you and my twin from?"

"Nova Scotia."

"Nova Scotia," Alice repeated.

"We're, well, I'm here for the skating competition in Central Park next week. Sophie skates as well, but... Do you skate?" he asked.

"No. I've always wanted to try though. It's such a beautiful sport. You looked so graceful on the ice."

"Graceful on ice but bumbling oaf up close?" he questioned with a smile.

"That wasn't what I meant. I'm sorry, I just..." Alice stumbled, face red.

"Hey, it's alright. I guess I forgot again that you're not Sophie and used to my teasing. I'm sorry." Jack smiled at Alice. "So, where are you from Alice?"

"I'm from Seattle. I..." Alice stopped short as the door opened to a woman who, even though bundled in a faded pink parka, with matching beige scarf, and knit hat, could have only been Sophie or Alice herself.

They stared at one another as Sophie removed her hat and scarf and came closer.

Jack looked from one to the other, and took a deep breath, as the waiter brought more meze and a bottle of wine. The waiter stopped in his tracks, stared from one woman to the other and then to Jack. "You are a lucky man!" he said, as he set the wine down and continued to stare.

"Thank you," Jack said dismissively, and the waiter walked away to a nearby table. Jack rose hurriedly, offered Sophie his chair across from Alice, and pulled out the one between them for himself.

"Hello," said Sophie, as she sat down across from Alice.

"Hello," replied Alice.

Both of their green eyes locked and then scanned the other. For Alice, it was as though she were seeing herself in a mirror. The dark, naturally shaped eyebrows, long dark lashes, straight narrow nose, with just a hint of an upturn at the bottom, the full lips, and even the long wavy hair were the same. The only differences were that Sophie's eyes held a hint of blue, her hair had a bit more brown mingled into the auburn waves, and her right cheek held a web of very fine scars.

Even their hands and the rhythm of their movements were the same, as each reached for her wine glass.

"Alice?" asked Sophie, breaking the spell. "Where were you born? Who are your parents?"

"I was born in Seattle. My parents are Edgar and Suzanna Morgan. You?" Alice asked Sophie.

"I don't know. I was adopted at age four," Sophie replied.

An awkward silence ensued, and the curious headwaiter returned to take Jack and Sophie's order, followed closely by another waiter with additional wine and water glasses.

After a brief look at the menus, Sophie and Jack pointed to their choices. The second waiter insisted on pouring wine for all of them, on the house, and it was not until another table required their attention, that they peeled their eyes from Alice and Sophie.

"May I ask what happened to your cheek?" Alice asked.

"When I was born there was some sort of growth and infection. I barely remember, but I was told it was the reason I was... well, the reason I was left at the hospital as a baby and that's where I lived most of the first three years of my life. When I wasn't there, I was cared for by one of the doctors in his home. Then something happened, perhaps it was just that I no longer needed constant care, and one day, instead of leaving the hospital to go to the doctor's home, I was sent to an orphanage and now I see you, and I wonder…"

"Could I be your sister?" Alice finished.

"Yes," Sophie whispered, as she stared at Alice's flawless complexion, wondering who she could have been. Then Sophie broke out of her reverie and smiled. "I do have wonderful adoptive parents. I did always want a sister though. Do you have any other siblings?"

"No, just me," Alice answered. "I mean, I'm sure my parents would have told me about… My parents would have never deserted their child." Alice tried to make herself sound believable, as she watched Sophie.

"You could always do a DNA test," Jack suggested awkwardly. "Or how about we enjoy this wine. What do you say we toast?" Jack raised his glass. "To new friends!"

"To new friends," Alice and Sophie whispered, as they clanged glasses, eyes locked.

Jack took in a deep breath as he looked from Alice to Sophie and back to Alice, as the waiter arrived with their food.

"Where are you staying?" Alice asked, after the waiter departed.

"We have a small apartment over a pub our uncle runs in Queens," Sophie answered. "I'll write the address out for you." Sophie took a pen from her purse and began to write on a napkin as she asked, "Where are you staying Alice?"

Alice felt embarrassed to say she had a company suite. She didn't want to flaunt her wealth in front of Sophie and Jack.

"I uhm…" Alice hesitated.

"What is it?" Jack asked.

"Do you need a place to stay?" Sophie asked.

At that moment, Alice wanted so much to say yes, but she couldn't lie. "No, no, I'm staying at the Alexandria Place. It's a guest house in Manhattan. The company I work for leases a suite," she added hastily, as Sophie and Jack's eyes widened.

"Sweet!" Jack said. "That's a beautiful building. Built in the nineteen twenties, I believe."

"I bet it's beautiful inside too," added Sophie.

"Would you like to come over? Perhaps we could talk more comfortably there," suggested Alice.

They all looked around as the café was becoming more and more crowded.

"Okay. That sounds like an excellent idea," Sophie concluded.

"I'll get the bill then," Jack said, rising and taking out his wallet.

"No, no," Alice protested. "My meals can go on the company account. I'll write it off as a business meeting. I insist," Alice said as Jack looked at her, contemplating for a long moment, before returning his wallet to his pocket. Then he waved the waiter back over.

"The bill please," he said.

"Certainly, was the food not satisfactory?" asked Sammy, noting their barely touched plates.

"The food was wonderful. We'll just have to take it to go tonight," Jack reassured.

"Certainly. Right away. The bill and some to go boxes. Will there be anything else?"

"No, that will be all. Thank you," Jack answered as the waiter glanced between Sophie and Alice, before going on his way.

Chapter Two

As they left the café, Jack walked on ahead. His mind was reeling with the discovery of Alice tonight and thoughts of what it could mean for Sophie. Jack had always felt more like a protective older brother to Sophie than just a cousin via adoption. At her request, he'd done some research already on the circumstances surrounding her adoption. He'd told her little of what he'd discovered though. It hadn't been pretty, and he had decided that there was no need to cause unnecessary heartache, but now there was Alice. Now Jack felt the need to know more himself, and he knew that no matter how much he wanted to protect her, Sophie wouldn't give up until she found out the truth.

"Do you skate?" Sophie asked Alice, as they followed behind Jack.

"No, but I've always wanted to try," Alice replied. "Jack said he was here for a competition next week. He skates wonderfully."

"You've seen Jack skate?" Sophie asked, surprised.

"I saw him on my way to the café tonight, when I walked through Central Park. He waved at me and… Well, now I know, he thought I was you."

"Jack!" Sophie called to him, and he stopped to let them catch up. "Let's stop at the Central Rink on the way."

"What for?" Jack asked.

"Remember when you taught me to skate?"

"Taught you? I barely did anything. You were a born natural."

"Exactly," Sophie said. "Alice, you said you want to learn to skate. I want to see if you already can."

"What?" Alice asked.

"Sophie. Just because you could..."

"Are you up for trying Alice?" Sophie persisted.

"I guess so. I don't have any skates though," Alice said.

"I'm betting you're a size eight?" Sophie asked.

"Yes."

"Jack, you have my skates in your bag still, don't you?"

"You know I do."

"Then it's settled. If we find out nothing else tonight, at least we find out if you can skate," she said to Alice.

When they arrived at the rink, Jack took out his skates and handed Sophie's to Alice. "Lace up tight and watch the blades," he warned.

"I'll help you," Sophie said to Alice.

Once he was laced up, Jack skated a few turns around the ice, hoping to help clear his head, before going back over to Alice and Sophie. "Shall we then?" he asked, extending his hand to Alice, whose palms, even in the winter air, were beginning to sweat. "We'll just try a few slow times around," he said, as she placed her hands in his and rose.

Alice followed Jack's lead, holding on with both hands only briefly while she got her bearings. "I think I'm okay to let go now," she said, after the first time around.

Jack released her hand reluctantly and stayed close, as Alice continued effortlessly around the rink. He was awe struck. She skated as though she had been born on the ice. Was this even possible? Jack looked at Sophie who looked equally awe struck.

Alice was awe struck herself. This felt so wonderful, so natural, with the wind in her face and her legs gliding along the luminescent ice. This was far easier than walking in three-inch heels. Something inside of her realized though that this wasn't natural. She'd seen children and even adults, struggle, and fall on the ice, after far more time than she'd been on it. Feeling slightly dizzy, Alice skated to the wall. Holding herself steady for a minute, as her head began to swim. Alice made her way over to the bench and sat beside Sophie.

"Wow! I don't know what else to say," Sophie exclaimed, as their eyes met again.

"How old are you, Sophie?" Alice asked.

"Thirty."

"Me too."

"That should have been our first question," Sophie said.

"I don't think we needed to ask," Alice replied, as Jack skated over to join them.

They walked the fifteen minutes to Alexandria Place in silence, each caught up inside their own thoughts and mixed emotions. Before they entered though, Alice stopped short.

"Oh no!" she said and motioned them back around the corner.

"What is it?" Jack asked.

"You mean, who is it?" Alice sighed.

"Who is it?" Sophie asked.

"His name is Albert Starling, and he's the last person I want to see right now, or ever for that matter," Alice answered. "I can't let him see me, us, he can't see us."

"Who is he?" Jack asked.

"He's the reason my parents sent me here. They think he's a good match for me, and I think he's a pretentious octopus, who only wants to marry the boss's daughter to work his tentacles up the cooperate ladder," Alice blurted, as she began to feel dizzy again and stumbled into Jacks arms.

"Whoa, easy there," Jack said, catching her.

"Are you alright?" Sophie asked, concerned.

Alice shook her head. "I'm fine. I had just hoped that he would leave me alone for one lousy evening. I'd better go in and face him. I just hope Leon didn't see me leave earlier and say anything to him. I'm sorry."

Just then Alice's cell phone beeped. Digging it out of her purse, she sighed when she saw five missed messages from Albert and two from her parents.

"What is it?" asked Jack.

"He's called my parents. The last text says that he promised to check up on me, and my dad gave him the key code for my suite. He wants to know where I am."

Sophie looked around the corner to the lobby where Albert stood talking with the concierge. "At least he's good looking," she said, turning back to Jack and Alice. "We could have a bit of fun with this."

"What are you thinking?" Jack asked.

"Look, Alice, if you're not interested in him, why not just walk in on Jack's arm, and maybe he'll get the point," Sophie said, matter of fact.

"She has a point," Jack agreed and offered his arm to Alice.

"You know what? You're both right. This is ridiculous. I'm a grown woman. Let's go!" Alice said, taking Jack's arm.

"You were right though too Alice. He shouldn't see Sophie, especially not if he's close to your parents," Jack said.

This time it was Sophie who sighed. "You're probably right, but hurry. It's freezing out here!"

"Okay," said Alice. "I'm on the 8th floor, room C. The code is 5587. Jack and I will distract Albert. We'll try to get him into the lounge and then you can sneak up and wait in my room. Let's do this!"

Sophie pulled up the collar of her coat and tucked her hair back as she watched Jack and Alice enter the lobby. As they entered though, the concierge left, and Albert moved away toward the house phones.

"How do you want to play this?" Jack asked. "Should we just

go over and say hello?"

Alice raised her eyebrow in a co-conspirator manner at Jack. "Why not?" she said, as their eyes met and lingered.

As Jack and Alice turned toward Albert, a group of about twenty people crossed the lobby, blocking their path. When they had passed, Albert was gone.

"Where did he go?" Alice asked, glancing around.

"Oh no!" Jack answered, as he pointed back out the doors to where Sophie waited.

Sophie, observing what had happened, began walking away down the block.

"Alice, go up to your room. I'm going to check on Sophie," Jack said hurriedly.

"No!" Alice replied.

"No?" Jack asked, irritated.

"If Albert did see her..." Alice started.

Suddenly Jack's phone rang. "It's Sophie," Jack said, as he answered it. "Sophie? Are you alright? Hello? Hello?"

"Come on Jack!" Alice said, pulling him out the door with her.

"Oh shite!" Jack exclaimed, about halfway down the block. "Get out of sight!" Jack muttered, pulling Alice behind him.

Alice ducked into an alcove about ten yards away, as Albert exited a pharmacy with Sophie in tow.

"I'm just glad you're okay. You had your father and me worried sick. I still think you should have let a doctor check out that cut," Albert berated Sophie.

"I told you, I'm fine!" Sophie said, as she touched the bandage that now covered the scars on her cheek. "I just used too much bath oil and slipped, and now I really would just like to get back up to my room."

"I'll walk you," Albert said curtly.

"Only if you insist," Sophie replied.

"I do," Albert said. "I do."

They began to walk back toward the Alexandria. Passing Jack, Sophie barely glanced up.

Alice pulled the hood up on her coat and turned to look into a shop window as they approached. She watched as they passed in the reflection, and Albert stopped, turning to look at Sophie.

"It's a big suite you know," Albert said, as he held onto Sophie's arm with one hand and brushed the hair back from her forehead with the other. "Perhaps I should just stay with you. Make certain you really are okay."

"No. No thank you," Sophie stated firmly, attempting to pull her arm from him.

"Come on Alice," he said, tightening his grip. "You know we're perfect together. Your father wants this. I want this."

"You both seem to be forgetting someone very important in your equation. Me. I don't want this! Understand?"

Alice stared at the reflection of them in the window, as she listened, wishing it really were her saying those words to Albert with the confidence Sophie projected.

"No, I don't understand, and I don't think you do either Alice."

Alice tensed at his words, as did Sophie.

"I will be spending the night with you. It's the company suite and I work for the company. Your father is my boss. Do you understand me, Alice?"

"I believe I'm starting to," Sophie replied.

"Good girl," Albert responded, and although he would have appeared to the casual observer to be guiding his girlfriend gently toward the Alexandria, his grip on Sophie's arm was almost painful.

As Albert continued on with Sophie, Jack turned and came

up behind Alice.

"Were you able to hear what happened?" he asked.

"He's taking her back to my room, and he's staying with her, all night," Alice responded, and Jack's face went ashen.

"Sophie will never stand for that," Jack said.

"He's not really giving her much choice Jack," Alice continued. "I felt like I was listening to a complete stranger. The way he spoke to her... It scared me. He said my father wanted him to stay with Sophie. I mean me. I don't understand why my father would want... I mean he wouldn't. He couldn't want..." Alice couldn't help shaking.

"Okay Alice. Calm down," Jack said, as he put an arm around her shoulder, and they crossed the street to be opposite the Alexandria.

"I am calm. I'm just confused. I've never been confused like this. Most of my life has been pretty predictable, but now nothing makes sense, and I think I'm getting a headache."

"Now that makes sense," Jack said.

"No, it doesn't," Alice muttered, rubbing her right temple.

"There they are," Jack said, pointing to the lobby, where Albert, still holding firm to Sophie's arm, had stopped to talk with the front desk manager, Leon.

"Leon should be off shift by now. What is going on?" Alice questioned.

"I don't know," said Jack, "but we can't do anything here except get spotted. Let's go."

"Where?" Alice asked.

"Back to our rooms at the pub."

"But what about Sophie?"

"She has her phone. I'm sure she'll contact me when she's able."

Inside the Alexandria, Leon walked with Albert and Sophie

to the elevators. It felt to Sophie as though the two men were in some sort of conspiracy, at which she was the center.

"Just let me know if you need anything else Mr. Starling," Leon said, as Albert and Sophie entered the elevator.

When they reached the suite, Albert entered the key code, pushed Sophie in in front of him, and closed the door hard.

"Now, tell me, what was the big idea?" Albert snapped. "What's with these clothes?" Albert stared at Sophie's well-worn jacket, sweater, and corduroy pants. Sophie turned away.

"My clothes are none of your business. In case you hadn't noticed, I'm an adult. I'll wear whatever I like," Sophie retorted.

"What has gotten into you Alice Morgan? You're not acting like yourself. I'm worried," Albert replied. "Look at me!"

"Worried? If your idea of worried, is behaving like a controlling brute, I'd rather you not!" Sophie stated, clasping her shaking hands. "Please leave me alone!"

"I thought we already had this little talk. I promised your father I'd keep an eye on you."

"My father? Really?"

"Don't get that way Alice. You know your parents only have your best interests at heart. Please don't give me any reason to concern them more," Albert said, as he loosened his tie, then threw his overcoat and suit jacket onto the sofa.

"You really expect me to believe that my father would ask a man to spend the night with me?"

"I'll be on the sofa, of course. Come on Alice. Why are you suddenly acting as though you don't trust me?"

"Why are you suddenly acting as though you own me? Why should I trust you?" Sophie interrogated with a raised eyebrow, as she looked Albert up and down. She had a hard time believing that she had ever called him good looking. She now realized that not only did he project the vibe of a viper, but he had a way of narrowing his eyes and twitching his nose when agitated, that under other circumstances, Sophie would have found almost comical.

"Call your father then. Go ahead," Albert said, pulling out his cell. "I'll call him." Albert started to dial, and Sophie walked to the window. As she looked out, she saw Jack and Alice walking away past a streetlamp.

Alice looked up to the window. Even though she couldn't see Sophie, she knew that she was there watching and nodded.

"Here," Albert thrust the phone at Sophie.

She took it and turned away. "Hello?" Sophie asked, cautiously. A few seconds passed and she hung up.

"So?" Albert asked.

"Voice mail. Now if you'll excuse me."

"Where do you think you're going?"

"To the toilet," Sophie replied, sarcastically. "If that's alright by you or do I need a hall pass?"

"Go right ahead," Albert replied, nonchalantly. "Just watch your step. We wouldn't want any more accidents."

Chapter Three

"What is it?" Jack asked Alice, as she gazed up at the window.

"Sophie. I can feel her. She's scared, but she's okay. I think she can handle Albert, maybe even better than I would," Alice answered.

"I don't doubt that she can handle him. Sophie's handled more than her share of forward men, but what if her accent slips? How long can she fool him, and what about everyone else? What time are you supposed to be at work tomorrow?"

"There is supposed to be a car here at 7:00 a.m."

"That gives us ten hours," Jack said, looking at his phone, which began to vibrate, as a text message came in. "It's Sophie. Thank God. She wants to know if there's anything she needs to know, and is there a way you can switch at the office tomorrow?"

"I'll be in a meeting first thing until at least 10:00. Tell her to just keep to herself and observe, take notes on any new financial numbers, but mostly I just listen and give feedback later. My briefcase is under the bed with my laptop. If she can bring a change of clothes and make an excuse to get there early, I'll try to meet her in the 4th floor ladies' room to switch before. Oh, and I take my coffee with one cream, no sugar, accompanied by one butter croissant. Also, I'd order the fruit and yogurt cup from room service for 6:00 a.m. I don't know if Albert would know that or not, but just in case."

"Got it. Anything else?" Jack asked.

"Ask her to text again in the morning, when it would be safe for me to call."

"Okay." Jack's phone vibrated again. "She has to go."

"That's all I have for now," Alice answered.

"Alright. Sent," Jack said, as he turned back to Alice. "Let's go." Jack glanced back briefly to the 8th floor window of the Alexandria, before walking ahead of Alice, in silence, toward the subway.

Once Alice and Jack took their seats, Jack asked, "So, how do you plan on getting into the office tomorrow without arousing suspicion?"

"I have a security code. I'll sneak in the back way and just hide in the ladies' room until Sophie is able get away from Albert." Alice saw the line of concern deepen in Jack's face at the mention of Albert. "He won't hurt her," Alice tried to reassure both Jack and herself..

"I have skate practice at 8:00 a.m. I can't miss it," Jack stated simply, looking straight ahead.

Alice could only look at him. His gaze was focused on his hands, much as the man who seemed to be examining his nails on her first subway trip, and she wondered, what could have been happening in his life? Could it possibly have been as odd as the situation she found herself in with Jack now? And what was Jack thinking? What could he think? They'd met just a couple of hours ago, and already their lives had become unbelievably intertwined.

All the way to the pub, they walked in silence. Neither one had any idea what to say.

On the way inside and up the stairs to the rooms, numerous people waved or raised their glasses in greeting. Like polite robots, Alice and Jack responded with quick waves and nods of the head, as they hurried by. Had Jack spoken? Alice couldn't even remember. There was a throbbing at the back of her head now that seemed to block it all out.

At the top of the stairs, Jack opened the door, walked across the sparsely furnished living room, and slumped onto the sofa. Alice closed the door behind her and leaned against it.

"Kitchen is there," Jack said, pointing to a small alcove with a two-burner stove and mini fridge under the counter. There was also a small microwave, and single basin sink. Above the sink, a small window looked out onto a neon sign in an alley. "Bathroom is there." He pointed across the narrow room to a door on the left of two. "The other room is the bedroom. That's where Sophie sleeps. You can have it tonight. I sleep here, but first, if you'll excuse me, I'm going down for a drink."

"I thought..." Alice started, and then seeing the weariness on his face, stopped. "Okay."

"Help yourself," Jack said, with a sweeping gesture. "But don't wait up," he finished, as he went past her out the door.

Alice, realizing that she was still holding onto the takeout bag from Turkish Delight, took it over to a small dining table next to the kitchen and sat as a wave of dizziness overtook her.

"Maybe I just need to eat?" Alice said to herself. The throbbing in her head had eased into an ache behind her right ear as she opened the food. Thirsty, she walked to the fridge for a bottled water. Finding none, she took a glass from the sideboard and ran it under the tap. At the first sip she screwed up her nose, but she returned to the table with it. As she ate, she looked around the small apartment. It was tidy, but she was certain that nothing in it could have been under fifty years old. It had a certain charm though, a hominess and Alice smiled.

Downstairs, Jack downed his drink and raised his glass for another.

"What's up with you tonight?" asked a broad man in his late forties from behind the bar.

"You wouldn't believe me if I told you uncle Quill."

Quill tipped a bottle of near beer to fill Jack's glass. "Sure you wouldn't be preferring a little of the real thing?"

"Oh, I'd prefer the real thing alright, but I have to at least place in this competition or we could lose the farm, literally."

"I wish your dad would let me help. I've got savings and I'm doing pretty good here," Quill said, looking around at the nearly full pub.

"Well, we both know that's not going to happen. I had to fight tooth and nail to get him to accept the prize money. He only agreed to that after I reminded him that it's my inheritance we were talking about, and even at that, he's still insisting he'll pay me back."

"Ben is a stubborn man, he is. So's my big sister though, and I'm still trusting God she'll pull through this."

"I wish the doctors had your optimism. Three months is a long time though and if she..."

"When she," Quill corrected.

"When she wakes up," Jack repeated, "There's still a lot of therapy to think about."

"Hey! Wipe off that glum face boy. My Beth has a multitude of prayers going up. Your mum's in good hands, God's hands. There's no hands better. You believe that Jack," said Quill with confidence.

"I do Quill. I do. It's more than dad and mom on my mind tonight though."

"Oh?" Quill enquired, a smile lighting his slightly plump, Irish bartender's face and making him look almost nymph like. "What's her name?"

"What? Who?" Jack asked, nearly choking on his drink.

"Come on son," Quill coaxed.

Jack took a deep breath and sighed. "Alice. Her name is Alice, and in some ways, even though I just met her, it's as if I've known her a lifetime."

"Now we're talking. Tell me all about her," Quill prodded.

Jack couldn't help it. He laughed aloud. "Well," he started, "think Sophie, only a whole lot more complicated."

"I see," Quill replied.

"Oh, and she's rich, with a family who keeps a pretty tight rein on her," Jack finished.

"That is complicated. Where'd you meet this lass?" asked Quill.

"In the midst of escaping her leash."

"Sounds interesting."

"To say the least."

Upstairs, Alice was lying on top of a quilt, embroidered with a blue and green leaf pattern, on Sophie's bed, staring at the ceiling. Her head still didn't feel right. Alice had never had a headache before, and if this was what they were like, she had a whole new appreciation for those, like her mother, who had suffered from them regularly. It didn't help that her mind felt as though it were running through a maze that kept leading to dead ends. After about an hour, Alice curled into a fetal position, and with her head buried in the pillows, fell asleep. It was anything but a peaceful sleep though.

Meanwhile, back at the Alexandria, Albert watched the screen of his iPhone. On it played a picture of Sophie curled up in bed. As he moved his finger, the image panned around the room.

"What is going on with you?" he asked himself, as he panned back to Sophie.

The clock on the desk blinked 1:00 a.m. as Albert received a text from Edgar Morgan. It read, "Check her cheek."

Chapter Four

North of Geneva: Dec. 6th 2018

At eight months pregnant, Magdeline was radiant, as she walked down the west corridor of the university's medical wing. She was looking forward to the first Christmas in her new home with Soren and the start of her maternity leave.

The scans had shown that all three babies were thriving, and it seemed that any of the concerns she had harbored, because of her own genetic abnormalities, were for naught. She still didn't understand the results, and they were the only thing that she had kept from Soren. Because of his own work and the concerns he had shared with her, she had decided not to worry him more unnecessarily.

She thought back to their wedding day nearly nine months ago, and how she had surprised him and herself by being able to walk down the aisle.

She still injected the sample she had grown of her own partial DNA string once a week, but the tests showed that her muscles were continuing to strengthen, and the process had even seemed helped by her pregnancy.

Right now, she needed to check on the growth of the new genetic strings. She hoped they would be sufficiently evolved before she went on leave, and she hoped that this time she had found the right sequence from a normal DNA sample to start trials on others who suffered from a similar paralysis as she had.

***

Alice woke up punctually at 5:30 a.m. and sat up before grabbing her head, as though to hold it in place. Blinking her eyes, she took a couple of deep breaths, as the dizziness subsided, and she took in the room around her.

It was still dark outside the window, but an ominous blinking was coming from the corner where she had left her purse in a chair the night before, and the soft glow of a light from the living area shown under her door. Alice swung her legs out of the twin bed and went to retrieve her purse.

Inside her purse, the light of her phone blinded her, as it blinked a message. It was from her father. It read, "Meeting rescheduled to 9:30. I want to teleconference the presentation. Nancy is unavailable at that time, but I trust you know it sweetie. Love dad. P.S. Bandage free. I'm sure you've healed by now."

"Oh no!" exclaimed Alice, as she clutched the right side of her head with one hand and the chair with the other. "Oh God. What is happening?"

Sophie woke up, rubbed her eyes and stared at the digital clock. It read 5:30. She switched on the bedside lamp just as there was a knock at her door.

"Alice?" called Albert's voice.

"What? What do you want?" Sophie replied, with more than a little irritation.

"We need to talk."

"Well, I need to shower, so you'll just have to wait!"

The doorknob turned, but the door didn't open. "You didn't have to lock it, Alice."

"I think you just proved that I did."

"I'll see you when you're ready then," he replied, as he watched her on the screen. He zoomed in on her cheek, but she turned into the bathroom before he could get a look.

Once in the bathroom, Sophie sent a text to Jack. "Alice okay to call now."

Jack was getting ready to scramble eggs for breakfast when Sophie's text came in, and he went immediately to knock on Alice's door.

Alice, still trying to recover her equilibrium, took a second to respond, which was just long enough for Jack to barge in.

"Call Sophie now," he said urgently, then caught her arm as she staggered to him. "What's wrong Alice?"

"Nothing, I need to call Sophie," Alice replied.

Jack hit speed dial and handed her the phone.

"Sophie. Hi. Don't worry about responding. We do have a little problem though."

"A little problem?" Jack broke in.

"There's been a change of plans. The meeting won't start until 9:30 now," Alice continued. "My father wants a teleconference, *live,* and he wants me to give the presentation. Bring my gray suit and tell Albert you want to go in at 7:00 a.m., as planned to use the gym. It's room number 330 on the 3rd floor. I'll meet you in the lady's locker room, and we can switch there. Albert will expect you to take off the bandage too. Tell him you want to keep it covered until after your workout for sanitary reasons, just to be safe. He should buy that. Also, if he doesn't go along with that, challenge him to a rematch on the cross-country machine, level seven, route four. His ego won't let him resist. My gym bag is the green duffle. It's all together. I'll be in the locker room waiting. If you've got all that, can you make some sort of obvious sound on your end?"

On the other end of the line Alice heard the toilet flush.

"Oh! That reminds me," Alice continued. "My makeup for the meeting would be the raven mascara and satin rose lipstick. No base or blush. Uhm, also the black pumps, and just throw the polka dot bag from my suitcase into the duffle, and we should be good. I'm so sorry about all of this Sophie."

Alice heard a man's voice in the background that she could only assume was Albert, and the toilet flushed again before the line went dead.

Alice closed the phone and looked at Jack's worried expression as he asked, "Is Sophie alright?"

"I think she's fine. In fact, I think she's better than I am right now," Alice said, sitting back on the bed and rubbing the back right side of her head.

"Well, if we need to be there in an hour and a half, we'd better eat and run. I'll finish breakfast. Aspirin is in the medicine chest," Jack said, as he exited.

Back in the kitchen, Jack poured the eggs into a pan, lit the stovetop, put down the toast, then took out a bowl from the fridge, and added the contents to the eggs. As he stirred the eggs, Alice came out.

"There's juice in the fridge, coffee or tea if you prefer. The hot water should be nearly ready," Jack stated, without looking at Alice.

"Thank you," Alice replied, as she sat at the small table set for two. The pain in her head seemed to come and go like intermittent pulses, and she massaged the back of her neck as another pulse radiated around it.

"Still have a headache?" Jack asked, as he brought the eggs and toast to the table.

"I've never had a headache before. Are they always this miserable?" Alice asked, as Jack scraped eggs onto her plate.

"You've never had a headache?"

"Never. Have you?"

"On occasion. Where does it hurt?"

"All over, but mostly it seems to radiate from back here."

Jack went behind Alice and began to massage her shoulders

and neck.

"That feels good," Alice said.

"Maybe getting rid of some tension will help," he said, as he worked his way up her neck and under the back of her ear.

"Ouch!" Alice shouted, as her entire body cringed.

Jack jumped back, startled.

"What? What is it?" he asked, as he moved back towards her to take a look at the last place he had touched.

"Don't touch it again. Please," Alice moaned.

"I just want to see. I won't touch. Can you lift your hair up?" Jack asked, as he knelt behind Alice's chair to look up under the back of her right ear. There was what looked like a birthmark there, and it appeared slightly swollen. It also happened to be in the exact same location as an incision scar Sophie had, Jack noted. He didn't know what the scar was from, only that it had something to do with the infection on her face that had nearly killed her as a baby. "There's a swelling back under your ear."

Alice tentatively touched the area Jack indicated and cringed.

"We really do need to talk Alice, but I want Sophie here too."

"I'll try to get away again after the meeting."

"Good. You'd better eat up. I hope it's up to your standards," Jack said, and took his place at the table. "I'm concerned about that swelling."

"I'm sure I'll be fine. I do need to eat though," Alice replied, and took a bite of her eggs. "This is delicious!" she exclaimed, as the kettle whistled.

"Thank you. My mother taught me how to cook when I was a boy," Jack sighed at the thought of his mother. "Tea or coffee?"

"Coffee, please."

"I'm afraid we're out of milk."

"Black is fine," Alice said, trying to read his face as he poured the water from the kettle into her mug.

At 6:45 sharp they were out the door and on the way to the offices.

The food and aspirin had helped her head to a degree, but the subway noise and bustle of the rush hour, threatened to overwhelm her, and she was grateful for Jack's arm supporting her to her stop.

"Do you need me to come with you?" Jack asked.

"No, you need to get to practice. I'll be fine."

"Text me when you're in."

"Okay."

Once at the offices, Alice punched in the door code, and headed up, taking the stairs to avoid any other early arrivals. She heard footsteps as she entered the hallway towards the gym room, but fortunately it was only a cleaning lady. If she had been in Seattle, the jig would have been up, as Alice had befriended them all there, and she would have been expected to stop and chat, maybe even have a coffee if they were on a break. As it was, none of them gave her a second glance and that was good, because it was 7:25 already, and Alice had just gone into the locker room, as the elevator arrived with Sophie and Albert, sharp on her heels.

"Aren't you glad that you changed before now?" Albert asked, chidingly. "I don't know what you were thinking, but then you really haven't been yourself since you got here Alice. I really think we need to go over that proposal before the meeting. I also think you need to take that stupid bandage off, pull your hair back, and..."

"And I think I'm sick of listening to what you think!" Retorted Sophie. "Don't touch me!" Sophie spun to face Albert as he reached to pull her hair back. Her hand, prepared to slap him, was caught sharply in his.

"You seem to keep forgetting our little discussion last night,"

Albert said.

"I don't forget. It's you that seems to be forgetting. You may work for my father, but he is still *my* father, and you'd better think twice before you lay a hand on me at just how much leeway your employ gives you with his daughter."

"Why you little..."

At that, Alice made an audible noise in the locker room, by throwing her shoes against the wall.

"Who?" Albert blurted, as he headed for the locker room, and Sophie grabbed him by the sleeve.

"Now, who's not thinking? That's the lady's locker room," Sophie stated, glared at Albert, and headed in.

"Thank God," Alice whispered, as Sophie turned into the shower area where she had been hiding, and they started immediately to swap clothes.

"What's taking so long?" Albert called.

"I'm putting my hair back!" Sophie snapped back, then whispered to Alice, "What a brute pig! I hope I didn't cause any problems, but I'm not very good at holding my tongue."

"I think you're amazing," Alice whispered. "I wish I could answer back like you."

"Maybe it's time you start." Sophie smiled, as Alice turned to leave. "Wait!" Sophie tossed Alice a bandage.

"Right. Thanks." Using Sophie as a mirror, Alice applied the bandage and hurried out.

"It's about time. Who else was in there?" Albert asked.

"No one. One of the shower curtains fell."

"Maybe I should look at it."

"I already fixed it, and aren't we short on time?" Alice retorted, in an attempt to come back at him as Sophie had.

"Something about you seems different," Albert said, climbing onto the bike. "I can't place it though."

"My hair's back."

"Yeah, right," Albert studied her, as they began the bike program.

Albert beat Alice easily this time, and he eyed her suspiciously. "Is that your way of trying to make up to me?"

"I didn't sleep so well last night," Alice shot a look at Albert, but unlike Sophie, turned away when Albert returned her gaze.

Albert looked at his watch. "Forty-five minutes. Get that ridiculous bandage off and get upstairs so we can go over the presentation."

Alice walked into the changing room to find Sophie waiting. "I don't know how to thank you Sophie," she said. "I'm so sorry about last night."

"It wasn't your fault. To be honest, it was kind of exciting. When do you think you can get away to meet again?"

"I'm hoping around one or 1:30, after our lunch. I have a plan, but it will only work if I can get my father to cooperate."

"I'll meet Jack at the rink, and we can eat at the sandwich shop next door. We'll wait there," Sophie said.

"I'll text you as soon as I can," Alice replied, as she pushed her gym clothes back into her duffle and pulled her hair into an updo twist.

"Ready yet?" Albert called, and before Alice had a chance to, Sophie answered.

"I'd like to see you pull on pantyhose and do your makeup in five minutes flat! If you're in such a hurry, just go on!"

"I don't know what's gotten into you Alice, but I don't like it," Albert called back. "I'll wait though."

Sophie bit her lip as she turned to Alice. "Sorry," she said.

"Don't be," Alice said, putting on her lipstick, and brushing on mascara, "I'll be there by 1:30. I'll find a way." As Alice turned back to Sophie, she grabbed her head in pain and nearly fell.

"What is it?" Sophie whispered, as she reached for Alice.

"I don't know. It's been coming and going since last night. I'll be fine though," Alice said. "I'd better go." Alice stood, and she and Sophie embraced.

"It's ten till!" Albert yelled.

"1:30," Alice whispered.

"We'll be waiting," Sophie replied. With that, Alice grabbed her gym bag and headed out.

Sophie looked up at the clock on the wall, shaped like a sandwich with pickles for hands and then back to Jack. "She'll be here. I know she will," Sophie tried to reassure them both.

"If she can," Jack said. "And I don't just mean getting away from Albert. I'm really worried about that swelling behind her ear."

Alice stared on, glassy-eyed, as Albert went on and on, talking. Her head still hurt, but she had to stay focused. When she had stumbled on the stairs that morning at a sudden wave of dizziness, he'd played mother hen and started asking her if she had taken her vitamins. Her vitamins? Yikes! I'm not five years old, Alice had thought. The truth is, she had accidentally on purpose forgotten to pack said vitamins, which her mother had shoved down her throat all her life.

It's ridiculous. This is all ridiculous, Alice thought. I need to get out of here and find out what's going on. Her attempt to escape earlier had been thwarted by her father, who cut her off with concern, and also wanted to make sure she'd taken her vitamins. What was it with men? He'd then signed off to take another call and asked that she call him back before the concert.

Not only did Alice not feel like going to the concert her father had arranged for her and Albert to take new clients to tonight, Alice didn't feel like being part of the company at all anymore. What did they even do? Really? She asked herself. They took over other companies to split them up and sell them off. That was the short answer. Her father had a reputation though of while lovingly selling company parts to new financially stable homes, he also allowed the previous owners an opportunity to continue working for him. In fact, by many, Edgar Morgan was considered a humanitarian in the business field, but was he really?

Alice was shocked by all the questions that raced through her mind about the company's practices and even about her own parents. Suddenly, she felt claustrophobic, as she sat in the restaurant conference room around a table with nine men in suits, as they twirled pasta, and dipped sandwiches, while talking about portfolios, and the validity of selling wholes or parts of companies. When Frank Amstead, owner of the pharmaceutical company in question asked Alice what she thought, her response was immediate. "Don't do it."

The shocked look of the other Morgan employees said it all, and the look on Albert's face terrified her.

"Can we talk privately for a minute?" Albert asked her.

From some new found source of strength, Alice answered. "No. I'm not done talking to Mr. Amstead. Mr. Amstead, may we speak privately please?"

"Certainly Miss Morgan. May I buy you a drink?" he asked, as he pointed to the bar.

"No!" Albert nearly shouted.

"Sir!" replied Mr. Amstead. "Miss Morgan is the owner's daughter. Is she not?"

"Yes," Albert replied, as everyone else looked on in stunned silence. "But she hasn't been well lately and..."

"Well, I am sorry to hear that you haven't been well miss Morgan," Mr. Amstead said, as he appraised her with raised brows.

"I'm fine. Thank you," Alice replied.

"You are not!" Albert blurted.

"Mr. Starling!" Mr. Amstead replied. "I suggest you learn some self-control. This company is still mine, and Miss Morgan does not belong to you either. Now, Miss Morgan has something to discuss with me, and I'd like to hear it. Nathan, Jeffery," he nodded to his associates. "Unless Miss Morgan would like you to join us, our meeting here is adjourned. Miss Morgan." He offered his arm to her.

"May I suggest an alternate meeting place?" she asked, as they turned out and toward the cloakroom.

"I believe that to be a wise idea," Mr. Amstead agreed, as he looked to Albert, who was clearly seething.

As they left the restaurant, Mr. Amstead handed a ticket to the valet, and asked, "What is with that young man Albert and you?"

"Nothing. Contrary to what Albert would have everyone believe, there is nothing at all between us," Alice answered, as Albert came out the door behind them.

"Don't do this Alice. You're not thinking straight," Albert called after her.

Alice had to restrain Mr. Amstead, as he swung around. At near sixty years old, Alice thought he could still probably knock Albert flat on his designer suit pants.

"You have no idea what I'm thinking," Alice replied calmly.

Mr. Amstead's car was brought around, and a chauffeur opened the back door for them to get in.

"At least speak to your father first," Albert continued, almost pleading.

"I will speak to my father, after our meeting," Alice stated, as she turned to face Mr. Amstead, who was glaring at Albert.

"We're done here," Mr. Amstead said, and the chauffeur closed the door.

After they were settled inside the car, Mr. Amstead asked, “Now what was it you wanted to talk to me about Miss Morgan?”

“Have you ever met my father Mr. Amstead?”

“Not as such,” he replied. “We spoke on the phone once and exchanged a few emails.” Mr. Amstead watched Alice patiently, as she tried to sort out a response.

“Mr. Amstead,” she began. “I’ve worked for my father’s company since I was sixteen. I have a master’s in business economics, and have participated in numerous transactions, always without questioning.”

Mr. Amstead continued to listen attentively, as she continued.

“Well, Lately, I have started to ask questions, and the more I ask, the more I find. I don’t want to hurt my parents. I don’t know if you’re aware, but they built this company together fifty years ago now.”

“I was not aware of that, but I think I’m beginning to understand a few things better. You didn’t choose to work there. Did you? You see, I may not know your father, but I knew mine, and I have a strong feeling that they are very similar. May I ask you a personal question Miss. Morgan?”

“Okay,” Alice answered.

“How much of your life do you feel is yours?”

“Honestly? None.”

“Well then, a word of advice. No matter how much you want to please your parents, don’t sacrifice your life to do so, especially not with Mr. Starling.”

Their eyes met and Alice asked, “Do you have children Mr. Amstead?”

“Two daughters,” he replied, with a proud smile.

“They are very lucky,” Alice said.

“Thank you.”

"No, thank you. I want you to know that it wasn't just for personal reasons that I advised you against selling to Morgan," Alice said.

"Honestly, it wouldn't have mattered. I am glad you did though," he continued. "I'd had a lot of questions myself already."

"You did? Albert seemed to think the sale was in the bag."

"Albert is one of those questions," he said.

"What? I know he was..."

"I don't just mean because of today. I did a background check on him, and after today, I'm positive that the only reason he was hired was for you," said Mr. Amstead.

"For me?" Alice asked.

"I think you know it too. That's why you had to get out of there. I could sense your tension all through lunch. Remember, I have two daughters. So, before we go any further, tell me, where is it that you would like to go?"

Alice looked at her watch. "I was hoping to meet some friends in Central Park, near the skate rink," Alice answered.

"Well, it seems we're on the right path," he said, as he pointed ahead to the park. "Which rink?"

"I didn't realize there was more than one. Do you know if one has a sandwich shop nearby?" asked Alice.

"I think I know the one," he replied, and pushed an intercom button. "Ed. Please go around to the eastern corner nearest the rink."

"I don't know how to thank you Mr. Amstead."

"You got me out of that meeting. There are some things I want you to promise me though," he said.

"What is it?" asked Alice.

"First, if we meet again, call me Frank, and second, that you'll make your life your own. You are an intelligent and beautiful young woman. I don't know what all may be going on in the company or with your parents, but my advice to you is to make your escape, so to speak. Now, aside from Albert, there are some fishy international holdings I found. Nothing that you could have been a part of, as all the contracts were dated 1980-87, but you should be aware."

"1980-87? But..."

"Yes?"

"It's nothing. Thank you again Mr....Frank."

"You are most welcome. I believe this is your stop," Frank said, as the car pulled to the curb. "If you ever need anything, feel free to call." He handed her a business card.

"Do you by chance remember the names of those companies?" Alice asked.

"Not off hand, but I'd be more than happy to look them up for you."

"Thank you," Alice said, as she exited the car and headed toward the ice rink.

Inside the sandwich shop, Sophie ordered another cup of tea and Jack wrung his hands.

"She's okay," Sophie tried to reassure him.

"How can you be so sure?" Jack asked, just as Sophie's phone beeped that she had a text. Sophie held up the phone for Jack. The message read, "Coming."

Chapter Five

Back in his office, Albert threw his cell phone across the room. "What the hell am I supposed to do?"

As his phone rang, Albert took a deep breath, before crossing the room to pick it up and answer. Alice's father was on the other end.

"She's in Central Park," Mr. Morgan told Albert. "I'm sending you the link to track her cell phone. Something is not right with my daughter, and it's your job to find out what, and take care of it. Oh, and if I ever hear that you used any form of force, or even threaten to do so, you will regret it."

"I would never actually hurt Alice Mr. Morgan," Albert replied, obviously shaken.

"Glad to hear it. Now, romance her, spoil her if you have to, even give in to a whim. Alice has never been prone to whims, but she also hasn't ever been on her own much, so this may just be a phase. I'm also sending a prescription for her vitamins to a local clinic. I want you to make sure she gets one ASAP. That may be what is affecting her moods. GDNA clinic is number 55 on 44th St. They should arrive by five this evening. Do you understand?"

"I understand."

"Good. Now find my daughter, and don't let her out of your sight again."

"Yes sir," Albert answered, as Mr. Morgan slammed the phone down on the other end.

Albert went to his email and hit the link that brought up a map tracing Alice's cell signal. "What did you get yourself into Albert?" he asked himself, as he grabbed his coat and headed out.

Alice stumbled in the snow as another surge of pain shot through her head, and she grabbed at a nearby tree to steady herself.

"Something is wrong now Jack," Sophie said.

"Now you think something is wrong?" Jack asked, confused.

"I feel it. Come on, let's get out of here and look for her," Sophie urged.

"And what if we miss her?" Jack asked.

"I'll find her," Sophie said, grabbing her coat.

"Hang on. I'm coming with you," Jack answered. Going to the register, he paid the bill and left a note with the hostess, that if a woman looking just like Sophie showed up, to ask her to please wait.

The snow had started falling heavily, and Jack reached into his pocket for gloves.

It was ten minutes later when they found Alice slumped by a tree. Jack ran to her and checked her pulse. "She's burning up," he said, and picked her up. "Call a taxi. I'm taking her over to the benches by the rink."

Sophie had walked only a few yards to get a clearer signal when she saw Albert. She ducked behind a tree, and watched, as he stared at his phone, moving closer and closer to where Alice and Jack were. Sophie knew Albert would get to them before she could without being seen, so she wrapped her scarf around her face and went to him.

"Albert," she called loudly enough so that Jack would hear.

Stunned, Albert swerved and stared at Sophie.

"What are you doing out here?" she asked.

"I was just about to ask you the same thing," he said, walking closer.

"I needed to think."

"Where did you get those clothes?" Albert asked, knowing

full well, everything in Alice's luggage. "You look like you just came from a nineteen eighties garage sale."

"I decided I needed something more practical for a walk in the park," Sophie answered, focusing hard on her accent and to keep her irritation at his insult out of her voice. She was in fact, having left her parka and other clothes at Alexandria Place, wearing her best woolen dress coat over her favorite sweater, jean combo, and new snow boots. Looking at Albert, she couldn't help thinking that she was dressed much more appropriately than he was in his three-piece suit and leather loafers.

Albert continued to move closer until he was right on her, scrutinizing her face.

"Look Alice, I want to apologize for my earlier behavior. Come on, It's freezing out here. Let's go back to the suite, change and go out somewhere nice where we can talk. I have a taxi waiting right over there," he pointed.

Raising her voice for Jack's benefit, Sophie glared at Albert and said, "I don't care that you have to pay that taxi to wait at the corner. I'm not going anywhere with you!"

"What is into you lately?" Albert shot back, grabbing her arm. Then he remembered her father's warning and abruptly loosened his grip.

In the meantime, Jack was feeling conflicted. He knew that Sophie had let him know about the taxi so that he could get away with Alice, but the idea of leaving her alone again with Albert tore at him.

Looking at Alice, Jack knew he had little choice. She was burning up with fever and only semi-conscious as he scooped her up and hurried as quickly as he could out of Albert's sight range toward the street. A few passerbys stopped to look, but on a Friday afternoon in December, those who did, had more important things on their minds like Christmas shopping, to really care.

When they reached the taxi, Jack told the driver that Albert had asked him to take them. The lie had felt slightly bitter to a man of Jacks morality, but he knew that it would have little effect on Albert and may help give Sophie the chance she would need to get away. The driver hadn't asked questions either. He had tired of waiting and was relieved to finally get going again.

"111 Cambia St.," Jack told the driver, as he got situated with Alice, who was starting to come around.

"Are you sure you don't want the hospital?" the driver asked when Alice moaned.

"I'm sure. She has medication at home," Jack answered, hoping that he was making the right choice.

Alice looked at him and groggily asked, "What happened?"

"You passed out. You have a pretty nasty fever brewing," he answered.

"Me? A fever?" Alice asked, bewildered.

"Just rest. I'm taking you back to the pub," Jack said, as he stroked her forehead. Their eyes locked for a moment. Jack looked away out the window, where the start of holiday rush hour was already at a near standstill. Alice had closed her eyes again, and Jack pulled his cell phone out, and dialed.

"Tom, this is Jack Wilson," he spoke into the phone. "I'm sorry to bother you, but I need you to look something up, regarding Sophie."

Back at the park, Sophie walked with Albert close on her heels. When he saw that she was headed for the subway entrance though, he grabbed for her elbow. "Stop it Alice. I can't go along with this."

"Fine. Leave then," Sophie replied in a nonchalant tone.

"You are not getting on a subway. Your parents would never

approve," Albert stated as firmly as possible, without drawing undue attention.

Sophie jerked away from his grip and continued walking.

"I'm calling your father," he threatened.

"So? I'm a thirty-year-old woman. I don't need his permission."

Albert opened his iPhone to dial anyway and was surprised by the blip of Alice's cell moving toward the other side of the city. Then, rather than Mr. Morgan's number, Albert dialed Alice's. When he heard nothing, he asked, "Alice?"

Sophie ignored him and continued down into the subway.

"Where's your cell phone?" Albert persisted, as he followed her toward the turnstile.

"Why? Did your big fancy one break?" Sophie asked mockingly, as she continued through the turnstile, leaving Albert stranded as he realized he had no idea where to acquire a pass, much less where she was going. He thought about jumping it, but a look from a nearby guard, who seemed to have read his mind, stopped him. Pushing his way through the crowd, he found an available ticket machine and bought a pass just to get through the turnstile, but by the time he passed through, Sophie was nowhere to be found.

Jack helped Alice into the pub and up the stairs to the apartment. "Just sit here," he said, as he lowered her to the couch. "Tom? Are you still there?" he asked into his phone.

"I'm here," came Tom Marshall's voice, loud and clear over the speaker.

"Who is that?" Alice asked.

"A friend from home. He's going to try and help us," Jack answered.

"I have a number here for the clinic where the doctor in charge of Sophie's care works. Let me call them and see what I can find out. I'll call you right back."

"Okay," Jack said. Hanging up the phone, he went to get a glass of water for Alice, and pillows to help her get as comfortable as possible. A few minutes later Tom called back.

"How swollen is the site?"

Jack pulled Alice's hair back.

"Ouch!" Alice jerked away.

"I need to see the swelling," Jack said.

"What does it look like?" asked Tom. "Size and color?"

"A bit like a pale pink robin's egg," Jack answered.

"I'm guessing it's pretty tender. Sophie?" Tom asked.

"He's talking to you," Jack whispered to Alice.

"Yes?" Alice replied.

"Where does your head hurt?" Tom asked.

"All over."

"Steady ache?"

"Steady ache in back and occasional pulses in front."

"Pulses? You mean throbbing?"

"No, I mean pulses, like light pulses and a couple of times like lightning bolts."

"Do you have anything to take her temperature with Jack?" asked Tom.

"Not here. I could ask Quill if I can borrow their baby thermometer."

"Never mind. I'm sending a prescription to a pharmacy that according to "Map Line" is just around the corner from you at 141, 8th Alley. The number there is 1-800-555-8585. Give them a call to find out when you can pick it up. In the meantime, keep some kind of cold compress on her, and buy a thermometer when you pick up the prescription. Call me back an hour after her first dose and have a temp for me. Got it?"

"Got it," Jack answered. "Thank you, Tom."

"Glad to help."

"And Tom?"

"I went by this morning. No change, but if your dad doesn't take it easy, she will outlive him."

"Right."

"We can talk more when you call back."

"Thanks," Jack sighed, as he hung up the phone. He looked over at Alice, half asleep on the couch, and went to the kitchen to make a cold cloth. He held it to Alice's forehead, and she moaned.

"I've never felt like this before," Alice whispered.

"Neither have I. Neither have I," Jack whispered back, as Alice closed her eyes, and fell back into a restless sleep.

Jack sat there lost in thought for several minutes, holding the cloth to Alice's forehead. Then the knob on the apartment door began to turn, and Jack popped up to alertness as Sophie entered.

"Sophie. Thank God! How did you get away?" Jack asked.

"Sophie?" Alice moaned, as she tried to sit up.

"Just lay still, and hold this to your head," Jack said, as he rewet the cloth, and Sophie sat beside Alice.

"I led him to the subway," Sophie said. "How are you feeling Alice?"

"Not so well. I don't think I've ever had a fever before."

"You've never been sick?" Jack asked.

"I had a cold one day."

"Only a day?" he questioned, with raised eyebrows.

"It was long enough."

"Don't you think that's a little odd?"

"My mother said it was because I took these special vitamins. I'm starting to think she was right."

"Why's that?" asked Sophie.

"I left them in Seattle." Alice grinned, "I was being rebellious, and now look at me."

"What did these special vitamins look like?" Jack asked.

"What difference does that make?"

"Humor me."

"Ugly," Alice answered, as her face twisted into a look of disgust that almost made Jack laugh. "They were brown, and the taste, I used to imagine they were what poop tasted like."

At this, Jack did laugh. "I'm sorry. They sound horrible."

"They worked though," Alice replied.

"Did your mom take them too?" Jack continued his questioning, as Sophie sat listening intently.

"No. She said they were something that you had to start taking really young like I did. It was a little weird, but I learned early on not to question mother too much."

"How do you mean?" asked Sophie, "What is she like?" Sophie and Alice locked eyes, and for a moment it was as though they were one. Sophie rubbed her head as a painful pulse of light struck, and emotions of longing welled up in Alice until tears brimmed her eyes.

Jack stared at them until he became too uncomfortable at the silence and intensity in their faces. He cleared his throat loudly, and the spell broke as they both turned to him. Then they both fell back on the couch, exhausted. Sweat ran from Alice's forehead, mingled with tears. Jack felt a wave of panic.

"Alice? Sophie? Alice?" he called, and Sophie's eyes flew open, and she immediately held the cloth back to Alice's head. Alice moaned.

"I'm sorry," Sophie said.

"It's okay," Alice replied.

Jack was now the one who felt like he was in a trance. He didn't know what to do, so he asked again, "How did you get away from Albert Sophie?"

"He was busy staring at his phone when I bought my subway pass, and once I was through the turnstile, he was clueless as to how to follow."

Alice laughed, and moaned at the same time. "Did you know it hurts to laugh when your head hurts?"

At that, Sophie giggled, and Jack smiled.

"I need to make a call," Jack said, as he looked at the clock on the microwave. "Then I'll need to run out to the pharmacy to pick up a prescription for Alice that I got from Tom. Do you two think you'll be okay alone for a while," he asked, as he went to the phone on the wall.

"We'll be fine," Sophie answered.

"Is he always this much of a worrywart?" Alice asked.

"Always."

"Well, judging by the events of the past several hours, I'd say I have good reason," Jack defended, as he called the pharmacy, and punched in the prescription number. "Okay," he said, hanging up. "I should be back in about twenty minutes. Keep the door locked."

Albert was still staring at his phone, looking at where the signal had stopped. He hailed a taxi and gave the driver the address. "111 Cambia St."

Chapter Six

Jack was returning from the pharmacy when he saw the taxi pull up in front of the pub, and Albert got out.

"Shite!" Jack said to himself. "How did he find her? I've got to warn Alice and stall him."

Jack hurried across the street to where Albert was standing in front, staring at the door, and then back to his phone.

Albert jerked around in surprise, as Jack came up behind him and asked, "Hey, can I help you with anything?"

"Uhm, hi," Albert said, as he took Jack in, and must have realized that he wasn't a vagrant or a thug, because he went on to ask, "What is this place?"

"It's a pub," Jack responded, barely able to keep the uh duh, inflection out of his voice as he looked at the large sign on the door that read, "McNaffy Pub. Family owned and operated since 1919", "In fact it's my family that owns it," Jack added. "Is there something I can help you with?"

"No. Well, maybe. Have you seen this woman?" Albert asked, as he flashed a picture of Alice.

Jack looked at it. "Can't say that I have, but then I'm just now going in. May I ask who she is?" Jack continued, as he opened the door and Albert followed him in.

"She's my sister," Albert lied. "She didn't show up for a family meeting and her, our dad is worried, so I said I'd look for her. I'll just show her picture around and..."

"Why don't you let me do that? There are some regulars in here that might not be so inclined to talk to a stranger, especially one in a three-piece suit, if you catch my drift," Jack said smiling, as he held out his hand for the photo.

Albert looked around at the other patrons, all in jeans. He didn't see Alice anywhere in the front room, and he was feeling more and more anxious as several pairs of eyes turned his direction.

"Come on. Why don't you sit down, and I'll show the picture around while you have a beer. On the house," Jack offered, and Albert reluctantly handed Jack the photo. "Don't worry. If she's been here, I'll find out. May I ask what makes you think she's here though?"

"Uhm," Albert stammered. "Her last phone call to us was from this number."

"Oh, I see. Well, I'll show this around then. What kind of beer do you drink?" Jack asked.

"Amstel. Thanks?"

"Jack."

"Thanks Jack."

"No problem."

Jack had Quill send over a beer, and went through the pub, stopping to talk to enough people, and hold the photo so that Albert would believe he was doing as he had said. Then Jack went through to the rear game room, out the kitchen, and dashed up the back stairs. Alice was asleep on the couch when he entered.

"What took so long?" Sophie asked.

"Here's the medicine," Jack said, tossing it to Sophie and going to Alice's purse.

"What are you doing?" snapped Sophie, as he rummaged through Alice's purse.

"This," he answered, taking Alice's phone. Going to the window, he dropped it into the dumpster below. "She can get a new phone," he replied to the look Sophie shot him. "That one had a bug. Its name is Albert, and he's downstairs."

"What? How?" Sophie gasped, and Jack pointed down to the

dumpster. "He was tracking her?"

"Bingo," Jack replied. "Now let's see if we can rouse her enough to take one of these."

A couple of hours later, Alice was awake and laughing as Jack told them about Albert climbing into the dumpster in the alley to discover her phone.

"I only hope he doesn't alarm my parents too much," Alice had said, at which point it was decided that she would use Sophie's phone to call and leave a message, knowing that being from an unknown number, it would not be picked up. Alice told her parents that she had simply needed some space from Albert. She said she had met and made a date with someone new that night, however on their way to dinner she had mislaid her phone in a coffee shop, only to find it gone once she had returned to look for it.

She explained that she was calling from the coffee shop manager's phone and would let them know once her phone was replaced. In the meantime, she was fine, but asked that Albert please be called off, as she was beginning to feel watched almost to the point of being stalked.

She said that her date was named Ernie, and that he was an upper-level manager she had met while getting off the plane in New York. She had checked him out through an online background check and had found nothing that they would object to. She only wished for some time to get to know him better herself before formally introducing him. She hoped that they would understand, and please get Albert off her back.

Feeling good that all the bases were covered, it was decided that Sophie, with Alice feeling very weak, would go to the Alexandria around midnight to collect Alice's things, and bring them back to the pub.

The next day Alice left another message for her parents,

telling them that due to Albert, she had simply decided it would be best to not be where he knew how to find her. She was terribly sorry if anyone was upset by her decisions, but she hoped they would understand. As for the episode with Mr. Amstead, Alice said that she had discovered, quite last minute, that there were some discrepancies, and had needed to make a spur of the moment decision, which she was certain was in the best interest of all concerned, as well as affording her the opportunity to dodge Albert for her date with Ernie.

Alice concluded with asking them to send any replies to her email, which she would be sure to check regularly. Also, since she wanted to avoid all unneeded contact with Albert, she would be attending the next meeting only by phone.

"Oh, what a tangled web we weave," Alice commented after the last message. "What if they figure it all out? I've never spoken or lied so blatantly to them like that before. They must know that something more is going on, and if Sophie is my sister, don't you think they might begin to wonder?" Alice asked, her mind racing to try to gather, and make sense of the past thirty-six hours.

"No. They won't know," Jack said, quite firmly, causing both Alice and Sophie to turn intense questioning looks to him.

"What do you know that you're keeping from us Jack?" Sophie probed. "Now that Alice is awake and feeling a bit better, I think it's time you filled us in. I've known for some time that you've been keeping something from me."

"You have, have you? I'd have thought you would have demanded answers before now then," Jack replied.

"Maybe I was afraid to know and didn't really think I needed to. Now, both Alice and I need to know what's going on," Sophie answered.

"She's right Jack. I'm really afraid to know, because I always thought I had known everything, but I need to know the truth,"

Alice said.

"We can talk after your conference call," Jack said. "I'm going to the market to get something for breakfast now," Jack continued as he grabbed his jacket and walked out, leaving both Sophie and Alice to stare after him.

"How did the meeting go?" Jack asked as he flipped pancakes an hour later.

"Alice is brilliant..." Sophie started.

"Until my, or our father, got on the line and I panicked,"

"I thought you handled it extremely well," Sophie said.

"What happened?" Jack asked.

"What always happens when I know he's displeased. I just froze."

"What did he say?"

"That I am to come straight home, back to Seattle today, and then he fired Albert," Alice said. "I've never heard him sound so angry. He didn't really yell, but..."

"He didn't have to," Sophie continued. "The tension and finality in his tone was..."

"Enough to chill me to the bone," Alice concluded.

"You aren't going though, are you?" Jack asked.

"Of course not. How could I?" Alice asked, her eyes meeting with Sophie, then locking firmly with Jack's.

"We need to know the truth, and that starts with you spilling everything you know. Now," Sophie ended.

Jack turned to serve up their breakfast plates, as both Alice and Sophie followed him with their eyes. He was being deliberately slow as he contemplated how to relate, as well as how much, to relate to them of what he had discovered.

Finally, Jack sat with his own plate. He poured fresh coffee for them all and began.

"One of the documents I found in Sophie's file was an

autopsy report." There was a moment of silence as Jack allowed this first bit of information to sink in. They both continued to stare at him as though they could pull more information from him with the intensity of their gazes alone, and they did. Jack continued, "The report said Jane Doe. Inside were test results for toxicology, blood, genetic markers, and a diagram consistent with facial deformation." His eyes locked with Sophie's.

"So, when did I die and what from?" she asked nonchalantly.

"A brain infection and suffocation, due to a genetic birth defect. Apparently, the deformation blocked your sinus cavity, and you were pronounced dead at four twenty on the morning of September15th 1988."

"That's two months before our birthday though," they said at once, and Sophie traced the fine scars of her right cheek. Alice hadn't noticed before, but one of the scars ran from just above her nostril to under her eye.

"Go on," Sophie prompted.

Jack looked to Alice, "Those pills..."

"Yes. They are similar to my vitamins. What are they Jack? Really? I know they aren't just vitamins."

"They're anti-rejection drugs, Sophie's doctor prescribed them."

"Why would Alice need anti-rejection drugs? I know I took them for my skin grafts, but..." Sophie questioned, as Alice sat silently.

"So, it was the vitamins that kept me from ever experiencing this before," Alice stated, as she tried to absorb the implications. "No wonder my parents were so adamant about my taking it. What would I have needed it for though? And why not just tell me the truth? I would have fought it a lot less and sure wouldn't have left it behind."

Both women looked questioningly to Jack, who could only

shake his head. “I don’t know the answer to that.”

“How did Tom know what to prescribe?” Sophie asked.

“I told him it was for you, so he’d send it, then described the symptoms. He called the clinic that treated you and called me back with the prescription.”

The truth was, Jack did have some idea, but he wanted proof before he tried to explain something, which to him, defied explanation. His biggest concerns right now were how to protect Alice and Sophie, place high enough in the competition, which was only a couple of days away, and what must really be going on behind Sophie’s façade of strength. No one could find out that they had been issued a death certificate, even before their birth, and not have a lot more questions.

Sophie felt behind her right ear. “I’ve always had a lump of scar tissue here that never healed as well as the rest. Since it’s hidden behind my ear though, I never gave it much thought, but Alice’s infection started behind her ear.”

Alice felt the lump behind her ear. “It’s still tender, but if you look, there’s a birthmark back there too.”

Sophie came around behind Alice as Alice pulled her hair up. “I can’t be sure with the other swelling, but that could be an incision scar,” Sophie said. “What if we both had an infection, but for some reason they were told I died, or what if they really just didn’t want me because I was deformed?” Sophie wondered.

“We can’t know what they knew,” Alice said, putting her hand over Sophie’s. “The parents I grew up with may be emotionally distant, but I can’t imagine them ever being that cold. Despite whatever is going on here, I have to believe they do love me, and if they knew you were alive...” Alice smiled at Sophie.

“It really doesn’t matter for me,” Sophie responded. “I had parents that loved me. What we do need to find out, is the truth about this." Sophie picked up the medication bottle.

"I need to know what's really going on with Morgan Acquisitions too. I can't ignore what Mr. Amstead said. I need to know the whole truth, before I can face my parents with it," Alice said.

"Somehow, I have a funny feeling that it's all connected, and if we answer one question, we'll find the answer to the other close behind," Jack stated. "You said yourself that Mr. Amstead's concerns were over acquisitions made before you were even born, and the fact that he owns a large drug company, I'm starting to see too many coincidences for them to be coincidences."

"I think we should all meet with Mr. Amstead," Alice said.

"No!" Jack responded, more harshly than he meant to.

"Jack? Why not? Alice may be right. He's obviously done research, and what he knows put together with what you know may lead to the answers," Sophie said. "You don't have to protect me, Jack."

"Or me," Alice joined. "I have his contact information, and I'm going to call him no matter what you think."

Jack looked into two of the most strong-willed faces he had ever seen. "You two are becoming more alike with every passing minute. Fine, call him, but don't let him know where you are." Jack looked at the clock. "I need to get ready. My rehearsal is at 2:00. So, let's get on with this call."

After Alice spoke to Mr. Amstead, it was agreed that Jack would meet with him at the café by the rink at six. Sophie and Alice were to stay put. They had both protested of course, but Alice was still battling an infection, and they had to concede that she was in no condition to risk even the slightest chance of getting caught.

"We don't know who all may be looking for you Alice," Jack

had said. "Before you knew to look out for Albert, but now, you wouldn't know who, and I'd bet my life that someone is still looking for you."

After Jack left for the rink, Alice and Sophie sat down to talk. They discussed their very different upbringings and compared the similarities that had always made them both feel as though they just didn't quite fit. Both had IQ's of over 170 and seemed to have inherent talents for skating, music, and math that they could not explain as coming from either parent, except for the accounting skills, which Alice had always attributed to growing up with her parent's business savvy. They had both taken to the violin and piano at early ages, and Alice had always wished that she had been allowed to nurture that skill more, but she had been directed to suppress her musical ambitions in lieu of more practical business and language skills.

Sophie on the other hand had always been encouraged, and played regularly in their church, and even taught classes. They were also both quick to pick up foreign languages. Sophie had picked up Gaelic and French from relatives and studied German with ease at only twelve years old. They talked for nearly three hours until they were startled by a knock on the door, followed by a woman's voice.

"Coming," Sophie called, as Alice ducked into the bedroom. Sophie opened the door to a petite woman of about forty, with a brown bob and a concerned expression. "Hello Beth. Is everything okay?"

"That's what I was going to ask you. Who were you talking to?"

"No one."

"I was sure I heard voices."

"Oh. You must have heard me rehearsing."

"Rehearsing?"

"Yes. I'm going to be in a play when I get home."

"Oh, well, you should have called. I'd be happy to run the lines with you. What is it about?"

"Sisters, but I think I have it all down now. Was there something I can help you with? Babysitting? Bussing tables? You know I'm here if you need me."

"No, no, Robby is with his grandparents, and we have Tamera's boys bussing today. In fact, I am completely free, so I was wondering if you might enjoy an outing to Macy's. You're only here for a few more days, and I've hardly seen you at all."

"Oh Beth. I'm so sorry. You're right. I've just been distracted the last couple of days. Jack is under so much pressure to win this competition. I'm not even sure I should have come."

"Nonsense! I was thrilled when your parents suggested you accompany Jack. I haven't seen you since you were a teenager. You deserve a vacation, and I'm here to see that you have one. Now let's get out of here while we still have some day left and do some Christmas shopping! I can't let you go home empty handed. Now grab your purse!"

"Uh?"

"Come on. No buts allowed."

"Okay. Let me duck in the bedroom and change really quick."

"You don't need to change. You already look beautiful, as always."

"I'll just be a minute. I promise," she said, ducking into the bedroom. Looking at Alice, she shrugged her shoulders. "I need to go with Beth," she whispered.

"Don't worry. I'm sure it'll be fine. Go and have some fun," Alice whispered back. "She's right. This is supposed to be your vacation. I'll be fine."

"I'll be back as soon as possible." With that, Sophie pulled on a different sweater, pulled her hair back, and was gone.

Alice looked at the bedside clock. It was already after 3:30 in the afternoon as she listened to the footsteps going down the stairs. For the first time now, she was alone with her thoughts. She kept thinking about what Mr. Amstead had said about having her own life, and she tried to imagine what that might look like now.

So many thoughts wove their way through her mind. She tried to think back to something, some clue from her past that might help make sense of all this. There were so many questions. Had her parents known about Sophie? Was Alice even sure that they were her parents anymore? That last thought was sobering. People had always told her that she had her father's eyes, but so did Sophie. In fact, Sophie's may have even been closer in color. People also told Alice that she had her mother's hair, but her mother had always colored and cut her hair short, so she could never really tell.

Alice had never known her paternal grandparents, and her maternal grandparents had died in a fire, years ago, along with any photos of her mother as a child. Alice went to the mirror and studied her face, but the more she looked, the more she doubted who she really was.

Chapter Seven

Back at the skate rink, Jack was suffering from a rare case of nerves and was having a difficult time focusing. He fell in two of his easiest jumps and couldn't seem to stay in time with the music. On the last slip his coach and close friend, Nick, told him to take a time out.

"What's up with you today?" Nick asked.

"I'm sorry. I just can't seem to focus for some reason. I guess, I just have too much on my mind," was all Jack could reply with.

"Look, I know you're worried about your mom. She's not worse, is she?"

"No, no change Nick."

"Okay then, I'm moving your next skate to the end of this lineup. Take the time to pull yourself together and remember why you're here. Okay bud?"

"Thanks Nick."

Macy's was bustling with shoppers as Christmas carols flooded the atmosphere along with sales announcements, and directions to the North Pole to meet Santa and his elves.

"What do you think?" Beth asked, as she held up a bright blue sweater.

"It's you," Sophie replied.

"Not for me silly. For you." Beth held the sweater up to Sophie. "It really brings out your eyes and that gorgeous hair. You should wear it down more. Oh, and with my coupon it's only ten dollars. Try it on."

Sophie and Beth were headed for the fitting room when out of the corner of her eye Sophie saw someone who made her catch her breath. It was the man from the Alexandria Place that Albert had been so friendly with. What was his name? Leon. That was it. Sophie made a quick U-turn into lingerie, praying that he hadn't seen her, and hurried to the other side of a rack behind a post where she could watch where he went.

"Sophie?" asked Beth. "What's wrong?"

"Nothing. I just realized I'm not wearing the right bra to try that sweater on with," Sophie replied, as she watched Leon's head disappear down the escalator to the next level down.

"But this rack is maternity. Is there something you're keeping from me Sophie?"

"What? Oh. Oh no. No, I just didn't look at the sign."

Beth looked at Sophie skeptically. "I know there's something going on. Both you and Jack have been acting odd the last couple days. It doesn't have anything to do with this new woman he's met. Does it?"

"New woman?"

"I assumed you would know. Jack was telling Quill about her the other night at the bar. Something about her being complicated."

"I think that's one you'll have to ask Jack about. Oh, this looks like a good bra to go with the sweater," Sophie said, pulling a teal-colored pushup from a different rack and turning toward the changing rooms.

"If you say so," Beth said, as she noted the $43.00 price tag, and followed Sophie.

A few blocks away Albert hurried down the street and into a subway tunnel. He was nervous as he tried to purchase his pass. The first two credit cards he tried were rejected. Then he took out a different billfold and pulled a card from it. That one processed, and he hurried to catch the next train toward JFK.

It was 6:20 now as Jack waited to meet with Mr. Amstead. Jack checked his phone for messages and then dialed Mr. Amstead's number. It went directly to a message that informed Jack that the related voice mailbox was full. Something was wrong. Jack could feel it. At 6:30 he decided to dial his hotel to see if Mr. Amstead had possibly been delayed there. The woman who answered at the front desk was full of talkative Christmas cheer.

"Happy Holidays! Meridian Hotel. This is Marin. How may I assist you today?"

"I'm trying to reach Frank Amstead, but I've forgotten which room he's in."

"Oh, Mr. Amstead, the lovely gentleman in 1225. Don't you think that's an appropriate number for him? He certainly is a popular man today! I asked him this morning if he'd consider being Santa Clause for our Christmas party. Not that he looks the part, but he has the kind of demeanor that I think would make children comfortable. You know, a kindness about him. The Santa we had last year made my daughter cry. She said..."

"Excuse me. I'm sorry, but I really need to get through to Mr. Amstead."

"Oh, certainly! I'm so sorry. I'm putting you through now. Merry Christmas!"

"Merry Christmas," Jack replied, as Marin clicked off, and the phone to Mr. Amstead's room began to ring. It rang twenty times. Jack was now positive something was wrong and decided to head over to the hotel.

A half hour later Jack arrived at the Meridian and headed up the elevator to room 1225. He saw a "Do Not Disturb" sign on the door handle and knocked, though he did not actually expect a reply. He tried to turn the door handle, but it was shut tight.

Jack really didn't know what he was doing. He couldn't break into the room. Could he? Down the hall he saw a maid get off of the elevator. Maybe he could claim he lost his key and she'd let him in. It had worked once at a roadside motel. Jack watched as she went around the corner, and he walked casually past, noting that after she entered the room, she slipped the master key card into a pocket of her cart. After she had been in the room a minute, Jack walked casually back, stopping by the cart, and nodding at a smiling couple headed for the elevator.

"Merry Christmas!" they said as they passed.

"Merry Christmas," Jack replied and then quickly borrowed the key card and a washcloth. He opened room 1225, leaving the cloth in the door to prevent it from relocking. Then he hurried back to replace the key card.

Back at the apartment Alice was restless. She had to be careful not to move around too much though, lest someone downstairs would hear her. She'd found some blank paper and tried to make an outline of her life and family as she remembered them in hopes that might jar some hint from her past. What she found is that it really didn't take very long. While Sophie and Jack had aunts, uncles, and cousins that they were close to, even some from other countries, Alice realized that aside from her parents, she had known only her mother's younger sister Claire, who had come to visit a few times when Alice was a child. Then Claire had married and moved to Alaska to live with her husband Jim, who had two children, Jeremy and Natasha, whom Alice had never met. Claire used to send birthday cards, and Alice would write back, but get no reply until her next birthday card.

The last Alice had heard from her aunt at all was eight years ago when she had sent a Christmas card and family picture. It was the only picture Alice had of them. In fact, she realized thinking back, that she'd stolen it. Alice had found the card in a pile on the entryway table of her parent's home. It had contained several photos, and Alice had put one in her purse. She had meant to ask her mother if she could have it, but for some reason never did. Alice thought of that picture now.

Jack entered the living room of Mr. Amstead's suite. It was a disaster. Papers were strewn everywhere, and on the carpet were ominous dots of red leading toward the bedroom. Jack thought about calling the police first, but he had to look. He had to be certain. He also wanted to know if there was any information still there that might help him to help Alice and Sophie. Jack noticed a bottle of brandy on the bar and thought about taking a slug to steady his nerves as he moved toward the bedroom door. Then decided he'd best be careful not to leave any prints, and instead slipped his gloves on. It was only after Jack saw that there was no dead body that he realized he'd been holding his breath. He let it out, then breathed in deeply.

There was a strange smell in the air, something medicinal, and Jack noticed as he followed more drops of what looked like blood toward the balcony doors opposite the bed, that there was a damp puddle of something on the carpet from which the smell emanated. There was also a smudge of red on the wall nearby. Jack held his breath again as he opened the doors and looked down. Nothing.

The bedroom appeared to have been ransacked, as had the living room. Only the bathroom seemed to be untouched. Then something caught Jack's eye. There was a blinking blue light coming from under the bathroom sink. Jack opened the cupboard to find a laptop. Since he didn't know of anyone else who kept their laptops behind the extra toilet paper rolls, he grabbed it, and tucked it into his jacket.

It was already 8:00 p.m. and Jack needed to get back to the

apartment. He hadn't been comfortable leaving them alone earlier, and now he was becoming downright scared. Albert had followed Alice's phone to the pub. What if someone went back with another photo?

Before leaving, Jack called room service so that someone from the hotel might find the mess and call 911. Then he looked through the peephole and waited for the hall to be clear before slipping out and down the emergency exit stairs into an ally where he called Sophie.

Sophie was having dinner with Beth when her phone began to vibrate, and she looked down to see Jack's name across the screen.

"Aren't you going to answer that?" Beth asked.

"Oh, no. I don't want to get stuck on the phone," Sophie replied, noting the time and growing concerned that Jack would, or even worse, *had* returned to the apartment and discovered her gone. When the phone stopped Sophie checked the voice mail and hearing nothing, said a silent prayer and started to slip the phone into her purse only to have it start vibrating again with Jack's name. "Would you excuse me? I think maybe I had better take this."

"Is it a man?" Beth asked with playful suspicion.

"As a matter of fact, it is. I'll be right back," Sophie answered, as she hurried down the hall and into the ladies lounge. Again, Jack had left no message, and again the phone began to vibrate, only this time it was a text from Jack... "Where are you? Are you alright? Please respond if possible."

"Please God, let them be okay," Jack prayed. Wind and snow whipped round him as he ran down the block trying to hail a taxi.

Sophie was now really getting worried. Had Jack returned to the apartment and found her gone or was something else wrong? She would have to word a response carefully so as to make sure and be reassuring in either case. "All is fine. Just caught up in girl talk. Are you alright?"

Jack sighed in relief as he got in the taxi and saw Sophie's message. He immediately replied. "I'll be home ASAP."

"Oh no," Sophie murmured, as she hurried back to the table. "I have to go Beth. I promise I'll explain later, but it's an emergency."

"Hold on, I'll come with you," Beth said, as she motioned for the waiter.

"Really. I can't wait. I have to get back to the pub before Jack knows I left."

"What? Why?" Beth asked, as she left some money on the table, grabbed her packages, and hurried to catch up with Sophie, who was already on her way out the door. "Wait up! This way! We'll need a cab," Beth called motioning toward a taxi queue.

Sophie turned to hurry toward the Taxi Beth had gotten and ran directly into Leon. Their eyes met and he began to reach for her wrists just as Beth called out, "Come on Soph!"

Leon turned, and Sophie dashed to the cab. She was shaking visibly, as she stared out the window to where Leon stood, stalk still, watching after them.

"Okay, Talk. What is going on with you? Did you know that man?"

"No." At least Sophie spoke the truth in that. She only knew who Leon was associated with and that was more than enough for her.

"You're shaking like a leaf Sophie."

"We need to change taxis," Sophie said, as she suddenly

realized that Leon was sure to track the number on this one.

"What?"

"Driver. Please stop at the corner. We'll take the subway from here."

"Sophie. What is going on?"

"I'll explain later, but we have to hurry."

Albert was sweating as he approached flight gate F8. He checked his ticket again and made sure that he had the appropriate identification with it, not the one he used to get through security. That one had the right face, but not the right name and he was thankful that the lady in front of him had made such a fuss over having her luggage gone through, that the guards had barely glanced at his ticket. It wasn't until he went to put it away, that he had realized his narrow escape.

Just then his phone beeped. Seeing that it was Mr. Morgan, Albert promptly hit the mute button, and grabbing some napkins from a food kiosk, stuck the phone and napkins in his pocket, rounded the corner to another gate, and discreetly deposited the napkin wrapped phone into the trash bin.

"Last call for flight S114 to Geneva," came a voice over the loudspeaker, and Albert hurried back to gate F8.

Somehow, Sophie and Beth made it to the apartment before Jack. Just barely though. They had seen Jack get out of the taxi just as they came around the corner, and Beth had distracted him long enough for Sophie to sneak in up the back stairs. She had no more than thrown her coat on a chair and joined Alice in the bedroom when his key turned in the lock.

At the sound of his entry, both women went to meet him in the living room.

"What happened?" they asked together, disturbed by the dark look on his face.

"He couldn't make it."

"What happened?" asked Sophie.

"Is he alright?" asked Alice, feeling a chill down her spine.

"I don't know. I hope so. When he didn't show and I couldn't reach him by phone, I went to his hotel room. I found this hidden under the bathroom sink."

As Jack withdrew the laptop from his duffle bag, he recounted what he had found.

"This is all my fault," Alice said, staring blankly at the computer. "If I hadn't... He has two daughters. I..."

"None of this is your fault," Jack tried to sooth. "He may be fine. Maybe he escaped whoever ransacked the place..."

"Then why wouldn't he have taken the computer with him or at least called?" Alice asked.

"I should have stayed home," Sophie said, "Stayed with Aunt Anne and..."

"Stop it! Both of you. This is no one's fault except the... except the bad guys, whoever they are. Both of you are victims in this, whatever this is."

"Let's check out the laptop," Alice said.

"There may be another problem," Sophie interjected. "And it would be my fault."

***

The stewardess was giving the in-flight safety demo as the jet sat, waiting permission for takeoff. There had already been a fifteen-minute deicing delay. The snow and wind were picking up again too. For the first time in probably twenty years, Albert found himself praying. He offered up a silent "Amen" as the plane slowly began to taxi down the runway. He still wouldn't feel safe though until he was gliding over the Atlantic at thirty thousand feet.

***

Alice waited for Sophie to go on as Jack asked, "What could you have possibly done? You've been stuck in here all day."

Sophie met Alice's gaze. She hadn't had a chance to tell her about Leon, and hadn't intended to tell Jack, but now, given the circumstances, she knew that it would be better to tell all now rather than to have him find out later.

"What? What happened?" Jack prodded, as he sensed a secret between them.

"Beth came by."

"And?" Jack asked, then continued before Sophie could answer. "You went out with her. Didn't you?"

"I told her to go ahead," Alice interjected. "It's supposed to be her vacation."

"Does Beth know about Alice?"

"Not yet, but she knows something is going on."

"Well, as long as you're back safe, I guess no harm's done."

"It's not Beth I'm concerned about. I ran into Leon, literally ran into him, and he saw my face up close."

"Leon?" asked Jack.

"He's the front desk manager from the Alexandria, who was so chummy with Albert," Alice replied to Jack. "What did he say?" she asked Sophie.

"He didn't say anything. He did try to grab me by my wrists, but Beth called to me, and I got away in a taxi with her before he could get a grip."

"He heard your name and saw the taxi?"

"Don't panic. We only took the taxi a couple of blocks and then changed to the subway. I'm sorry Jack."

"Let's not worry about that now. At least he didn't track you here," Jack said as he went to plug the computer in.

"Jack?" Alice asked.

"Yes? Please don't tell me you went out too."

"No. I was just wondering how your rehearsal went?"

"About as well as the rest of this day," he replied with a sigh.

"I'm sorry Jack," said Sophie.

"It'll be okay. I don't know how, but I have to believe, it'll be okay." Jack forced a smile at both of them. "We're in this together. Now let's see if we can figure out what this is," Jack finished, as a file list populated the screen.

Chapter Eight

In Seattle, Suzanna Morgan was pacing the antique, hardwood floor of their Montlake home. At seventy-seven Suzanna was a petite woman of five foot three, who wore her hair in a stylish short bob, dyed a similar shade to Alice's. She had always worried that Alice might do something like this. She assumed that it would be as a teenager though, when they at least still had some legal control. She knew that what the doctors had said was true. Despite all the controls, Alice was still human, and the human nature of any child couldn't be controlled, much less the obedience of an adult. In fact, Suzanna had to admit that at least a little part of her was proud. She could relate to Alice's recent disobedience, and it made her feel as though she were more completely her daughter. It remained however that Alice's behavior posed dangers that Alice had no way of knowing and mustn't ever be allowed to discover.

The call had come from Leon three hours ago, but they still hadn't been able to locate either Alice or Albert or find out anything more about the mysterious Ernie. Dampness threatened to spill over Suzanna's eyes, and she wiped them quickly with her sleeve, leaving behind mascara streaks on her pink angora sweater. *"Darn it!"* she thought. She would now have to go upstairs and change. She could not allow Edgar to know. She had never allowed herself to shed a tear for Alice or any of them, and she couldn't start now.

Suzanna had just started up the stairs when she heard the

crash from Edgar's office. Assuming he had thrown something again in his frustration, she continued up the stairs to change.

***

Alice browsed through the file list, as Jack paced, and Sophie made coffee. There were hundreds, but so far most of what she had opened appeared to be personnel files or drug information related only to Mr. Amstead's company. It wasn't until she reached the end and started over at the beginning, that a name or rather a date, caught her attention. The file was AIH0/AIH7. She had ignored it at first and then she remembered, Mr. Amstead had said all the files were from nineteen eighty to eighty-seven and AIH corresponds numerically to 198.

When Alice double clicked on the file, instead of any information, she got a password box. Clicking on the "forgot password" icon underneath, she brought up list of three questions to answer.

"What is it?" asked Jack, as he paced behind Alice.

"I think this must be the right file, but it's password protected, and I need to answer the security questions to get the password."

"Do you know the answers?" Jack asked, as Sophie came over to look.

"It depends. If he created them after we spoke, then he would have made them something he knew I could guess, but if not..."

"They look like children's riddles," Jack cut in as he read, "What's red on the face and yellow inside?"

"Are you thinking what I'm thinking?" Sophie asked, smiling at Alice.

Alice laughed as she typed the answer, "Albert", and the answer highlighted in green.

"One down. Two to go!" they cheered.

"I don't believe it. What's next?" Jack asked.

"It's a cryptogram, like the file name, but not as simple," Alice said. "Can you hand me some paper and a pen? I'll write it down so we can all work on it."

"Right here," Sophie said, handing her the note pad and pen from beside the phone, which chose that moment to ring. Sophie looked at Jack.

"Let me get it," he said, crossing to the phone in two long strides. "Hello?" Jack answered. "Hey dad," he continued, and Alice breathed a sigh of relief. Sophie and Jack however, seemed to still be holding their breath. Jack had not told Alice anything about his mother's condition and had, in caution, until he was more certain about Alice, asked Sophie to not say anything either.

Jack listened on the phone without response for what seemed to Alice an unusually long time, and she was sensing an uneasy tension that seemed to be affecting Jack even more strongly than had the rest of the day's events.

"Okay. Thanks dad. I'm going to hand you over to Sophie now."

Sophie took the phone, and Jack grabbed a couple of mugs of coffee to bring back to the table. "So, let me see what we have here. I used to be pretty good at cryptograms," he said to Alice, with a forced smile.

"Is everything okay?" Alice ventured.

"Fine," he said as he took a sip from his mug.

"Jack? What's wrong?"

"Nothing. Did you want some cream for your coffee?" he asked, rising and going to the refrigerator.

Alice looked to Sophie, who looked to Jack. "I forgot, we're out of cream. I'll just run downstairs and get some," he continued and without a beat he was out the door.

Sophie had gone to the window with the phone. She was just

as silent as Jack had been, as she gazed out the window. Alice wanted to go to her, but she knew that no matter how close they had become and how much they had been through together in the past couple of days, there was something going on now that she was not a part of and couldn't be, until they decided to let her in.

***

Suzanna knocked on the door to Edgar's study. She had pulled herself together, changed into one of Edgar's favorite negligees, brought a bottle of wine, and some glasses from the pantry.

"Edgar?" she called gently. "Can I come in? Let's work on this together." When there was no answer, she tried the handle, but the door was locked tight. "Edgar? Sweetheart? Are you alright? Edgar?" Putting her ear to the door, she heard nothing. She tried the door again. "Edgar?" A sense of panic swelled in Suzanna's bosom as she threw on her coat, grabbed a set of keys, and ran outside into the pouring rain.

Her house slippers were soaked by the time she reached the patio and the outside French doors to the study. The first thing that struck her was that the shades were drawn. Putting the key to the door, she discovered it already open. What she saw next was darkness, as she felt herself hit the carpet and a warm trickle of blood run down her face.

Chapter Nine

The first rays of dawn made their way in through the kitchen window, as Alice scrolled through the data on Mr. Amstead's laptop. All of the companies were research based in biotechnology. And all of the transactions were made thirty-one to thirty-seven years before. What was really odd was that it wasn't one or two simple acquisition transactions to buy out the companies or even transferal of stock. Instead, there were multiple back and forth, high dollar wire transactions between not just Morgan and the individual companies, but cross-company transactions. It was as though they were all working together on something, but what? Alice was sure that none of these companies were listed in Morgan's current portfolio either. How had Mr. Amstead even gotten ahold of this information? Alice wondered.

The alarm on Jack's phone began to ding. He stretched on the couch and with eyes still closed reached to turn it off. "It can't be 6:30 yet. Can it Soph?" he moaned, as he rolled into a semi-upright position.

"I'm afraid so," Alice replied, looking at the clock.

At her voice, Jack's eye's popped open. "Didn't you ever go to bed?" he asked, as he watched her staring at the computer screen.

"Apparently not," she answered, giving him a wry smile.

"Find anything?"

"Nothing that makes any sense, but then again, that's why Mr. Amstead was suspicious in the first place. What I really need to do is to get into the company database to research if there are any other records, but that's not easily done without arousing a lot of suspicion, and I think I may be looking at a lot of that already."

"Have they always worked this hard to keep tabs on you?"

"Yes," she said, thinking back to the man in her photos. "But they never really had to. This is my first major rebellion."

"Wow! You may be fast at learning everything else, but you're at least fifteen years behind the curve on that." He smiled and winked at Alice as he walked over to start making some fresh coffee.

"Do you know of someplace that I could get on the internet Jack? The internet has been disabled on this," she said, pointing to the laptop. "I imagine, to keep it from being traced, but I want to get on and at least do a check into who the companies listed here are or were. I figure if I can't get into the Morgan database to look for them, maybe I can find some reference to Morgan in theirs."

"And just how do you intend to get into their files?"

"I'd have to hack in," Alice said, as she picked up her mug from the night before and crossed over to where Jack stood by the sink to rinse it out.

"You know how to do that?" he asked, turning to look at her. The way the sunlight struck across her cheeks, reminded him of a painting of an angel he'd seen once on a cathedral wall in Ireland.

"Yep. It's usually relatively simple. Morgan's files would be another issue though, and they would know it was me."

Jack mentally shook himself to focus back on what she was saying. "Is it simple enough that you could teach me?" he asked. "I don't want either of you two going anywhere today."

"Do you know computer code?"

"You mean all those ones and zeros?"

"Binary. Yes!" Alice answered hopefully, her emerald gaze

turning to meet his eyes.

"No," he said, turning away to check the progress of the coffee when he realized he had still been staring at her.

"Oh," Alice replied. "Well then, I'm afraid I'll just have to be extra careful. I…We need answers, and to get them I'll have to do this."

"Good morning you two," came Sophie's voice from the bedroom behind them. "I'm sorry I fell asleep on you. Did you sleep at all?" she asked, glancing from Jack to Alice.

"I sacked out on the sofa, Alice hasn't slept at all though," Jack said, turning to Sophie. It amazed him that even though they looked nearly identical, their effect on him was incredibly different.

"You should go get some rest Alice," Sophie said.

"She's right," Jack agreed.

"I don't think I can. I have to figure out how Morgan was involved with these companies," Alice responded, as she turned to the finishing coffee, and poured a mug of the rich black liquid. She sniffed it. "This should help wake me up."

Sophie went over to pour herself a mug, looked at Jack, and back to the coffee. "I think this could perk up a corpse."

Jack made a grim smile. "Exactly what I need," he answered, and opened the fridge to pull out some bread, jam, and butter.

"So, what do you need to do in order to find out about the companies?" asked Sophie.

"Find another computer that I can hack in from."

"Oh. Okay."

"You're not going anywhere," Jack said, as he put bread in to toast. "Neither one of you. I have two preliminary skates today, and I don't want to be worrying about you two running into Leon or whoever else may be out there looking for you."

"It would be better if it were a public computer, in case they trace the hack," Sophie said.

"And what would you know about it?" Jack asked.

"Just what I've seen on television, but..."

"No! Absolutely, positively no! Got it?" Jack asked, looking from Sophie to Alice and back to Sophie's defiant face.

"We could go in disguise," Sophie suggested.

"That's a great idea!" Alice agreed, as Jack rubbed his temples and took a long swig of coffee.

"And where would you get said disguises?" he asked.

"Beth."

"No! I don't want anyone else involved, especially after what happened to Amstead."

"We don't actually know what happened to him," Sophie countered.

"Exactly!"

"And after yesterday, Beth is kind of already involved."

"Maybe, but she doesn't need to know any more that could put her in danger. Come on Sophie. You can't really want to involve her?"

"Of course not Jack, but Beth's no dummy, and she's going to ask questions, so I think it might be safer if she knew what she was getting herself involved with. You know as well as I do that she'll involve herself, whether she knows what it's about or not."

Jack sighed in exasperation, as the toast popped up, and both Sophie and Alice stared him down. "Okay. I give! I never could argue with the logic of a woman, much less two of you. I still don't think you should say anything about Alice though."

"Oh? Then what is she going to think when I tell her I need two different looks?"

"Two?"

"Jack's right Sophie. There's no reason for you to put yourself at risk again."

"B.S.! Yes, there is! First off, two is less conspicuous than one, and second, we're in this together. This is as much about me is it is about you Alice!"

Just then somebody knocked at the door.

Jack motioned for Alice and Sophie to go into the bedroom.

"Is everything okay in there?" came Beth's voice from behind the door.

"Fine Beth," Jack said, as he went to the door and opened it. "You might as well come in on this now though."

"Come in on what?" Beth asked, brow raised. "Is it about your mother?"

"No," Jack said raising a finger to his lips.

"What? What's wrong Jack? Sophie was acting strange yesterday and..."

"Sophie, Alice, come on out."

"Who is?" Beth started to ask, as she looked up and both women entered the room. "How?" Beth stuttered, blinking to make sure she wasn't seeing double.

"I'm Alice," Alice said, extending her hand to Beth, who grasped it warmly, and looked into her eyes.

"We think we may be twins," Sophie added.

"Well, I can see where you might get that idea," Beth replied, as she let Alice's hand go, and looked at Jack. "Does Quill know?"

"No." Jack answered, "and I hate to ask you to keep a secret, but if you could, just for now anyway, it would be best."

"And why is that?" Beth asked.

"We met by chance a couple days ago, and things have been rather, how should I say...?"

"Mysterious," offered Sophie.

"And confusing," added Alice.

"To say the least," Jack concluded, as he walked to the kitchen to take a bite of his now cold toast and a drink of his also cold coffee.

"Okay. Now fill me in," said Beth, moving to sit on the couch. "Make it quick though, before Quill comes knocking for me to feed Robby."

"Robby?" asked Alice.

"Aye. He's just four months. He was asleep when I came up, but he won't be much longer," she said, looking at her watch, and then anxiously back to Sophie and Alice. As if on cue they heard crying from below. "I'll be back as soon as I can," Beth said, hopping up from the sofa and making her way to the door. "Right back."

No more than five minutes later Beth was back, nursing a hungry Robby, but completely focused on the story being recounted to her of their last few days.

"What can I do to help?" asked Beth.

"I need to get on the internet. Preferably somewhere public with a large bank of computers," Alice told her.

"Why can't you just use the pub's connection?"

"I don't want to risk it being traced."

"Why would it be if it's not from your personal IP address?"

"Because I'll have to hack in."

"Oh, okay then."

"We need disguises too," Sophie added.

"That makes sense, I guess. I have some wigs downstairs I can bring up."

"Perfect," Jack sighed in resignation, "I guess I'll leave you three to it. I have to run, but I'll be back about four, so if for any reason you aren't going to be back yet, please call me," Jack said, grabbing his duffle bag, and heading for the door. "And please, please, please, be careful!"

After Jack left, Beth left Robby with Sophie and Alice and went downstairs for the wigs and her makeup case. When she came back, she was even paler than her normal white Irish complexion.

"What is it, Beth? What's wrong?" asked Sophie. "Is it?"

"No. It's Jack. It looks like he needs a disguise as well," Beth said, as she showed them the sketch in the paper.

"Oh no!" they said in unison.

On the third page was a quarter page size sketch of Jack with a caption that read, "Wanted for questioning in the disappearance of multi-million-dollar businessman missing from a local hotel under highly suspicious circumstances. If spotted, DO NOT APPROACH. Please contact the NYPD IMMEDIATELY."

Chapter Ten

Jack wiped at his face as he felt several pairs of eyes on the subway scrutinize him. He knew he didn't have egg on his face, maybe toast crumbs, but the looks he was getting were downright disconcerting. Then when he got up to street level, he was met by Nick, who yanked him into an ally.

"What the hell! Nick?"

"That's exactly my question. I'm just glad I found you before anyone else."

"What are you talking about?"

"This. What is this about? Do you know this dude?" Nick asked, showing the paper to Jack.

"You must be kidding me!" Jack said, as he read the caption. "What the hell else could possibly go wrong?"

"Well..." Nick started.

"I really don't want to know," Jack stated, cutting him off. "What am I supposed to do?"

"Pray Jack. Pray hard that nobody who knows you sees this. Come on, wrap your scarf around your face and pull on this hat. You can tell me all about it when we get to the locker room. Here, let's switch coats too, just to be safe," Nick added.

An hour later, Alice had become a raven-haired vixen with bright red lips, and Sophie a platinum blond with cotton candy pink lips.

"I feel a bit overdone," Alice said, looking in the mirror.

"You look great Alice!" Sophie encouraged.

"Yes, you do, if I do say so myself!" Beth agreed.

"If you say so. It just isn't me."

"That's the point!" Sophie reminded her.

"Good point."

"Even Jack wouldn't recognize you two!" Beth said, standing back to admire her handy work. "We will need to do something about the clothes though, or at least the coats. Alice, you can wear my trench coat. It's long on me, so it should fit you fine, and Sophie can wear my ski jacket, and to complete the look, a pair of reading glasses. Oh! And some pale plum blusher over a little of this green tint concealer stuff to help hide the scars," Beth finished, as she dabbed at Sophie's cheek.

Jack hadn't been able to talk to Nick. When they got to the locker rooms a whole team from Toronto was there showering from their dawn practice. Jack wasn't sure what he could have said anyway. Alice in herself was shocking enough, but this thing, whatever it was, just seemed to keep growing. It was bad enough that Beth was now involved, but at least she was family. She would have found out soon enough anyway, but the idea of bringing Nick into it was too much. Yes, they had known each other since Jack had started skating at age twelve and he knew Sophie as well.

In many ways Nick was far more than a coach, he was a big brother figure. He knew what was going on with Jack's mother, and Jack knew that Nick would do anything he could to help. He also knew that he couldn't lie to Nick.

So, what the hell was he supposed to tell him? Jack wondered, as he pulled a red Olympic ski mask of Nick's over his face. He felt like a bloody criminal on ice wearing the thing, but he could have been the president, and no one would have recognized him.

He bent over and took a deep breath as he double checked the laces on his skates. He thought about his mother. He needed to focus on his routine. For her sake, he had to focus.

He looked up to see Nick across the rink watching him, waiting. He could do this. He had to do this. He closed his eyes and pictured the farm, his mother's smile as she stood in the soft summer sun feeding the chickens. It was with that image held in his mind that he began.

Jack warmed up with a few laps and a couple of single spins, then completed three triples with perfect landings, and after a couple turns, a combination he'd been working on all year. He recognized Yuri and Calvin as they came onto the ice. Yuri was by far the stiffest competition for the individual skate. There were other people watching from the benches now, so Jack knew he was still safe from having to explain anything to Nick for a while yet. He skated over to the side where Nick waited as Yuri and Calvin warmed up with laps. He needed to stretch, have some water, and observe Yuri's practice.

"That was a good run out there," Nick observed. "Much more focused than the last two days."

"Thanks. I have to do this Nick. You know I do, for my mom."

"I know. How is she?"

"Fighting."

"That's good," Nick nodded, clasping Jack's shoulder. "I called the committee to tell them about your accident, and they were really understanding about the need to keep the bandages on your face. We wouldn't want those burns to get infected," Nick added, as Jack saw two of the judges and Yuri's coach coming down the bleachers beside them.

"How'd it happen?" asked one of the judges with a concerned look.

Before Jack could think of a reply, Nick jumped in. "My friend here considers himself a bit of a chef as well as a skater, and some cooking oil tried to cook his face."

"Ouch! That's why I stick with takeout and the microwave. That must hurt like the devil!" the judge replied.

"Are you sure you're okay to skate tonight?" asked Yuri's coach.

"He'll be alright," Nick said.

"You do know that any drug use, even a pain killer will disqualify him?" the coach continued.

"He's using a topical. It numbs the face a little and makes it hard to talk much, but he's good to go on the rink. You should have seen his practice just now."

"Good," replied the judge. "We'll look forward to your performance then."

Jack just nodded to the men as they walked away and resisted the urge to rub his hand down his face. Then he and Nick watched Yuri give a flawless practice.

"Look," Nick said, "some of the other coaches, including my roommate, are having lunch together today. Why don't we grab something from the sandwich shop, go to my hotel room instead, and you can tell me all about everything then? Right now, stretch it out and I want to see that combination again."

It was 11:00 O'clock when Alice and Sophie finally headed out after letting Beth add some finishing touches, like fake eye lashes for Alice and some eyebrow plucking and pencil for both of them. Beth had excused herself to go help Quill with the lunch rush, and Sophie and Alice left via the back stairs to avoid being noticed by any of the regulars as well as Quill. They caught a cab two blocks over and went to Times Square where Beth had told them of a large internet café. On arrival to the café, they grabbed a couple of venti mocha's and found an empty terminal towards the back but facing the door.

"Okay. Where's the list?" Alice asked, as Sophie pulled it from her purse. Alice started on the first one. Not wanting to take time to read through all of the files, Alice downloaded everything that she thought relevant onto thumb drives they had picked up at a shop on the way. It took nearly two hours to complete all of the downloads, but fortunately the place wasn't raided by FBI, and they made a seemingly clean get away.

It was nearly three by the time they returned to the pub, and much to the relief of their rumbling stomachs they were greeted with pub sandwiches and a note from Beth, saying that she had to run out, but she hoped all had gone well and she would be back around 4:00 O'clock.

Nick sat across from Jack, his mouth wide open as he tried to absorb the implications of what Jack was trying, with as much caution as possible, to explain.

"So, you went to get something this guy had for Alice, who you think is Sophie's twin, separated at birth, and found a blood trail in his room? Then you made sure that the cops were called, but you left. Why was that?"

"Because I sort of broke into the room."

"And you did that because?"

"When he didn't answer the phone or the door, I was worried. I just wanted to check for Alice that he was okay, and since I'm not family or have actually ever even met this guy, it wasn't like they were going to just let me into the room."

"Okay."

"So, you understand?"

"Not completely, but I do know you're not a killer. My concern for you buddy is that even though I was able to think up a cover for the competition, there's not a hell of a lot I can do to help you through customs when you leave next week. And you better pray to God that none of the people who know your face, see that sketch," Nick said, "Especially Yuri. He and his coach would have a field day. You're real competition for them and they'd love to see you out."

"I know. Right now, I'm hoping that whatever happened

with Mr. Amstead clears itself up before I'm due to leave."

"You better pray that it doesn't clear itself up by them finding his corpse somewhere."

"Thanks. Like I hadn't thought of that possibility myself."

"I'm sorry Jack. I know you had enough on your mind before. I'm just worried about you and about Sophie. I'd like to meet Alice though. Maybe I can be a more objective judge of her."

"This isn't her fault."

"I didn't mean that it was, but you've only known her a few days and just look at how she's already affecting your life. I could run a background check on her."

"No. She needs protection, not checking on. She's had more than enough of that in her life already!"

"How would you know?"

"She told me."

"She told you?"

"And I saw it."

"What aren't you telling me Jack?"

"It's just this guy she works with. I saw him. He follows her. He tracked her cell phone for God's sake! That's why I went to see Amstead and not her."

"Do you think this guy had something to do with Amstead's disappearance?"

"I don't know, but I wouldn't put it past him. Hey," Jack said looking at his watch, "we'd better get back to the rink. The girls are expecting me back around four."

"Here," Nick said, handing Jack his cell phone. "You'd better give them a call. I forgot to tell you that when I talked to the committee, they moved the single's preliminaries to 4:00 O'clock. You're right though, we'd better head out before my roommate gets back."

Jack put the mask back on and phoned Sophie and Alice as they went down the back stairs and out the hotel service entrance. Then he and Nick cut across through the park to the back side of the rink. It was busy as they made their way down the side steps and into the locker room. Several of the guys looked up and stared at Jack briefly, but most were too preoccupied to notice the masked man.

"He's wearing it to protect the bandages. He got burned last night. Okay?" Nick said to the gawkers.

"I'd stare at me too," Jack said, as he passed a mirror.

"At least it's not black. You don't look too much like a criminal."

Back at the apartment, Sophie listened to the message from Jack and gave a sigh of relief that he at least knew what was going on and was so far okay.

Alice turned and watched her expectantly, as she went to the kitchen and cleaned off their lunch plates.

"Nick, his coach, intercepted him this morning at the station, and he's telling everyone that he burned his face with cooking oil and has to wear a ski mask to protect the bandages. They also changed his place in the lineup, so his rehearsal isn't until 4:00. That means it will be nearly 6:00 before he can get back now," Sophie told Alice.

"That's good. I was thinking that I'll need to get some money, and I should try to do it before they decide to put a restriction on me, if they haven't already. I should have thought of it before, but I'm so accustomed to using my cards. Those can be traced though, and when I paid the taxi driver, I gave him my last fifty."

"Won't they trace it if you use your ATM card too?" Sophie asked.

"Only to the machine, so I'll just need to make sure and use one several blocks away. The problem with an ATM is the five hundred dollar a day withdrawal limit."

"How much money are we talking about here?" asked Sophie.

"As much as possible. Normally I could call my dad's secretary to wire funds, but I'd rather not bring her into this."

What they agreed on was simple. It was Saturday, and the banks were already closed. The pawnshops and gold exchanges, however, were still open. Looking up nearby locations, Alice and Sophie, along with Beth, made their way to five different shops. Fortunately, Alice had brought some gold jewelry, as well as a watch from Cartier with her, which together netted them nearly twenty-five thousand dollars. Unfortunately, it was not all in cash, a few thousand was and the rest was in checks made out to Beth, which she would cash for them on Monday.

By the time they completed the transactions, it was nearly 7:00 O'clock and they all needed to get back to the pub."

"I've never seen that much money at once in my life!" Sophie exclaimed, as she entered the apartment with Alice.

"I just hope that it's enough," Alice said, concerned.

"It's a year's wages for my dad," Sophie said.

"I'm sorry Sophie. I didn't mean... I just don't know what's going to happen or what we might need," Alice explained. "I've always wanted more adventure in life, but I'm just not sure how to handle this."

"None of us are Alice," Sophie said, sitting beside her.

Nick had loaned Jack money for a taxi back to the pub, but Jack asked the driver to stop a couple of blocks away at a small chapel instead.

It was still only 5:30, but it may as well have been midnight. The air was still and eerily quiet in the pitch dark. The thick clouds had begun to dust the streets with soft white powder. Jack could hear people on the next street over, where shops and cafés abounded, but here the only sound he heard was of someone, probably Mona, he thought, playing the organ.

Mona was the elderly caretaker who lived above the small sanctuary. Jack already knew he didn't dare to show himself at service in the morning. For now, he would pull the mask off, say hello to Mona and light a candle for his mother and maybe even one for himself. He wondered for a moment if lighting a candle for oneself was sacrilegious, but then he thought, it wasn't about him. None of it was, and so he lit the second candle with a prayer for wisdom, strength, and safety for all of them. God had put them in this together and Jack must have faith that God would bring them through it together too.

Chapter Eleven

When Jack returned to the apartment, he found both Sophie and Alice huddled over computers.

"So, how was your day ladies?" he asked, as Sophie ran over to hug him.

"We were getting worried Jack. It's nearly 8:00."

"I'm sorry. I didn't realize I'd taken so long. I thought it might be appropriate to the situation if I stopped by the chapel tonight, lit a couple of candles, and sent up a few big and I guess pretty long prayers," he said, as he shrugged out of his coat.

"I couldn't agree more," Sophie responded. "There's some beef stew and sandwiches in the kitchen that Beth brought up from the lunch leftovers."

"I thought I smelled something good. You didn't answer my question though. What did you two find out?" Jack asked, looking at Alice.

"Nothing yet, but there must be something here somewhere," she replied.

"Beth brought her computer over so that we could both work and look through two companies at a time. I can't believe how much information there is," Sophie said.

"Most of it is meaningless, but we used three thumb drives to load it all," Alice added. "How was your practice, Jack?"

Jack smiled that she had thought to ask. "All things considered, it actually went really well. Thanks for asking."

Alice couldn't help but smile back.

Sophie fixed Jack a plate and brought it to the table along with a carafe of water, and a fresh coffee for herself. "Have a seat and we'll tell you all we can. Did you want more coffee, Alice?"

"Yes, but I'll get it myself. I need to tear myself away from the screen so that I won't become too mechanical as I scan through and miss something important."

"Have you two eaten?"

"We had a late lunch, but now that you mention it, I am getting hungry again," Sophie said.

"Allow me," Alice said, as she put two more plates together for herself and Sophie. "I need to feel like I'm doing something besides messing up your lives."

"You're not messing up our lives," Jack said.

"Jack's right," Sophie agreed. "This isn't your fault."

"We're in this together Alice. And God will bring us through it together. I have to believe that. Okay?" Jack added.

"You really believe that?" Alice asked.

"Don't you?" he asked, realizing that he knew nothing of her faith.

"I don't know. My parents went to church on Christmas and Easter, but that's about as far as my experience with God goes. Speaking of my parents though, I really should call again to at least leave another message. My mom is probably worried sick. She's used to talking to me at least twice a day. I really should have thought about it while we were out, but ..."

"You do realize that she's part of this?" Sophie cut in.

"It's possible she didn't know," Alice tried to defend. "She may have been told you died."

"Come on Soph. We've all watched enough television to know that things like that do happen."

"I guess it's possible," Sophie admitted. "I'm sorry Alice."

"Don't be. I have thought it myself. I just..."

"She's still your mother. I understand. My adoptive parents will always be my parents too. No matter what."

"I'd love to meet them."

"And I'm sure you will," Jack started "but first we need to…"

"Wait a second! Jack, do you remember the name of the doctor on my death certificate and where it was issued?"

"Sophie, I…"

"I know you didn't tell me everything."

"I told you as much as I could be certain about. Right now, we have enough to do. We need to focus on finding a link between Morgan Acquisitions and the other companies that you downloaded information from."

Sophie glared at Jack before acquiescing with a sigh. "Okay, I'll let it go for now, but as soon as we get home, I want to see everything you have. No matter how small of a scrap, it's my life and death, and I want to see it. Don't even try to protect me or you'll have to protect yourself from me! Understand Jack?"

"I think I get your meaning fine, but that brings up another problem. I'm a wanted man. How am I supposed to get through customs to go home? Lying to the skating committee is one thing, but customs isn't just going to take my word for it. I'd have to have signed medical proof."

"What about Tom?" Sophie asked.

"For one thing, if someone found out, he'd lose his license, and for a second, he's in Nova Scotia."

"How much does your passport photo look like the sketch?" Alice asked. They don't know your name, so it's possible you won't be recognized."

"She's right," Sophie agreed. "Especially if we change your hair and you have a few strategically placed bandages, you can still show your face enough to pass, but not look so much like the sketch."

"The photo is about eight years old. It might work. They usually don't pay too much attention. I guess I should be more concerned about one of the pub patrons or someone from the rink recognizing me," Jack said, picking up his plate and trading his water glass for a mug of coffee. "Do you mind if I take a look at some of these files?"

"Be my guest," Alice said.

"And as far as calling home, Alice is right, Soph. She needs to keep suspicion to a minimum, especially after the incident with Mr. Amstead. In fact, I wouldn't be surprised if the police wanted to question her too. Just make sure you call from a pay phone in a different vicinity and keep it short Alice," Jack said as he gazed at the lists that she had up on the computer.

"I'll go do that now," Alice said.

"Oh no. Not alone," Jack said, stopping her in her tracks as she started to pull on her wig and coat."

"Why? No one will recognize me."

"Maybe not, but this isn't like walking around the Alexandria. This isn't the area for an evening stroll. Besides, do you even know where a phone booth is?"

"No," Alice admitted.

"There's one by the supermarket. We'll pass it on the way to church," Sophie said.

"Okay," Alice consented, taking off the wig and going to top off her coffee.

Jack stared at the computer. Something looked familiar about one of the companies called "Scangentech." Jack could have sworn he'd seen that name while looking for information on Sophie. He clicked on the file. The company was founded in 1937 and had been based in Canada with research centers in France, Germany and Switzerland. "Research for what though?" Jack asked himself, apparently not completely to himself though as both Alice and Sophie turned to look at him.

Scangentech turned out to be a company that specialized in biological scans to dissect variants of genes in animal DNA.

They had attempted to conduct scans of human DNA, which were inconclusive because, due to the possible radioactivity, they could only obtain authorization to scan corpses. The date on this particular file was 1983. Scangentech supposedly went bankrupt in 1988 and ceased all further genetic scanning and research. If that were true, Jack wondered, why was he so certain that he had seen the company's name in connection with his research on Sophie?

"What is it, Jack?" Sophie and Alice asked in unison, causing Jack to jerk and look first behind one shoulder and then the other where each now stood.

"You two just scared the bejesus out of me! A minute ago you were sitting in front of me. I didn't even see you move."

"You were awfully focused. What did you find Jack?" Sophie asked, as both women leaned in to read over his shoulder.

"I found that I'm suddenly claustrophobic," Jack answered glancing from Sophie to Alice, whose faces were almost touching his as they read. "It's probably nothing. I just thought I'd seen that name somewhere before, but if they went out of business in 1988, then I'm probably wrong and I've just seen something similar somewhere. Anyway, I don't see any references to Morgan Acquisitions."

"They have to be current," Alice answered. "Otherwise, I wouldn't have found these secured files online. Maybe we, I mean my parents bought them out and they resumed business." Alice clicked on a file that was labeled "Year End 2013." "Here it is. If we go back through this list, it looks like they reopened in 1992," she said, clicking on the "Year End 1992" file. The file said that after receiving private funding from anonymous donors Scangentech re-launched their research into human genetic scanning using embryonic cells. Multiple tests are to be conducted both invitro and pre-fertilization in the hope of finding a gene therapy solution to multiple birth defects, including retardation and autoimmune diseases.

"Maybe it was funded by wealthy AID's patients?" Sophie speculated.

"That still doesn't give us any reference as to how or why Morgan Acquisitions is connected to them though," Alice said.

"They could have been a donor," Jack said.

"No. My parents are known to be philanthropists, but the business side is into ownership, not rescue." Alice clicked on another file. "This just says that it is privately owned by the shareholders, but there should be a list of shareholders somewhere, and based on that we would be able to see who has the controlling interests." Alice continued to scroll through the file, but no individual names were listed, only other companies. It was one of these companies, "Firebranded Computing," that caught Alice's attention. "I've seen that name before in our accounting records."

"What do you know about them?" Sophie asked.

"Nothing really. They've been on the books since before I started working. They're just one of hundreds of names listed in our acquisitions."

"You said you saw them in accounting records?" Jack questioned.

"Yes, that just means that there's been recent payments made to us through them, which just says that they are active and making a profit."

"I wonder if all of Morgan's connections to the companies Amstead listed are second hand," Jack said.

"That would explain why none of them are familiar to me."

They spent the next few hours going through the other files and found a couple of other similar connections, where the companies had gone bankrupt only to come back to life with the aid of companies that had been bought out by Morgan

Acquisitions. All of the companies also seemed to be related to bioengineering and other genetic research, but they were rescued by companies in other fields from computing to construction.

It was 1:30 in the morning, when they were startled by a knock on the door. "Jack? Sophie?"

"It's Quill," Jack said looking at Alice, who took her cue to go into the bedroom, as Jack went to open the door.

"Hi Quill. What brings you by at this hour?"

Quill entered and looked around the apartment.

"Since when did you two become computer nerds?" he asked eyeing the two computers on the table. "And where'd you come by the second. That's looks quite the upscale model."

"A friend," Jack replied simply.

"That's not why I'm here though. I want to know what's goin on with this?" Quill asked, pulling out a copy of the paper.

"I... Well, I was..."

"Oh, for God's sake Jack, just tell him," Sophie stated. "Or would you prefer me to?"

"Sophie! I don't..."

"I know! *You* don't want anyone involved! Well, I think that should really be up to Alice and me. Alice, come on out and meet my uncle Quill."

"Alice? Oh, dear Lord in heaven!" Quill exclaimed as Alice came out from the bedroom.

"Hello," Alice said, extending her hand to Quill. "I'm Alice."

Quill shook her hand, but otherwise stood stock still, only his eyes glancing back and forth between Sophie and Alice. Then a smile lit his face and he started laughing and turned to Jack. "Now I understand what you meant when we were talken the other night. What I don't understand is how this gets you connected in a possible murder. So, like the lass said, just tell me what's goin on," Quill finished, as he took a seat at the table.

The next couple of hours were a long succession of questions, answered usually with even more questions. There were a few things agreed upon though. Namely, that as far as any of the patrons who knew him would know, Jack had gone back to Nova Scotia Friday, but Sophie would be staying on a few days longer. Alice would buy a ticket from a local travel agent and pay cash. Then Quill and Beth would take them all to the airport Tuesday morning and pray they all got to Nova Scotia safe and sound. From there, they would all go over the information that Jack had located on Sophie's birth and visit the hospital where she had lived the first few years of her life.

At 4:00 am Quill looked at his watch and decided to head to bed, with the suggestion that they all do the same. He and Beth would expect them all over for breakfast in the morning. Jack obviously needed to lay low, and so he would watch Robby while Sophie and Alice, in costume, would join them at church.

After Quill left, Jack was exhausted, but too tense to go to bed.

"What is it, Jack?" Sophie and Alice asked in unison.

"Would you two please try to stop doing that? It's a little disconcerting."

"What?" they both asked.

"That. Speaking in unison."

Sophie and Alice looked at each other in silence, but something inside of them both smiled.

Chapter Twelve

Sunday morning arrived way too fast for everyone. Fortunately, they didn't have to be at church until 11:00. Beth waited breakfast, but had been up with Robby, nearly since the rest of them had gone to bed. Sophie and Alice seemed to be on timers, and both awoke at 7:00, looked at each other, shrugged, got up, and got dressed. Jack had been right. They did seem to be becoming more and more in tuned with each other. It was as though they maneuvered that morning by mind reading. Neither said a word the whole time they were getting ready in the small bedroom and bath.

They had both heard Robby fussing, and simultaneously looked at Jack snoring on the couch, smiled, and headed down to help Beth. The men seemed to be on similar timers as well, both got up and slugged to breakfast at 9:30. Jack looked at Robby, who was currently sound asleep, crossed himself and mouthed a silent thank you to God.

Beth looked at him. "You do realize he won't stay this way long?"

Quill went over and bent to kiss Robby on the forehead. The baby squirmed. Quill winked at Jack. "Good luck to ye uncle Jack."

"Wait a second Quill. If you're my uncle, how can I then be uncle to your son?"

Quill rolled his eyes and poured two large mugs of coffee, handing one to Jack. "You'll be needen this." He looked at the women who had been chatting away over their own coffees for nearly two hours. "You all look well rested."

"Slept like a baby," all three said together, and laughed as

Jack rolled his eyes.

"God help us. It's contagious," Jack said, going to the kitchen where an array of eggs, bacon, sausages, and potato pancakes awaited.

"Aren't you ladies eating?" Jack asked.

"We ladies couldn't wait on you men and went ahead," Beth said.

"We might have some more before we go," Sophie and Alice added in sync.

"Please try not to do that in church. The last thing we need is an exorcist following you home," Jack said, only half joking.

Quill chuckled. "He is right about that."

At church, Alice went in disguise and was introduced as a friend of the family. Beth had lent her a prayer book and gave her the general idea of the order of service. Alice had only seen segments of Mass on television, and although the church was tiny compared to the large Presbyterian Church she had attended at the holidays, she enjoyed taking in the beauty of the artwork and the priest's ornate robes. The only church leaders she remembered wore business suites. Being Advent, they focused on the story of Christ's impending birth and the prophecies surrounding it.

Alice watched as the Advent candle was lit. She had seen and heard some of this before, but listened intently, wanting to connect on an even deeper level with both Sophie and Jack. Alice had always wondered what it would be like to have a sister, and she had decided that as strange as the situation was, she liked it. She was glad that she had met Sophie and Jack. Her mind strayed to Jack, his smile, the way he was so protective of them, yet she felt it was a respectful protectiveness, rather than the controlling one she was used to. Alice was thinking of Jack playing with Robby when Sophie nudged her. It was time for communion, and Alice followed suit with Beth and Quill in the lead. She was surprised when she tasted actual wine from the challis where she dipped the bread. She had always been used to grape juice in separate little cups that resembled glass thimbles.

Back at the pub, Jack watched Robby as he sucked and chewed on the trunk of a rubber elephant toy as though it were a stick of bubble gum candy. While his eyes were on Robby though, his mind was on Alice.

A week ago, he hadn't even been sure she existed, and now she was thick as thieves with Sophie and coming home with them. Now Sophie was going to insist on seeing all the research Jack had done on her, and she would know that he knew she had been from a multiple pregnancy. There had been no number specified other than multiple.

She would be angry. He knew that much, and he knew that she would insist on finding out about the possibility that there may be others out there. Frankly, the idea terrified Jack. If Alice thought she had been an only child and Sophie had suffered near death from a birth defect and even been proclaimed dead, then what might have happened to any others? Could the answer be in the photos he had found? He hadn't been able to bear looking at them too closely. What if they had suffered with a deformity as Sophie or with even worse defects?

Could others have survived and been adopted out like Sophie? Maybe in a child smuggling ring? Jack shook his head and tried to think rationally. Alice didn't have any reason to believe she had been adopted. And how was it connected, if it even was, to the gene sequencing, biotech and other research companies that lurked mysteriously in the recesses of Morgan Acquisitions?

My God, Jack thought, could they have been some sort of

weird Nazi like experiment? Human Guinea pigs? They weren't exactly normal. Both of their brains learned and adapted far beyond the scope of any other human Jack had ever met. He thought back to that first night they met and how quickly Alice had taken to the ice, even though she claimed she had never so much as tied on a pair of skates before. Neither one of them seemed too overwhelmed by the situation either, at least not nearly as much as he would have expected and in fact felt himself. The speaking in stereo was beginning to freak Jack out a little too. He'd heard that twins could read each other like that sometimes, almost psychically, but how far might it go with them? They had definitely not been normal births of normal children, and why did Alice need the same anti-rejection drugs that Sophie did? She hadn't had any skin grafts or organ transplants.

It didn't make sense, and yet Jack couldn't help but find himself somehow instantly attracted to Alice. He didn't want to be. For one, it was a little weird after having grown up with Sophie, but he had never been attracted to Sophie, at least not in the same way. Then again, he supposed that it must be like someone who dated any other twin.

His mind was getting off track though. Robby had taken note of his distance and began to fuss for attention, and Jack also noted, sniffing the air, that Robby needed a new diaper.

Quill and Beth called after the service ended to say that they had all been invited for lunch over at the O'Brian's and asked if Jack would mind staying with Robby a bit longer. Beth had left two bottles of breast milk in the refrigerator.

Jack couldn't very well say no. He owed them for so much and in a way, he was relieved to have some more time, for the most part, on his own. In fact, it had worked out perfectly. Robby had fallen asleep in his arms midway through the second bottle, so Jack laid him in the basinet beside the sofa and stretched out to take a nap of his own.

He was exhausted, more mentally than physically though, and he decided that he was in desperate need of help, so he reached for the Bible on the end table and opened it randomly, with a prayer for wisdom, to Psalms.

It was 3:00 O'clock when Jack heard a rap coming from the front door of the pub. He sat bolt upright. Robby started to fuss, and Jack put a finger to his lips. He could see the child preparing to wail and quickly grabbed the rubber elephant from the play pin just in time.

As Robby shoved the trunk back in his mouth, Jack noted the flashing of red and blue below the window. There was another rap at the door, and Jack prayed for Robby to stay quiet. Thankfully, the prayer was granted. They still hadn't left though. The lights were still flashing. Perhaps they were coming around to the back, Jack thought.

He picked up Robby, who was getting really squirmy in the basinet. He also appeared to be tiring of the elephant. Jack rocked him in his arms and grabbed the rest of his bottle. Then he heard voices. A minute later he heard the back door open. His heart was beating wildly, and then the knob to the apartment door turned.

"How did it go?" Beth asked, as she came in and Robby reached for her.

Jack let out the breath he'd been holding.

"That well?" asked Beth at Jacks sigh.

"He was perfect Beth. What happened out there though?" he asked.

"Just your standard police enquiry, asking if we were harboring a wanted man," Quill responded. "Relax Jack. I told them I did know someone who looked like the sketch, but he'd already gone, so it must not be."

"What if they check flight records and find out you lied? I'm still scheduled to skate tomorrow too. You know how important this is Quill, but if they know my name now."

"Aye. They don't though."

"They don't?"

"No. All they were told is that someone matching the drawing had been seen frequenting this pub. The tip wasn't from anyone who knew you. So, I told them it looked like a lad named Fergus who had gone home to Ireland for Christmas, leaven Thursday. If they check, they'll find a Fergus, Dublin bound before it had even happened."

"Thank God for Fergus!" Jack exclaimed, sitting back on the sofa.

"Indeed, that was quick thinking Quill," Beth said with a smile, as she kissed him while in the same move passing Robby into Quill's arms. "I think we all need to just relax. It's Sunday. There doesn't seem to be much else we can do for now. Tomorrow's a big day so let's do something to distract ourselves," she said pulling a box of dominoes from a shelf.

"You'll have to show me how to play," Alice said.

"You've never played Dominoes?" Sophie asked in surprise.

"My family was never big on *play* of any kind," Alice answered.

"In that case, we'll teach you!" Beth said smiling.

"Sure. Why not?" Jack said, and a smile crossed his face as he looked at Alice. "So, what did you think of church Alice?"

"It was different. I liked it though, and lunch was wonderful! The O'Brian's were so welcoming and friendly. I can't believe I only met them a few hours ago. Have you met their dog Mac, Jack? He's a gigantic Saint Bernard, and he tried to climb on my lap!" Alice exclaimed, with a huge smile.

Jack couldn't help smiling at the image, and everyone else smiled too. For the rest of that Sunday, they were almost like a normal family. They played a few rounds of Dominoes and later went to the pub, which was closed on Sunday, and Quill unlocked the billiards table for them to teach Alice that as well. They all ended the evening with near beers, pastrami sandwiches, and smiles.

Jack was up at 5:00 a.m. Monday morning for Nick to pick him up and head in early to the rink. The schedule and rankings had been posted the night before, and Jack was scheduled for a 9:00 a.m. skate that morning, with his final skate at 2:00 that afternoon. Currently he was ranked third in the individual skate, right below Yuri and another skater he didn't recognize. He'd need to get into first though.

Jack focused on his mother as he headed out to the rink to warm up. It was only 7:00, still dark except for the bright electric lights around the ice. A cleanup crew was just leaving, and the rink was smooth and free of the overnight snowfall. A few flakes were still falling, illuminated in the bright lights. Jack prayed the weather would hold. He was used to this rink and preferred to skate outdoors, rather than the alternate indoor rink.

He knew he should have been here yesterday to practice, but he'd been leery of showing his face, mask or no mask. He was feeling the day off though and slipped on the triple axel landing. As he circled around the ice, he saw a patrolman walking by, and his heartbeat quickened as the officer stopped and chatted with Nick. He had to shake it off.

Nick started the music for his routine to cue him. The officer was still watching. Jack took a deep breath and pictured his mother. It was a decent practice run. At least he felt in time with the music, but he'd need to have his whole heart in it and perfect timing to beat Yuri. Jack looked up and noticed the officer clapping. He waved as he turned to leave. Jack waved back and skated over to Nick to stretch and take any notes he may have.

"You looked pretty good," Nick said. "Unfortunately, pretty good isn't good enough. I know you have a lot of distractions, but I know you can pull this out too."

"Thanks Nick," Jack said, as he stretched.

"And Jack, you can't let the police make you nervous," Nick whispered.

"Yeah, I know."

"He thought you were good, and he hoped the mask or any pain from the burns wasn't interfering. He's just a nice guy walking his beat. I've gone through all the main papers today and there's not a thing. I didn't see anything yesterday either," Nick added.

"I'm glad, but at the same time it seems a little strange for the whole story to just disappear like that," Jack said.

"Remember, this is New York. There's a million stories every day to take its place."

"Right," Jack said, as he watched other skaters file into the locker room, but in his mind, he thought there was a lot more to it. A cover up? Perhaps even police involvement. Potential murder stories didn't just die out overnight. He couldn't think about that now though. For now, he would just be relieved by the fact.

Back at the pub, Sophie and Alice also noted the sudden disappearance of the story in the papers.

"I'd say somebody is hiding something," Commented Sophie, as she went through the last of the papers.

"What scares me is that it may all be my fault," Alice said, getting up from reviewing the files from Mr. Amstead.

"Why do you keep blaming yourself Alice?" asked Sophie.

"Because it was me who went off script. I can't help but

think everything would have been fine if only I'd stuck to what I was sent here to do and not gone wondering off for Turkish food or... Mr. Amstead was such a nice man Sophie. You didn't talk to him. I've never had anyone be so understanding or stand up for me the way he did. He almost punched Albert," Alice said, half laughing and yet wanting to cry at the same time. "Jack would have been able to focus on the competition. I know it's important to both of you. I don't know why, and I don't need to, but I had no right to...to...to," Alice stuttered as she started to cry. "I'm so sorry. I don't know what's wrong with me."

Sophie came and put her arm around Alice. "There's nothing wrong with you."

"I'm selfish."

"What?"

"This whole mess is because I did what *I* wanted to do. I remember once when I was five. I wanted to learn to play the violin, so I snuck into the music room at school and was practicing on one that was just sitting in a chair. I didn't know that it was sitting there because it needed repairs. I broke it and my parents told me that the boy whose violin it was hadn't been able to perform that night because of me, and that he'd been counting on that evening for a long time, but I ruined it because I was selfish and did something without asking permission. I felt so bad that I started to cry then too, and I was told to stop feeling sorry for myself, because that was even more selfish. And here I go again," Alice concluded, as she wiped her eyes.

"You were five," Sophie tried to sooth.

"Exactly," Alice said pulling away and turning to face her. "I was old enough to know better. That's the one thing from church that was instilled in me every Easter. Jesus was totally unselfish, but I am selfish."

"You're being way too hard on yourself Alice. Yes, Jesus is totally unselfish, but He's also the son of God. You, we are human and that's the real point of Easter. It's not for us to feel guilty, but to understand God's forgiveness that he gave to us through Jesus. He understood that we're human. He created us Alice, and He loves you."

"Do you really believe that?"

"Yes! I know it! And there is nothing that you did that was selfish. What seems selfish to me are your parents and I'm glad that for whatever reason, they didn't raise me. I'm sorry that you had to grow up that way."

"They gave me everything."

"Except compassion and honesty. I know you don't want to think badly of them, but you know now that they lied to you."

"I know, but they're still my parents, and they did teach me the ten commandments too. The first of which is to honor your father and mother. I didn't even remember to call yesterday."

"That's only one of the commandments and not the first," Sophie stated going to get her Bible. "It sounds to me that they only let you learn what they wanted you to learn. Did you ever have a Bible?"

"Not one of my own. I asked about it once and they told me it was unnecessary when there were plenty in every pew or at the library if I really wanted. So, I put the idea out of my mind."

"You can have that one if you like."

"I can't do that. It's yours."

"It's just the one I have when I travel. Please, take it."

"Thank you, Sophie. I'm sorry I'm being so emotional. I..."

"It's alright Alice. It really is alright. If I were you, I'd probably be far more emotional," Sophie admitted, as they embraced and she meant it. She may have been sick as a young child living in the hospital, but even there she felt loved and genuinely cared about, and her adoptive parents were amazing. She missed them. She had always wondered about her biological parents, but now that she knew what she did, she really didn't care. And that was what Sophie thought was selfish about herself. She was truly glad to know Alice. They were sisters. But as important as learning the truth was now, especially for Alice, Sophie suddenly found herself not sure if she wanted to know any more.

***

Back in Seattle, the Morgan's secretary, Charice dialed the Morgan's home line again. It was highly unusual for at least one of them not to be in the office before her, much less for them not to have called. Charice had been worried by 9:00 AM. and after she had called both Alice and Albert in New York as well with no response, she was doubly worried. She had asked everyone, but no one had heard from them. She even called the New York Offices, but it seemed that all of the Morgan's along with Albert had mysteriously vanished. Charice wasn't worried about Albert though. She'd only spoken with him twice over the phone, but she knew she didn't like the man. She knew Alice didn't like him either. If anything had happened to any of the Morgans though, Charice wouldn't hesitate to suspect him.

Chapter Thirteen

Alice donned her disguise, and Sophie pulled her hair up and took her wig with her. At least one of them needed to look like the passport photo when the ticket was purchased. Beth was needed at the pub through the lunch rush, but she would try to meet them at the rink by two. On the way to the travel agent, Alice stopped at a pay phone and left another message for her parents. Then just to be safe, she stood on lookout duty for Leon or Albert. She doubted they would be in this neighborhood, but Albert had shown up here before, and the last thing they needed was for him to spot Sophie, now bandage free and do...What? Alice didn't know what he might try, but she did know that she didn't want to find out.

As it turned out, all of the flights into Halifax and elsewhere in Nova Scotia were booked solid with people flying home for the holidays. And with severe winter storms predicted the next week, the best option was to take the train, which was filling up fast as well. The next option was to fly into Quebec or Montreal and take a train from there, which would be twice as expensive.

Sophie excused herself and went back out to talk to Alice. It was decided that they would hold three seats for the two-and-a-half-day train ride leaving the next afternoon. That way they could discuss the best plan with Jack and be back at the agency with their decision before closing when the seats would have to be either paid for or released.

Next, they hopped in a taxi, where Sophie donned her wig and went to the rink to find seats for the competition. Beth had promised to bring sandwiches and a thermos later. The couple's competition was already in progress and the stands were nearly full, but they managed to get seats in a section on the side where they could still have a good view, and Beth would be able to get in with Robby and the stroller.

Beth arrived at 1:55 with a bundled and sleeping Robby, and they all eagerly unwrapped the still hot roast beef sandwiches that had been tucked into his diaper bag along with a steaming thermos of apple cider. Jack was eighth in a lineup of ten and a light snow was just starting to fall.

Jack was in the locker room saying one last prayer before he headed out. This was it. "Oh, dear God, please help me to be my best so that I may have the means to help others. Namely my parents. Dear Lord, please let it be your will to bring my mother back to us and for my dad, not to lose their farm and for Sophie and Alice..."

"Jack! You're on deck," Nick called to him.

"Amen," Jack concluded.

Alice was absolutely enthralled with all of the skaters and secretly wondered what it would be like if she were out on the ice. She obviously had a natural talent for it, and she wondered how that was.

Alice, Sophie and Beth all held their collective breath as Jack came up to the rink. Beth and Sophie said prayers in Gaelic and even Robby popped his eyes open and seemed to be watching intently, though it may have been more at the snowflakes that were lazily floating down around him.

Jack skated a near perfect program to music from "The Phantom Of The Opera" and scored a 9.3, the same as Yuri who had skated before him, which meant that the final score would be based on a review of the tapes, combined with the scores of the morning skates. The next two skaters scored a 9.2 and an

8.9. Not knowing how the morning had gone, Sophie realized that this was going to be tight and the winners unknown, until the closing ceremony that night at nine.

Nick didn't recognize Sophie in the wig, but he did know Beth and headed over to let her know that he had ordered a taxi for Jack to get back to the pub if she wanted to join him.

"Thank you, Nick," Beth said. "Thank you for everything. Tell Jack we'll meet him at the corner for the cab."

Nick couldn't help but be drawn to the blond sitting beside Beth and caught himself staring until Sophie turned to look at him. At first, he turned away, embarrassed, until he realized she was staring and smiling back at him. Then she removed the glasses and winked at him, and he realized it was Sophie. Alice stayed turned away, not wanting to intrude, and Beth chuckled to herself, then turned to Nick, inviting him to dinner."

"I'll try to make it by for a bit, but I have to be back here by eight. I'll see you soon though," he said, sending a wink back to Sophie before heading off. Damn! He thought. She looked just as good as a blond!

When they met Jack at the taxi, Sophie and Alice joined him for the ride back to the pub as Beth, who didn't have a spare car seat hiding in the diaper bag, continued on with Robby in the stroller to the Subway station.

Both Sophie and Alice congratulated Jack on his skate, but he was still on edge. He wouldn't know his placement until later that night, and they had all agreed it best that Jack not actually attend the ceremony. Nick would accept in his place any winnings and let him know.

Nick was scheduled to return on the same flight the next day, which was the next thing they all needed to discuss.

They had not filled Jack in on exactly how much money Alice had been able to obtain, and he was surprised that it was enough for more than one ticket. Jack, as they had thought, wouldn't hear of Alice making the journey alone. He also thought that his odds of not being recognized were better if he joined Alice on the train. Sophie on the other hand would fly home as scheduled and do what she could to ease the introduction of Alice into the picture. Thinking about it, Jack was now glad that Nick knew as well and could be there with Sophie.

Their interest in each other hadn't escaped Jack either, and though he had his concerns, he had far fewer concerns with Nick than he would with anybody else. The fact was though, that he was also concerned for Nick. Would he be able to handle whatever they may discover about her? Jack shook the thought away. What would it matter? He thought. Would it matter to him about Alice? No. Regardless of whatever experiment he feared they may have been a part of, they were human. Jack had always loved Sophie like a little sister, regardless of how obviously superior she had been to him in school and even on the ice. No, it wouldn't matter, and they could deal with it together.

Sophie and Alice had gone out again to complete the ticket reservations, and on the way back Alice decided to try her ATM card, knowing that even if they tracked her account, it wouldn't post until after they had gone the next morning. She was surprised, but thankful that they had not frozen her account in order to force her home, and she withdrew her maximum $500 daily limit with the hope she would be able to do the same on the way to the station in the morning. Then she would not only have more cash but looking at her account would show her moving in completely different areas.

They didn't hear from Nick until 10:00 that night. As it turned out Jack had come in ahead of Yuri, but so had someone else, which had put Jack in second place. It was still a $10,000 pot, but Jack had been counting on the $25,000 in order to pay down enough of the medical bills and the back taxes on the farm. Still not wanting to let Alice in on the crisis at home, he excused himself to give Quill and Beth the news.

***

As soon as office hours were over Charice headed to Montlake. It was about 6:00 p.m. when she finally made her way through the traffic and into the Morgan's drive. The night was pitch black and overcast with just a slight glow from the moon filtering through the clouds. The security lights came on as she walked up to the door and rang the bell. After a minute, she rang it again. She waited a couple of minutes and then walked around the house toward Edgar's office. She felt a little funny sneaking around, but the house sat up on a large lot and was surrounded by a privacy hedge, so she doubted any suspicion would be aroused. She wished that she had thought to take the spare key she knew Edgar kept in his office. As she circumvented the house, she tried the doors and looked in windows. Aside from the kitchen though all of the curtains were drawn, and the only light she saw came through an upstairs window. A shiver spiraled down Charice's spine. Had she seen a movement or was it her imagination? Making her way back to the front of the house, she rang the bell again and called at the same time. She heard the phone ringing inside, but there was no answer, and it was starting to drizzle ice cold drops from above.

Going back to her car Charice made a decision and called her boyfriend Max to meet her back at the office. Charice knew that the police would do nothing at this point, but she was positive something was wrong. Max was an ex-army General that Charice had started seeing last year. He had come with her to several office functions where he had met the Morgan's. He had liked them, and Charice was certain he would help. Besides, it wasn't really breaking and entering if you had a key.

Two hours later they were back at the house. Charice hadn't wanted to wait, but Max had convinced her to stop for dinner on the way back.

When they arrived it was pouring rain, but Max wanted to ring the doorbell again and then check around the outside of the house himself before going in. Charice went with him and froze when they got to the side of the house.

"What is it?" asked Max.

"There was a light on upstairs before," Charice told him.

"Are you sure it was this side of the house?"

"Positive."

"Alright, let's continue around and keep your eyes peeled for any footprints."

They finished circling the house but saw nothing. Max insisted that they try calling one more time. This time the machine said that voicemail was full.

"Okay," said Max. "You only have the key for the office door?"

"Yes."

"Is there an alarm?"

"Yes, but I know the code. I've had to come by before when they were out of town to get papers, etc."

"Okay, let's see if there's anything there."

Upon opening the door to the office Max switched on a flashlight until Charice found the light switch and went to disarm the alarm.

"That's strange. The alarm wasn't armed," she said.

"Do you see anything else out of the ordinary?" Max asked.

"No, but don't you smell that?"

"Yeah. It smells like the place has been sanitized. They have a maid though, right?"

"Seera. She only comes on Wednesdays. I know because I authorize her hours," Charice answered, as she started to pull off the driving gloves she had on.

"Leave those on Char. We don't want our prints all over everything."

"Right," she said, replacing the gloves. "I'm really worried Max."

"I know. Now look closely at everything okay. I'll take some photos so we can look later as well," Max said, as he tried the door that led into the rest of the house. "I don't suppose you know where the key for this door is?"

"No, but I'll keep my eyes peeled," Charice answered, thumbing through some mail stacked neatly on the side of Edgar's desk.

After checking through the mail and finding nothing odd, Charice moved to the computer. Once booted, she tried signing in with her company password to see what Edgar had been working on last. It didn't work though. That was odd. She'd logged on only last week. Of course, she couldn't access his private files, but now she appeared to be locked out completely.

"He must have been working on something he wanted to keep hushed up. I can't get in."

"You didn't have any problem at work though. Did you?"

"No, but that won't show me what he was looking at. He keeps copies of all the files from the office, but he's on a different system here, so what he accesses from home doesn't show up on the office computer files. I found the key though, I think," Charice said as she picked up the key, which had been exposed when she adjusted the keyboard.

"Let's see what there is to see in the rest of the house."

"Remember, I know I saw someone here earlier. They could still be in the house. Maybe hiding," Charice finished.

"It could be them too. I admit this is odd, but they may just have decided they don't want to be bothered. It's not a crime to hide out in your own home," Max added.

"What if they're hurt or being held hostage upstairs?"

"I have a better idea."

"Oh, thank God," Charice said, now visibly shaking from the possibilities racing through her mind. "What is it?"

"The police won't come if we report them missing this soon, but if we trip the alarm they'll come. We have photos, so let's mess things up a bit. Grab what you can and set the alarm. I'll throw one of the rocks from the planter through the glass and we run like hell. Got it?"

"Roger that," Charice said, pocketing the keys, mail and the phone, from which she hoped to be able to access the full voicemail box. There was a book on the desk as well that looked interesting, so she figured, what the hell and grabbed that too as she knocked over the pens and nearly the computer, before Max grabbed it.

Max knocked several items off of shelves, and semi attempted to pry the lock on the file cabinet with a letter opener to give the whole thing a more authentic aura of robbery.

Next, Charice set the alarm and locked the door. They did their best to obliterate their footprints as Charice hurried to start the car. A minute later Max had slammed a rock through the door and hopped in the car.

"Drive normally," he said. "It'll take a minute before the police are alerted, and we don't want anyone to pay attention to us," he finished, as he stashed the computer in the back seat.

Chapter Fourteen

Jack and Alice made their way through the crowded station, sticking close together. Alice was not the only one sporting a disguise that morning. Before they left, Beth had arrived with Quill's electric razor and bandages, just in case they did run into someone who knew him. Jack had insisted she stop short of shaving his head, and just short of it is exactly where she had stopped and borrowed some of Quill's Grays Away hair color to turn what was left from his natural dark brown to ebony. Alice barely recognized him herself.

Quill and Beth had taken them all to the airport, but they had to get back to the pub for the lunch crowd, so Alice had insisted on paying for a taxi to the train station. So far everything had gone smoothly, and they were getting ready to board.

They were sharing a private sleeper car on the upper deck of the "Super Liner." Alice had never been on a train before and despite everything else, she couldn't help but feel a little thrill at the new experience. What she had dreaded being a boring week of business had in fact turned into quite an adventure! She kept the emerging smile to herself though.

"Would you like the upper or lower bunk?" Jack asked, as he stored the luggage.

"What?"

"These seats turn into a bed, and that up there," he said pointing to a latch in the ceiling, "pulls down into an upper bunk."

"Oh!" Alice gasped, and blushed slightly at the reality of sharing such close quarters alone with Jack. "Whichever you want is fine with me."

"I've always been an upper bunk boy," Jack said with a sardonic smile, as he sighed and plopped into a seat, relieved to be aboard and exhausted from a sleepless night.

Alice felt really bad for him. She knew it was because of her that Jack was basically a fugitive, and that worrying about this whole mess was probably why he hadn't placed first in the skating competition. She had known that it meant a lot to him, but it wasn't until she saw the look on his face, after receiving the news from Nick, that she realized how much. Neither he nor Sophie had yet divulged the reason, but Alice knew they needed the money. In fact, that was why she was most concerned with getting as much cash as she could to take with her, and why she had asked Sophie not to mention the amount. Sophie understood. Alice could tell. They really could read each other.

Jack picked up a newspaper that was left in the seat beside him and started randomly flipping through. He glanced up at Alice, who appeared lost in her own thoughts, as she gazed out the window. His eyes lingered on the slant of her cheek, and she turned to face him. Their eyes met for a minute in silence before Jack said, "I'm going to check and see if there's anything in the news today."

"I just hope he's okay," Alice replied, conscious that she was also likely to blame for Mr. Amstead's disappearance.

"Me too," Jack replied, turning back to gaze blankly at the print in front of him.

A couple of minutes later they were underway, and a steward came by to check their tickets, followed by a gentleman who handed them a menu and asked if they would like anything from the galley.

Jack and Alice replied in unison. "Coffee please."

Alice laughed. "I guess it's not just Sophie I do that with."

Jack smiled.

"Jack?"

"Alice?"

"I was just wondering. We never really had time alone to talk, just about normal things, and get to know each other. Yet, here we are, sharing a sleeper car. I just feel..."

Jack cocked his eyebrow. "Awkward?"

"Not exactly. Do you? Feel awkward, I mean?"

"A little."

"Oh."

"Maybe overwhelmed is a better word."

"I'm sorry."

"Alice, It's not you. What I mean is, it's not just about you. I was feeling a little overwhelmed before I even met you," Jack said, figuring that she would find out about his mom sooner or later. After all, she was on the way home with him, and they had two days to spend alone together.

"I know. I mean I know there's something else that's been bothering you. Is it about your skating?"

"No. This competition was connected to it though. The fact is Alice, it's my mom. She's in a coma and it doesn't look good. My dad mortgaged the farm to help with the medical bills, and I was hoping to get the first prize money to help pay the mortgage back."

"Oh Jack, I'm so sorry and I distracted..."

"Stop Alice. Please. I chose to be a part of this. You can't help who you are any more than Sophie can, and you're helping Sophie to find out just who she really is and where she came from. These are questions that have haunted her through her whole life. This isn't going to be easy for either one of you, and I think you know that."

"What haven't you told us Jack?"

Just then the porter arrived with their coffee tray.

Chapter Fifteen

The smell of chlorine permeated the air, and it was cold, very cold. Her mouth felt like it was stuffed full of cotton. She tried to scream, only to realize her mouth *was* full of a cotton like material. She was thirsty, very thirsty. She fought to open her eyes. They felt as though they were swollen shut. Perhaps they were. Her arms were stiff, strapped to something. Each other? Handcuffs? Her wrists were too numb to tell. The cold and chlorine burned as she took a deep breath through her nose. She heard a thudding in her ears like a drum, the beat getting faster. Dear God, it was her heart, she realized. She was having an all-out panic attack. She had to calm herself, take a deep breath. It burned so bad. She fought to move, to open her eyes. It must be a nightmare. She had had them before. All she had to do was wake up. She forced her eyes open, only to shut them tightly against the brightness of the light that beamed into them. She was still seeing spots behind her closed lids.

"I was wondering when you might wake up or if you even would," said a voice, that seemed to come from somewhere behind her.

She felt a warm trickle of blood dribble across her lips from her dry, burning nose, and then her whole body swung upwards. A wet cloth dabbed at her face to blot the blood away. She tried again to open her eyes. The light was still too bright. She tried to turn her head, but she couldn't. There was something around her head, holding it in place. Her ankles were strapped down too. She was pivoted again so that she faced the floor, and she watched a drop of blood from her nose hit below, and then she looked into his eyes as they stared up at her through the clear glass. Her mind screamed, "Edgar!" and she blacked out.

His eyes were taped open, his head held firm, as though in some sort of vice, forcing him to stare up at her. He saw the drop of blood as it splashed above his face. Her eyes were swollen, but he could see the terror that they held as they found his, then suddenly she had been turned away. At least she was alive! For how long though? How long would either of them be kept alive and for what purpose?

***

Sophie stared out the window as the plane lifted off into the gray New York sky. She shivered.

"Are you cold?" asked Nick.

"Not really. I was just thinking about something Jack said and it..." She trailed off, not wanting to talk or think anymore about her own death certificate. When she did, it gave her the creeps.

"I'm sure they're fine."

"I know they are," she said, turning to face him. "I think I'd know if they weren't, I would feel it. Does that sound odd?"

"Not at all. Siblings, family members, even lovers often have that kind of, I don't know what you call it, not really a psychic, but a spiritual connection."

She smiled at him. "You do understand. Do you have that?" she asked, as their eyes met. Her heart caught in her throat. "I mean with any of your family?"

"Not yet," he smiled.

Just then the plane gave a violent shudder. Sophie gripped Nick's hand, as the sky seemed to fall out from under them.

A few seconds later the intercom came on. "This is your captain speaking. It looks like we're in for a rough flight. Please keep your seatbelts fasted at all times."

A stewardess staggered down the aisle checking seat belts and handing out extra vomit bags.

***

"So?" Alice asked, and then eyed him over the rim of her coffee cup.

Those eyes were unnerving, and he had a brief image of Sable, his family's barn cat, just before she pounced on an unsuspecting mouse. He wished there was a hole he could climb into.

Alice set her cup down. "Jack, I'm an adult and so is Sophie. We have a right to know."

"That's part of the problem. I don't know what it means. I didn't do all that well in biology, and I'm definitely not a geneticist, but I could tell enough to know that what I saw didn't fit. I found an old box of files that belonged to the doctor who supposedly signed Sophie's death certificate. I had tried to locate him. I went to the hospital that issued the certificate only to find out that it was shut down. I asked around and discovered it hadn't ever been a hospital, at least not the kind with a regular maternity ward. It had been a lab that specialized in genetic research."

"Where?"

"Quebec."

"I want to see it."

"There's nothing to see. I told you, it's closed down. I think it was slated to become some sort of shopping center."

"So where was this box?"

"Inside."

"So, there was something there."

"No. Well, nothing aside from a few homeless drunks huddled around a fire. I brought them dinner and some beers, and they showed me how to get inside."

"They lived there?"

"Outside. Although, I suppose a few of them probably snuck in when the elements were bad. Quebec gets pretty cold in the winter, but no. Most of them were afraid of the place. They said it was haunted. It was a nasty looking thing. There was a fence around it a good twenty feet high and at one point you could tell that it had been topped with barbed wire. You could even see what looked like camera mounts. To tell the truth, if they had still been in business, I'm pretty sure I couldn't have gotten in."

"How did you get into the building?"

"A broken padlock. Once inside, I could tell it had been used as a hangout for druggies. There were hypodermic needles and other medical paraphernalia all over."

"Did you see anyone inside?"

"You mean ghosts?"

Alice rolled her eyes. "Addicts."

"No, and no ghosts either, just in case you were wondering."

"And?"

"Can you pass the coffee please?"

"What?"

"Never mind," Jack said, reaching across Alice for the carafe.

"Oh. Sorry."

Their eyes met for one brief electric moment, as he leaned back into his seat and continued. "Anyway, I do have to admit the place was a little creepy. I made my way down the corridors wearing a head torch, not really expecting to find anything. I was just curious. Then I saw the nameplate beside where a door used to be. At some point there had been a fire and most of the office was charred ruins. The only thing intact was a metal lock box. I found it back in a storage closet. The lock had been pried open, probably by some kids looking for money or more drugs. Inside were some files. They were barely legible and spotted in mildew, but I was able to clean them up a bit. I still didn't expect to find much, if anything connected to Sophie." He paused, as he remembered his first look through the files.

"You did find something though. What Jack? What did you find?'

"You don't want to know."

"I need to know."

"I found photos, photos of babies, some not even fully developed. Do you know how abortions are performed Alice?"

"No."

"Well, that's what some of the pictures were of."

"Do you still have them?"

"Trust me. You don't want to see them."

By the look on his face, she felt inclined to believe him. Jack had gone a sickly shade of blotchy grayish white and a little green around the gills at the memory.

"What connected Sophie?"

"Some of the photos were of live babies. One was of Sophie and the growth she had on her face. There was another copy of her death certificate attached."

Alice felt a chill run down her spine. "I wonder," she said. "I wonder if there could be any pictures of me in the file?"

"Possibly. There were a lot. I doubt it though. You're too perfect."

"What?"

Jack took a deep breath. "The babies in the photos all had some kind of deformity. Some were minor enough as to barely be noticeable. Each one was labeled. I stopped reading after I found Sophie's though. I couldn't stand to look at them."

"Where are they?"

"I wonder that too sometimes. If Sophie's alive, then some of the others might be..." He looked at her, realizing that wasn't what she'd meant. "They're safely locked away."

"What if we have other siblings?" Just considering the possibility struck her hard, and the tingling in her spine increased. Then another thought hit hard.

"Jack?"

"I suppose it's possible."

Alice turned away, suddenly overwhelmed by the new thoughts swimming through her mind. "Jack?"

"Are you alright Alice?" he asked, gingerly reaching out to touch her shoulder.

"What if my parents aren't my parents either?" She turned back to face him. "Think about it. The vitamins. There was something wrong with me too. What if we're just part of some crazy genetic experiment? That would explain why my parents were always so protective. Watch this," she said, pushing up the sleeve of the sweater she wore. Then she took a nail file from her purse and pressing it firmly against her arm, started to scratch.

"What are you doing? Stop!" Jack tried to grab the file away, but she got up, dodging him.

"Don't worry. I just want to show you something. Look," she said, showing him the bright red scratch on her arm.

"You've hurt yourself. You should put something on that," Jack said, worried. What the hell was she doing?

Alice just shook her head and pulled the sleeve back down. "It'll be gone in a couple of hours," she said, sitting back down and taking a sip of her now cold coffee. "I'm not normal Jack. You know that. I've always known that. I just never understood why or how. I'm not going to hurt myself Jack," she said, firmly, to the very concerned face staring back at her.

"Like Sophie, I need to know who I am. What I am."

"You're human. And so is Sophie, maybe not average, but who wants to be average?" he questioned, attempting a smile.

"Average sounds pretty nice right about now." She tried to meet his attempt at a smile with one of her own. "Something to eat sounds pretty good about now too."

"I'll ring for the porter," Jack said, pulling a call cord.

Chapter Sixteen

The sky was still gray, but the rain had been reduced to an icy drizzle as Captain Shane McDougal followed detectives Dave Asher and Lidia Yarnok around the perimeter of the house.

By the time officers had arrived the night before, the perpetrators of the break in were gone. Calls to the residence raised no reply via home phone or mobile on record. A brief search of the home had found no one and no signs of foul play, but something told Shane that this was no random crime.

He rubbed his nose. That was his version of gut instinct or smelling a rat. The hairs in his nose always tickled when something was off. To not be able to reach the homeowners was the first oddity, but then again letting voice mail pick up when you are on vacation and letting your mailbox fill up isn't that odd. He'd done it himself, on his honeymoon with Patricia. He'd gladly do it again if... But this was Edgar and Suzanna Morgan. Patricia had known Suzanna. In fact, he'd been to a party here once with her. Some fundraising gig he thought to himself, as he tried to remember what it had been for.

"Captain?" Detective Asher called, and Shane looked up. "Take a look at this. I couldn't see it last night in the dark."

"What is it?" Shane asked, as he looked at the side of the house where Asher was pointing.

"Rope and scuff marks. The walls are too rough to get a shoe print, but it looks like there's some rope fibers up there by the window and I bet you if we check, we'll find the window unlocked."

"I'll check," Yarnok answered, and headed into the house.

"You're saying that somebody scaled the walls?"

"Sure looks that way."

"Why would somebody go to the trouble of going in through an upstairs window and then throw a rock through the glass doors to the office downstairs?"

"Your guess is as good as mine on that."

"You were right! It was unlocked," called Lidia from the window above.

"This is no amateur break in," Dave added. "Whoever was here knew what they were doing. They smeared their prints and messed the office up so bad, it'll be a while before we can tell what, if anything, aside from the computer is missing."

"The Morgans," Shane said, as he walked back around to the office.

"What?"

"The Morgans are missing."

"I think he's right, and not just since last night," Lidia added, as she entered the office from the main house.

"What do you mean?" Shane asked.

"I looked at the answering machine. It's not just full, it's been full since Sunday morning."

"You're sure?" Shane asked.

"I skipped through the dates on their calls and the last one recorded was dated Sunday."

"Okay. Let's grab the machine and get it to the station, and then let's get a forensics team out here ASAP. We need to listen to all those messages and then get over to their offices to talk with their employees. We need to know the last time anyone saw or spoke with them!"

"I'll bag the machine," Lidia said.

"On it!" Dave said, heading back to his car.

Lidia was inside bagging the awkward answering machine when Shane entered.

"Here, I'll hold the bag."

"Thanks. I haven't seen one of these for a while," she said as she maneuvered all the cords in.

"The Morgans have a daughter," Shane said. "I want you to find her and talk to her."

"Finding her will be easy. She works for them."

"You know her?"

"Not really. We sort of graduated college together."

"What do you mean sort of?"

"I mean we did. We were in the same literature class."

"You remember someone in your college lit class, but you didn't really know her?"

"She was only fifteen or sixteen and looked like a model. A little hard to forget. I remember she was upset one day because her parents insisted she drop some elective and focus on more business, so she'd be prepared to come to work with them."

"Are you sure she did?"

"Oh yeah. She was featured in the alumni yearbook."

"What's she like?" Shane asked. "I only knew about her because Patricia knew Mrs. Morgan and... Anyway, I'd appreciate you talking to her and if you have any insights?"

"I remember her as quiet, studious, under her parents' thumb, and everyone was jealous of her, but they liked her too. She was really nice. She even helped me with my homework once."

"That must have been humbling, especially for you Yarnok," he teased.

"It was," she agreed, as they walked back out to the drive.

"Forensics is on their way," Dave said. "About ten minutes out. Did you want me to question the neighbors?"

"No, I'll wait and hold the fort here until forensics arrives. You two get back to the station. Take the machine to Selma and listen to it in the lab then write up a report. I want Lidia to head over to the Morgan's offices. Dave, you follow her after you listen to the machine."

The detectives headed out, and Shane sat down by the front door to wait. He rubbed his nose again as a strange sense of déjà vu overwhelmed him. He couldn't get Patricia out of his mind. It was the not knowing that was the hardest to overcome.

***

"Thank you for flying today with Skyline Airways. We look forward to serving you in the future," said the cheery announcement, as they stood to retrieve their bags from the overhead compartment.

The landing had been the only smooth part of the flight, and Nick and Sophie moved aside to let several passengers, who didn't look so well exit before them.

Nick's brother Matt met them outside baggage claim. "Where's Jack?" he asked.

"He'll be along in a couple of days," Nick answered. "The flight was overbooked."

"Oh, hey Sophie! How are you? Can we offer you a ride? I brought the bug, so it'll be tight, but I'm sure Nick won't mind the walk."

"Very funny bro!"

"It's alright guys, I have a ride."

"Your parents knew when you were coming in, right?"

"I think so, but it's my friend Shannon who's picking me up and... There she is," Sophie said, as a blond with eighties style big hair pulled up in a blue Volvo.

"Then I guess I'll say farewell for now," Nick said, as he smiled and carried her bag over to Shannon's car.

"For now. I'm sure I'll see you around once Jack gets back."

"Or before. I mean if you'd like?"

"Maybe I'll come by the rink."

"And we can have lunch?"

"I like lunch," Sophie said, as Nick put her bag in the car.

"Come on dude!" Matt called. "I have ten minutes before they charge me another five bucks for parking."

Sophie smiled, as Nick rolled his eyes and nodded with a smile.

"You'd better get going."

"Yeah. Tomorrow? For lunch?"

"We'll see," Sophie responded, not wanting to come off too easy. She thought he could wait at least forty-eight hours. The problem was, she realized that she didn't want to.

Nick chuckled under his breath and headed off with Matt.

"What was that all about?" Shannon asked, as Sophie situated herself in the passenger seat.

"I don't know yet."

***

Charice was just getting ready to go on her lunch break when Detective Yarnok arrived asking about Alice.

"Has something happened?" Charice asked, hoping to find out what the police may have discovered about the whereabouts or fate of Edgar and Suzanna. "I've been a bit concerned. I haven't seen any of the Morgans since Friday."

"Is that unusual then?"

"Highly. Alice, I do know is supposed to be on a business trip in New York, although she should have been back by yesterday as well."

"So, you don't know where Ms. Morgan is?"

"No."

Lidia recognized the look of true concern on Charice's face, as well as the awkward note in her voice that said she was hiding something, and decided that she had found her starting point for questioning.

"How long have you known the Morgan's Ms.?

"Ryan."

"How long have you known the Morgans Ms. Ryan?"

"Thirty-one years. I started here as a college intern."

"Do you have a few minutes to talk?"

"I have as long as you need. Join me for lunch?"

Lidia was a little taken aback. Ms. Ryan seemed unusually anxious to talk, a rarity in the field of police questioning. This was one of those times, she was sure Shane would have considered a real nose scratcher, as she followed the Morgan's secretary into Mr. Morgan's office.

"Do you always eat in the boss's office?" was her first question.

"No, but I do often have business lunches with them. Besides, it's the most private place to talk," Charice offered, as she entered a well-appointed lounge with a kitchenette that lay between Edgar and Suzanna's respective offices and began to prepare her lunch.

"Please have a seat officer."

"Detective Yarnok."

"Would you care for some coffee, or can I offer you anything to eat?"

"Coffee would be great. Thank you."

"Cream or sugar?"

"Black. When did Alice Morgan leave for New York?"

"On the 5th."

"And what was the purpose of her trip?" Lidia asked, as she watched the secretary. Ms. Ryan was obviously on edge and Lidia was about to discover why.

After taking the phone and computer last night, Max had helped her hook it up to the office network, where using Charice's password they had been able to get access into the files. The problem was that the files had told them nothing. Most of them were old acquisitions from before Charice had started working there, and the others were encrypted, so they had decided to turn it over to the police once their investigation took off, which it seemed to be doing now. Charice needed only to make sure that it would go beyond investigating the break in they had staged. She was afraid to hear the answer to the next question she would ask the detective, but she had to know.

"Detective Yarnok? Just please tell me, are the Morgans dead?"

"What makes you ask that?"

"You're here and they're not. Please, just tell me that much."

"We don't know. Now is there something else you want to tell me?"

"They're missing."

"We know. That's part of why I'm here. What is it you're hiding Ms. Ryan?"

"And you promise to keep investigating even though it's been less than forty-eight hours?"

"Have you seen them or know of someone who has in the last forty-eight hours?"

"No, but the break in was just last night."

"Ms. Ryan, please. We believe they have been missing since before the break in, at least since Sunday, so no, we are not going to stop investigating. Now, will you please tell me, what are you hiding?"

"I was at the house last night."

"At the Morgan's? Are you saying that you broke in?"

"Yes. I mean no. I had a key, to the office only. I sometimes do work for them when they're away on business trips that requires me to access files for them from their home office."

"Go on."

"I was worried when Mr. Morgan didn't come in yesterday. You would have to know him to know how unusual that is. Mrs. Morgan rarely comes in anymore, but Edgar, Mr. Morgan is often here six days a week."

"So, when you couldn't get ahold of them, you went by to check on them?"

"That's right. The voice mail was full and that never happens, so I knew that something was wrong. I was going to check the rest of the house, but I was scared. I saw a light and someone moving in an upstairs window, and so I set the alarm and threw the rock through the window as I left so that the police would come."

"Why not just call us?"

"And say what? That I was snooping around and saw someone, who may or may not have been one of the Morgans moving around in their own home? You see, I didn't believe you would actually do anything unless there was an obvious crime. Something has happened to them, and I want you to find them before it's too late! Please Detective Yarnok! Please!"

"Did you go alone last night?"

"The first time, yes."

"First time?" Lidia asked, raising an eyebrow at Charice.

Yes. It was the first time that I saw someone, and I got scared. I also had left the key at the office, so when I came back, I had a friend with me."

"And this friends name is?"

"Are you going to arrest us?"

"Not unless I discover that you're lying. Tell me, does your friend do rock climbing?"

"What does rock climbing have to do with anything?"

"How did your friend get into the house?"

"He didn't. I told you, I had a key, but only to the office. There's a key to the main house there, but we didn't go in because I had seen someone before, so we decided to set the alarm off to bring the police."

"What did you do in the office? It's important you tell me everything so that we don't waste time."

"We looked around for any sign. There was a strong smell of sanitizer..."

"Sanitizer?"

"Yes. Didn't you smell it?"

"Not this morning, but that may be because it was ventilated overnight through a hole in the door. I'll check the initial report to see if the responding officer noted it. What else?"

"I took the phone and the computer."

"And why would you do that?"

"Because my password wasn't working on their system, so we hooked it up to the office network."

"Your friend is a hacker?"

"No! Like I said, I have worked from the Morgan's home office before, so when I tried to sign in last night and couldn't, it was odd. I thought if I could find out what Edgar had been working on last that it could be a clue."

"Where is the computer now?"

Charice pointed to Edgar's desk. "In there."

"You realize it'll have to come with me? The phone too."

"Of course. Look, detective, we want the same thing here."

"Okay. For now, we'll say I believe you, I still need your friends name and to contact Alice Morgan."

"Let me call him. He can come here to meet with you. Please?"

"Alright. If he can come right over, I'll go along with that. I'd like you to show me what you did find on the computer, and it sounds like this may be the best place to access that."

"It is. Thank you," Charice said, as she dialed Max's number.

Lidia dialed headquarters at the same time to request a

computer analyst.

"He's on his way," Charice said, as she hung up. "He should make it in the next forty-five minutes."

"And I should have an analyst here in about an hour. In the meantime, how do we get ahold of Alice Morgan?"

"Like I said, I was expecting her back in today, but I'll just get her itinerary. Her home and Mobile are in my phone, under 'A' for Alice," Charice said, as she went out front to collect Alice's itinerary from the New York trip.

***

They had eaten in relative silence, and the porter had just left with their dishes.

"Look," Alice said, and pushed her sleeve up to reveal the skin on her arm, to show just the faintest pink mark where the jagged red scratch had been.

"What the?" Jack asked. "How?"

"I don't know. Just like I don't know how I was able to skate so well. It must have something to do with the genetics lab though and however it was that my birth came about."

"I don't want you to take this wrong Alice, but is there anything that you know you're not good at?"

"Baking, sewing and Swahili. I could never get my tongue to cooperate. Also, I can't yodel."

"Fascinating," Jack said, unable to keep himself from laughing at the very serious expression she suddenly had.

"What's so funny?"

"Nothing. That's a fascinating list and I think, I think I just need to laugh at something, anything. It's not you."

"It is too me, but it's okay. I like to see you smile," she said, smiling back at him.

"Ditto," Jack said. "You said you wanted to know more about me. Did you mean that?"

"Of course."

"Okay, then what do you say we try to not think about all this? And just for one evening we do get to know each other like two normal people who just met on a train? It's not exactly like we can do anything tonight anyway."

"I think that's the best idea I've heard in a long time," Alice agreed.

"Okay then," Jack said, wondering to himself just how to go about talking to Alice as though she was normal. He wanted to slap himself. He had said it himself. She's human, but the fact remained she was no normal human. Then again, how do you define normal in this world? He was only making himself more and more nervous, and the silence was getting way too long for comfort.

That's when Alice got up and went to the door.

"Where are you going?" Jack asked.

"Don't worry. I'll be right back," Alice replied, as she opened the door.

Jack thought about following her, but she wasn't going anywhere. She was just standing in the aisle facing out the window on the other side. Maybe she just really needed to get away from him. He definitely hadn't been the best company. Hell, he couldn't even treat her like a normal person. Jack closed his eyes, suddenly feeling like the world's biggest jerk.

Then the door slid open, and he looked up to see Alice facing him.

"Hi," she said, holding out her hand. "I'm Alice, and it looks like we'll be sharing a compartment."

It took him a second to catch on, but then he stood and smiled, holding out his hand. "I'm Jack, Jack Wilson. Nice to meet you Alice," he said, as they smiled and shook hands.

"So where are you headed Jack Wilson?"

"Home for Christmas in the wild farmlands of Nova Scotia,

not too far from Halifax. You?"

"I'm running away from home," Alice said, only half joking. "I'm going to visit my sister. She lives just outside of Halifax as well."

"Well then, we should get to know each other. Who knows, maybe we'll run into each other once we're there as well."

"Tell me about your hometown."

"Well, It's pretty small, and most everybody knows everybody else. There's this great little café and bookstore down by the sea. They make a killer cinnamon latte, and the ham sandwiches are amazing. Right now, there's a really cool Christmas light festival going on too. They have just about every kind of holiday food you can imagine, gifts for everyone and lots of music and dancing. There's a gigantic Christmas tree in the town center, and on Christmas Eve, just after dark hundreds of boats of all kinds and sizes, decorated in thousands of lights form a parade down the coastline and back."

"That sounds wonderful!" Alice exclaimed, really looking forward to seeing it herself.

The next few hours were wonderful! Jack and Alice talked about everything from literature to baseball. It was midnight before they even looked at the time again. They were both tired, but neither one wanted to sleep, knowing that in the morning they would need to again look at the reality of their situation. They didn't even pull out the beds, but Alice nodded off with her head on Jack's shoulder and he with his head against hers.

Chapter Seventeen

The morning came all too soon as the train whistle blew, and sunlight streamed in through the window. The intercom announced that they would need to change trains at the next stop.

They both stretched and stood to go to the small toilet in the corner of their cabin.

"Ladies first," Jack said, smiling at Alice through sleepy eyes.

Alice looked at herself in the small mirror over the sink. She ran her fingers through and repined the wig she wore, then used some tissue to clean up the circles of eye makeup that had smudged as she slept. As she did this, she looked into her eyes. She stared back at herself. There wasn't a single line on her face. Her teeth were straight, but she smiled in some satisfaction that they were slightly stained from all of the coffee she enjoyed. It was funny, she thought, so many people she knew were obsessed with trying to look and be perfect, and here she was actually wanting to find more imperfections. She brushed and rinsed her mouth, spat, and straightened the clothes she wore as best she could. She looked into her eyes one more time and wondered who she was. "Where did you come from? Who did you come from?" she asked herself.

She was startled by a rap on the door.

"Are you alright in there?" came Jack's voice.

"Yes. Sorry. I'll be right out," she answered, wiping away a tear that had suddenly appeared to trickle down her cheek.

"All yours," she said, as she stepped out.

Jack could see it in her eyes, even though she didn't look at him. They were back to reality, whatever that may be, Jack thought. Little did he know just how close they were to being hit with even more.

***

Sophie was relieved to be home in her own bed again, and for a moment she was able to believe that nothing had changed, but the fact was that her whole life had changed. She had a sister, and even more questions about her own birth. It had been so hard not to tell her parents everything. She didn't want to make them any more a part of this than they already were, and she knew that on some level it hurt them that she even wanted to know.

Alice was a reality though that they were soon to meet, and Sophie still didn't know the best way to tell them or how much to tell them. She did know that no matter what he promised, Jack was likely to continue playing the part of protective surrogate big brother. That meant that she needed to find out what he was keeping from her before he returned.

Sophie stretched and reluctantly jumped out of bed. She pulled on some sweats and opened the shades to look out the window of her studio cottage to the main house where her parents lived. The day was gray, and there was a light snowfall that dusted the path across the yard. There was also smoke coming from the chimney, signaling that her mom was up, and that there was coffee, and breakfast being prepared. Sophie knew they were expecting her to join them and tell them all about her trip. They had wanted that when she arrived yesterday, but she had needed time to consider, and so had gone with Shannon to the Christmas bazaar, and then to her house for dinner. When she had arrived home, she had claimed to be too tired and promised to fill them in on everything in the morning.

Sophie looked through the camera she had taken to New

York. Beth had taken a picture of Sophie and Alice together. Sophie pulled on her boots, coat, scarf, and hat, grabbed the camera, took a deep breath, and headed to the house for what was certain to be an interesting breakfast.

***

Charice and Max had spent several hours with the detectives and analyst, looking at the files, writing down names and trying to contact Alice, Albert, or anyone who could tell them where they were. Alice had not gotten on her scheduled flight from New York or any other flight on record. They were also informed that she had not been at the company suite, and that meetings had been canceled due to her disappearance as well as Albert's. At the request of the police, Charice had also checked Alice's company account, and noted that she had taken the maximum daily withdrawals.

"You don't suppose they decided to run off and get married, and the whole family is having some secret wedding getaway?" asked Dave.

"Ha!" exclaimed Charice. "Alice can't stand Albert. Mr. and Mrs. Morgan set them up, but as loyal as she is to her parents, she would never marry that man!"

"You don't like him very much?" asked Shane. He had arrived just after the offices officially closed. Technically he'd been off duty for hours, but he wanted to stay close to this case.

"I've never actually met him," Charice admitted, "But I have spoken to him on the phone and seen the look on Alice's face when his name is mentioned. So no, I don't like him."

The next morning Dave had gone back to the office to continue questioning the employees, while Shane and Lidia met again with Charice and Max at the station. They had received a call that morning from the NYPD, who were also looking for Alice and Albert in connection with the disappearance of Frank Amstead.

"And the plot thickens," Shane said, shaking his head as the sergeant handed him the report on Mr. Amstead's disappearance in New York.

Selma was next to come in with information. The messages retrieved from the office phone were different from those on the home answering machine and had included the message left by Alice that verified Charice's description of Alice's feelings toward Albert.

"Well, maybe she did run off after all, only not with Albert," Dave said, eyebrows raised.

"No," Charice replied adamantly.

"I agree," said Shane. "I think all of the disappearances are somehow linked, but not to a wedding. Can you get the transcripts from the last meeting in New York?" he asked Charice.

"I should be able to. I'll call right now," she replied.

"Good! And let's get a search warrant for Alice's apartment. I also want an international A.P.B. put out," Shane said. "On everybody!"

"International?" Dave asked. "We already checked and there aren't any hits on their passports."

"Yeah. International," Shane confirmed, looking at his watch and then turning to Charice as she hung up her phone.

"That's odd," Charice said. The lead secretary said there are no transcripts. What she does know about the meeting is that it didn't go well. She said that Albert was in a horrible tizzy when he got back, and she thought she heard him throwing things against the wall in his office. It seems that Alice walked out of the meeting, leaving with Mr. Amstead and no sale. What really surprises me though is that I didn't hear about it before now."

"There's something more personal going on here," Shane

said, rubbing his nose. "You and Max are free to go now, but I'm assigning police surveillance to you both."

"Why?" Max asked. "We're not going anywhere, and I can protect us."

"Humor me. I've got too many missing people already, so you can either leave with surveillance or I can arrange a cozy room for you behind some nice safe bars. Your choice."

"Okay, I get it," Max said, rolling his eyes. "I have a lot going on though. It is Christmas and I have commitments. I volunteer at a soup kitchen, and I'm stage-managing a Christmas pageant at the VA. We start dress rehearsals this week."

"Admirable. I'll tell the officers to help out as volunteers too."

"If you insist."

"I do and illegal as it was, I appreciate your help too," Shane said, holding his hand out to Max. They shook. "Okay," Shane continued pointing to two officers who had appeared in the doorway. "Follow officers Samson and Hinder, and I'll be in touch."

"Just find them. Find them all alive," Charice said.

"That's the goal," Shane said, putting a hand on her shoulder.

Chapter Eighteen

Alice stepped off the train and into the bustling station in Quebec. They had an hour before their next train left and decided to grab a bite to eat and a paper at the concession stand. Alice had something else she wanted to check out too.

"How far was the lab from the train station?" She ventured to ask Jack.

Jack raised an eyebrow at her.

"I'm just curious."

"It's sure to be a shopping center by now anyway," he responded.

"Exactly. So, there's no reason not to tell me. Besides, we only have another forty-five minutes, not even enough time for you to worry."

Jack considered for a minute. What difference would it make to tell her? If he didn't, she would probably spend the rest of the trip annoyed at him. So, Jack shrugged his shoulders and told her. "It's just the other side of the tracks around the corner from the station."

"Show me."

"Why? There's nothing there and we need to get to our platform."

"Oh, come on Jack! Like I said, I'm curious. Let me see the shopping center. It's not like I'm going to race in and run up my credit card. I just want to see the spot, the spot where I may have been created."

"Alice."

"What?"

"I just wish you wouldn't talk about yourself like that."

"I'm just trying to face reality. Now come on. I'm going with or without you."

"It's freezing out here!" Jack said, as they stepped out onto the snow blown walk a minute later. Light flakes dusted their heads, as Jack looked at the time. "Come on. We'll have to hurry."

"This is beautiful!" Alice exclaimed, as she took in the front of the station and its surroundings. "It's nothing like I had imagined. I expected a run-down industrial neighborhood. This city is beautiful!" She continued, as she hurried to keep up with Jack.

They both stopped as they rounded the corner and Jack pointed. "It was right over there. I guess they changed their minds about the shopping center," Jack said, as they looked at the hotel sign. Jack looked at his watch as Alice stared. "We need to go."

"Okay," she said, turning away to follow him back to the station.

They made it to the platform just as the last call to board was made.

Jack sighed in relief, as they settled into their seats.

"What did you think was going to happen?" Alice asked. "You thought I was going to try something. Didn't you?"

"Try what? No, I just wanted to make sure we made our train," he said, pulling the newspaper, breakfast croissants, and bottled juices from the bag of purchases they had made before their little sightseeing expedition. She was right he thought. He had been concerned. He couldn't really explain why though. He had known there would be nothing there of consequence, but still, something about her demeanor bothered him. He couldn't put his finger on it, but he felt as she was the one now hiding something from him.

Alice sipped her apple juice, and bit into the ham and cheese croissant. It was good, she thought, as the landscape began to move through the window. She was certain that Sophie would be more than willing to help with the idea that was brewing in the back of her mind. She just needed to make sure that Jack was home safe first with his parents, and that she left him in a position where he would not have to worry about the expenses or the authorities. He had done enough, and he didn't need to be involved any deeper.

***

The picture really had spoken a thousand words when Sophie had shown it to her parents at breakfast. Her mother had gone speechless at first, and her father had burned his finger on the coffee pot, but after a minute they had recovered. Dad sucked his finger, as mom chatted about preparing for company, and they both said that they were happy that she had discovered she had a sister.

Sophie hadn't told them about anything else. They knew nothing of Mr. Amstead or of the common traits Sophie and Alice shared aside from their looks. In fact, they seemed relieved, thinking that now that she and Alice had met, all of Sophie's questions were answered, and her research into her origins would cease.

It was a good thing they couldn't see her now as she had broken into Jack's apartment and was snooping around. Technically, she hadn't broken in. She did have a key, but she still felt like a thief as she spied through his drawers, careful to place everything back just as she had found it.

She had just searched through Jack's sock and underwear drawer when she was startled by the sound of a key in the door. Surely there was no way Jack could be back already. She was certain that their train wasn't scheduled to arrive until early the next evening. Frantically, Sophie looked around, and just as the front door opened, she ducked behind the bathroom door. She then tiptoed into the tub and careful to be quiet, drew the shower curtain closed. She thanked God that he had a dark blue cloth curtain on the outside and not just the clear liner. She looked up to the frosted window just over the bath tiles and prayed that she wouldn't have to use it. Sophie focused her breathing and listened. Someone was moving around, and she thought that she heard the refrigerator open. Then she heard the distinctive sound of a drink opening, and popcorn popping in the microwave. The television turned on next, and Sophie sank down to lay waiting in the tub.

***

Her nose still burned, but she was warmer now, and as she woke, she noticed that her eyes no longer felt swollen, and her mouth was cleared of the gauze she had previously been gagged with. She tried to move her legs and found them stiff, but free of bonds.

She opened her eyes to find herself lying on a comfortable bed in what looked like a hotel room. She also found that she wasn't alone. Another woman lay on another bed next to hers.

Suzanna walked over to the door and found it locked. She needed to find a way out of here, to find Edgar and escape. Her heart started beating fast at the memory of the last time she had seen him. She forced herself to breath circularly until her heart rate slowed, and then made her way over to the other side of the room to look out the windows, and at the other woman.

The windows appeared to hang out over the edge of a high bluff, and there was a beach far below that seemed somehow familiar, as did the woman when she turned to look at her. She couldn't see her whole face as it was turned into the pillow, and the dark hair fell over the other side, but Suzanna was certain that she knew her from somewhere.

Tentatively, she touched the woman's shoulder. There was no response. The woman was breathing steadily. Suzanna could tell that much. She shook the woman's shoulder more firmly, but still, there was no response. She had clearly been drugged.

Something else caught Suzanna's attention as well. She had not noticed it at first, as the woman lay in a semi fetal position, wearing a lose sundress. She was otherwise slim, yet a telltale bulge in her abdomen noted that she was also clearly several months pregnant.

The next thought that crossed her mind, at first seemed odd. She wondered who would wear a sundress in December? Then she looked out the window again, and it hit her where she was. She clutched the windowpane to steady herself. It had been thirty-one years ago, but she could never forget.

***

He knew that she was there. He had smelled her lotion as soon as he entered and had seen the door to the bath close. He wondered how long she would hide in there, and then he wondered how long before he would need to go in there himself. He shouldn't have opened that second bottle Nick thought to himself as the movie ended.

He chose another film, wishing that she would just give herself up and come out to join him. Of course, she didn't necessarily know who she'd be joining. Should he just go in and expose her? His bladder was telling him yes, and he headed toward the bath.

Sophie held her breath as she heard him enter. She tried to think of who else would have a key to Jack's apartment. His dad and any number of his friends that he may have asked to pick up mail and look in on his plants while he was away. Nick? No. Nick had been in New York with them. He wouldn't come by now, yet she could have sworn that she smelled his aftershave. Any number of men could use that same scent though.

She must be in the tub, Nick realized as he closed the door. How would he explain himself? Not that it was him who needed to explain, but he had been there for two hours already. What if she wasn't dressed? He thought suddenly. No, she had been there searching, just like Jack had thought she might. He needed to do something fast though, because he really needed to take a leak.

"Sophie?" he called out.

Sophie froze. It was Nick! And he seemed to know she was there. She glanced furtively up at the window.

"Come on. Game's up. Come out and join me for a movie," he said, as he drew back the curtain. He couldn't help but laugh as she looked up at him so innocently.

"You scared me to death!" she stammered. "Why didn't you let me know it was you? I thought you were a robber or a murderer."

Now it was his turn to look innocent as he replied, "This face only kills with its good looks."

"Oh brother!" she said, climbing out from the tub to stare him squarely in the face.

He loved looking into her eyes, but he really did need some privacy. "Would you mind waiting on the couch? I actually came in here with a purpose and I don't need an audience."

It took her a second before she blushed deep red and excused herself into the living area.

"So, what are you doing here?" she asked, as he returned.

"I thought we had a date," he replied, grinning and handing

her the bag of popcorn. "I hope you like thrillers," he said, settling back on the couch as though he were quite at home.

Not really knowing what to say, Sophie decided to just try to relax and enjoy the film. She had wanted to see Nick again and maybe she could perfect her own story.

***

Back on the train Jack had found a story in the paper that caught his attention. A man had been found dead and badly beaten in New York in an empty apartment, and the description fit that of a prominent businessman gone missing just days before, said the article. The name was being withheld pending official identification.

It went on to say that NYPD was still looking for the suspect who had been seen leaving the man's hotel on the day of his disappearance.

There seemed to be nothing further as Jack flipped through the pages, and thank God, no sketch of his face.

"What is it, Jack?" Alice asked, as she watched him searching through the paper.

"Nothing. Well, not exactly nothing, but it does look like this is all," he said, handing her the paper folded to the brief article.

"Oh no!" Alice exclaimed, as she read. "It can't be him. He's such a nice man and he has a family."

Chapter Nineteen

It was going to be another long day for Shane. It was only 1:00 in the afternoon, but he was exhausted. He couldn't sleep though. Usually cases didn't affect him personally, but this brought back too many memories. It had been five years and yet...

Her photo stared at him from the bookshelf. He couldn't bring himself to put it away, and now it felt almost as though she were trying to tell him something.

"What is it sweetheart?" he asked the photo. "Where are they? Where are you? I know I'm a cop and that people disappear all the time, but not high-profile businessmen. Not whole families from different sides of the country! Not my wife! I need you Patty. I need you." He sobbed, as the picture stared silently back at him.

He laid down on the carpet in front of his desk and stared at the swirling patterns of the ceiling. The swirls curved one into the other. He closed his eyes, and he saw hers looking back at him. She had bought a silk negligee, sapphire blue, just like the color of her eyes in their most inner ring. One of the straps had slipped from her shoulder and she smiled seductively. They had been trying to have a baby for three years, and while nothing could be found to be wrong with either one of them, every month had been another sad disappointment. That's why she had left him, or so he willed himself to believe. No matter how hard it was, it was easier to think that she was safe somewhere with someone else and maybe even with someone else's baby, than to let himself dwell on the other option. There had been no sign of struggle. He had simply come home one day to find her gone. Her suitcase and a few articles of clothing were gone too. There had been no real grounds for investigation. Of course, he hadn't let that stop him.

She hadn't had any family. Patty had grown up in a convent. A good Irish Catholic girl, his mother had said. Patty had said that his parents were like the parents she never had. How could she have just left without a note or a word to any of them?

Shane's mom had passed three years ago now, and his dad had gone to live with his sister Raina. None of them ever believed that Patricia had left on her own, but even with all the resources at his fingertips, Shane had been unable to find any trail to follow.

That brought his mind back to the Morgans. Where was their trail?

Selma knocked on his door, and he called for her to come in.

"Back problems?" she asked, as she looked down on him, stretched out on the floor.

"No. I just wanted to try thinking in a different position."

"Did it help?"

"Not really," he said, standing to face her. "What do you have?"

"I got a call on the DNA results from the body they found in New York and it's strange."

"What's strange?"

"The lab tech called me herself. She said that officially they were saying the results were inconclusive, but that there's no way they could be a match, not even as a relative."

"That is strange," Shane said, as his nose hairs began to dance a tango. "I'll call the chief in New York and see if I can find out what's going on."

"No! I mean please don't. Monica, the technician called as a favor. We went to school together. If they find out..." Selma said.

"I got it. Don't worry. I'll consider it privileged information. There's something really weird about this whole case."

"Agreed."

"Have you found something else Selma?"

"No, nothing. That's what's so weird it's almost like…I'm sorry," she said, glancing to Patricia's picture.

"I was just thinking the same thing. They knew each other."

Selma looked at Shane. "How?" she asked

"Patty was involved in helping with some of the fund-raising events they held. She'd met Mrs. Morgan at an event somewhere before we met. I don't even know what it was for. Maybe if I'd paid more attention before, she would still be here."

"Don't go there again. This could just be the lead we were looking for five years ago."

"I hope you're right on that," Shane said, as his nose hairs settled into a slow Cha-Cha. "I'll have Myers see what records he can find on the Morgan's philanthropic endeavors, and maybe he can come up with some donor and contractor lists or anything else. Thank you, Selma!"

The confirmation from Selma that he wasn't crazy for thinking there could be a connection, was exactly what Shane had needed to be able to focus forward.

***

They were halfway through the movie when Sophie turned to Nick and asked, "Aren't you going to ask me what I was doing here?"

"No," he replied simply, with a smile, eyes still focused on the television.

"What?" asked Sophie. "Why?"

"Because I already know."

"Oh really? Okay then Mr. Psychic, why am I here?"

Nick paused the film and turned toward her. The expression on his face was serious now. "The file's not here Sophie."

"You know?"

"Jack asked me too..."

"To keep an eye on me! I just bet he did!" Sophie said, rising from the sofa and throwing a cushion at him. "I do not need his protection or yours! I'm a grown woman and this is my life! My life that I have a right to know about!"

"Sophie please. Calm down."

"Calm down? You know I almost believed you," she continued, riveting him with a glare of steel. "I bet you think I'm stupid, that I believed you really wanted to spend time with me when all you are is an overzealous babysitter. Well, I am not a baby! And I won't be treated like one either."

"Sophie. I don't..."

"Save it Nick!" she said, as she grabbed her, coat, and purse, and stormed out.

There was only one other place that Jack would hide something, Sophie thought and that was at the farm. Sophie was just closing the door to her car when Nick jumped in beside her.

"You shouldn't leave your door unlocked like that," he said matter of factly.

"Get out!"

"Look. I just don't want you to waste your time."

Sophie fought to hold back the urge to deck him. Damn! Why did he have to be so handsome?

"You're right, Sophie. Okay. Please don't hit me," he said, reading the look on her face.

"I'm glad you agree. Now please get out of my car."

"I have the file, Sophie."

"You have it?"

"Jack asked me to get it. He figured you'd be trying to hunt it down. He knows you pretty well."

"It's my file."

"Yes."

"Have you looked at it?"

"No. I can't. It's in a lockbox."

"Locks can be broken."

"Are you sure you really want to do this?"

Sophie glared at him again.

"Okay. Okay," he said. "My apartment is only a few blocks away. Just don't tell Jack I gave it to you. I'd like to survive to see the New Year."

Sophie started the car.

"And Sophie," Nick continued. "I do want to spend time with you."

They drove the half mile to Nick's complex in silence. Sophie didn't know how to feel about what he had said. She wanted to believe it, but she needed to keep her guard up and focus on finding out the truth about where she and Alice had come from.

***

Alice shivered as she woke from the dream to discover that she had kicked off all of the covers. She drew them back up around her, and curled into a fetal position, as the dream replayed in her mind.

She was very young, maybe two years old and they were visiting with her aunt. Why did she dream of Aunt Claire? She hadn't seen her for years, yet she was never far from Alice's heart. In many ways she felt a stronger bond with Claire than she did with her own mother. Her mother had told her that her aunt had passed away just before the Christmas card had arrived. She'd died in a car accident. Alice had never met Claire's husband or children and had never been to Alaska. The dream had been so vivid though and definitely not in Seattle or any place Alice recognized aside from her dreams.

It was freezing cold, and Alice had been sitting on her aunt's lap in a rocking chair, bundled in her arms. There was a large window overlooking a barren field of snow. Her aunt had been crying and Alice had put her arms around her, which seemed to make her cry even more. The next thing she remembered was being put into a green car. It was a nice older model with black leather seats. Alice had thrown off her coat and was crying as she waved goodbye to her aunt. Snow was falling outside, but Alice had pulled off her sweater and kicked off her shoes. She had felt very angry at the end of the dream as her aunt faded from site and her mother had turned around to try and cover her with a blanket. She threw it off and curled away from her mother's touch as she shivered in the car seat. That is when she had woken up.

She uncurled herself, and lay staring up at the bunk above her, blankets tucked under her chin. She could hear Jack softly snoring above, closed her eyes, and replayed the dream again.

Her aunt had said something to her. Why couldn't she recall what it was? Then she reminded herself that it had just been a dream, and she wondered what her parents were doing. Were they worried about her or were they just angry? Both, she supposed.

Alice got up and peered through the curtain of the train. It was snowing, just as it had been in her dream, big fat flakes that shimmered in the moonlight. She picked up Jack's watch that he had left beside the window. She hadn't been asleep long. It wasn't even 9:30 yet. They had both felt drained as much from the recent events in their lives as from their thoughts of what the future may hold. They had decided to splurge and ordered a bottle of wine to share over dinner and had shortly afterward found themselves yawning. An image of Mr. Amstead passed through Alice's mind as she stared out the window. She tried to pray, but she wasn't really sure how she realized. What did she even believe? Alice didn't know how long she stood there, gazing out at the falling snow, mind crowded with images, and so many questions that she couldn't even begin to make sense of. She snapped out of it when someone banged loudly on the door of their cabin.

Jack sat bolt upright, banging his head. "Shite!"

"Open up! I know you're in there," came a slurred voice from the corridor.

Jack jumped down from the bunk, glancing at Alice as she stood, startled, with her back against the window.

"Who are you?" Jack called, as he checked to be certain the door was securely locked.

"Come on Gil. Let me in. I brought the beers."

Just then, a voice came from the compartment next door.

"Hey Lenny. We're over here. You got the wrong compartment man!"

"Sorry," came Lenny's voice again, followed by a resounding belch and the sound of the next-door compartment, opening and closing.

Jack let out a sigh of relief and turned to Alice. "Are you all right?"

"I'm fine," Alice said, as she went back to lie on her bunk and snuggled under the blankets. She rolled toward the wall, and Jack climbed back into the upper bunk, clicking on the reading light.

"The light doesn't bother you, does it?" he asked, wishing she would open up to him. He was sure she had been up before the drunk came to their door, and he really wanted to know what was on her mind.

"It's fine. I'm halfway back to sleep already," she lied, as she faked a yawn.

"Good night then," Jack sighed.

"Good night."

***

It took Sophie only a few seconds to snap the lock, and she hesitated only a few more as she offered up a silent prayer before opening the file, which lay inside. Nick was sitting on the carpet beside her. He had just finished kindling a fire in the fireplace, but a shiver of ice ran through him as Sophie began to spread out a series of photos.

Sophie was numb. She had braced herself for the worst and the worst is exactly what seemed to be laid out in front of her now.

"Sophie?" Nick asked.

"I'm fine. They're only old pictures and I have to look at them," she said. Then she picked up a pile of other papers and began looking through them. A number of them included some kind of scientific equations, that even though Nick had aced Calculus, appeared far beyond him. He reached over to pick one up and recognized that what had at first appeared to be a foreign equation, was really a much more basic equation that included elements from the periodic table.

"This reminds me of a biology test. Wait here, I think I still have an old textbook somewhere with the periodic chart," he said.

"Never mind," Sophie said, reaching out her hand to stop him, as he began to rise. "I understand it," she continued, as she stared at a long string of equations on another page. "At least I understand the idea, but..."

"What is it Sophie?"

"It should be impossible," she said, then she glanced at the photos, shuffled the horrific images of deformed infants and aborted fetuses into a pile, and flipped them over.

"Sophie?"

"I'm fine. I can look at those later. Right now, they're just a distraction," she answered, as she looked through the pages in front of her. "He must have put the certificate somewhere else."

"What certificate?"

"My death certificate."

"Death certificate?" Nick asked as another chill ran down his spine.

"Yep. Didn't Jack tell you? I'm dead, just like them," Sophie said, glancing to the stack of photos. "Or at least someone wanted everyone to think I was."

"Sophie." He couldn't think of anything else to say as he watched her study the pages.

She looked up at him. "It's okay Nick. I think that maybe being dead is why I'm alive."

"What is it that you said is impossible?"

"In simple terms, it says that eight halves can equal one whole. Only it's not exact halves. It's multiples of different fractions with common and uncommon denominators that form two with a common denominator, only the fractions have then been separated into several different subcategories and then reorganized and reduced into a single whole. Only it's not possible because there are too many fragments or fractions. They are basically saying though that two, four, or even five can be made equal to one."

"That makes no sense."

"It does in terms of procreation. Two people come together to form one baby. This is taking it further though and saying that there can be more than just two parents."

"Like when a dog has puppies by two different fathers?"

"Yes. Only in that case, each puppy still only has one father.

This is trying to prove that one egg could be fertilized by two fathers."

"Wouldn't that just mean twins with different fathers though? Right?" Nick asked, trying to grasp what she was implying.

"If the egg splits, yes. These equations though are fusing it all together, thus the three being able to equal one."

Nick picked up the photos, commanding back the bile that rose in his throat as he looked through them. "They weren't experimenting with puppies here though," he said, as he looked at a horribly deformed fetus."

"No, they weren't, and I wasn't..." She stopped herself as the reality of what she was saying sank in. "Yes, I was, but Alice wasn't deformed. They succeeded."

"What are you saying?"

"That's what this is. What Alice and I are. Oh, dear God! What am I?" she said, suddenly getting up and moving away from Nick before he could touch her.

"You don't really think that you and Alice were part of this sick experiment?"

"No, I don't think. I know. It's the only explanation that makes sense."

"It doesn't make sense though. It's not possible Sophie."

"All things are possible. Even the Bible says that."

"No, it says all things are possible with God. God wouldn't do this," he said, standing, and throwing the pictures onto the dining table.

Sophie moved to get her coat and purse. "I need to leave," she said.

"Sophie, please, let me drive you home."

"No, Nick. I'll be fine, really. It's just that it's getting late, and I completely lost track of time," she said, glancing at a clock above the stove, which read 9:45. "My parents are probably worried," she continued, even though she had phoned them earlier to say she'd be late.

Nick was by her side as she opened the door to discover that nearly a foot of fresh snow had fallen and was still coming down in thick clouds of fluffy flakes.

"Call your parents and tell them you're staying with a friend."

"What?"

Nick felt his face flush as he realized how that must have sounded. "I didn't mean... I meant that I could sleep on the couch."

"It's just a little snow."

"You can't see two feet in front of you!"

Sophie turned to stare indignantly at him.

"Your parents will worry a lot less if they don't think you're out in this."

Sophie had turned away, reached her car, and was trying to wipe the thick layer of snow from the windshield.

"Come on back inside Sophie," Nick urged.

"I'm going for a walk," Sophie said, kicking the tire of her car and heading toward the street. Nick followed, and she swung around to glare at him. "Alone! Don't you get it? I need to be alone!"

Nick watched her fading into the whiteness. He couldn't even begin to imagine what she must be feeling, especially if what she was presuming was true. It couldn't be true though. There had to be another explanation, didn't there? He thought, as he began to follow Sophie's tracks. He couldn't leave her out here alone. The wind whipped hard at him. In his hurry to follow Sophie, he hadn't thought to grab his coat, and within minutes, his sweater was sure to be soaked through. He rubbed his reddening hands together, praying that she would turn back soon.

She didn't turn back though. Sophie's mind was reeling. She understood now why Jack had been so afraid for her to see the file, if only for the photos alone. Did he have any notion of what the equations meant? She thought back to the files on Mr. Amstead's computer that they had looked through. It was all starting to make more and more sense to her. The logical side of her was somewhat relieved to at least have some comprehension of what she was. The other side of her screamed that it wasn't logical at all, and all she wanted to do was sit down and cry. She still had no idea of who she was in the sense of the parents she had come from, yet as she saw her adopted parents through the living room window, she knew exactly who she wanted to be. She considered joining them, but she wasn't prepared to answer questions.

It had taken her over an hour, but Sophie had made her way home, though how she had been able to find her way, Nick had not a clue. He hadn't realized where they were until he had followed her footprints into the drive, and recognized her parents through the window, as they sat in front of their Christmas tree watching something on television. Sophie hadn't even stopped, but had passed by on a path around the side to her own cottage behind. Nick was shivering like crazy, and with no explanation other than "I was following your daughter," to explain himself to her parents with, he had no choice but to knock on Sophie's door and confess the same to her.

"What are you doing here?" Sophie asked as she opened the door.

"Freezing!" was all Nick could manage through the chattering of his teeth, as Sophie pulled him through the door. In the light, he looked horrible. His hair was white with snow, his skin not a healthy pink, and his clothes were soaked.

"Oh, my goodness! Nick. You have to get out of those wet

clothes, or you'll have hypothermia."

"It may be too late for that," he chattered, as he tried to pull off the soaked through sweater.

Sophie had to help him lift it over his head and unbutton the shirt he wore underneath. "What are you doing here?" she asked again as she lit the wood stove and got a towel for him.

Nick took the towel and sat in a chair by the stove to remove his shoes and his pants. Then he realized what he was about to do and asked where the bath was, and if she minded him taking a hot shower.

"Oh, well, of course. Go ahead," she mumbled. "It's over there," she said, pointing to the open door beside her bed.

Nick breathed the steam in deeply, as the heat from the shower began to bring back the circulation in his limbs. The sensation of pins and needles pricked at his fingers and toes, and for a moment he thought of just filling the tub and submerging himself in the heat. Then he realized how tired he suddenly felt and thought about Sophie coming in to discover his nude body asleep in her tub. He smiled at the thought of how he had found her in Jack's tub earlier, as he lathered up with jasmine scented body wash. At least he'd come out smelling like something she liked, he reasoned. What could he come out wearing though? It would take at least an hour in a good dryer before he could put his clothes back on. He had stood another good ten minutes in the shower pondering just what would happen when he got out, when Sophie knocked on the bathroom door.

"I have something dry for you to put on," she called. "Can I just step in and leave them on the toilet seat?"

"Sure. Thank you," he called back, suddenly all too aware of the transparent shower curtain that surrounded him.

Sophie had snagged a pair of Jack's jeans and a work shirt

that he had left there for when he would come over to go fish with her dad. Fortunately, it had been laundered, and left on a shelf above the dryer in the garage, where she had been able to procure it unseen.

Sophie was all too conscious of the need to avert her eyes as she opened the door to the bathroom, which had been turned into more of a steam room. As she lay the folded clothes down though, she couldn't resist sneaking just a peek. He had turned away toward the wall and was cloaked in steam, but she could still make out the muscular outline of his back and below. She blushed, and then turned to quickly leave.

She had left just in time. The water was beginning to turn cold, and Nick hurried to turn it off, and exit into the still steamy warm room, where he toweled off and dressed quickly.

He wondered for a moment just what she was doing with a set of men's clothes. Then he recognized Jack's shirt, and he was suddenly very thankful that he was her cousin. Though obviously not blood related, he knew that there had never, and never would be anything more than a kind of brotherly and sisterly relationship between them. Alice was a different situation all together though, and Nick couldn't help but wonder how their trip together on the train was going. They were due to arrive the next evening.

Jack was bound to find out and be angry that he had allowed Sophie to see in the box. He had trusted Nick to protect her, but he hadn't been able to deny her right to know. He felt that despite it all, he had done the right thing. And he had tried to protect her. Shoot, he'd almost killed himself following her for over an hour in a virtual blizzard, and now he promised himself that he would go out there and behave like a perfect gentleman.

Chapter Twenty

Alice awoke to the whistle of trains. A thin ray of sunlight was coming in through the curtains, as she stretched, and got up to use the tiny restroom, dress, and apply her disguise before Jack would arise.

Jack was already awake. He had been practically all night really, dozing off only for a few seconds at a time. The clatter of the tracks seemed to be somehow agitating his mind, not allowing it to come fully to rest. He could also hear the drunken man chattering away with his friend through the wall. Jack rubbed his eyes and yawned. He wanted badly to sleep but knew that he wouldn't be able to. He thought about his mother and wondered what he would find when he arrived home later this evening. Would there be any change? He wondered what Sophie had been up to, and what all she had told her parents. He wondered about the man in the newspaper and if it really was Mr. Amstead. How long before NYPD caught up with him? Dear God, how he wished he could just flick a switch and shut off his mind to get a few hours of sleep.

Alice appeared a few minutes later. "Every time I put this thing on my head, I feel like I'm getting ready for a costume party. I almost scared myself in the mirror," she continued, smiling up at Jack, who had rolled over to face her. "Are you hungry?" she asked him. "I'm starving!"

"A little, I guess." he said, smiling at her and dropping down from the bunk to pick up the menu.

"I feel like a huge stack of pancakes with whipped butter, maple syrup, and bacon." She continued.

"We'd have to actually go to the dining car for that," Jack

answered.

"Yes, and we are well over the border, and in disguise, and I'm starting to feel a little claustrophobic. Come on Jack. This is my first real train ride. I don't want to spend the whole time cooped up in here. I think the fact that we never leave our cabin makes us look more suspicious than anything."

He had to agree that she had a point. He also needed to walk a bit, and hiding in here really did make it look like they were doing just that. Of course, he was sure that the porter only thought they were lovers, but still, even lovers come out from their nest from time to time, and being around other people might help to calm all the thoughts and concerns clattering around in his head. How did she always seem to stay so blasted calm he wondered?

"Okay, you have a point. Just wait for me to change so we can go together. After we ordered the wine last night, I'm sure they think we're newlyweds or something, so we need to stick together."

"Alright," Alice agreed, as he took his change of clothes into the toilet.

***

She was laughing, not at him, but with him as he twirled her around the floor. He couldn't help thinking his life was perfect now. She seemed to be that perfect piece that made his life complete. Oh God, how he loved her. It was her eyes that had first caught his attention and held it now as she gazed into his. A warm breeze blew leaves into a gentle dance around their feet as sunlight glinted through the trees. Then the breeze turned into a sudden wind that howled and blew the leaves up in a funnel between them. The sky turned dark, and all the limbs of the trees were bare. His arms were empty as well and a cold dense fog was settling in all around him. He tried to see through it to look for her. He called out her name but could hear nothing but the strange forlorn howling of the wind as it seemed to push him backwards. He was falling backwards through the fog now.

Shane awoke with a start, and it took him a minute to realize where he was. He had spent the night on the floor of his office. He looked at his watch. It was only 5:00 a.m., but that meant the coffee shop on the corner would be open and a fresh cup of coffee sounded like just the ticket. He could get a sugar and caffeine pick me up all in one cup. What was it Patty used to like? A double dolce. That was it. That's what he needed. Strange, he thought, that a cup of coffee could make him feel somehow closer to her.

The weather, when he stepped outside gave him a strange feeling of déjà vu that he was somehow back in his nightmare. Then again, he was, but he had a renewed determination to wake up from it. No matter what else he found, he was going to find Patty too.

As he stepped inside the coffee shop he was greeted with the sound of "Jingle Bells" and a cheerful looking teenager in a Santa hat. Patty would have loved it, he thought. Christmas had always been their favorite holiday. He smiled at the young clerk and took out his wallet as he stared at the prices. Five bucks for his drink of choice. Hell, he thought, that was probably about how much they paid for the whole can of coffee back at the office, and it brewed twenty pots.

"One venti dolce latte Please," Shane ordered.

"Yes sir. Coming right up. Would you like whip or extra foam on that?" the young man asked with a smile.

"No. Thank you for asking though," Shane answered, trying his best to return the smile.

As the barista made a smiling Santa face in the foam of his drink, Shane stared into the pastry case, and decided that he'd need his strength from something more solid than coffee. He didn't want it from doughnuts or any of the other Christmas goodies that seemed to magically appear in the lunchroom either. All were slathered in sugar, and usually topped with some kind of frosting and little red and green sprinkles. Shane grabbed a banana, and ordered two ham, cheese, and egg bagels. Gave the young man behind the counter a fifty and told him to keep the change.

"Merry Christmas!" Shane added as he headed away from the cheery coffee shop. He took a sip of his drink. Wow! Sweet, but with a kick. Perfect!

***

Alice and Jack had just sat down in the dining car of the upper deck and had a great view! Alice had to admit that though this wasn't how she had dreamed of adventure, she was excited! Here she was running from both her parents and the law with a handsome man on a train in a foreign country. She had met a sister, which she always wanted, but never dreamed she would have, and was on her way to discovering, no matter how unsavory it may be, truths about herself that she had never imagined.

She thought back to the dream of her aunt and wondered what it meant. It wasn't the first time that she had dreamed of her, but it was the first time she had ever felt that there might be some meaning to it. Before, Alice had always assumed that any dreams that had family aside from her parents were just her subconscious way of helping her fulfill her wishes. Alice had always longed for family. She remembered how jealous she had felt at times of the other students, especially at college, when they would talk about going home at the holidays and being crowded in a room of twenty plus people around gigantic turkeys and children playing under foot.

Alice smiled up as a waitress came to take their orders. "I'll have the pancake special with bacon," Alice told her.

Jack, appetite suddenly coming back at the smell of the surrounding patron's meals, ordered the same.

The waitress had just brought them their plates and a pot of coffee when the train came to a complete stop, and the whistle blew.

"Where are we?" Jack wondered aloud, as he looked out the windows.

Just then an announcement came over the loudspeaker. "Due to the blizzard conditions that the region experienced last night, the track ahead is currently blocked. We hope to be able to reinstate our journey within the next few hours. We apologize for any inconvenience and thank you, thank you for your patience."

***

Sophie tried to act natural as she traipsed through the knee-high snow that lay across the yard to join her parents for breakfast. She needed to be with them. They helped her feel normal. Nick would go around the way they had come into her place the night before and knock on the front door on the pretense of being in the vicinity. She hadn't anticipated this much snowfall though and prayed that Nick would be convincing as to why he would be out in it.

"Good morning!" Sophie said, as she entered the kitchen.

"Good morning Sophie," her dad called back from the living room. "Mum is in the garage counting our supplies," he continued, as he came out to kiss her cheek good morning.

Nigel O'Hare was a small man at five-foot six, balding, in his early sixties, semi-retired primary school science teacher, turned chicken farmer, and aspiring author, who adored his daughter.

"Are we expecting another storm?" Sophie asked, already concerned about Jack and Alice.

"We are, but not until tomorrow. When and how did you make it home last night? I didn't see your car."

"That's because I left it in town and hiked in," she said, figuring that honesty was best, at least in her own case.

"You hiked back? Sophie, do you realize how dangerous it was out there?"

"It wasn't so bad da. I actually would have come by last night, but I had already said I might stay with Shannon, and I was really beat."

"Why didn't you just stay in town with Shannon love?"

"Dad," she said in a voice meant to gently remind him that she was an adult. "Shannon had a date, and I didn't want to be a third wheel."

"Okay sweetheart. I'm just glad you're safe."

Just then there was a knock on the door, and her dad went to open it as she went to the kitchen.

"Nick! What a surprise! What brings you out here so early and in all this snow? Come on inside. Please, you must be freezing! Would you like some coffee son? Sophie, look who's here!" Mr. O'Hare continued, coming into the kitchen with Nick. "Get the lad a cup of coffee will you, and I'll go retrieve your mum."

"You heard the man," Nick said with a wink. "I'll take it black," he continued, as she poured cream into a mug and poured a coffee, which she sipped as she turned to face him.

"Wipe the smug look off your face, and I'll think about it," she said with a wink of her own.

Nick bit his tongue and managed a more serious look as he sat at the table. Sophie couldn't help herself. She broke out laughing at him.

"Some hostess you are!" Nick teased, and Sophie had to turn

away to pour his coffee.

"Serves you right," she said, as she turned back, biting her lip to keep a straight face, and handed him the coffee.

"What's all this going on?" asked Sophie's mom, Lily O'Hare, with a smile as she came in. "It's good to see you, Nick. What brings you out this way so early?"

"Aye? I was wonderen the same thing," Sophie's dad added, as he came in and sat at the table across from Nick.

"I have to stay in shape come rain, come shine or even snow, and I wanted to come by and see Sophie anyway."

Sophie stiffened.

"Oh, well that's nice," said Sophie's mom, turning to give her a smile. Lily O'Hare was fifty-eight, but with barely a line on her face, could have easily passed as Sophie's older sister. She had kept her figure and maintained that her long brown wavy hair was still natural thanks to a secret passed on to all the women through the French side of the family.

Sophie cocked an eyebrow at Nick.

"So, what is it you're wanting to see our girl about Nick? Mind you, we've barely seen her ourselves since she got home."

"I owe her lunch and wanted to see if she was free to let me make good on it today."

"You don't owe me lunch Nick," Sophie put in.

"Yes, I do. Remember I said at the airport that..."

"I remember, but you really don't. And like my parents said, I've barely spent any time with them, so I think I should just stay in today."

"We promised we'd both meet Jack and Alice at the station. They're due in at five-thirty, so I thought we could just go in a bit early and have lunch at that new restaurant across from the station."

"Oh, that's right!" exclaimed Sophie's mom. "I'm so excited to meet Alice. I pulled the cot out from the garage, so if she wants to, she is more than welcome to stay here with us."

"Well, it sounds like it's all been worked out then," said Mr. O'Hare. "Sophie, can I just have a quick word with you before you go?"

"Sure da. What is it?"

"Not now. It'll hold till after breakfast." He turned to Nick. "You will stay for breakfast, won't you Nick?"

"Well, I..."

"Of course you will Nick," her mom added. If you don't mind waiting fifteen minutes or so while I pull it together."

"Not at all," Nick said with a smile as his stomach let out a growl of hunger. "Not sure I could make the trek back without."

Sophie was tense. All she had wanted was some more time to herself, but it was clear that wasn't about to happen. She would wind up walking back into town with Nick and then it would be the four of them again. Sophie really did want to spend time with Nick, and she could hardly wait to see Jack and Alice again, yet she treasured her time alone too, and she had had virtually none at a time when she needed it more than ever to sort things out. It had been hard enough before when she didn't really know who she was, but now she felt that she knew more who she was than what she was. She wanted time alone with Alice, and prayed that Nick and Jack, as well meaning as she knew they were, would back off and give them some space. She wondered if Alice had been able to drag anything more from Jack.

"Dad?" Sophie asked.

"Yes?" he answered, breaking off in mid question to Nick about the competition in New York.

"Would you mind having that word now, while mom fixes breakfast?"

"Well, I hate to leave Nick here all alone, but..."

"What do you mean all alone?" asked Sophie's mom. "I may

be cooking, but I am still here and capable of conversation. So go on and have whatever word it is you want with our daughter."

Sophie and her father went from the kitchen and into the closet, which was also known as his office. It was a tiny room originally meant to be a laundry, but the plumbing had been messed up, and it was now home to a small desk, with an outdated computer, and a couple of file drawers.

"What is it dad? Is it about Mum's Christmas present? I picked up a nice scarf for her in New York."

"No. In fact I'm not sure what this is," he said, as he reached into a file drawer, and pulled out a large manila envelope, which he handed to Sophie. "I was hoping you might tell me though."

Sophie looked at the envelope. It was postmarked from Seattle. She looked up at her dad and read the concern on his face.

"I have no idea where this came from. The only person I've ever met from Seattle is Alice, who I only just met in New York and is on her way here."

"And you didn't request any records or anything from her family? Please just tell me you're letting the questions about your adoption go. She'll act happy for your sake, but having Alice come here scares your mum and me."

"Why da? You're my parents no matter what. I just need to know where I came from."

"We don't want to lose you."

Sophie embraced him and could feel him tremble as he hugged her tight. What was he really afraid of? Did her dad know more? They'd always said it was just a standard closed adoption, and that they knew no more than she did. But something inside of Sophie knew that her dad's reaction was more than fear of losing her to a family she'd never known.

She let go and looked at the envelope again. There was no name or return address. "This is really odd. It doesn't even say who it came from."

"That's why I thought maybe you..."

"I didn't. I didn't request anything from Seattle."

"Well then, I guess you may as well open it, and solve the mystery for both of us," he said, a smile back on his ruddy face.

"Breakfast!" came a call from the kitchen, followed by Nick's voice.

"You better come and get it before I eat it all!"

"We better go. This is probably just some ad. I probably got put on a list and they want to sell me international insurance or some such junk," Sophie said, tucking the envelope under her arm and opening the door.

"You're probably right, especially after all your shoppin in New York. Maybe it's a catalogue for online shoppin. You will tell me though, and settle your old da's curiosity, won't you?"

"Of course, da," Sophie replied, as they passed through the living room, and she curled the envelope to tuck it into her coat pocket.

***

Shane opened up the paper as he sipped his drink. It was his third 'Dolce' of the day. It was far too sweet for his personal taste, but it did the trick, in more ways than one he thought as he looked at Patty's photo.

They had managed to keep the Morgans off of the front page of the paper itself, but Shane was irked to discover a large photo of Edgar and Suzanna on the front page of the business section with a headline reading: "Seattle Tycoons Reported Missing". He read the article, and it was nothing but two columns of speculation. One suggestion was that they had stolen funds from the company they had sent their daughter to meet with in New York. It went on to suggest that when Mr. Amstead, the CEO of said company had decided to back out that they had him killed. It was then noted that their daughter, who was wanted for questioning in the case had disappeared. Certainly, they were all planning to rendezvous.

The next suggestion was that Edgar Morgan had been taken ill, and that his wife and daughter were with him at some undisclosed medical facility outside of the country.

The last suggestions of this particular article were that the entire family had been either kidnapped and was being held for ransom or that they had already been murdered by a disgruntled employee of either their company or one that they had acquired.

Shane felt certain that the correct answer was none of the above.

He wondered who had leaked the story to the press, then he realized it would be a waste of time to try and find out. There were way too many people, and he was sure that even without the police involvement that many of them had to have realized the Morgan's absence. Charice had certainly been concerned.

Shane closed the paper and opened the file back up to review the pictures from the crime scene.

Chapter Twenty-One

Jack and Alice sat in silence. She could read Jack's discomfort and desire to get back to their cabin, but Alice was certain there was no need for alarm. Besides which, if they left now, they would not only be conspicuous, but starving as well.

A porter came around to hand out complimentary magazines and newspapers. He was followed by another railway employee who was checking to see if anyone would be likely to miss connections and require new routing.

Jack stayed turned toward the window, as Alice gave their destination and took a paper.

Out of habit she turned to the business section. She was enjoying her coffee as she read an article about mining in Canada. When she turned the page for the rest of the article, she was caught off guard as the faces of both her parents looked up at her from a photo attached to a small bottom corner blurb. The title read, simply: "Vanished".

Alice's heart beat faster as she read:

"Business acquisitions magnets and international philanthropists Edgar and Suzanna Morgan have seemingly vanished from their home in Montlake WA. USA.

The couple who sources say are usually at their downtown Seattle offices six days a week stated that neither they nor their daughter Alice have been seen or heard from for nearly a week. Local police at this time are not commenting".

It took Alice a minute to catch her breath as she held the paper higher, and pretended to continue reading, not wanting

Jack to see her face, which she was certain would be a dead giveaway that something was wrong.

Would they have planted this to flush her out? The thought left her mind as soon as it had crossed it. No, if they were truly that eager to find her, they would do so without making anything public. Her parents had more than enough resources at their fingertips to have multiple private detectives hunting her down. They had the NYPD already helping them as well. Then she wondered if the NYPD had planted the article to draw her out. She had heard of them doing such things, but unlike her parents, they wouldn't be likely to risk that she would be scrutinizing the business section. No, they would have not only placed the article in a more blatant location, but it would most likely have also included a photo of her for readers to be able to identify.

After dismissing these scenarios, the only one left was that her parents were indeed missing. The next thought that came to her mind was of Mr. Amstead. Could the same people who had taken and possibly murdered him also be responsible for the disappearance of her parents?

***

They had just made it back to Nick's apartment when the snow began coming down again.

"What do you say I make us some nice hot tomato soup? I can make up a nice fire too, and we can check to make sure that their train is still on schedule."

Sophie's teeth were chattering. Her boots had not thoroughly dried from the night before, and her toes were nearly numb with the cold.

"Okay, you win this one too," she said.

"What? So easily? Are you going soft on me Sophie?"

"No, just numb with cold. My boots got wet inside last night, and they're still a bit damp with ice."

"In that case, can you help me grab some more wood from the pile over there? I don't want us to need to come back outside until we head to the station."

Nick piled the logs into the fireplace and lit some kindling. The fire roared to life, and Sophie moved closer, taking her coat off. She pulled the envelope from the inside pocket and began to tear it open.

She pulled out two, eight by ten photographs and gasped at the images.

"What is it?" Nick asked, as he turned toward her.

Sophie handed him the photographs.

"Dear God! Who are they?"

"I don't know. The one could be Mr. Amstead, but he doesn't really match Alice's description."

The man in question had to be close to eighty. The picture only showed him from the waist up. He had a slightly square shaped face, which Nick guessed twenty or so years ago had been well chiseled. His head was held in a brace in such a way that he would not have been able to turn it. His eyes were taped wide open, staring straight ahead in fear. His chest was bare aside from four wired electrodes, and he appeared to be strapped down on some sort of gurney. What looked to be a rubber gag, stretched across his jaw from one side of the gurney to the other. Attached was a larger center insert, which filled his mouth. It left red marks across the lower part of his face, and there was a large ugly bruise above it on his right cheek.

The other photograph was of a woman, roughly the same age. She was dressed in a flimsy slip, her hands were bound above her head, which was fitted into a similar sort of brace as the man. There were what looked to be fresh stitches in a zigzag formation across her right temple down to her eye. Both of her eyes appeared to be swollen closed.

Sophie sat, and Nick looked in the envelope to see if a note of some kind had been included. There had not been.

"What does it mean?"

"I have no clue. Let me see the envelope."

Sophie handed him the envelope as she stared into the fire. A new kind of chill was running through her blood, and it wasn't just about where her blood had originally come from, but about just how much danger who she and Alice were may be putting the lives of those they loved in. It had to be some kind of a threat. Someone had to have connected her to… To what exactly? How would anyone have known where to find her, much less about her connection to Alice and all the craziness that had arisen since? It had to have something to do with that though. Less than two weeks ago her life had been boringly normal, that is as far as she knew. She had not really thought that the search for her parents would turn up anything much out of the ordinary. Could somebody else know what Jack had found? There had to be some reason that these terrible photographs had been sent to her. It was the Seattle postmark and the date of their arrival that pointed to her meeting Alice as the link. Had someone discovered their connection? Someone who was able to trace her address? It sounded crazy, but then again so did many of the things she had learned since her first meeting with Alice.

Why send pictures of an older couple though? What did these people have to do with genetically manipulated fetuses or Mr. Amstead's disappearance? They looked old enough to be her grandparents or… The thought hit her out of the blue. She thought back to the description Alice had given of her parents. She snatched the photos back from where Nick had sat them on the other side of the coffee table. She gasped as she became more certain.

Nick looked up from his examination of the envelope.

"Alice's parents."

"What? Are you sure?"

"No and yes. It should be easy enough to look up a current photo of the Morgans online though."

"How would anyone in Seattle know or even think to send them to you?" Nick asked, as he brought his laptop over and started it up.

"There's no way to know how many people are involved in this, and any one of them could have seen us together on that first night that we met, traced me through Jack or... I don't know. I don't know! I just don't know." She put her hands over her face and tried to hide the gathering tears.

Nick cautiously put a hand on her shoulder, and when she didn't pull away, slid his arm around her. At the same time, he hit search images for Edgar and Suzanna Morgan, Seattle WA USA.

Sophie couldn't look at him, but his arm felt too good to push away. She knew she should, but she didn't have the strength. She leaned back against him and wiped her eyes but kept them closed. She didn't want to look.

Nick looked, as the image filled his screen. There was no doubt. The people on the screen were the same two in the photographs that Sophie had received. He lowered the screen, sighed, lay back on the sofa beside Sophie, and closed his eyes. What the hell had he gotten into, he wondered for the umpteenth time. Then he turned his head and looked at Sophie to find her looking back at him.

"You were right. It's them."

Sophie nodded and looked down. "I don't even know how to feel. They, at least in a way, are my parents too."

"Your parents are home safe."

"Safe for how long? Somebody else knows about me."

"They weren't part of it though. The Morgans knew what was going on, about the experiments. They must have. That's why..."

"I hope you're right on that point, but still... I don't know. And how am I going to tell Alice?"

***

The first thought that went through his mind when he awoke was that he must be dead. His eyes were still closed, and he debated about whether to open them. The bed was soft, and the fragrance of fresh flowers and the sea surrounded him. Heaven, he thought. He'd actually made it. Even after all he'd done. Slowly, he opened his eyes, and awareness crept back as he tried to stretch. He felt the ache in his muscles, and knew he'd been wrong. He was still very much alive.

The events of the past few days came rushing back. The call from Meschner, the conversations with Albert, and the awful realization that everything was coming undone. They hadn't even given him a chance to handle it on his own. Meschner had said there were too many leaks. He had tried to play along. Tried to protect them, but they had sent in what Meschner referred to as a cleanup team. Then he wondered, just why was he still alive?

Sitting up, Edgar looked around him. He was in what looked like a hotel room. The open balcony was lined with tropical plants and looked out over the sea. He arose and walked outside. Looking down, he guessed that he was about five stories up, and a shiver ran down his spine as he realized where he was. He went back into the room and tried the inner door. To his surprise it opened, but instead of a hallway, he found himself in an office.

A man in his mid-thirties, with blond hair, and strikingly

vivid blue eyes, looked up from behind a desk with a smile. "So nice to see that you're awake. We weren't sure you'd make it. Your heart rate had shot up to quite an alarming level."

"Who are you and where is my wife?" Edgar demanded.

"I suggest you keep calm Mr. Morgan. Everything will be made clear soon enough."

"My wife?"

"She should be fine, as long as you both cooperate," the man replied with a sigh, as he stood and motioned for Edgar to sit. "Would you care for some coffee Mr. Morgan?" he asked, going over to prepare himself a cup.

"Water," Edgar stated, following the man with his eyes and still standing.

"Please, please do sit and try to relax," the man said, as he handed Edgar a bottle of water. "The others will join us shortly, and we can go over everything together."

"What others? Where is my wife?"

The man smiled and shook his head as he sat with his coffee, and Edgars eyes bored into him. "I wonder," he replied, "why don't you ask where your daughter is?"

Edgar felt like a shot had ripped through him, as the man behind the desk continued to smile. He sat abruptly on a chair beside him, his eyes never leaving those which seemed to gleam maniacally at him from behind the desk.

"Where is my daughter?"

"Your daughter?" the man laughed. "Which one?"

"I only have... Alice. Where is Alice?"

"Now that is the billion-dollar question, isn't it?" The man winked and turned toward another door as it buzzed and slid open.

The man who entered looked nearly identical to the man behind the desk, and he was followed by another near duplicate. The only difference was a slight variation in height, hair and eye color.

"Welcome Carl and Jonathon," the man said, and waved them in. "Mr. Morgan here has been getting anxious. Where is Mathias?"

"He's checking on the women," Carl said, with a snort.

"I do hope he's not allowing any sentiment to cloud his thinking. If he's not here in five minutes, I'll go check on them myself. Mr. Morgan, please do excuse the hold up. In the meantime, allow me to introduce you to my brothers. In fact, allow me to introduce you to myself," he said with a chuckle. "My name is Richter, and I am thirty-seven years old. To the right is my brother Jonathon, he is thirty-five and on the left is Carl, who is thirty-four. Mathias, who you will meet next is thirty-eight, but I'm afraid that he can be a bit of a dolt sometimes. He lacks the understanding that men like us all have, that to effect perfection, you must let go of those attributes that promote mistakes. You know what I mean Mr. Morgan? I'm sure you do since you were such an integral part of founding our work. A literal founding father we might say," Richter concluded with a wink.

Edgar took in each one of them. How was this possible? They were all older than Alice and there were four of them. It couldn't be. Alice had been the first survivor. Dr. Meschner had assured him. None of this was supposed to be here anymore. It had closed down years ago upon the death of the other three partners. Dear God almighty! Then it clicked. This is why Meschner had been so concerned about tracking Alice still. He knew!

"You'll excuse me Mr. Morgan, while I go to retrieve our wayward brother. I trust Jonathon and Carl will be good company."

Carl rose and went to the coffee machine. "How would you like yours Mr. Morgan?"

"I wouldn't."

"Very well. Jonathon?"

"Vanilla latte. Thanks Carl," Jonathan added, as he touched Edgar's hand. Edgar turned and saw a different look in Jonathon's eyes. They were a deep aqua and seemed to be trying to express something that he could not say. As Carl turned back to them with the coffee, Jonathon once again took on the same stoic expression he had when they entered.

Suzanna had paced the room a thousand times, until she was exhausted. Surely someone would come, explain something or at least tend to the other woman who remained sedated. Suzanna had found some water, fruit and protein drinks in a mini fridge as well as a clean set of clothes hanging in the bath. She had changed and forced herself to eat a banana to keep up her strength, but it felt like a lead brick on her stomach. She couldn't get the image of Edgar's face out of her mind, and she had nothing except her own mind to keep her company. A part of her wondered if they were merely trying to drive her insane. The truly ironic thing is that they were holding her on her own property, and she knew that even if she escaped, there was nowhere to run.

She and Edgar had bought the island with exactly that purpose though. It had needed to be secluded. A tear rolled down her cheek at the memory of what this place had been intended for. It was meant to make dreams come true. Their dream and others for the perfect children. Children who would fulfill their parents every dream. Children who would never suffer the ravages of disease, whose talent, beauty, and intelligence the world would envy, and it had, but at a gruesome expense. That, they had learned to live with though. They had Alice, and that was what Suzanna clung to as a way to sedate her conscience.

Her heart leapt at the sound of beeps from the other side of the door, and she sat upright, wiping away the moisture from her eyes.

"Hello," Mathias said simply, as he quickly closed the door behind him and went over to the woman on the other bed.

"Who are you?" Suzanna asked, as she watched the man gently push back the hair from the woman's face.

Mathias looked up. "Are you alright?" he asked. "If there's anything you need..."

"Where is my husband?"

"In my brother's office, I believe, waiting for me to arrive."

"And who are you? Who is your brother and why are we here?"

"I apologize. My name is Mathias. As to why you have been brought here, well my brother will explain that to your husband shortly. Has she stirred at all?" he asked, as he looked at the woman on the bed with a genuinely concerned expression.

"No. Who is she? I know I've seen her before somewhere."

"She's ..."

"Mathias!" came a stern voice from the doorway as it beeped open again.

Suzanna turned to see a double of Mathias, but the resemblance was clearly only physical. The man in the doorway stared icily at Mathias, and then turned to smile broadly at Suzanna. "Ah, Mrs. Morgan. You appear nearly as recovered as your husband. I'd love to stay and chat but..."

"Richter!" Mathias cut in. "She shouldn't still be out," he said as he stroked the woman's forehead.

"You interrupted me brother."

"I'm sorry, but..."

"Not to worry. See," he said, lifting the woman's dress to show a small monitor and some fluid strapped to her thigh.

"It's on a timer. When will you learn to trust me Mathias? I have everything under control. Now come along brother."

As he opened the door, Suzanna charged at him. Richter simply ducked back, while keeping his leg in the doorway and Suzanna tripped over him. She fell face first onto the cold, hard floor with a scream of terror, and pain as she felt the bone crack. Mathias ran to her side and glared defiantly up at Richter.

"Leave her be Mathias. Stupid woman and after I released you into such a beautiful room," he mocked, as he dragged Suzanna moaning in agony back into the room. He left her on the floor and shut the door. "Come along Mathias. She'll live, but she needs to learn not to provoke me, as do you with your foolish concern."

Chapter Twenty-Two

Alice turned the page of the paper. She could feel Jack's gaze, and she lowered it to take a sip of her cold coffee.

"What is it?" he asked as soon as their eyes met.

"Nothing. Except that my coffee's cold," Alice said, screwing up her nose.

Jack took his own empty cup, filled it with hot coffee and pushed it across the table to her. She smiled back, picked it up, and took a sip, and Jack reached over to snag the paper away.

"Hey! I was..."

"Hiding something from me. You stared at the same page without shifting for ten minutes. I want to see what was so interesting so..." He stopped, as he spotted the blurb on the Morgans. "Oh, dear God. Alice..."

"Shush. It's not that big of a deal. I'm sure it will go back up and our interests are diversified enough," she said, as a couple passed by. "I'd love some more eggs, honey," she continued, one dark penciled brow cocked at him as the porter passed by.

"Are you sure sweetie? I was thinking about more bacon and coffee myself," Jack asked, and Alice smiled.

An attendant passed by and took their additional order. He smiled at them. "Wise decision," he said. "A lot of people are getting off. There's a small commuter station up ahead, and people are getting off to walk it for a cab into town. The station is bound to be chaos. We're not the only train backed up. Where are you headed?"

"Home from our honeymoon," Alice said with a smile. "Are they thinking it will be more than a couple of hours delay?"

"Congratulations! Well done mate!" the attendant said, with

a smile and a nod to Jack. "As for the time, it depends. If they can clear the tracks before the next storm blows in, then yeah, we should be moving in a few hours. If not, then we'll be stuck overnight. If you want, they'll try to get you on a bus, but it won't really be any faster. So, my advice is stick with the train, but try to get a room in town. Bacon, eggs, and coffee, coming right up," he finished.

"Thanks for the tip," Jack said.

"Anytime. Oh, and the best place in town is "The Coriander Inn." Very romantic," the attendant said, and winked at Jack as he headed off.

"You sure you don't want to head back to the cabin Sweetie?" Jack asked, with a tense smile, as he looked around at more people entering the dining car. "I was just thinking it's a little crowded in here. I'm sure they could bring our order to us."

"No, I feel like showing you off for a while," Alice said, reaching to take his hand as another couple walked by. "It sounds like we'll have plenty of time to be alone later."

Damn! She was good, Jack thought. He knew, inside that she must feel overwhelmed, confused, and scared. God knows he would be or rather already was. First Amstead, now her parents, and here they were stranded on a snow-bound train unable to do anything, and just praying not to be recognized.

The attendant brought the coffee, fresh cups, and cream. "It's all on the house," he said. "Honeymoon special. I'm off shift, but my name's Walt. Just make sure that the waitress who brings your food knows you're on my list."

"Thank you, Walt," Alice said with a smile.

"Yes. That's very nice of you," Jack added.

"Stay warm!" Walt said with a wink and headed off.

They had just drained the coffee and were watching out the window as fresh snow came down sideways, when another announcement was made.

"We regret to inform you that due to increasing winds out of the west, our journey will be indefinitely discontinued. Please return to your seats as soon as possible. When your carriage number is announced please take all luggage with you to the front of the train. To make this as orderly as possible, you will not be permitted in the front carriage until your carriage number is announced. An attendant will be going through the train with additional information."

***

Nick checked the train schedule and saw that Jack and Alice's train was going to be delayed due to severe snow accumulation and high winds.

"It looks like they won't be making it in today or even possibly tomorrow with this blizzard coming. So, you might as well sit down and try to relax," he told Sophie, who had spent the last hour pacing back and forth in front of the fire.

"Relax? Are you kidding? How far away are they?" she asked, coming to look over his shoulder at the map. "Maybe it's for the best. She and Jack can have some more time together before they have to start worrying about her parents too. Maybe I can..."

"What? Maybe you can do what Sophie? Look at it out there," Nick said, as he pushed the drapes aside to reveal swaying trees. "We're lucky the internet is still up. We'd better call your folks before the lines go down."

Sophie grabbed her coat. "I'm leaving before the snow buries my car."

Nick jumped in front of the door to bar it.

"Get out of my way, and don't try to follow me again."

"Neither one of us is going anywhere Sophie!"

"Damn it, Nick! Get out of my way! I need some time. Alone! Please! I haven't had a minute to myself since this whole thing started," Sophie said, as she furtively tried to push Nick out of her way. He grabbed her arms, and she started to sob. He pulled her close, and she tried to push him away. "I mean it!" she snapped, as he felt her knee rise between his legs. "This is your last warning! Don't push me, Nick!"

He released her, and she ducked into the bathroom, slamming, and locking the door behind her.

"Come on Sophie. I'm sorry. I really am, but I can't let you go out there. I'd never forgive myself if something happened to you." And Jack would kill me, he thought.

He could hear her moving around. It sounded like she was hitting or throwing something, what he couldn't imagine and then silence.

"Sophie?" He knocked on the door. "Sophie?" Oh crap! He thought, the window! Nick flew outside as fast as he could against the strengthening wind.

She was already in the car, attempting to start the engine. Thank God, they hadn't dug it out, he thought as the engine turned over. There was no way she could actually go anywhere.

When she saw him coming, Sophie locked the door and yelled at him. "What part of alone don't you understand? I'm obviously not going anywhere, so just let me sit in the privacy of my own car!"

"Sophie."

"Go away Nick!" she screamed and turned away.

Nick made his way back inside. He pulled up a chair by the window where he could keep an eye on her and poured himself a cup of tea. It was going to be a long night, but regardless of what she thought, he did understand her need for space, and he hoped that she would understand his need to protect her. He grabbed his phone, called Sophie's parents, and plugged in the charger to make sure the battery was as full as possible. He hoped that Jack and Alice would somehow be able to call. Sophie had taken the photos of the Morgans with her, but the other files were on the counter. Nick picked up the folder and started looking through it. The images were horrible, and he turned them aside to read through the other papers.

***

Lidia and Dave looked through the closet in the high-rise apartment owned by Alice Morgan, or rather Morgan Acquisitions. After checking all of her financial accounts, home, and utility records, even her insurance, they had found that everything leads back to one place, Morgan Acquisitions. Aside from her driver's license and passport, not a single thing was in Alice Morgan's name.

"Damn!" Lidia exclaimed. "I knew she was under their thumb, but this is crazy! Everything she has is owned by her parents. If I were her, I would have run away years ago!"

"Don't feel too bad for her. She was of legal age," Dave answered. "If she really wanted to, she could have insisted on having things in her own name."

"Probably easier said than done when it's your parents, and they're the ones who gave you the only job you've ever known. She rebels, they could cut her off at the knees. Not really as much of a choice as it may seem," Lidia put in. "Wherever she is, I hope she's alright."

"You're not going soft on me, are you Yarnok?" Dave asked.

"Not a chance. Wow! Look at this. Not what I was expecting to find. Looks like she was trying to keep it hidden too," Lidia said as she opened a shoebox of dog-eared romances and self-help books on attracting the man of your dreams and how to make friends. Underneath she also unearthed a bunch of CDs of romantic love songs and dance music. "Welcome to the secret life of Alice Morgan."

"Yeah, look in here too. I just found something with Alice's name on it."

"What is it?"

"A museum membership and would you believe, a card for the YMCA. Look at this. It looks like she was taking classes in CPR," Dave said, as he pulled a folded registration slip out of the pocket of sweatpants, he'd found in a laundry bin.

"Interesting."

"I wonder what's in here," Lidia said, as she pulled out a lock box from behind some shoeboxes. "Shoot! It has a built in five-digit combination lock."

"We'll have to wait until we get it back to the station and pry it open. Anyway, I think I've covered my side of the closet. My whole bedroom as a boy wasn't this big."

"Shall we do the desk or the kitchen next?" Lidia asked.

"You do the kitchen. I'll take the desk."

"Deal."

"I'm surprised she doesn't have more of a home office," Dave commented, as they walked back into the main living area.

Lidia continued on to the kitchen, while Dave went over to inspect the corner by the balcony where a small computer desk and a two-drawer filing cabinet stood.

"I'm sure she would have taken her laptop with her, but no desktop, and only one drawer in her filing cabinet has anything in it."

"I'm starting to get the feeling that Alice's work at her parent's company was under pretty tight wraps too. You know, what goes on at the office, stays at the office," Lidia called from the kitchen.

"Maybe, but it just seems odd. Maybe she had another computer and..."

"And somebody took it along with some files? Could be, but

there's no sign of a break in, so someone with a key? Then again, maybe she just preferred to leave work at the office. If you think about it, it's not so odd. We're not supposed to take home case files."

"True, but still, when your family owns the business? And look at Edgar Morgan's office. He certainly took work home with him."

"Just one more way Alice decided not to be like her parents. Oooh! Okay, I seriously wish I'd gotten to know her better. This is a refrigerator after my own heart, and the cupboard too. Hey Asher! Look at this. She has a stash of cookbooks hidden up in the top cabinet behind the food processor, and the...I don't know what this is?"

"Pasta Maker," Dave said, as he came over to the kitchen. "Don't you cook Yarnok?"

"Sure. Remember the 4th of July?"

"Yeah? You're telling me that you did those burgers and dogs?"

"Don't forget the chicken and watermelon."

"No kidding? So, what was Rick doing in the kitchen so much?"

"Dishes."

Dave laughed, and looked through the foodstuffs. "Not bad. She has good taste in wine and ice cream anyway, and a well-balanced array of frozen fruits and vegetables, even bacon, cheeses, whip cream, and whole milk. So, what are we looking for in here again?"

"It tells us about her. Gives us a more well-rounded profile. For example, the milk is dated tomorrow. There's an open bottle of wine with no more than one glass worth missing and apples on the counter. This is someone who wasn't planning to disappear. The coffee pot has some build up and there's a print or two on the microwave, so she's not OCD clean, but at first glance you still feel like you walked into a show room photo. The trash is empty. She would have dumped the milk if she had meant to be gone longer, and she wouldn't have bought the apples or left the open cheese in the fridge. She meant to be back. The single missing glass of wine combined with what we found in the closet, also tells us that she was alone."

"Noted. I'll go check out the bath."

"Wait up Asher. You said only one file drawer had anything in it. What was it?"

"Receipts, copies of tax returns, some old school records, and a couple of newspaper articles relating to Morgan Acquisitions," Dave answered.

"Let's take a closer look at those receipts," Lidia said, as she closed the last kitchen cupboard and followed Dave into the large living room and over to the office area. Another wall was lined with a built-in bookcase. A majority of the books were in different languages. She had taken note of random titles to look up their meanings later. "You know what's odd here Asher?" she said, as she scanned the shelves again and adjoining wall.

"Yep. There's no family photos anywhere."

"Exactly! Now let's see those receipts."

"There's some pretty fancy restaurants here. Some concerts, conventions, bookstores, department stores, dry cleaners, beautician, garden store, some grocery receipts, and a separate envelope labeled: tips, donations and incidentals, with ATM withdrawal slips. Funny, these grocery receipts don't seem to match the groceries in her kitchen."

"She didn't put the YMCA in here either. These receipts are only the items she thought her parents would approve of. Note how she's labeled the withdrawals."

"You really think they kept that tight of a reign on her?"

"More and more all the time. I'm almost expecting to find a hidden camera somewhere."

"If there is, it'd probably be in the overhead lighting. I'd look, but I'd need a fire ladder to reach."

"I like the high ceilings."

"Yeah, but the cleaning and heating expense. Speaking of which, did we find out if Miss Morgan employed any cleaning service?"

"According to Charice, the same maid who did her parents' house was paid to come in once a week, but when I talked to her, she said that there was never much to do, and she and Alice would usually just sit and have coffee. Occasionally Alice would even ask her for laundry tips. She may have been under her parent's thumbs, but she seems to have had a strong independent spirit."

"Maybe one that landed her in trouble. Remember what we were told about the meeting in New York? Maybe this is a case of parents kidnapping their own child? You know, like one of those intervention deprogramming treatments they have for people who join cults," Dave suggested.

Lidia chuckled. "Yeah, but if that were the case, it wouldn't have been their wall that somebody scaled."

"Or better yet, maybe it was Alice that arranged the intervention for her parents," Dave went on.

"Anyone ever tell you that you'd make a great conspiracy theorist Asher?" Lidia asked then looked at the time. "We'd better get a move on. Let's take a quick look at the balcony and then the main bath. I checked the guest bath while you were in the other bedroom and except for a roll of TP, it's as untouched as her guest room."

They spent all of ten seconds on the balcony taking in a few rose bushes planted in sturdy pots and a bistro table set under a couple of hanging green something or other plants. Then they ducked back inside, shivering from the arctic like wind and drizzle.

In the bath they found the typical soaps, towels, TP, and feminine products. The medicine cabinet revealed only two items, a tube of half used toothpaste and a prescription bottle.

"I wonder what we have here?" Dave asked as he opened the bottle and took a whiff. "Oh man!" he said cringing. "These smell nasty. Take a picture of this label to have deciphered."

Lidia clicked photos of the pills and bottle. Then they locked up and headed to the station to brief Shane.

On the way back to the station they decided to make a side trip to the YMCA.

When they arrived and showed Alice's picture to the man behind the reception counter, he recognized her immediately.

"Oh yeah. She's not someone you forget," he said with a wink at Dave. "I've been wondering where she was. She used to come by a couple afternoons a week. She aced the CPR class, and I should know. I volunteered to let her practice on me."

"I bet you did," Dave replied with a smile, and Lidia kicked him.

"What my partner means is, when was the last time you saw her?"

"Not since the CPR training. Is she alright? I mean usually when cops come around asking questions it isn't good news."

"That's exactly what we're trying to find out. Is there anything else you remember about her?" Lidia continued.

"I'm afraid not, but Melinda might. She leads the class, and I saw them talking a couple of times."

"Would Melinda happen to be here today?" Dave asked.

"Actually, yes. She's in the middle of another class right now, but if you can wait, say fifteen more minutes, she should be down."

"Thank you, Steve," Lidia said, reading his name badge and pushing her card across the counter to him.

"No problem. Feel free to help yourself to some Christmas

cookies and cider too," Steve added, pointing to a small table by the window. "I hope she's okay."

"You didn't have to kick me so hard," Dave said, as he walked beside Lidia with an exaggerated limp. "I was just voicing what you were thinking."

"That may be so, but we don't want to risk intimidating any potential witnesses. Here, keep your yap busy with this," she said, handing him a white frosted, tree shaped cookie, with red, green and blue sprinkles.

Chapter Twenty-Three

It had been over three hours, even though they had been one of the first to get off the train. Special off-road vehicles with front plows had been brought in, to shuttle those needing assistance and to transport the checked luggage. Jack and Alice had trudged with the rest of the passengers on foot to the station. Walter had been right. It was chaos. It seemed every minibus in the town must have been employed as well as the taxis, and with two other trains affected, as well as the regular commuter crowd, just making their way through the station with their bags was a treacherous endeavor. It was nearly impossible to decipher where what line began for transportation or luggage. Staying behind a family that cut through the crowd with their double stroller, Jack and Alice had finally made it past the mayhem and decided they may as well go the rest of the way by foot too. After walking a few blocks away from the station, they found a phone booth and were able to phone The Coriander. They had been in luck, sort of anyway. There was only one room available, and it had only one single bed.

"We'll take it," Jack said, and proceeded to get directions. Fortunately, it was only three blocks away as the wind gusts were becoming difficult to walk in without losing their balance. In fact, Alice had to grab onto the light posts more than once, and Jack actually did go down on a patch of ice.

"Maybe you should put your skates on," Alice suggested, as he pulled himself up and hefted his bag back over his shoulder.

"I was thinking skis. Look," he pointed. "there it is. Thank God!"

They made their way across the street and up the concrete stairs of the Inn, which had thankfully been covered in a weatherproof traction carpet and swept of the accumulating snow.

"So, how are we playing this sweetie?" Jack asked with semi sarcasm. "They'll probably ask for ID even if we pay in cash, so let's have our story ready."

"I know," Alice said. "I thought about it while we were in line to get off the train. Sophie and I made photocopies of each other's passports in case we needed them when we bought the tickets or for an occasion like this. I'll just say I lost my wallet with my cards and ID in the crush of people, but I still had my change purse in my pocket with my cash and the copy of my passport in my luggage."

"And me?"

"We can say they were together in a separate bag?" she suggested.

"Okay. Your purse and my wallet were in a backpack that in the hurry and chaos got left on the train, and we have to wait until the weather calms to get it back."

"Sounds viable… sweetheart."

"Ladies first sweetie," Jack said as he opened the front door for Alice.

As it turned out, the woman at the reception was so frantic with calls from other people looking for a room, that she simply had them sign in, took the first night deposit in cash, and handed them a key. Then they followed the sign that pointed up the stairs to the wing where their room number was located.

Room thirteen was nice, but small, and the twin bed was hardly romantic. It had clearly been inserted into an extra space at the corner of the second floor. There was a gas fireplace insert on the inner wall next to a bath, which was only slightly larger than the one on the train. On the other side of the bed, in front of a large window, they had managed to wedge in two small chairs, and a table. Just to the right of the bed, on the same wall was a small armoire, and to the left, a small table with a mini fridge underneath, and a clock radio on top. The wall in front of the bed and just next to the door hosted a mounted flat screen TV.

Dropping their luggage on the chairs, they both collapsed across the narrow bed.

"I guess I'll take the lower bunk tonight," Jack said, motioning to the floor. "Just let me know which side I'm least likely to get stepped on."

"I was thinking we should try to call Nick and Sophie again."

"I've been thinking the same thing, but I somehow doubt we'll get a better connection now, and all I got on the line before was static. My guess is that the cell tower is out. I could try my dad on the landline. I'll head down and see if there's another phone. A landline is probably better anyway, just in case. I've heard they're harder to trace," Jack said, as he pulled himself upright once again and headed downstairs.

It was the first time in days that Alice had gotten a moment to herself. Had she been at home, she might have curled up with a good book and a glass of Merlot. She was beyond wanting to be alone with her thoughts. They were far too confusing. She stood up and went to move her bag from the chair to the armoire. Upon opening the armoire, she found an extra pillow and blanket, which she pulled down for Jack. She also found a visitor guide sitting on a lower shelf next to a coffee pot. She took everything out, turned the gas fireplace on, and lay back on the bed. She flipped through the pages of the visitor guide, then rolled to the other side of the bed to look in the mini fridge. It was empty. She took the coffee pot and sat it on the table by the window, found a plug behind the drape, removed the coffee packets that were stuffed in the pot, and filled it with the tap from the bath.

A few minutes later the aroma of coffee filled the room. She had tried the TV, but got only static, so she sat staring at the pink and white striped wallpaper, and the few prints of what looked like an old English village that adorned the walls, until the coffee finished.

Suddenly she realized that she hadn't found a mug to pour it in. She went back over to the armoire and opened a drawer under the shelf to reveal a mug, extra towel, and a Bible. Alice took the Bible and mug back to the table with her, poured herself some coffee and began to read. "In the beginning God created the heavens and the earth."

***

The wind howled down the chimney, and Nick looked up to see Sophie still sitting in her car with the engine running. She appeared to be writing something. He looked at the time. It had been over an hour and the sky was turning dark and ominous. He thought briefly about going out to try and coax her in again but decided against it. She'd come in when she ran out of gas to keep the heater running, and the last thing he wanted was to spend the night with her mad at him.

He still couldn't make sense of the papers. It was like reading a foreign language, where he could sound out the words, but their meaning eluded him. He looked at the photos turned upside down and noticed that a few of them had been marked with an 'X' in the upper left corner. He flipped one over. It was of an obviously premature baby girl. Her veins were still visible under the delicate skin. One side of her head appeared somewhat caved in, and her legs were badly twisted. One foot also appeared to be clubbed, but her eyes were open. She had at least been born alive, and Nick cringed as he wondered what the sadistic bastards had done with her.

He flipped over the other photos with 'X's'. These appeared to be all of the botched abortions in which the child had survived, at least long enough for them to be photographed. He also noticed that each one had a date stamp in the lower left corner. Nick now forced himself to look more closely at each of the 'X'd' photos. There were a total of ten, but it was the eighth one that caught his attention. The little girl appeared nearly full term and fully formed. The only deformity was an angry looking bulge that obscured the right side of her face. He looked at the date. The month and day were off, but the year was right, and he knew. He was still staring at the picture when the sound of the door opening made him look up. It was her. He immediately put the photo down and closed the file.

"Hi," he said simply.

"So," she said. "What's for dinner? I'm starved."

"Take your choice. We have frozen pizza or frozen pizza." Their eyes met in momentary silence.

"I'll take the pizza," Sophie said, and Nick got up to take the box from the freezer.

***

"According to Charice, Alice walked everywhere and only occasionally used a company car, but Melinda, the woman we talked to at the YMCA stated that Alice drove a lime green Fiesta," Lidia said. "She also told us that Alice always had to rush off after the classes, except for one night when she stayed and swam laps for two hours. They had chatted a few times, and Melinda invited Alice to go dancing one night. Alice had accepted, but later called to cancel, because of a last-minute business dinner she had to attend."

"I double checked with DMV, and there aren't any vehicles registered in her name," Dave added.

"Maybe she borrowed it from a friend," Shane suggested.

"Who? Aside from her parent's friends, people at work, and Melinda, she didn't really have a social life," Dave replied.

"She did have the museum membership. Maybe she made some friends there or maybe her manicurist," Lidia suggested.

"Do we have photos of all the receipts?" Shane asked.

"Not all. I mean she had receipts for everything from pillowcases to her toothpaste."

Shane sighed as the door opened and Selma entered.

"Hey Selma. What do you have for us?" Shane asked.

"Okay guys. I have the toxicology report on that prescription, and it's not exactly what it says. According to the label it's just a high potency vitamin blend to boost immunity."

"What is it though?" Shane asked.

"It's an anti-rejection medication and not just your standard anti-rejection drug either. See this line around the capsule?" Selma asked. "There are actually three different medications contained in layers around each other. In fact, the one on the inner layer is the high potency vitamin labeled on the bottle. The outer layers though are two anti-rejection drugs."

"So, what are they for?" Dave asked.

"Not a clue. We'd need to get our hands on her medical records for that."

"We can't do that though. Can we?" Lidia asked.

"Not at this point," Shane said. "What we can do though is find out who her doctors are and try to trace any hospital visits. That could also be where she formed other friendships. What could that combination of drugs be used for Selma?"

"Honestly? I've never seen them used together before. The one isn't even on the market in the U.S."

"You're saying that you can't get it here then?"

"Come on now. You guys have worked enough cases to know that you *can get* pretty much anything. My guess though, due to the unique design, is that it's at least manufactured overseas, and the vitamin blend is definitely Asian. What makes it really hard to trace is that there isn't even a doctors name or any other traceable markings on the label."

"You two are positive there aren't any medical files at her apartment?"

"Positive," Dave and Lidia answered in unison.

"There was one item though that we can't be sure about. She had a lock box in her closet with a built in five-digit combination lock," Lidia said.

"I said we should bring it, but Yarnok here kept me on the straight and narrow," Dave put in.

"Believe me. I may be more curious than anyone. It seemed to us that the things she kept most discreetly were the things that wouldn't fit the image. Things she probably didn't think mommy and daddy would approve of. The things that made her seem more human," Lidia concluded.

"Okay," Shane said. "I want you, Yarnok to go back with Adams and see if one of his gadgets can open that lock. Photograph everything, even if it's a receipt for toothpaste. Then on your way back, stop by to drop off the key and have another talk with Charice. She seems to be the person closest to the whole family so maybe she can fill us in on the medical mystery."

***

Back in New York, Leon slammed his cell phone closed and headed up to the Morgan's suite. He was pissed! He hadn't heard from the man; he knew only as 'The Lead" in nearly a week. What the hell was he supposed to do? It was enough that he was supposed to babysit Alice during her stay, but this was ridiculous! He hadn't been paid either. He'd gone to the offices to see Albert about that, only to find that he had disappeared off the face of the earth. He'd thought about just cutting him lose, but the man had not only seen his face when he managed to rip the mask off but must have a ton of his DNA under his nails. Leon had been surprised by the older man's strength. He'd been told not to hurt him, but what choice had he had? He seemed to be recovering pretty well from the stab wounds though. They were mostly superficial. Thank God. It wasn't like he could just call a doctor and the last thing Leon wanted was a murder rap.

Maybe he could contact the family for ransom? Then he could skip the country. A warm tropical island sounded good right now.

Chapter Twenty-Four

Alice had read up as far as Eve eating the forbidden fruit, when she heard the door opening. She laid the Bible to the side and looked up at Jack.

"Any luck?" she asked.

"No. There's nothing but static on all the lines. I think the lady at reception is relieved though. She has a lobby full of people now, and the staff were unloading extra food supplies, and bringing some cots, and blankets to the lobby. I overheard people talking, and it sounds like this is going to be a mega storm. The hotels are full, and they're trying to get people to a shelter set up at a local school." Jack was standing in front of the fire, warming his hands. "I also heard that the electric is already out in half the town, and a lot of hotels will have to ration power, so the generators hold out. We really lucked out!" he said, turning to Alice. "This place was built before electricity came to town, and they kept what they could on gas."

Alice went over to join him by the fire as a gust of wind made the window shudder.

"Afraid of storms?" Jack asked.

"No, not that I've really experienced many, but I like storms. I think they're romantic."

"I'd probably agree if it wasn't for either having to shovel out of them or deal with flooding every year," Jack said with a smile.

"Do you mind if I take a shower?" Alice asked.

"Not at all. I was just thinking about the same thing. I probably need one," Jack said, as Alice gathered a change of clothes.

The water was soothing as it ran over her body. She had taken her pill that morning, but was feeling, for her, oddly fatigued. She felt behind her ear. There was no swelling, and she didn't seem to have a fever. A million thoughts should have been filling her mind, but only two questions nagged at her. If God was the creator of man, but she had been created in a lab somewhere, what did that make her? And Jack. Was it even possible for there to be anything romantic between them? She knew she should have been more concerned about her parents, Mr. Amstead, Sophie, and everyone stuck in this storm, but right now all she could think about was Jack. She was glad that they were stuck here, but she was suddenly feeling unusually anxious at the same time.

Stepping out of the shower, she wiped the steam from the mirror and stood for a moment looking at her reflection. She didn't like her body. She knew that was ridiculous, but she felt like there was something missing. A scar, a wrinkle, even a pimple would have been welcome. People had always told her that they envied her complexion. She sat on the toilet and tried to say a prayer. "God?" she asked. "If you're there, would you please give me something, some visible flaw to prove that I'm human?"

Jack looked around the room and opted for setting up his makeshift bed at the foot of the bed, where he could at least keep his feet near the warmth of the fire without blocking the restroom.

He wondered what was taking Alice so long. Jack walked over to the window and looked out. In the past half hour, the blizzard had gone into full swing, and all he could see was a falling white haze against a dark sky, dimly lit by a streetlamp. He sat down and began to take off his shoes to dry by the fire.

He took the first one off and realized that his feet smelled awful! He pulled the shoe back on, deciding not to subject Alice to his feet until after he had bathed. He looked around the room again, realizing that despite being cramped, it did in fact have a romantic aura about it that he wished it didn't. It had been difficult enough sharing space alone with Alice on the train, but at least the train had felt more public with the voices and footsteps of people constantly passing by their cabin. There was no romantic fireplace or any other decor. It had been... safer.

He needed to stop thinking about her, at least until they were back in a less intimate setting, but how? Why wasn't he thinking about his mom? He was still fifteen thousand short of what his dad needed to hold off the bank and...

Alice came out of the bath. She had changed into jeans and a brown turtleneck sweater that gently accented her curves. The glow of the fire glinted like rubies in her damp hair.

Jack needed to do something. "I'm going back downstairs for a bit," he said. "I might be able to help them set things up."

Before Alice could respond, Jack had closed the door behind him.

***

Suzanna groaned and nearly blacked out again from the pain. Her left leg ached as she lay still, and sharp stabbing pain shot through her at the slightest movement. Her mouth was dry, and she could see water, she just couldn't reach it. Maybe she could use her arms to pull herself along the floor and then, what? She still would not be able to reach up to where the bottle of water sat on the counter. It seemed to stare at her now, mocking her just as Richter had. The mini fridge was all the way in the other corner of the room, but she knew she had to get there. She couldn't, wouldn't let them beat her. Suzanna

Morgan was a survivor, and even at age seventy-seven she still worked out twice a week, swam, and played tennis weekly, usually winning against much younger opponents. It was with these thoughts that she pulled herself forward. She cried out in pain but was determined not to black out. She didn't stop, until inch by inch she had crawled to where she was now laying in front of the mini fridge. She took a minute to catch her breath and let the shock waves of pain subside back into a mere throbbing ache. She took a fresh water out and, careful not to choke herself, sipped it slowly until she had drank half of it. Reaching up on her other side, she snagged a corner of blanket from the bed and pulled it down. Stuffing it under her head, she lay back, exhausted. She closed her eyes and thought of Edgar and then of Alice. What had they done? She wondered. What had their dream become?

The woman awoke to the sound of agony. She was groggy as she gradually opened her eyes to try and locate the source. It had sounded as though it were right beside her. She could hardly keep her eyes open. Her whole body felt heavy. She ran her hand down and felt the swell of new life growing inside of her. She felt a little lower to the box attached to her thigh. Now she understood why she was so tired. The wailing had ceased, but she could feel the presence of someone else in the room. She forced herself to stay awake as she pulled to remove the box. She knew her fumbling with it was bound to leave a nasty bruise, but she had to be awake to help herself, and the babies, and whoever else she was certain was trapped in here with them.

Edgar stared at Jonathan as he attempted to explain as much as he could before Richter or Carl, who had stepped out to make a phone call, returned.

Jonathan had reassured Edgar that both he and Suzanna were safe for now, and that he and Mathias did not agree with Richter's plan.

"Richter is a bit like Hitler," Jonathan explained. "At first we all went along with him. He was very convincing, and we believed that what he was doing was for the benefit of all mankind. It was when the deaths began that we started to question him. Richter doesn't like being questioned. He believes that he is some kind of god and has no belief in any other god. He wants to use this project to create a perfect race and he's not alone. He..." Jonathan cut off as the door began to open.

Richter nodded to Jonathan and to Edgar. "I apologize that Mathias here kept you waiting."

Mathias, now accompanied by Carl, nodded at Edgar with what appeared to Edgar as a look of pity. He then moved to the counter to get himself a drink as Richter's eyes followed him disapprovingly.

Richter cleared his throat. "Shall we begin gentlemen?"

Edgar stared at Richter in silence as he spoke and explained just what it was that he expected from Edgar and Suzanna.

Edgar cringed inside as Richter spoke, and the feelings of guilt felt as though they were eating him alive.

There was only one thing Richter needed in order to proceed with his mission - Alice. They had planned to wait until after the other babies had been born. So far, this pregnancy had been a success and if it continued well, then they would have the fulfillment of the needed gene pool of what Richter termed perfection. In all honesty they would not have needed Edgar or Suzanna, but with Alice missing, they had to try every tactic to locate and bring her in now. They would need to hold them all together until they knew the infants were viable for harvesting. If something happened and they turned out to be unviable, they could try again, and this time they would use Alice as a secondary carrier. They could not proceed without Alice though. Richter considered her as his mate, his closest female genetic match. The others had all been flawed and should have been disposed of within the set time frame. Unfortunately, they had not all been allowed to expire as they should have. Richter had said that the old doctor had been too soft, and that meant that those poor souls would now have to have a purpose found to legitimize their existence. There were a multitude of experiments and services that Richter could make use of them for, and this was the purpose they must serve for their survival for as long as, well for as long as they would survive it. Afterwards it would be up to Richter, Carl, Jonathan, and if he could handle it, Mathias to finish their disposal.

It was after this revelation that Edgar had been given an ultimatum. Richter had said he would be generous and give Edgar until the next morning to sleep on it. The choice was quite simple really, Edgar and Suzanna could either help them get Alice, and they could all live out their lives in the house Edgar had built on the opposite beach or he could watch as his wife was tortured in front of him. How much did Edgar think she could endure? Richter did not consider himself a killer, but he had to acknowledge that she could easily die of natural causes like say a heart attack or a stroke. Richter would be sure to keep Edgar himself functional though for as long as possible.

"Exactly how *can* we help you? We don't know where Alice is any more than you do!" Edgar had protested.

Richter had laughed in response. "That may be," he continued. "Wherever she is though, I am certain that she will either eventually check her email, watch the news or read the paper. So, you and sweet mother Suzanna are going to help us make a little video. We have already sent some very interesting photos."

"Sent where? If you know where she is then why in hell..."

"Now, now Edgar. It's not polite to interrupt. Allow me to finish. As I am sure you know, Alice is hardly an only child. In fact, all of us here are one-eighth brothers to her. It seems eight, not five turned out to be the golden number, however Alice was the exception. Did you ever see the pictures of the others?" Richter asked.

"Of the miscarriages you mean?" Edgar asked hopefully, realizing full well and feeling quite nauseated by what Richter was telling him.

"It is most unfortunate that they weren't all allowed to perish. Of course, we had our suspicions, but it didn't really matter as long as they didn't meet. Who would have thought that they would ever be in New York on the same week, much less meet? We have copies of the camera footage, if you would like to see? It's really quite incredible. As stupid as it was for him, I have to say the doctor did an excellent job with the reconstructive surgery, you could almost believe they were the same woman. Anyway, after she was spotted in New York, it wasn't that hard to find out where she lives and send the package to her. My guess is that they will contact each other again soon, and Alice will see just how much fun you and Suzanna had while you were strapped to the boards."

Edgar was speechless.

"Well, I think I have shared more than enough with you. I am certain that you understand and will, of course come to the only correct conclusion."

Jonathan then led Edgar back to his room as he slipped something into his pocket.

Genetically, Mathias was viable, Richter thought, as he and Jonathan left, but Richter realized that he was also much more of a liability. Still, his genes would be useful, much as their other sister's. If only the bitch doesn't miscarry again. If she aborted naturally again, there would be too much scar tissue to use her for more breeding.

Chapter Twenty-Five

It was nearly 8:00 PM. Alice had taken a nap and read through the Bible to the story of Babel and was pondering it when Jack returned.

"I'm sorry I was gone so long," he said, as he held up a large sack. "They were really busy and grateful for the help. They gave me this food bag. There's some sandwiches for dinner and sweet rolls for breakfast as well as some fruit and drinks."

"Jack?"

"Yes?"

"It's just that I know you must be worried about your mom, but..."

"I can't go there right now, not when I can't do anything."

"I know. I'm sorry Jack. I was just worried about you."

"Don't Alice. None of it's your fault. Let's just wait out this storm and make it across to Nova Scotia safely. I can't think beyond that right now, so can we just eat and get some sleep?" he said far more coldly than he had meant, as he took the sandwiches out of the sack.

They ate in silence. Jack knew he should apologize, instead he scarfed down the sandwich and then went in to take his shower. When he came out, he found Alice sound asleep with the Bible lying open beside to her.

***

Sophie and Nick also ate in an awkward silence. She wasn't angry with him anymore, but neither one of them could think of something safe to say. Nick didn't think that it was a wise time to bring up what he discovered in the photos. He would wait until Jack and Alice were here. They had started to watch a movie, but ten minutes in, the power went out. They had finished eating by the light of a camp lamp and gone to sleep early, with Nick on the couch and Sophie in his room.

Sophie breathed in deeply of his scent on the sheets. She lay there listening to the whistling of the wind, but she had slept little the night before and drifted off within minutes.

***

Before Shane left the office that night, he made a call to someplace he hadn't thought to visit in five years. He then told everyone that he would not be in the next day, but he would be available by phone, and to make sure and contact him with any new information.

On his way home he stopped at Westlake center and did some Christmas shopping for his sister's family. He also bought something else on a whim. He knew it was silly to buy a new one while all of her others were boxed up in storage, but Patty had loved scarfs. He could always give it to his sister later, but for now it helped him reaffirm that he wasn't giving up hope.

The sisters had agreed to meet with him between morning prayers and the Christmas craft show, which they had also gotten him to agree to help them set up. He smiled as he set his packages down in the foyer. Then he turned on some Christmas music, nuked a microwave meal, and poured a glass of Patty's favorite wine. He knew some people would say he was in denial, but so be it, he thought as he sat back on the sofa. He looked around the living room and decided there was something else he wanted this year too. He hadn't had one since Patty disappeared, but suddenly he wanted very much to have a Christmas tree.

***

Alice awoke the next morning to the smell of coffee. She stretched and took a moment to realize where she was.

"What time is it?" she asked, as she sat up.

Jack couldn't help but smile, as he took in her mussed-up hair and sleepy eyes. She had always appeared to wake up fully awake and somehow perfectly groomed. "It's 8:00. You slept nearly twelve hours."

"That's impossible," Alice said, as she sat up, yawned and stretched again. She ran a hand over her face and felt an unfamiliar bump on her chin. Rolling to the other side of the bed, she got up to use the restroom, and investigate. She pushed back the turtleneck she had fallen asleep in and was shocked when she found a pimple just under her jaw line. She stared at it for a minute, then washed her face, and ran her fingers through her hair, which for some reason seemed dryer than usual. She looked at the pimple again, shrugged her shoulders, and smiled.

Jack had opened the drapes to reveal the work of the night's blizzard. There must have been at least five feet of fresh snow on the ground, and flakes were still gently floating down on what had turned out to be a surprisingly sunny morning.

Jack turned and handed her a mug of coffee.

"Thank you," she said, as she sat and took one of the sweet rolls he had set out and a banana. "How did you sleep?"

"Not quite as well as you, but it wasn't so bad, as far as floors go."

Alice sat on the bed, and the Bible peeked out at her from under the pillow. She felt the pimple under her chin again, as she remembered her prayer. Smiling, she offered a silent "Thank you." Then said to Jack, "Let's go out and build a snowman."

"What?"

"A snowman. I don't know if I've ever made one before,

unless you think we're going to be able to go out on the train today?"

"I don't think we'll be able to get out the front door today!" he said looking at the child like light in her eyes. "But I'll go down and check in a bit. Something about you seems different today Alice."

"It must have been the good night of sleep," she said, biting into an apple filled bun.

A few minutes later Jack went downstairs, and Alice changed into fresh clothes, making sure to wear a sweater that revealed her chin. She nearly forgot to put the wig back on and had to hunt down the bobby pins that had fallen on the floor.

When Jack returned, he said, "You're in luck. With the raised porch and the roof keeping the majority of snow off of it, we can walk right out. In fact, there are some children downstairs getting ready to go play in the snow right now."

Jack could hardly believe he was doing this, but ten minutes later they were both rolling snowballs, and dodging the ones being fired by the children. After the snowball fight, he helped Alice roll, pack, and stack larger snowballs into a snowman. He stood back and smiled proudly at their creation. He had a pinecone nose, a mouth of a red zip tie, sunglasses hooked over two Styrofoam cup ears, and was topped with green and brown pine needle hair.

Jack took a picture with his cell phone of the snowman and Alice. "You make a cute couple," he said, as Alice struck several poses.

"Okay. Now you."

"What?"

"I want to take a picture of you. Honey," Alice added, as a family with three children came outside.

"I'd be happy to take a picture of you together," offered the man, as his children took off running across the field of white, while their mother watched after them.

"Thanks!" Alice said, and Jack went over to join her.

"Get a little closer together," the man said. "I heard you two are on your honeymoon."

The man took several shots of them in various poses and insisted on at least a couple of them kissing.

"You only get one honeymoon. You need to have as many memories as possible. You'll need them to look at later, when you ask yourself why? Trust me," he said, as he looked at his offspring pelting their mother with snowballs.

Alice had never been kissed, and she trembled as Jack lowered his mouth to hers. She wrapped her arms around him and opened to his kiss.

Jack was surprised by her responsiveness. He could feel her trembling, but he felt no resistance. If anything, Alice Morgan was quite passionate, and he felt his resolve of the night before melting into his own passion.

"I'll just leave the phone up here. Don't forget to come up for air," they heard the man say with a chuckle.

Separating, they did both gasp for air. They stared at each other for a long moment before Jack suddenly let go and turned away.

"Did I do something wrong?" Alice asked.

Jack turned back to her. "No," he said, as he grabbed her and kissed her passionately again.

Chapter Twenty-Six

Shane set out before daylight. He only planned to be gone for the day, but it was Friday, so just in case, he tossed in his go bag. It was only a couple of hours to the convent, but that was without traffic, which he knew would start backing up the freeways in the next hour. He also wanted to stop back by "Stoney's" for breakfast.

An accident on the 5 freeway had made it worse than he imagined. It was already a quarter of eight when he pulled his silver Suburban into the parking lot of Stoney's just off state route 2.

The rain was snow up here, and Shane double-checked to make sure his chains were still in the back. He hadn't used them since the last time he and Patty had been up here six Christmas's ago. They had spent a week up at Leavenworth, a Bavarian village and major tourist destination a little further east. He considered calling to see if there were any rooms available for the night there. It was only half an hour from the convent. After pushing aside his golf clubs and some rarely used fishing gear, Shane found the chains and headed inside.

He entered the restaurant to the strains of "What Child Is This" and a sign that read "Seat Yourself." Shane slid into a booth by a window in the back near the kitchen. It was the same booth they had sat in on their way home that week.

"I remember you!" the waitress said with a bright smile.

"You do? I haven't been here in nearly..."

"Six years! Way too long! Did you bring the family?"

"Family? I think you must have me confused with someone else."

"That's mighty strange. You're a cop. Right?"

"Yes."

"And five years ago, your wife and her brother were headed up to meet you in Canada. You were going to adopt twins."

Shane felt his heart stop.

"You okay honey? You look white as a sheet. Did something happen to them?" she asked, looking suddenly very pale herself.

Shane didn't know what to say, as he pulled his wallet out and opened it to a picture of Patty.

"That's her," the waitress said, sliding into the booth across from Shane. "What happened?"

"When did you see her?" he asked. "And what did the man look like?"

"It was five years ago. Around this same time of year. Yes. I remember because I was getting ready to go off shift and to my daughter's High School Christmas play. So, it would have been a Saturday night."

"Are you sure?"

"I've been working here for twenty years, and I've had the same schedule for ten. Tuesday through Friday mornings and Saturday afternoons."

"Marion," Shane said, looking at her name badge. "My wife disappeared five years ago, with no trace, on a Thursday evening. You're the first person I've found who claims to have seen her after. What else do you remember?"

"Ike!" Marion called to a man coming toward them. "This is Mr. Uhm...?"

"McDougal," Shane filled in, reaching up to shake the man's hand.

"He's with the police and..."

"I have a few questions I need to ask Marion here in regard to a missing person."

"Certainly. I'll have Marsha cover your tables," he said, looking around at the three other patrons. "Can I get you anything officer?"

"Coffee and French toast with bacon would be great. Thanks," Shane said, and turned back to Marion.

"The man she was with, I remember he seemed a little odd, and she did seem a little nervous, but I put it down to becoming a new mother."

"What did he look like?"

"The opposite of her, but then siblings can sometimes. He had pale blond hair and intensely bright blue eyes. He was sitting, but I'm still usually a pretty good judge, so I'd say six foot one or so, and slender."

"Would you be willing to sit with a sketch artist?"

"Of course. Anything I can do to help," Marion replied, as Marsha brought them both hot coffees.

"Do you happen to know where in Canada they were heading?"

"I'm afraid not hon, but there can't be that many orphanages anymore."

"You're sure she said it was an orphanage?"

"Yes. Outside of foreign charities, you don't hear that term too often, so it kind of sticks."

"I don't suppose there's any chance that she mentioned this brother's name?"

"Not as I can remember, but this might be important."

"Yes?" Shane asked, leaning across the table.

"Can I see the picture again?"

"Sure," Shane said, pushing the photo toward her.

"Yes, her eyes were darker, a deep chocolate brown. I remember because of how opposite they appeared to her brother's."

"And you're still positive that it was my wife?"

"Yes. She told me that she and you had stopped here before, on your way back to Seattle from Leavenworth, and I had waited on your table. You had been trying to conceive on that trip?"

Shane felt his face turning pink. "Did she tell you that..."

"About the miscarriage?"

"It was definitely Patty then," Shane said, not quite sure what to feel.

Marsha came with his French toast and bacon, but all Shane could do was stare at it.

He looked up as Marion spoke again. "The man with her didn't call her Patty though. He called her Eve and joked about naming the babies Seth and Able. That's one of the things I found odd about him. He seemed more enthusiastic about the adoption than she did, and like I said before, she seemed nervous. If this man was abducting her though," Marion continued, "why didn't she try to get some kind of message to me? She could have easily written something in the bathroom, on the receipt, or the cash for that matter. Another thing I thought was odd. He insisted that she pay cash for the bill, and he said he didn't have enough U.S. currency, but it didn't look Canadian."

"What do you mean?"

"Well, that would be the normal foreign currency someone might have around here, but his money, he did take out his wallet and look at it. Anyway, it was full of what looked like a mix of foreign currency along with a few one's that he plopped down for the tip. I couldn't tell you what country or countries, but not Canadian."

Shane looked at the time. If he still wanted to talk to the nuns today, he had better get going.

"Thank you for all the information Marion. Here's my card if anything else comes to mind, and I put my cell number on the back. Call me anytime, and I'll try to get a sketch artist to come out in the morning. Could you meet them here before your shift?"

"Sure. Like I said, I'm happy to help. I pray she's okay."

"Thank you, Marion and Merry Christmas," he said, putting a fifty on the table. "Keep the change."

"Did you want a to go box?"

"Thanks, but no. I've got a meeting to get to. Your help means more to me than you can know Marion. Get yourself something nice with that," he said, trying to form a smile as he nodded to Marion and headed out.

***

Sophie glanced at Nick sleeping on the sofa, as she sat at the table. Looking through the files, she noted the pictures that he had separated out. When she came to the one of herself, she immediately turned it over. She had seen it before, but instead of becoming numb to them, the pictures seemed to hurt more. The thoughts that kept going through her head were like torment. Could any of these be her sisters or brothers? She had ascertained from the files that they were all multiple embryo pregnancies, and she knew that this was what she and Alice had been from.

Why? Why was she spared? What for? She had been raised to believe that God had a special purpose for each and every life, but what possible Godly purpose could allowing success in such horrific experiments have? From what she could tell, this was the Frankenstein version of genetics, and to think that she was one, rocked her understanding of God and creation to the very core. She tried to reason that these experiments were only physical. God gave us our spirit and that is what makes us human. She told herself it was no different than someone who had a kidney transplant or the skin graft that she had been told she had. It shouldn't matter, but it did.

She had wanted so much to just know who her biological parents had been so that she could better understand herself. Yes, her spirit was the most important part of who she was, but still, she knew that many characteristics of our personalities are inherited from our family. We can overcome them, but they are still one of the roots of who we are. That is even so in the Bible. There was a reason that Jesus was descendant of David, a reason that Isaac rather than Ishmael held the promise, and that Jacob was favored over Esau.

No matter what, Sophie suddenly felt stronger than ever that she needed to know everyone she had come from. At least if she knew, she reasoned, she could know what tendencies to be aware of. For all she knew they could have inserted her with DNA from a mass killer. She couldn't fathom what the plan was. What if she was programed to go berserk? What if there was some chip in her head? She wondered, absently touching the incision scar behind her ear. She had never been big on conspiracy theories, but the file she had in front of her topped many of the strangest theories out there.

Nick stirred on the sofa and opened one eye. He wished she wouldn't keep looking at those. He understood now why Jack had made such a big deal about keeping them from her. He wanted to go over to her, put his arms around her and just make it all go away, but he couldn't. He couldn't do a damned thing, and it was making him crazy inside. One thing he could do though was make them some breakfast.

"It looks like a nice day," he said, looking out the window as he got up and went into the kitchen. "Shall I put some coffee on?"

"The power is still out," she said simply.

"Then I guess I'll just have to do this the old-fashioned way and boil the kettle on the stove. Thank God for gas!" he said, as he filled the kettle and lit the burner. Then he pulled out the flour, eggs, milk, and butter. "I hope you're in the mood for pancakes."

"Pancakes will be fine. Thanks Nick," she said, without looking at him. "I wonder how Alice and Jack are doing."

Nick sat the mixing bowl on the counter and went to sit with Sophie at the table.

"You're really worried about how she'll deal with this," Nick said.

"Of course, I am. She grew up thinking that she already knew who she was, but now her whole life has been turned upside down. No matter what, it's clear that she loves her parents, and I have to show her these," Sophie said, pointing to the photos of the Morgans. "I at least knew that I might find something I didn't like when I started looking into who my parents were. I never imagined this though. This is insane! Alice also doesn't have a faith base. Look at me!" she continued, as she stood up. "I am not handling this well. How is Alice supposed to? I don't even know what we are, much less who. I mean, what kind of sick monster does this? And what if the sick monsters behind it turn out to be the people Alice has spent her life calling mom and dad? How? How can anyone deal with that?"

"I don't know. I don't know Soph."

At that moment the kettle began to whistle, and Nick rose and went to make their coffee.

"I'm sorry I was so hard on you yesterday Nick."

"Forget about it," he said, handing her a cup of coffee and going back to whisk the pancake batter.

Chapter Twenty-Seven

Edgar was torn. This was crazy! There had to be another way. He wouldn't give in to a terrorist and that was exactly how he viewed Richter. If anything, he wanted to find a way to tell Alice to stay hidden wherever she was, and he knew that Suzanna would agree. Yes, they had wanted a perfect child, but not so much for themselves as for her. With the DNA they had chosen, Alice was programmed not only to be highly intelligent, but also healthy, athletic, and beautiful. She was someone who could make it anywhere, succeed at anything, and look good doing it.

The rejection hadn't been part of the plan. They had hoped that with the DNA being injected into the developing embryo that it would all develop and blend organically together, and that the donor DNA would be so much a natural part of her as to defy rejection. Unfortunately, this had been the one area they had not been able to perfect in time.

Yes, the results had been tragic. That's why they had closed everything down, or so he had believed. He was aware of continuing research of course, but it was his understanding that no human subjects would be involved. Then again, he should have known.

He had assumed that the donations from the DNA bank had been destroyed in the fire, but now he guessed that they had simply been removed. Maybe they were even sitting down the hall. Thousands of samples of characteristics that had been obtained, most through willing donors, and some who were no longer around to donate, by other more covert methods. For example, the DNA sample from a survivor of the plague. He knew that someone in the European branch had needed to literally dig that one up. The idea was that not only could people who otherwise had difficulty conceiving, in fact have a child who would have not only their own family genes, but they could add additional DNA to make the child stronger, healthier, smarter, and more talented in whatever areas they chose. It was a project that was intended to make dreams come true. Now though, Edgar Morgan found himself standing in the middle of the worst nightmare he could imagine.

He wished that he were a younger man so that he would have the chance of overpowering Richter, though he had a feeling that Richter was not lacking the genes for increased muscle development. Through the shirt he wore, Edgar could tell that although he was no body builder and fairly slender, Richter was solid.

What Edgar didn't know, was just how much he could rely on Jonathan and Mathias. Carl seemed to be in step with Richter, but...

The knock on his door startled him. He was even more startled when he looked up to see Alice standing there in front of him.

"Alice?"

"Not a bad replica, is she?" came a voice from behind the woman, and Edgar felt a chill run through him as he stared into the eyes of Richter, or at least he thought it was Richter, but how could he really be sure?

"That will be all for now Annie. You may go join the others."

"Yes," she replied, and left them.

"I thought you might appreciate our latest endeavor."

"What is it?"

"Why Edgar, that's not a very nice way to talk about your daughter."

"That was not my daughter!"

"Oh, but that is where you are wrong. She, just as I do, has some of your DNA. Her physical features are cloned from Alice's DNA. She was grown from stem cells taken at birth from Alice, however her heart, lungs and kidneys are synthetic. The latest models used in emergency transplants when no donor match is available. They will never grow ill or deteriorate, only need to be occasionally upgraded. Eventually we will replace all of her bones and joints with more durable bionics. She already has visual and audio implants. Real blood pumps through her though, and her brain, her brain is the most amazing achievement to date! The tissue is organic, but we discovered a way to program it with tiny, microscopic implants, allowing us to stimulate where and when a certain region is more active. For instance, the region of the brain responsible for language is stimulated while we play recordings in French or any other language. Everything that is played during the stimulation period is retained in that brain region. We do have to be careful only to teach one language at a time or we risk confusion, but she is fluent in French, German, Italian, Russian, Danish, Japanese, Chinese, Greek, Latin, Hebrew, Hindi and of course, English. Oh, and let us not forget that she is only four years old."

"What?"

"Isn't she amazing? She only has one real flaw. She's sterile, which brings us back around to our earlier conversation. I need Alice. So, tell me Edgar, what do you suggest?"

"I suggest that you go to hell!"

"Not quite the suggestion that I had hoped for. Maybe a visit to your wife will help to motivate a change of mind. Come along and let us see how she is coping."

As they started down the hall, Edgar took note of where each of the security cameras was located.

"You may be surprised to discover that I don't have cameras

in my guest rooms. You see I find no need for that sort of voyeurism, and I feel perfectly safe in saying that my guests have no better place to go."

During the night, a doctor had come to set Suzanna's leg and had left her resting less than comfortably on the bed. He had been given strict instructions not to give her any pain medication. Richter wanted to be sure that movement would be excruciating. The doctor had been worried enough by her pain though to defy Richter and administer a mild painkiller. Moving would be painful, but he feared not relieving the initial pain could trigger a deadly heart attack, especially in a woman of her age.

The other woman had only just reached Suzanna, when she heard the beeping of the keypad, and dashed back under the covers, pretending to still be sedated. She wondered how long they had intended to keep her under.

After the doctor had left, she waited until Suzanna's pain subsided enough for her moaning to stop. They had wound up whispering through the night, and in the morning the woman had managed to help Suzanna out to sit on the balcony and fixed her a plate for breakfast before going back inside to bed. They had a plan of sorts, but they would have to wait until the right moment presented itself.

Richter could barely suppress his astonishment at finding Suzanna on the balcony, much less with a cup of coffee at her side.

She turned, at first with a glare of contempt, but as Edgar ran towards her the contempt turned to relief.

"Edgar!" she cried, as he knelt beside her and clasped her face in his hands.

"How touching," Richter mocked, "But not really my style. I do believe I'll leave you two alone to discuss that pressing issue

I was telling Edgar about. I'll be expecting your final answer when I return," he finished, exiting and locking the door.

Edgar turned as he heard the movement behind him.

"Edgar. Do you remember Patricia? She used to assist with certain charity events?"

"I do, but what on earth are you doing here?" he asked.

She was silent for a moment as she rubbed a hand over her abdomen. "I'm having twins. I can't have them here though."

"Patricia and I have a plan dear," Suzanna cringed, as she turned.

"Suzanna?" Edgar said, placing a hand on her arm.

"Broken tibia. Sometimes the nerves spasm when I turn wrong. I'll be okay dear. We have to do this. Do you know what it is they're planning to turn our dream into Edgar?"

"I'm afraid I do. So, tell me, what is this plan?"

***

Shane had made it to the convent just in time after having to pull over to put his chains on. Sister Margarita had greeted him in her office with tea and frosted sugar cookies in the shape of angels. Then she handed him the file with a look of dismay. "I'm sorry Shane. I don't know how it happened, but your wife's medical records appear to have vanished. The Mother Superior and I are the only ones with the key, so I really can't begin to explain."

"Don't trouble yourself too much Sister."

"It is troubling though. We want to protect the privacy of our children. I don't suppose you would care to investigate?"

"Have there been any other missing files?"

"Not that I've noticed."

"I'll tell you what. I'll take a look at the cabinet the files are in and dust for prints. I'll let you know what I find, and you check to see if any other children are missing files. Okay?"

"Thank you. I always said Patty was blessed when she found you. You're a good man, and you know I'll do whatever I can to help find Patty. In some ways, she was like the daughter I never had. Do you know why she was never adopted?"

"No. Why?"

"Because she was never up for adoption. Her father was still alive. He may still be. I haven't heard from Thomas in years though."

"I'm afraid I don't understand. How is it that he left her here without at least signing away his rights?"

"Dr. Thomas started off as a specialist in tropical diseases. He went with our mission teams on many overseas trips and was a major contributor to our order. It's because of him that the Mother Superior survived a serious bout with Malaria in 1980. So, when he showed up one day after a year of research in Europe with a one-month-old baby, we couldn't very well turn them away. He said that her mother had died in childbirth, and he had tried to care for her himself, but couldn't and work at the same time. His services had been requested in a remote area of Indonesia, and he begged us to care for Patricia. He wanted to be sure that she was with people he trusted. He gave us her birth certificate and a case of clothes and toys for her and well, that's really the end of the story. He set up a trust fund for her care too. It was even enough to cover college and he made an additional generous donation to restore our chapel."

"Did Patty ever know this?"

"No. He asked us not to tell her. He thought it was better for her to think she had no parent, than to think she had one that deserted her to run off to the jungles. As far as she ever knew, both of her parents were dead. I still have a copy of the birth certificate in another file if you would care to look at it?" Sister Margarita asked.

“Of course,” Shane replied, trying to absorb what he had learned as he followed her into another office.

Chapter Twenty-Eight

According to the rail system, once they finally got through, Jack and Alice's train would be delayed until the next day. Around noon the plows had finally made it to Nick's Street, and he and Sophie went to dig their respective cars out. They called her parents and Jack's dad to give them the update. Sophie's parents said that she should just stay in town, as the plows were not likely to make it to them until the next day. Sophie sighed.

"If you really want some time alone Sophie, you could always stay tonight at Jack's," Nick suggested.

"I think I'd like that. Thank you, Nick."

"Of course, you'll have to dig your way in."

Sophie turned an icy that's not funny glare on him.

"If you ask really nice though, I'll come help."

Sophie rolled her eyes. "I can do it myself you know," she said picking up the shovel.

"I'm sure you can, but I'd rather you let me help."

"Okay. You can help, but first, how about we finish off that pizza."

"Sounds like a plan," he said, following her back inside. How had she done it? He wondered. He was completely at her mercy.

When they arrived at Jack's, to their dismay, they discovered that the plows had pushed several extra feet of snow into their way. By the time they were to the door it was growing dark, and they were both exhausted and hungry again.

Seeing that Jack had pretty much nothing except popcorn in the kitchen, they opted to walk into town.

The town was aglow with Christmas lights and cheer. Despite the blizzard, the Christmas Bazar was in full swing. They stopped at a stand selling Gyro's and found a table in the covered pavilion that looked onto the town square and a giant spruce covered in twinkling white lights with vivid red and gold ornaments.

Nearly every other table was packed with families, about half of them tourists. Pastor Blake spotted them and came over to say hi and inquire about Jack.

Pastor Blake was only fifty-three, yet he seemed to have an almost grandfatherliness about him, that often caused people to think he was at least ten years older, and was a constant source of embarrassment for his teenage son and daughter.

"Hi you two. Hey Sophie, I'm a little surprised that I haven't seen Jack back around yet. I was sure he would be back by now. I went by his place after checking in on his mom on my way here and the walk was clear, but he didn't seem to be around. Didn't he come back with you?" he asked Sophie.

"Unfortunately, he couldn't," she replied.

"Oh. Why was that?" asked pastor Blake.

"The flight was overbooked," Nick answered quickly.

"Too bad, but I'm not surprised, and with the weather, well anyway, I just hope he isn't held up too long. This Christmas is bound to be hard on him and especially his dad. If you talk to him, tell him I stopped by and said a special prayer over his mom."

"Thank you. I will Pastor."

"See you both Sunday? It's the pageant, and we've got a special surprise for the youngsters this year, two camels cloistered in the barn. The poor things are probably freeze'n their humps off."

Nick bit his tongue in an effort not to laugh, and nearly choking in an effort not to spit the mouth full of cocoa on

Sophie that he had taken just before the Pastor's last comment."

As soon as pastor Blake was out of range, Sophie did burst into laughter.

Nick coughed and leaned back enjoying the glow of the Christmas lights and laughter in her eyes. He liked her laugh. He hoped that soon she'd be able to laugh more.

After they finished eating, they walked down the street through the booths and throngs of people. They stopped for a couple of minutes to listen to carolers, and then continued back to Jack's where they said goodnight.

That evening Sophie took advantage of the solitude. A part of her had wanted to invite Nick in, but she really did need this time to herself, and said a silent prayer of thanks to God that she could have this night.

The first thing she did was to run a hot bath. Sinking into the water she laughed at the thought of the last time she had been in this tub and the memory of Nick's face when he had caught her.

After her bath, she borrowed one of Jack's shirts, popped a bag of popcorn and curled up on the couch to watch "*The Sound of Music.*" She knew every line, and sang along with every song, allowing herself to escape into another world, a happier world. Even that world though had been tainted by the Nazi's. They had escaped though. Sophie had always believed in happy endings, and she tried to hold on to that belief as the credits rolled, and she made her way into the bedroom. For a moment she felt almost like Goldie Locks. She had slept in her bed, Nick's bed, and now Jack's bed. She stretched and clicked the bedside lamp on. Then she picked up the Bible Jack kept next to the lamp, turned to Psalm 31 and read;

1.In You, Lord, I have taken refuge; let me never be put to shame; deliver me in your righteousness. 2. Turn your ear to me, come quickly to my rescue; be my rock of refuge, a strong fortress to save me. 3.Since you are my rock and my fortress, for the sake of your name lead and guide me. 4. Keep me from the trap that is set for me, for you are my refuge. 5. Into your hands I commit my spirit; deliver me, Lord, my faithful God.

"I do have a spirit. No matter what, I believe that you gave me a spirit and Alice too. Please help us. Amen," she concluded, then rolled over into a deep sleep.

***

Shane was glad he had thrown in the go bag. He wasn't, however spending the night at a nice hotel in Leavenworth, but in a monk's cell at a nearby monastery that Sister Margarita had arranged for him as he continued his journey up into Canada.

He knew there was nothing left for him to do here aside from sleep. The cell was comfortable enough and did have electricity at least, but there was zero phone service and no internet. Still, he had discovered more today about Patty and her disappearance than he had in the last five years of investigating. He knew that a sketch artist was set to meet with Marion the next morning, and discovered only two likely candidates for the orphanage, if that was indeed where they had been headed.

Marion had called and left a message on his phone while he had been helping the nuns. She said that she remembered Patty and the man driving a midnight blue Mercedes. That told him it wasn't a rental, and Marion had also been sure that it had Washington license Plates.

***

After the kiss, Jack and Alice had walked in silence through the snow. Eventually they found themselves back at the train station, where they discovered that they would be able to leave on either an 8:00AM train or one leaving at noon the next day.

"Let's make it the noon train, if that's okay with my wife here?" Jack said, looking at Alice directly for the first time since the kiss. "After all, we don't have to check out until eleven, so we might as well enjoy our breakfast."

"I think that sounds like a good idea," Alice agreed, holding his gaze.

They had continued their walk through town, occasionally commenting on the Christmas decorations or popping into a shop. By two, they realized that they had missed lunch, and stopped into a local diner. Jack bought a newspaper from a machine out front, and they slid into a corner booth in the back. It was a cheerful place with old time Christmas carols coming from a jukebox and 1950's décor. They browsed the menu, and after a few moments a waitress in a pink uniform and red Santa hat came over to take their order.

After she left, Jack divided the newspaper, and they both began to flip through it, praying that nothing new would be there.

It was Jack that saw it first. He hadn't recognized the building in the photo at first, but something in the headline made him read the article.

"Missing Man Escapes From Popular Guest House."

"A prominent businessman who had gone missing from his own Manhattan hotel a week ago under suspicious circumstances, escaped his kidnappers by making paper airplanes with a note and sending them down from the eighth-floor suite where he had been held by a yet undisclosed

employee.

The man said that when he saw a patrol car parked below, he knew he had to take his chance. Eventually one of the airplanes landed on the officers' window and the man was rescued.

Aside from a slightly infected stab wound the man appeared to be in good health, and after making a statement to the New York Police Department and the Federal Bureau of Investigation, was on his way home to be reunited with his family."

Jack folded the paper to the article and pushed it across the table to Alice. "What do you think?" he asked, as she looked up.

As Alice read, she felt flooded by a sense of relief. "It must be him. That's definitely Alexandria Place. It must have been Leon."

***

Soren Anglistan slid his card into the lock, and then placed his head into the scanner that conducted not only a retinal scan but checked his ear print in order to match it to the information stored in the chip on the card he had inserted. Soren would then be through the first door. At the next, he would have to punch in three codes, which were changed on a nineteen-hour basis. Nineteen had been decided as a nice, odd time frame of which anyone with thoughts of tricking their way in via kidnapping, or God forbid decapitation of authorized personnel, would not be likely to consider. Yet even after that, there was a third door. The third door was sneaky. It required voice recognition, but not the standard recognition of someone simply stating their name. For this lock they would have to sing their way in. This meant that not only was a wider vocal range measured, but each individual had their own choruses that they were assigned to sing on a rotational basis. The last time Soren had come through he had sang the chorus to Bon Jovi's

"You Give Love a Bad Name." That meant that this time he had to sing the chorus to "Amazing Grace." Whoever had thought up this security system, certainly had a sense of humor, he thought. Soren couldn't carry a tune to save his life, but that was okay, as the system recognized his vocal fluctuations over any talent, or rather lack thereof.

Once inside, Soren strolled down the corridor, lined with halls of vaults that contained over a billion samples of DNA, much of it from those who had long departed this world. Soren couldn't help but feel a sense of awe as he walked past the hall of royalty, so dubbed because its vaults contained the DNA of royalty from Katherine the great of Russia to Prince Harry of England. The vaults were organized by nationality and date of life. He stopped and gazed down the hall as possibilities filled his mind. He considered that he was about to be a father and what this could mean for his own children, and then he continued on to his purpose for that day. He passed rows of vaults containing samples of famous athletes, doctors, linguists, financiers, politicians, musicians and authors, which made up some of the other categories that filled the nearly four-mile-long underground storage facility.

Eventually he came to another set of doors. The first needed only a simple palm scan, the second needed literal blood to get through. This was where they kept the maximum-security DNA samples, and a DNA sample was exactly what was needed to enter. Soren stuck his finger into the hole from which a needle pricked it and analyzed the blood sample. He would have to wait patiently now as his blood was scanned for markers to verify his identity. There were only three people in the world allowed into this vault, and therefore the process was relatively quick.

This vault always made Soren's skin crawl. It was where samples of people like The Prince of Wallachia, Caligula, Idi

Amin, Hitler, Pol Pot, Torquemada, Jeffrey Dahmer, Anthony Morley, Joseph Vacher, Leonarda Cianciulli and Bela Kiss were kept, along with various other war criminals, serial killers and psychopaths. These were the samples that Soren believed the world was better off without. It wasn't his decision though, and he only prayed that the motive behind the research was as he had been led to believe. He had been told that the goal was to find similar genetic markers that could result in early diagnosis of tendencies toward psychotic and or criminal behavior. The goal was then to observe, and if the tendencies began to manifest, to counteract with the addition of DNA from someone like Mother Teresa perhaps. The ultimate goal they said was to breed out evil.

Soren himself had been brought up by a devout Catholic mother and a Lutheran father, and this fought against the scientific reasoning in his mind. He knew he was among the minority who both practiced science and yet held a firm belief in God. It was his parents who had encouraged him though. They explained to him that the heart of science was not against God, but in harmony with God.

In this vault though, Soren felt anything but harmony. It was as though the DNA in here was indeed alive and screaming of the chaos that its once living souls were now suffering in the torments of hell, which is where he thought, they most assuredly had all gone.

Soren couldn't wait to get out of there. He must treat each sample with care though, lest he have to return. Eventually he had the requested samples secured, and he crossed himself as he exited the vault along with Hitler's pals Ilse and Karl Koch secured in the bag on his hip.

Chapter Twenty-Nine

Ben Wilson arranged the flowers beside Anne's bed at the care center, and then sat in the chair beside her. "I talked to Nick honey. You remember Nick. Anyway, he said that Jack would be back tonight. I'm sure if his train gets in in time, he'll drop by to tell you all about New York." Ben brushed the hair back from Anne's eyes. "You have such beautiful eyes Annie. Oh, how I wish you'd open them for me," Ben continued, bending down to kiss her forehead. "I miss you. I know you're in there though, and I want you to know that I'll be here for you. It doesn't matter what happened that night or who you were meeting. All that matters is that I love you."

Ben had told her this a hundred times now, praying that she heard and would be encouraged to open her eyes. He needed her. It really no longer mattered if she had snuck out to see another man. That man wasn't here, and Ben would be. Maybe he had been wrong, but if she were meeting one of her lady friends, why would she have been so secretive, and it also wasn't the first time he had caught her in a lie about where she was going. He had tried to follow her twice, but both times she had turned down a long narrow lane, and he knew that if he followed behind, she was bound to spot him. He also knew that at the end of that lane were rental cottages.

Ben picked up her hand and kissed it. He looked at the clock, and then back down at Anne as he stifled tears. He had a meeting later that morning with the bank, and he had to convince them to extend the loan. He knew that Jack had not placed as he had wished, but he prayed the bank would accept the lesser amount and hold off. If not, Ben would not only lose their home and livelihood, but also the ability to pay for Anne's care.

Ben jumped, as he was broken away from his thoughts by a knock on the door.

"Hi Uncle Ben. I hope it's not a bad time."

Ben smiled up, as he waved Sophie in.

"How is she today?"

"No worse," Ben answered, trying to sound positive.

"How are you?"

"Just glad that the plows came early this morning, and that Jack will be back tonight."

"You heard from him then?"

"He rang Nick this morning. I'm surprised he didn't call you?"

"You know, he may have tried. I'd forgotten to charge my phone though. I'm sorry I didn't make it by the farm when I first got back."

"On the contrary my dear, I think you would have been sorry if you had. I'd have put you to work!"

They both smiled, and Sophie handed Ben the flowers she had picked up on her way over, as the door to Anne's room opened again.

"Tom, hi!" Sophie said.

"I see you're feeling better Sophie."

"Oh yes. Much," she stumbled a little having forgotten that it was her he believed he had sent the prescription for in New York.

"Were you sick Sophie?" Ben asked, looking worried.

"Just for a couple of days while we were in New York."

"Well," said Tom, "I was over helping my dad at the hospital this morning, so I thought I would swing by and look in on one of my favorite patients."

"How is your dad doing?" Ben asked.

"He just got back from a month in Kosovo, and you know him, he's already making plans to head back to the Congo after Christmas."

***

Edgar had made his move and taped a video appeal to Alice. He claimed Suzanna and he had argued about it, she being more than willing to sacrifice herself. He wasn't sure that Richter had bought it, but it had at least bought them some time.

Patty knew through Mathias that the helicopter was fully fueled for takeoff the next morning. All they had to do was get to it. Therein lay the catch. Patty had been given more sedation, which of course had been removed, but she knew that they were monitoring her heart rate, and that if they noticed too much increased activity, someone would be there in a flash. Therefore, the timing was key. She would have to lie as calm as possible until the security switch at ten O'clock that night. She knew that there would be a few minutes of distraction in between, while they did the routine transfer of earpieces and radio frequencies from Richter over to Carl or Jonathan. At that time, she would go to the balcony, and using the curved leg of the patio chair, pull down the fire escape ladder to the left, which led up to the helipad on the roof.

Patty knew that since Richter would be in his mandatory sleep time, Carl or Jonathan would be the one who would come to check on her. She prayed it would be Jonathan as no one, not even Jonathan or Mathias, it seemed, was certain how deeply Carl's loyalty to Richter ran.

This however would be the easiest part. Edgar could walk on his own, and how he would get there depended greatly on where he was able to position himself. Suzanna however could not walk on her own and would therefore need to be carried either up the ladder or down the halls and up the elevator, all of which were well monitored. The ladder to the roof would be best for all. Edgar on his own could make the ladder if he made it to the room, but with Suzanna strapped to his back, they could very well both fall, and there was nothing but a few hundred feet of air between the ladder and beach below. Patty knew that Edgar would not leave without Suzanna, so somehow Mathias or Jonathan would have to get to her and take the risk of Richter discovering that they had helped her.

Once they got to the chopper though, there would be one more obstacle. Who would fly it?

Edgar said he had brief flight training sixty years ago, but a lot had changed. Mathias was the best choice, if he was able to get there once the alarm was raised. She knew that Richter would not rest long without being on the scene, and that meant that he would have a sharp eye on Mathias. Jonathan? It was not likely, regardless of his sympathies, that he would risk the allegiance he had with Richter. Overall, there were way too many dangers, but after weighing the danger of attempted escape against the other options, it still won out. Even if they all perished, it would be better than allowing Richter to succeed.

Patty thought of Richter as Mengele reincarnated.

***

Dr. Thomas Marshall Sr. hated himself for this in so many ways. He knew it was his fault that she was in this position to begin with. She had only wanted to help her son and adopted niece. What sort of man was he? All he seemed to do was run away. What made him feel really awful was that so many people acted as though he were some kind of saint, when in fact he felt more of a devil. Not that that had been his intention, but the road to hell was paved with good intentions, and his road was well paved.

He had been on call when she first arrived at the hospital that night. Hell, he'd heard the crash. That was when he realized that they knew where he was and likely knew all about Sophie as well. It was her saving grace that she didn't know who her parents were or remember who he was.

It was Anne finding out that they feared. They didn't know that she had found out from her son, and that was accidental when she had been looking through some old things in her barn to sell and ran across the old lock box. She had known the combination and looked inside to see what was in it. What she had found had shocked her so much that she had gone directly to him.

She had realized that these were the items Jack had confided to her that he thought it better if Sophie didn't know about. Since he was a doctor though, Anne had correctly thought that he might be able to help her understand what she had found. For a moment he had wondered why Jack hadn't come to him, but then he'd realized that unless Jack suspected a connection, he would tell no one. He was like his father in that respect, self-contained and not prone to asking for help. Anne knew this too, and for that reason she had kept her meetings with him a secret.

He had tried to protect her. No, he had tried to protect himself, carefully trying to steer her away from the truth. She had been acting more and more suspicious of him though and Anne had a terrible poker face. He had hoped to be gone on a permanent trip, perhaps even disappear into the jungle before she started to air her suspicions to anyone. He would have hated to never see his son again or Sophie, but in his own defense, he would have given up his life before taking hers.

A part of him was worried that they would come back to finish the job. Then again, deliberate killing, at least past full gestation, had never been on their agenda. Anything pre-forty week, they deemed a necessary mercy miscarriage, or as with Anne, they could justify an accident. An accident could go either way, and therefore they did not consider it murder. It was creation that interested them, and he had no doubt that if Anne ever did come around, that they would not hesitate to make her another specimen. He suspected that they were waiting to see what kind of brain function she would have. Would she be able to move? Speak? Remember? Then they would fly in and appear as heroes with their specialized treatments. One thing they would make very sure of; She would not divulge anything that could put the operation at risk.

***

Shane had spent the last three hours talking to Yarnok as she briefed him and took notes on other checks he wanted them to run.

The face from the sketch had turned up no database hits yet, but Asher was going to send it to a contact at Interpol to see if they could get a hit.

As far as the orphanage went, it appeared to have been nothing but a mislead. So far no one he had spoken to remembered anyone fitting the description of either Patty or the man she was seen with. Granted it was Saturday, and he had been told that the director at each facility would be back on Monday. He would take vacation leave until Tuesday and over the weekend, he would circulate Patty's photo and a description of the man at airports, train, and bus stations. Then on Tuesday, if he were still empty handed, he would circle back west and return down to Seattle via Vancouver and the I-5. He would stop at the port as well, to be certain that all transit routes were covered. Granted they may have continued into Idaho or even up to Alaska, but Shane could only go so many directions at a time.

There was one thing that had made his nose twitch when he spoke to a caregiver at the second children's home. He had seen a woman there cleaning and something in her features had struck him. He had only glimpsed her briefly in semi profile from behind but made a note to inquire about her Monday.

***

Nick had taught a class that morning, and then called Sophie to tell her that Jack had phoned with their arrival time, and to see if she would have dinner with him again.

Sophie had said yes, and then after meeting Shannon for coffee had headed back over to the care center with some CD's she had found at the Christmas bazaar. She knew that music often helped in brain cell regeneration of people in comatose states, and Ben had mentioned wishing that he had a better selection to play for her. Sophie had chosen two music CD's that she was sure Anne would like along with one book on CD by a motivational speaker who herself had overcome a major brain trauma.

She was surprised when she looked through the window of the door to Anne's room to see not Tom, but his father sitting by her bed. Well, at least Auntie Anne wouldn't be lonely today. She stopped short of opening the door and saying welcome back though. There was something strange in his composure, and fear that something bad had happened while she was out gripped her heart. Dr. Marshall appeared to be crying.

Chapter Thirty

Something had changed, was changing with both Alice and Jack. Ever since their kiss it was as though some invisible barrier had been broken through, and then the relief of the article that set their minds more at ease about the fate of Mr. Amstead. Jack had also been able to get through to his dad. He found out that his mother's condition remained stable, and let his dad know that he would have the prize money for him. Unfortunately, it would now be Monday before it could be deposited, but his dad had reassured him that it would be fine. Even if he had to write the check today, it wouldn't process through until Monday.

Then they had gone back to the guesthouse and sat together on the bed, where Alice had asked Jack questions about what she had read in the Bible and pointed out the now two blemishes that had appeared on her jaw line.

They went back out and walked through the town looking at the Christmas lights together and stopped by a local church to watch a Christmas pageant. After that they had joined in with a group of carolers, and finally made their way back to their room around midnight, where they turned the fire on and fell, exhausted, still fully clothed onto the single bed together. Jack's arm draped across her, and she laced her fingers with his as they fell into a deep sleep.

She watched as the girl struggled to make her way across the room. Her face was hidden behind a strange blank mask and red curls flowed down just one side of her head. She wore mittens on her hands and oversized mouse slippers. Alice was curious. She wondered who the girl was, but then the girl looked straight at her, and Alice stumbled to hide behind a woman's coat.

"It's okay baby," the woman said, reaching down to stroke Alice's head.

As the girl moved closer though, Alice began to cry, and then the girl started to make muffled grunts, and drool trickled from under her mask. Alice screamed.

She woke up in a cold sweat, her heart pounding in her ears. "Rosie! Rosie! Rosie," she kept repeating, as Jack tried to calm her.

"It was just a nightmare Alice," Jack said, as he smoothed her hair back.

She turned suddenly to face him, and the look in her eyes startled him. "Rosie," she repeated, staring hard at him. "I don't want to be like Rosie."

"Rosie?" Jack ventured.

"Noooo!" Alice cried out, and then collapsed into tears.

Jack didn't know what to do. She just lay there quaking and sobbing until finally her breathing slowed, and she began to snore.

Jack on the other hand could not go back to sleep, and lay there in silence until the sun rose, offering up the occasional prayer, and wondering what was happening now. She had looked like a woman possessed when she looked at him, and it chilled him to the bone.

When she finally awoke again at eight in the morning, she acted as though nothing had happened. She looked up at him all smiles, stretched and asked. "So? Did you make enough for me?" referring to the coffee he was having.

He poured her a cup and asked. "How did you sleep?"

"Better than I can ever remember. How about you? You still look a little tired. I didn't steal all the covers, did I?"

"No. I guess I'm just used to more room to stretch out."

"Well, tonight you will finally be home and I..."

"Alice?"

"I'm going to have to face reality. Whatever reality may be. Right now, I'd like to take a shower, and go downstairs for breakfast. Do you need in?" she asked, gesturing to the bathroom.

"No, go ahead. Just save me some hot water," he said, and raised his cup to her as she turned, picked up her bag, and disappeared into the bath.

By nine they were downstairs enjoying breakfast in the dining room. Most of the other guests had gone out on earlier trains, and the only other people in the dining room were the family they had met outside the day before.

Jack and Alice hated to be anti-social, but the children acted as though they were hyped up on way too much cocoa, and the family soon left to check out. The man gave a wan smile, and a wave, as his wife tried to corral their young.

Caroline, who managed the guesthouse, greeted them warmly, but thinking them to be newlyweds, did not intrude on their meal. They enjoyed fresh crapes and slabs of ham with freshly brewed organic Columbian coffee.

They decided to walk back to the train station, and by 11:30, were situated back in their car. This time, however, due to the massive backup, they were sharing a car with two sisters. The women were friendly, and Alice thought that they would never stop asking her and Jack questions about how they had met and what their wedding had been like. Then they wanted to see pictures, and Jack and Alice had needed to think fast. Jack had said that they were all packed in their checked luggage. The sisters had both been taken aback by that, and couldn't understand why they wouldn't have them nearby, not only to protect the precious memories, but to be able to share. Alice had then had to concoct a story about wanting only to share the professional pictures that would have color corrected the rash that she had unfortunately broken out in on her wedding day. She pointed to the two pimples, claiming that they were the residue of her extreme nervousness. The sisters looked at her with sympathy, and then slipped into stories about their own mutual anxieties, and the therapies they had each undergone to overcome them. They departed the train, none too early for Jack and Alice, with much encouragement and well wishes.

They had been alone for a couple of stops until they crossed the border into Nova Scotia, at which point they found themselves joined by two men, who seemed quite the opposite of the sisters. At first Alice was thankful for their silence, but at one point she had glanced up, and for an instant her eyes met those of one of the men as he stared over the top of the paper he pretended to read.

She reached for Jack's hand, and he squeezed hers. Then she suggested ordering some more coffee. When it arrived, Jack asked the men if they would care for any. They answered in French, "Non." Of course, in this region, that was not unusual, but Alice couldn't help feeling uneasy. She felt as though they were both somehow there for her, and for a split second the image of Albert flashed through her mind.

She sat her coffee down and faked a yawn, laid her head on Jack's shoulder, and closed her eyes, wondering if Jack was sensing the same vibe.

***

Sophie waited until Dr. Marshall had left before going back to Anne's room. She was relieved to note her aunts slow, steady breathing, as she placed one of the CDs in the player next to her bed. She took Anne's hand in hers and asked casually what she and Dr. Marshall had been talking about. She was stunned when she felt a light squeeze in response.

Sophie didn't say a word to anyone about what had happened. Perhaps it had just been a reflex? She didn't dare to get Jack's hopes up. Sophie had sat with Anne for almost another hour before a nurse came in to change the bedding, with no further response.

On her way to meet Nick she saw Dr. Marshall again with Tom walking through the Christmas stalls. They appeared cheerful enough as they both waved to her from across the street. She waved back and continued on to the post office to send some cards she had managed to write that morning. Sophie couldn't believe how close they were getting to Christmas. She thought about Alice and wondered what she would like. Sophie knew of course that Alice could easily buy anything she wanted, but from the description of her family Christmases, Sophie wanted to make sure that this one was extra special. Alice was part of their family now, and that meant that she would be included in every way. Sophie wished that she had more resources of her own. Right now, she felt as though she had only bad news for Alice. She would have to show her the pictures of both her parents as well as the babies, and regardless of how painful it would be, she knew it had to be done tonight. Waiting would only make it worse. She closed her eyes as the images flooded her mind. It was the photos of Alice's parents that worried her the most. What had happened to the babies had happened, and they couldn't turn back the clock, but for the Morgans the clock might still be ticking, only she had no idea for how long.

By the time Sophie met up with Nick, she had run through a thousand scenarios in her mind. She would be direct and give Alice the envelope with her parent's pictures to her immediately. After that, it was up to Alice.

***

Alice herself had been thinking much along the same lines. Her parents were missing, and her hands were tied. In many ways she was feeling very selfish, as she stepped off the train and onto the platform of the station that evening. The two men had disembarked at the previous stop, which had given Alice some much needed time to talk alone with Jack.

Jack also had picked up a strange vibe from the men, but since they hadn't actually done anything other than gawk a bit at a beautiful woman, which Jack could hardly blame them for, he decided to let it go and focus on their return and all that it might mean. He still hadn't figured out how to explain Alice and prayed that Sophie had covered that end. Alice was still wearing the wig, so at least no one would be seeing double right off the bat. There were also the files and photos that he knew they would both insist on looking at. Add to that the original issues of his mother's health and hanging onto the farm, and Jack suddenly wanted to get back on the train and disappear. In fact, he was starting to think he was having an anxiety attack. He had never had one but was pretty sure that how he was feeling now must be close to one. Then there was Alice herself, who despite it all had stayed calm. He looked at her, and mentally pulled himself together. He was falling in love with her. No, he was in love with her. He had been falling in love with her since that first night at the Turkish Delight Café.

They spotted Sophie first, and the women converged in an embrace. When they parted, Sophie held out the envelope.

"Don't open it here Alice," Sophie cautioned.

"What is it? What's wrong?" Alice asked.

"It's about your parents."

"I saw an article about them in a paper. I know that they're missing."

"Alice, they're not just missing. My parents received these before I even got home. Somebody else knows about me."

Chapter Thirty-One

Claire had gone down every year for Christmas to see her, but this year she knew she wouldn't make it. The cancer wouldn't let her and probably never would again. A part of her blamed them for that too. All of the injections, hormones, and scans that she had endured, she knew they must have contributed.

Her real concern now had nothing to do with her own suffering. She'd been dealing with that ever since she lost her husband in a hunting accident ten years ago. Then his daughter decided that she wanted to, as she'd said, be free and swing both ways. She had left college to run off with another girl and live in Paris. Her husband's son had married and moved to Australia. She had thought that the woman was no good and had tried to warn him. He reminded her that she was not his *real* mother, stopped talking to her, and Claire had not heard from either of them since.

None of them knew anyway. Well, her husband had known part of it, and she often wondered if that stray bullet had really been an accident. No, right now she was thinking about her girls and her sister. She had received the photo's a week ago as a warning, but she didn't give a damn what they did to her. She had already lost everything else.

She pulled herself up in the bed and took a pain pill before attempting to get up and move to her computer. She had realized where they must be in the middle of the night. She didn't know the exact location, but she was certain that the police could find it. She just needed to figure out who to tell.

She stopped short as soon as she turned the computer on,

and the video appeared. She had underestimated them. She didn't think that they knew, but the video proved that they did know where Rosie was, and God only knew what they would do. Claire had to do something. She had to find a way.

***

Richter looked in the mirror and gave himself the injection. This had to work. He had sent out scouts to assess the situation and had placed the order for the next stage. He was so close to making the world right, at least as far as he saw it. The way he saw it, everybody had a purpose, they just needed to understand where they fit and stay in their place. His place was the top, and he wanted Alice to join him there. Together they would create a utopian society to rival anything Hitler or Stalin had ever imagined.

***

Alice stared at the pictures as they drove over to Nick's. Everyone was silent until they arrived. The one bright spot seemed to be that Mr. Amstead had been found alive.

Jack tensed, and Sophie cocked an eyebrow in a "This is our life, and we don't need your protection," look, as she picked up the files, and took them to the table to go over with Alice.

Jack just sighed and went to call his dad. Ben had been fortunate at the bank, with them accepting twelve thousand for now with another ten percent of the two hundred and eighty thousand total, plus interest, of course to be paid in allotments of every six months. The first allotment they wanted by January fifteenth. It was an impossible situation. That would be over five thousand a week! Basically, the bank was giving them just enough leeway to have a home for the holidays, and then get out before they came in and took it all. This was going to be one hell of a Christmas. Everyone was getting a lottery ticket and a prayer request.

After he got off the phone with his dad, Jack went to sit on the couch with Nick, who didn't seem to know what to do with himself either.

"So?" asked Nick.

"Don't ask. I think they're in a whole other universe," Jack continued, as he watched Alice and Sophie. "They really don't need us."

"It only looks that way."

"Yeah, but why is it that we need them so much more?"

"Good question. What do you say we take a walk and go get some of that famous Christmas beer over at George's pub? On me."

"Right now, it would have to be. Thanks Nick. I would like to talk privately," Jack said, as he gathered his coat.

"Jack and I are going for a walk. Call us if anything new comes up or, well just call us if you need us," Nick said to Sophie and Alice, who barely looked up.

"Okay," they said in unison.

They found a booth in the back corner in the upstairs section of the pub where they could talk. Jack stared into the foam in his mug, as they sat in companionable silence for ten minutes before he finally spoke.

"She had some kind of crazy nightmare last night. She woke up screaming and sobbing and repeating the name Rosie. She was terrified, but then she went back to sleep, and when she woke up this morning, it was as though she'd forgotten all about it."

"Rosie? Not Sophie?"

"No. She definitely said Rosie."

"Maybe it was just a nightmare. She could have seen or heard a story about someone named Rosie. People do have nightmares."

"She had a nightmare on the train too I think."

"What do you mean?"

"I woke up, and she was over against the window. There was something in her face, her voice."

"Did she say anything about it?"

"No, but I can't help thinking that she's remembering something. Maybe she knows more about who she is than she is consciously aware of, things that may have happened when she was really little. I don't know, and I don't know what to do."

Nick half smiled at that, and replied, "I know exactly how you feel. I wish I knew how to help Sophie."

It was Jack's turn to smile. "You're in love with her."

"Is it that obvious?"

"Yes. Don't worry though. It's equally obvious that she loves you."

"I could say the same for you and Alice."

They smiled at each other and raised their beers in a toast.

"To Alice and Sophie."

"To Sophie and Alice."

"What do we do though? On the one hand, I think Alice is a hell of a lot stronger than I am, but..."

"I know. I think that there might be more too," Nick said.

"More of? You think there could be other sisters?"

"Maybe, but there had to be other children. This is obviously a big operation. Think about it."

"I have, and you're right. We know from Amstead alone that there were multiple companies involved through Morgan. The records I found in Quebec, Alice and the Morgans based in Seattle, and there have now been at least two kidnappings since they met. So that means that this, whatever mad experiments Sophie and Alice were part of, are probably still going on. This has been going on for over thirty years."

"I don't think we should be trying to handle this on our own. It's too big."

"What do you suggest?" Jack asked. "That we present Alice and Sophie as proof to be poked and prodded by even more crazy doctors? You know that's what would happen."

"They won't let this go though. They can't. I'd probably feel the same way if I were them."

"Even if there wasn't the addition of the Morgans being kidnapped, I couldn't let it go either. I just don't know if there's anyone that it's safe to talk to. I have to protect them."

"*We* have to protect them."

They returned an hour later to find a note.

"We were exhausted and went back to my place to sleep. We'll call you in the morning."

Sophie

***

Patty tugged at the ladder. It wouldn't budge, and it was only seconds before Jonathan was there.

"Just relax," he said, as he picked her up and carried her back into the room. He looked at Suzanna, who stared back, as he lowered Patty onto the bed. He grimaced, as Patty bit into his shoulder. "You have to calm down if you don't want Richter to come."

At that, she pulled back and just glared at him. "Why won't you let us go? You're not like him, so why won't you help us?" She was beginning to sob, and Jonathan looked away. He wasn't comfortable with emotion. He stood in front of the door to the balcony, facing out, and spoke to her reflection. "It isn't safe."

"I won't have my babies here. I won't let him take them," She sobbed.

"Now isn't the time. You'll have to trust me."

"Trust you? You just give me one good reason why I should."

"You said it yourself, I'm not him. I'm not Richter." He paused. "There are guards on the roof with even fewer scruples about the sanctity of life than Richter. They would have shot you on sight."

"Edgar!" Suzanna cried under her breath.

"I'll go check on him," Jonathan said and left.

Edgar had challenged Carl to a round of chess, hoping that it would help him to gain insight into this other brother. They were still playing when Jonathan entered.

"Is everything alright?" Carl asked without looking up.

"Fine. We should move them soon though."

"Move?" Edgar asked.

"Yes, as soon as I get back."

Edgar looked questioningly at Jonathan.

"I have some errands to run. I suggest you tell your wife and Patricia to relax. I would hate to see them get hurt."

Carl glanced up, and noted the red mark on Jonathan's shoulder, where it was bleeding from Patricia's bite. "Don't forget to change your shirt," he said.

He slipped into the room just after Jonathan turned the corner down the hall.

"Matty!" Patty said with a smile, as he entered.

"Are you ready to go?" he asked.

"Jonathan said that they posted armed guards on the roof."

"I just came from the roof. No one was there. We don't even use guns here, at least not the kind that kill. I've told you that before. Did he hurt you?"

"No. I don't understand though. Why?"

"He can't let you leave."

"But I thought...?" Suzanna asked.

"Jonathan isn't a bad man like Richter. He doesn't agree with Richter's goals, but that doesn't mean he's on your side either."

"And how do we know that we can trust you?" asked Suzanna.

"You don't. How do you know if you can trust anyone though?"

Suzanna stared at him. He was right of course, but he looked so much like his brother that she had to wonder if this even was Mathias.

Richter listened as he typed in the coded responses and smiled. He may not have cameras in the rooms, but he had no qualms about bugging their conversations. He was surprised that they had seemed to assume that the lack of cameras meant the lack of listening as well.

He got up and looked in the mirror. His body ached, and he gave himself another injection hoping that he would have the samples he needed without delay, and he headed out.

***

"Will you fly the helicopter for us?" Patty asked Mathias.

"Of course. I want to leave too."

"I couldn't get the ladder to come down."

"Really? It's probably stuck," he said, as he went out onto the balcony. He reached for the ladder, and it pulled down easily. "Now get on my back."

Suzanna's heart raced as she watched Patty climb onto his back. She wished she could move. She felt so helpless. Even if she and Patty did get to the helicopter, what about Edgar? How would he be able to get away now that Jonathan was aware of what they had planned? She couldn't go without him. She was contemplating this when she heard the scream.

Chapter Thirty-Two

Jack crashed on Nick's couch that night. They had stayed up until two in the morning, as Nick showed Jack what he had discovered about the pictures and talked. They had both been surprised that Sophie and Alice hadn't taken the files with them.

It was nearly nine before Jack awoke to Nick shaking him awake.

"Hey buddy. Jack? Wake up. It's almost nine, and I haven't heard from the girls."

"What?" Jack asked as he sat up and rubbed his eyes. "Have you tried calling them?"

"Of course, but it just goes to voice mail. I tried calling Sophie's parents too, but there was no answer. Something doesn't feel right."

Jack was fully alert now. "We shouldn't have left them alone," he said, as he pulled on his shoes. "We'd better go check it out."

Five minutes later they were on the road to Sophie's. When they pulled up to the front of the house the family van was gone, and aside from the strings of Christmas lights around the door and windows, all was dark.

They ran around the back to Sophie's cottage. No one was there either.

"Maybe they just got busy talking, and then went into town," Jack suggested hopefully.

"You're probably right. Maybe they even went to the early service at church. They are early risers, and with Alice's new interest in the Bible, that would make sense. We should just relax and go get ready for church ourselves."

"You're right. It's a good thing they can't see us right now."

They tried to relax, as they headed back to town, but neither said anything else until they reached town and turned toward Jacks. That's when Jack spotted the van and Sophie's car.

"There's their cars. I guess we were right. They came into town early."

"I hope they didn't go knocking on my door and wonder where we were," Nick said, and they both laughed.

Nick dropped Jack off so that he could shower and change, and they agreed to meet at the front of the church.

Jack arrived first and greeted Sophie's parents as they approached.

"Welcome back Jack!" they said, as they embraced him like a long-lost son.

"Where are the girls?" he asked.

"They said that they were heading over to meet you and Nick."

"They must be with Nick then. He took me home so I could get some fresh clothes."

"They're quite a pair," Sophie's mom said.

"You can say that again!" Jack agreed.

Just then Ben came up the walk, and Jack suddenly realized that he had not explained Alice to his dad.

"Dad! Excuse me," he said to Sophie's parents.

"Good to see you finally back son!"

"There's something I need to tell you about my trip."

"I want to hear all about it," Ben said.

"I met someone in New York."

"A lady?"

"Well, yes, but..."

"Is that the real reason you came back late? I understand if it is."

"It's kind of a long story, and I don't want you to go into shock or anything, but she's..."

"Did you bring her back with you? Where is she?"

"Listen dad, there's something that you should know about her."

"Well why don't you just introduce me?"

"I will, but there's something you should know first."

"What? Is she a communist or an atheist or something?"

"She's something all right."

"That's great then. I'm sure I'll love her, and something positive like this is just what I need right now. I'm happy for you son. I just wish your mom could meet her."

"Me too dad. I want to tell you something before you see her though."

"She has three eyes? A tail?"

"Dad, please. It's just that she looks a lot like..."

"Your mom?"

"Sophie."

"You and Sophie aren't? I know she's adopted, but is that why you were talking with the O'Hare's?"

"No. It's not Sophie dad. I said that she looks like Sophie. A lot like Sophie. As in they're probably twins."

Ben took a moment to try and absorb what Jack was telling him, and then said. "Are you saying she found her actual biological family?"

"Maybe. Alice wasn't put up for adoption though."

"Oh. So?"

"The whole thing about their parents is really complicated."

"So, I'd guess. What's she like?"

"You'll like her," Jack said, as the church bells rang. "In fact, she should be here by now. I'll see you inside dad."

"We'll be saving you both a seat," Ben said, as he waved to the O'Hares and headed inside.

Jack went back over to Sophie's parents as an ominous sensation spread through him.

"There's Nick and Matt," Mrs. O'Hare said. "I wonder where the girls are."

"I'm sure they'll be along," Mr. O'Hare said. "They probably got distracted on their way through the market. I'm going inside. I wanted to say hi to Ben before the service starts. See you soon," he nodded to Jack.

Nick and Matt greeted them a minute later on the steps. "I thought you'd all be inside with Sophie and Alice," Nick said, as he looked at Jack.

"They said they were going over to your place," said Sophie's mom. "Haven't you seen them?"

"Not since last night."

"Don't worry," Jack told Mrs. O'Hare. "We'll go look for them and meet you inside."

"Okay, but why don't we try calling them first. There's no need for you two to wander off and miss the service," she said, as she pulled out her cell, and called Sophie. It rang once and went to voice mail, where she left a message.

"I'll send them a text too," Jack said.

"I think I'll head on in if you don't mind," Matt said. "Mindy's doing a solo today, and I promised her I'd sit up front. So, I don't want to be sneaking in late."

"Go on bro. We'll catch you later," Nick said, and Matt hurried inside.

Mrs. O'Hare stayed with Jack and Nick while the text was sent. Jack had a sense that she was uneasy as well.

They could hear the music starting inside. "Come on in. I'm sure they'll be along," said Mrs. O'Hare. "They're probably just stuck in a line waiting to buy a Christmas gift or something," she continued, as though trying to convince herself, as she climbed the stairs into the church, and Jack and Nick followed her in.

Mrs. O'Hare went around the side, and slipped into the pew beside her husband, while Nick and Jack slid into the rear pew. Mr. O'Hare and Jack's dad turned to look back at them, and they nodded.

"They'll sit back there so as not to cause disruption when the girls arrive," Mrs. O'Hare whispered to her husband, and reached to hold his hand. He squeezed it gently as they rose to sing the next hymn.

Alice had spotted them right away and pulled Sophie aside to explain that she had seen them on the train. "I had the wig on then, but I could swear they were watching me, and we know now that they know about you."

"I think we should go now," Sophie said.

"I agree," said Alice.

"We should at least leave them a note though," Sophie sighed. She hated the thought of leaving her family and Nick, especially at Christmas time.

"Maybe we can have this all figured out and be back before Christmas," Alice said. "You believe in miracles. Right?"

"Right. Do you still have the cash on you though?"

"Right here," Alice said, patting her bag, "and my passport. You?"

"Yes."

They wrote a brief note, walked to Nick's, and left it under his windshield. Then they walked another block and got on the Christmas shuttle, a holiday bus that mainly shuttled tourists and the elderly between holiday markets and events. They stayed on until the end of the line at the Cunard Event Center, on the Halifax waterfront. From there they took another bus to the airport, where they purchased two one-way tickets to Quebec.

Part Two

Chapter Thirty-Three

"They left," was all Nick said as he handed the note to Jack. Jack read it.

We can't stay here. It may not be safe, and we can't put you or our families at risk anymore. The men from the train are here. Please don't worry. We'll be fine.

Love,
Alice
&
Sophie

"Don't worry! What are we supposed to tell Sophie's parents? My dad? I don't believe this!"

"The men from the train, tell me about them again. What did they look like?" Nick asked. "If they're following Alice and Sophie, then we need to find them."

"They were both thin, about six-feet tall I'd guess, black hair, nothing special that I can recall except that they made us uncomfortable. They spent most of the trip behind newspapers. They were wearing long gray overcoats. Not terribly distinct," Jack said, frustration filling his voice. "Sophie's parents are already worried. I have to talk to them."

"I'll come with you. We'll think of something. If these guys are no good, then they should know to look out for them too."

Jack looked at his watch. "I need to go see my mom before I do anything else. Would you mind picking up something for dinner? I missed breakfast and lunch."

"No problem. Shall I meet you at the care center? I've been meaning to stop by and see your mom too."

"Sure. Thanks Nick."

***

Claire knew what she had to do. It was the only way. They had sent her the invitation when her cancer had first advanced to stage three. She had rejected it flatly. She had been ready to go, but now she composed a letter directly to doctor Meschner. She hated the idea of being a Guinea pig again, but it would give her a way inside.

It was funny, she reflected. For years she had been angry at her big sister for subjecting her to this. She had been happy to carry a child on her sister's behalf, but when she had signed the agreement, she had not worried to read the fine print. This was for her only sister after all. She had not dreamed what the consequences would be.

***

Patty didn't know where she was. She opened her eyes and saw stars dancing above her, and a light breeze brushed her cheek. She pulled herself up and froze. She was no more than six inches from the sheer cliff. Looking up, she realized that the drop had not been nearly as far as it had felt, perhaps twelve feet. Actually, she had not fallen at all.

She remembered the jolt she felt in her heart when she realized what was about to happen. Richter himself had been at the top of the ladder reaching to haul her up. She had batted Richter's hand away and grabbed instead onto a rope that Mathias had tied to his belt. She remembered screaming as

Richter reached for her, and she kicked off, preferring death to being locked away again. She remembered swinging out over the open air, but then something had happened, and she had swung back in toward the cliff side and landed where she now was.

The area was only about five by eight feet. The cliff above stuck out over her head at an angle. Climbing back up would be impossible. She looked around her for the rope but saw no sign of it. She must have let go when she swung onto this ledge.

She felt the babies move and sighed a sense of relief. Then she moved as close to the Cliffside as she could, leaned back against it and closed her eyes.

***

Jack had spent the night at the O'Hare's after visiting with his mom. He had found the CD's that Sophie had bought and turned one on for her as he left. He had told her everything as kind of a safe rehearsal for what he would say to Sophie's parents.

They had not reacted with the disbelief he had expected. Of course, he hadn't gone into their suspicions about the genetic research. How could he? He didn't understand it himself. What he had told them about was Mr. Amstead, Albert, the disappearance of Alice's parents, minus the photos received by Sophie.

Mrs. O'Hare had sat silently and looked inquiringly towards her husband as she asked. "Do we dare to call the police?"

"No. She's a grown woman now anyway, and they left a note. The police would nah be able to do a thing."

"What do you mean *dare* to call the police?" Jack had asked.

"Nothing," Lilly O'Hare replied. "It's just that once the police become involved with missing persons, well it's the results you often hear that are so scary. Her da is right. It has not yet come to that. They didn't actually go missing. There is the note. Do you think perhaps they might have gone to Seattle to inquire into the investigation of Alice's parents?"

"Since they didn't say, it's hard to guess. I would imagine they hadn't much time to formulate a plan before they left the note. Hopefully, once they do, they'll call," Jack said.

"I only wish they'd have called us first," Mr. O'Hare had said, as he flipped the outdoor lights on. "Do you really think these men represent a danger?"

"There's no way to know. Their being in town may be no more than coincidence, and their looking at Alice on the train no more than natural attraction. There's really no evidence to say they aren't just tourists. I have to admit that they did make me uneasy too though. There are too many unknowns in all of this, and after Alice's parents went missing, well I hope you can understand why both Alice and Sophie, as they could easily be mistaken for one another, might overreact."

"So maybe they just panicked, and they'll be back in the morning," Mrs. O'Hare said hopefully.

"Maybe," Jack tried to comfort with agreement.

Afterwards, Nick had gone back home, and Jack had slept on the O'Hare's couch. Now he rubbed his eyes, as he awoke to the aroma of the coffee and bacon Mrs. O'Hare had put on.

When she saw he was awake, she poured two mugs and went to sit with him on the couch.

"What all did you find out about Sophie's adoption?" She asked.

Jack looked at her, startled. He hadn't told her that he had looked into it, and he was certain that Sophie wouldn't have.

"I had a call from the hospital that looked after Sophie as a baby. They said that someone had been inquiring, and you're the only one she would have asked to do that," she said simply.

"Not much that made sense," he responded, with the only

honest answer he dared.

Just then Mr. O'Hare came into the living room. Lilly smiled warmly at Jack and went to greet her husband good morning.

They were sitting around the breakfast table, staring at the food, more than eating it, when Jack's phone rang. It was Nick. Sophie had called him from a pay phone. She wouldn't say where they were but asked that he reassure her family that they were okay. She had run out of time on the phone before he had a chance to ask her anything. He doubted that she would have answered anyway. At least for now they were alright.

Chapter Thirty-Four

Shane reached for his phone and saw that it was Yarnok calling. He yawned and noted the time was five in the morning.

"What's happened?" he asked, as he held the phone to his ear.

They had discovered the green Fiesta, Melinda claimed Alice drove. The reason they hadn't been able to locate it before was because it had been registered in another name, however, Alice Morgan was listed as a designated driver on the insurance. It was the night security that patrolled the garage where it was kept, who had brought it to the attention of the police after seeing the article about the Morgans having gone missing. He had recognized Alice as their daughter and thought it prudent to report that he had not seen her for an extended period of time either. And she herself had told him that she would be gone only a week.

"So, whose name is it registered in?" Shane asked.

"According to the guard, the owner is a Mr. Haggle, who we discovered used to live in the same building as Alice. It seems he became disabled in an accident last year, and she helped him by driving him places and running other errands."

"So, he put her name on the insurance, which makes her a legal driver of the vehicle."

"Exactly!"

"And where is Mr. Haggle now? I think we should have a chat with him."

"Mr. Haggle is in a coma at Harborview Medical Center after an aneurism burst last month, caused by the before mentioned accident. However," Yarnok continued, "The guard did let us take a look in the car."

"And?"

"We found a gym bag, a second cell phone and an iPad. The cell is one of those pay as you go, but we'll check out where it's been, and Selma will be in at seven. The iPad is on her desk. Sorry to call you so early, but I knew you'd want to know."

"You know me. I was about to get up anyway. That orphanage director is supposed to be in at seven. I'll call after I meet with her for any updates. Tell Asher and Laben I said good work."

"Will do, and for what it's worth, we're all praying that you find her."

"Thanks," Shane said, as he hung up, got out of bed, and into the shower.

An hour later he had left his key at the front desk and was sitting in a café just across the street from the orphanage.

He had just finished his waffles, refilled his coffee and looked at the time. It was still ten minutes before seven, as Shane looked out the window. He recognized the man from the sketch immediately, as he looked around before putting the key into the door of the orphanage and entering.

Shane pulled out his wallet and left a twenty on the table.

When he got across the street to the door it was locked again. Apparently, he would have to wait another eight minutes, but at least he knew that he had returned to the right place, and he was determined not to leave until he got some answers.

***

Selma was intrigued, psychologically that is. Alice Morgan was very interesting. For a prodigy, who still supposedly lived under her parent's thumb at age thirty, she seemed to have developed a rather well balanced, although secret, second life.

The iPad had contained music lists that included many of Selma's personal favorites. The emails were mostly between her and five people, which included Mr. Haggle, Melinda, and three international contacts who appeared to be students from China, who had been sponsored by Alice through an international educational aid program. They were the only three contacts on the Facebook page Selma found as well. Most of the communication was lighthearted, but some was deeply personal confidences that the students shared with Alice about their families, dreams, their concerns. Alice was empathetic, briefly mentioning how controlled she sometimes felt by her own family. Selma found stunning pictures of Mt. Rainier and the Seattle waterfront at sunset as well as some from Bainbridge Island and other areas of the peninsula. It was the last file of photo's she clicked on that caught her attention. They were at various locations, a farmers market, a concert, a park, a museum, and the ferry dock. In the background of each one the face of the same man appeared. It was a face that Selma had seen just the day before, in a sketch of the man last seen with Shane's wife.

Selma called Shane's cell to tell him what she had discovered.

"Thanks Selma. I'm about to meet the guy face to face myself. I saw him enter the orphanage here just a few minutes ago. Do you think she knew him?"

"He is either way in back or to the far side of the photos. I get the feeling she was being followed, knew it, and this was her way of documenting it."

"That means he may work for Morgan Acquisitions. Tell Yarnok to take the sketch to Charice and see if she recognizes him. I've got to go. I'll check in when I'm done here. Thanks again," Shane said, as he put the phone in his inside jacket pocket and entered into the foyer of the orphanage.

***

Alice and Sophie enjoyed omelets with sweet breads and coffee in the hotel restaurant as they talked. It was hard to believe that they were now sitting on top of the spot where they may have been born? They had both agreed, though they still had their concerns, that what mattered was who they had become regardless of how they had become.

"It doesn't seem to be getting any better," Alice said, referring to the blemishes on her jawline and a new one that was sprouting out at the side of her nose. I know that this is normal for teenagers, but I'm not a teenager, and I've never had an injury last more than a few hours," she continued, pointing to the bruise on her arm where she had bumped it getting off of the crowded bus the day before.

Sophie looked at the bruise and the acne. "The one we put the cream on last night looks a little better. If I didn't know you better, I'd say you were normal," she said with a half-smile.

"I did ask for this though."

"What do you mean?" Sophie asked.

"When I was at the bed & breakfast with Jack, I asked God to give me some physical imperfection to make me more human. I was thrilled when I first found the pimples. I guess I hadn't really expected an answer, but now I'm wondering," Alice said.

"Wondering about God or the pimples?"

"Both. That was probably the first real prayer I've ever said and this," she said pointing to the pimple under her chin, "was an almost instant answer. I've also been more fatigued though lately. I can hardly believe that I slept over ten hours last night. What I'm wondering is if there is something different or missing in the pills I got from your doctor, verses what I was taking in Seattle?"

"That would make sense," Sophie responded. "I have a feeling that if they were the same, I might not have this," she said, pointing to the pale scars on her cheek. Do you think that there really could be another of us, I mean another sister who looks like us and is alive out there somewhere Alice?"

"Yes. I think I may have even met her once."

"Me too."

"You do?"

"I don't remember much from before my adoption, but sometimes I dream about another little girl that I see in a mirror behind me. She looked a lot like me, but there was something not right about her. Then I remember hiding one time. I don't remember why, but I had to hide and there was somebody else there. I couldn't see her, but it was another little girl. I could feel her long hair as she lay there beside me hiding in the dark. I used to think it was just a nightmare, but now I'm starting to think that maybe it really happened."

The waiter came and refreshed their coffee. He gave them both an appraising smile and asked if there was anything else he could get them. They thanked him for the coffee, but it took him a moment before he realized there was no reason for him to continue standing at their table and he moved on.

"I was thinking," Alice said. "We might want to change our look a bit. I'm sure the waiter is innocent enough, but we're too easily noticed."

"Agreed."

"The library doesn't open until noon today, so why don't we both go to the mall. We need clothes anyway, so we might as well get our hair done?"

"I've always wondered what I would look like with a black bob," Sophie said.

"I was thinking of a rich mahogany for me, like that woman over there." Alice inclined her head to a woman in the lounge area.

"I can see that on you," Sophie said. "There's something else Alice."

"What is it?"

"Saturday, I went to visit Jack's mom, and I saw Doctor Marshall, not Tom, but his dad. I had thought he was out of the country. That isn't what bothered me though. I got the strangest sensation when I saw him with her. He was crying. After he left, I went in to sit with her, and I could have sworn I felt her squeeze my hand."

"That's great! Did you tell Jack?"

"No. It may have just been my imagination, but..."

"How well do you know this Dr. Marshall Sophie?"

"He came to town with his son Tom probably twenty years ago now. Jack and Tom have been great friends for years, but his dad is usually off providing care at missions in third world countries. He's supposed to be one of the top doctors when it comes to tropical and rare diseases."

"Do you think he's somehow involved?"

"I don't know, but the way he looked with Aunt Anne was beyond a normal doctor patient or even friend reaction. In fact, I was scared after he left that something awful had happened to her, but there were no nurses around and her breathing appeared normal. Then when the nurse came in later, she assured me that there had been no change."

"What could that have to do with us though?"

"Nothing, I guess. It's probably just my imagination, but..."

"What is it, Sophie?"

"I felt something odd when he looked at me too, but Dr. Marshall and I hardly know each other. Like I said, he's usually overseas. I really only know him through Tom and Aunt Anne wouldn't be involved."

"Unless she knew about what Jack found," Alice ventured.

***

Anne wanted to open her eyes, but they felt so heavy, and her body felt so weak, as though she had been run over by a semi-truck. She could hear voices, and wherever she was smelled slightly antiseptic. She must be in the hospital she thought, but why? And why was she so tired, she wondered as she drifted back to sleep. She could hear Jack's voice in her dreams telling her the whole crazy story, only it wasn't crazy. She had to wake up and tell her son and Sophie and who was the other name he had mentioned? She had to wake up, but she couldn't yet. She needed to rest. The headlights were coming directly at her. There was nowhere to go. She cranked the wheel to the right and screamed.

The nurse at the desk bolted to alertness and raced into Anne's room to find her sitting straight up, eyes wide with shock. The nurse hit the alert button and went to her side, just in time to catch her as she slumped back onto the bed.

***

Patty covered her eyes from the sun trying to comprehend what she was seeing. Below on the beach were men picking up what looked like body parts. To the left behind her, she had also discovered a narrow cave. She cowered back towards it as the men looked up. They were most likely down there to look for her body, yet hers was altogether. She wished she had a pair of binoculars to see what was really happening. She had backed about three feet inside of the cave now and prayed that they hadn't seen her.

The cave was dark, and she wondered briefly about what might lurk inside. She could hear water dripping from somewhere further in, and she was growing desperately thirsty.

Slowly, she began to make her way further into the cave as

her eyes tried to adjust to the lack of light. She turned so that she could crawl, searching out in front of her with her hands before proceeding.

Eventually she felt water drip on her, and the floor of the cave sloped down as she entered into a larger cavern, almost large enough for her to stand up in. A few minutes later she saw a beam of sun streaming in from somewhere as it glinted upon a small stream of water, maybe two feet across, flowing down the cave wall into a small waterfall on her right.

Patty scooped up some of the water for a drink. It tasted slightly odd after five years of bottled water, but it was refreshing. After drinking her fill, Patty leaned against the cave wall, trying to make out where the sunlight was coming in from. She knew that she had been moving at an angle and eventually made out that the light must be coming from the cliffs facing the west beach. She was also able to make out that the cave veered off into three different directions a few feet ahead. Patty continued following the water, and its hopefully gradual downward flow to the beach a couple hundred feet below.

Chapter Thirty-Five

Shane showed his badge and asked about the man he had seen entering the building just ten minutes before. The girl said that she had been there for less than five minutes though and did not recognize the man Shane described, but that she would be happy to escort him back to the director's office.

Along the way Shane saw the same woman again that had made his nose itch on his previous visit. She was at work, mopping down a hallway as they passed.

"Who is that?" Shane asked as he stopped to watch her.

"No one. She just helps with the cleaning."

"Everybody is someone," Shane said. He was going to ask her name, but his guide was already turning the corner down the hall. He would have to inquire of the director.

"There. Her office is the second door on the left. If you will excuse me, I need to get back to the front desk," she stated, stiffly stalking off back down the hall.

"Certainly," Shane said, as he went to the door she had indicated and knocked.

"Come in Sandra."

Shane opened the door and cleared his throat. The woman looked up from behind a large mahogany desk. "You're not Sandy, are you?"

"Afraid not ma'am," Shane said, as he walked closer and showed his badge. I would like to ask you a few questions."

"You appear to be a little outside of your jurisdiction Mr. McDougal. I'm afraid I won't be able to help you."

"Please. I would just like to know if you have ever seen this woman," Shane said, as he took out a picture of Patricia.

The woman or rather Director Karstinson, as the nameplate on her desk claimed, took the photo hesitantly and gave it a brief look before looking back up at Shane.

"I'm sorry," she said, handing the picture back to him. "I suggest you go now Mr. McDougal."

"I wanted to ask you about someone else here as well. The girl who is mopping in the hallway, with red hair, what's her name?"

"I'm afraid that I am not at liberty to answer that. Now please, I have work to do. Please leave via the rear exit at the end of this hallway," she said, as she looked back to her computer, while pointing to the left.

Shane stared at the woman until she met his gaze.

"What is going on here?" Shane asked.

"I'm going to suggest this only one more time," she said, looking at her watch. "You are way out of your jurisdiction." She raised an overly penciled eyebrow. "Leave via the exit at the end of this hall and do it now. Do you understand?"

Shane nodded, unsure exactly what she seemed to be trying to tell him. On the outside it seemed like a basic get lost, but that last look had started a jig inside his nose, and he felt a sudden urgency to obey her instructions.

As Shane exited the door, she had directed him to, he saw the man again, and the girl was with him. Shane stood back and watched as the man directed her into a silver Nissan hybrid, taking careful note of the license plate. Shane's own car was parked across the street on the other side of the building. Ducking back inside, he raced down the hall and out the front door just in time to see the man turn out of the back parking lot. Shane waited until he turned the corner and dashed across the street to his own vehicle.

They were just two blocks ahead of him as he turned down the next street. Shane was forced to sit at a red light as they continued, and he saw them turn left. He couldn't lose them. His nose was on high alert. He had to find out who they were.

Shane dialed Yarnok and read the license plate to her, as he continued his pursuit. He followed them for another twenty minutes to a small municipal airstrip, where he watched as they prepared to board a helicopter.

He was watching through high-powered binoculars when the girl turned. He felt as though he had been struck by lightning as she seemed to stare straight at him, but he was certain that there was no way she could know he was there. Still her eyes, which were an intense almost unnatural green, pierced him as he realized that he was looking into the face of Alice Morgan. Only it wasn't her face. Beneath the piercing eyes, a long scar ran down each cheek to the corners of her mouth, and one side of her forehead was slightly concave, with a scar that ran down behind her right ear. The other side of her face had a defined droop to it, as if from a stroke. The man was talking to the pilot, as she continued to stare towards him, and he noticed that she was making repetitive motions with her hands. It looked like some kind of sign language.

Shane pulled out his phone and used the camera video function to try and catch it. Unsure, he held the phone camera lens up to the binocular eyepiece. Then the man returned and guided her onto the chopper, and Shane noted as she stepped up that her left leg was twisted at a right angle. Shane jotted down the call number of the chopper and called Yarnok again.

***

Edgar felt groggy as the sunlight streamed in on his face. He rubbed his eyes as he tried to remember what had happened. The last memory he had was playing chess with Carl. Jonathan had come in with a bloody spot on his shoulder.

Edgar slowly opened his eyes. He wasn't in the same room

anymore. He sat up, realizing that he was now wearing pajamas. Had he put them on? Looking around, he knew almost instantly where he was, and he turned to the other side of the bed, hoping against hope to find Suzanna there. It was empty though, and he wondered how she was. Would he ever see her again? Were she and Patty still back at the clinic or had they made their escape?

Slowly he stood up and went to the glass doors leading to a patio that sat just above some large rocks before the sandy shore. Seagulls squawked overhead, and he watched them as they dove in and out of the sea, flying free. He turned away suddenly. He was restless. He needed to do something.

Edgar made his way through the house, opening every door. Had they really left him out here all alone? In the living room he stopped and stared at the painting on the wall that seemed to stare back at him. He had commissioned it as an anniversary present for Suzanna. Alice had been just two years old, and they had brought her here only the one time, after that last trip to Alaska. In the portrait, Edgar and Suzanna were sitting side by side, as together they held Alice in front of them. The artist had done well in changing Alice's then tear streaked face into a smile. It had been over two months before she would even hug them, much less smile for them.

"Damn!" Edgar wondered how everything had gone so terribly wrong! He had thought that was all in the past though, but now the tear-streaked face of that little girl filled Edgar's mind, and he realized that they had failed as parents even then. He didn't want to fail again, but what could he do? He was isolated now. That had been the purpose of this home though. It was to be a place where they could completely retreat. For that reason, they had not even installed a land line, and they would be more than three miles across the island from the clinic. Now here he stood in this dream retreat turned virtual prison, or maybe he wasn't totally isolated.

Taking one last look at the portrait, he turned back down the hall and opened a secret door behind a wall panel. Making his way up the stairs he felt a flutter of hope as he saw it was still there.

***

Suzanna Morgan had lain awake that entire night. No one had come back to the room, and she couldn't stand it. She had first heard Patty's scream and then could have sworn she had seen two shadows fall just before the sound of the chopper's propellers filled the air. No more than a minute later she had seen the lights of the chopper as it took off.

Lowering herself gingerly into the chair beside the bed, she had used her one good leg to scoot it along as a kind of wheelless wheelchair. She first made her way to the restroom. The last thing she was going to do was allow them to make her wet herself. Then she painstakingly made her way to the balcony, stopping to rest and get some sustenance from the refrigerator.

When she finally made it out onto the balcony it had been just over an hour and she was drenched in sweat, but she had made it. Her fear was that Patty and Mathias had not.

As she looked over the edge, her miracle appeared to have been granted. She saw no shattered bodies lying on the beach below. Her relief was only momentary though as she wondered where they were. She was certain that at least Patty had fallen, and there was no way anyone could have survived a fall of that distance. Had a cleanup crew already retrieved the bodies? Of course, they had, she thought.

Had Mathias fallen too? She wondered. Would even Richter take off just after watching his own brother fall to his death? Something had not sat right with her from Mathias entrance last night though.

The wind was starting to gust, and the sunny sky was suddenly becoming most appropriately overcast.

Suzanna knew that she should try to make her way back inside before the threat of rain made itself manifest, but she was exhausted and dreaded being alone in the sterile room. The wind was cool, but nothing like the cold that chilled your bones in Seattle at this time of year, so she opted for scooting her way under the overhang of the balcony above and just sat, staring, not even knowing what to think.

***

Soren didn't know what to make of it. His shift had ended two hours ago, yet he found himself glued to the file before him. He had come across it quite by accident when he had gone to the archives to retrieve a previous test result requested to be faxed to a lab in the Northern Mariana's. Soren had no idea what to do with it. He still could hardly get his mind around the implications. According to what he was looking at, there had been human test subjects involved with experimental DNA injections into unborn fetuses for over forty years.

Chapter Thirty-Six

Alice and Sophie looked at each other as they left the salon. Sophie sported a black bob, and Alice's hair was now a rich mahogany that had been straightened and cut diagonally on the sides with long layers down her back.

Their next stop was a department store, where they purchased jeans, sweaters, and some good walking shoes. They also bought some prepaid cell phones, then grabbed some Chinese from the food court, and headed back to the hotel with their bags before going to the library.

There was a part of each of them that wanted to avoid finding out more, but that wasn't an option as they each sat down at a computer. Alice searched newspaper articles on business dealings and research of the various medical and pharmaceutical facilities, while Sophie focused on individuals such as the doctor who had signed her death certificate, and any others who were listed as having worked at the hospital where she had convalesced as a child. Alice also decided to contact a friend whom she thought could help, and asked him to run not only company names, but a background check on her parents.

Duyi was studying to be a computer programmer in Hong Kong. In fact, Alice had sponsored him when he came to the states to participate in an internship with Microsoft. Creating a new email account and giving the number from the prepaid phone, she emailed him her request.

***

Ben Wilson sat by Anne's bedside, as he waited for the test

results. He had raced to the clinic as soon as the call came. He could hardly believe it. Would God bring her back to him for Christmas? Then the thought struck him that she would be coming back to nothing. The farm was sure to be repossessed, leaving them with no home. Still, though it may be selfish, he needed her. He could deal with anything as long as his Anne was by his side. No matter who she had been meeting that night, he begged God to bring her back to him.

He had thought about calling Jack, but didn't want to get his hopes up, especially since he seemed to be dealing with so much in regard to Alice and Sophie.

Ben looked up at the sound of the door opening as Tom entered. Tom smiled, as he looked from the results on the clipboard he carried and back to Ben.

"Well?" Ben asked a bit impatiently.

"It looks good Ben, there's substantial increased brainwave activity, in fact from the looks of this..." he trailed off.

"What is it Tom?"

"Something is preventing her from coming around, and we still don't know why. Judging from the reaction the nurses witnessed, it sounds like it may be due more to psychological trauma rather than physical."

"That's good though. Right?"

"Yes. In that there is a higher likelihood of full recovery and no, because we don't know what it is, and as long as she's unconscious... Well, the point is we're kind of back to square one. Obviously, there was some physical trauma from the accident, but even then, according to the tests we thought she'd recover. Then the brainwave activity waned and stabilized into a chronic condition. The lack of activity from being in a prolonged coma seemed to be degenerative rather than restful and healing, but if the coma is due to psychological factors there's no way to project a prognosis. She could go either way.

If we at least knew what it was that was keeping her in this state, we might be able to do something, but as it stands all we can do is wait. This may have been the beginning of recovery or, well I hate to say it, but you have to be aware that it could be the opposite. If she's reliving a serious psychological trauma, it could be dangerous. Can you think of anything at all, any stressors she may have been going through?"

Ben sighed. All he could do now was think about what he so desperately wanted to forget and wonder about whomever she'd been meeting. "Nothing I can say off hand. I'll um, I'll try to think back, and I'll let you know if anything comes to mind," Ben said, as he turned away from Tom to look at Anne and fought back the tears that threatened to fall.

"Okay. You know where to find me."

"That I do. Oh! Tom, please don't say anything to Jack."

"He might be able to think of something you wouldn't."

"I can ask him in my own way, without getting his hopes up."

"Okay," Tom said, as he watched Ben worriedly. The man seemed almost more emotional today than he had when she'd first had the accident. Hard as it was, he would respect his wishes though and say nothing of Anne's episode to Jack. He should ask the nurses the same he thought as he closed the door.

***

Edgar tinkered with the radio controls. He had had the radio room installed for a combination of reasons and one of those had been to basically have a ship to shore link in case of an unforeseen emergency such as this. There was a similar unit installed at the clinic, and he would have to be careful to use a frequency that would not be intercepted. At first, all he got was static. The sky was overcast which he knew could cause problems with the reception. It had been so long since he'd used one of these. It took about an hour of fiddling with knobs before he finally heard a reply. It wasn't in a language that he understood, but perhaps they could understand him or at least relay him to someone who could.

Patty could see an outlet up ahead now. She had been gradually descending for quite some time but was still nervous about how far above the beach she may actually be. She looked for a place as the cave narrowed, where she could brace herself and see her position without risking a perilous fall.

Clinging to some roots that protruded through the wall of the cave, she eased herself down, not letting go until she found another solid hold. Her heart was beating so hard she could hardly breath, as she grabbed hold of the next root and it broke off. A scream escaped, as she slipped and felt the other root, she still clung to, begin to give way.

When she finally felt stable enough to look, she opened her eyes, and realized that the beach was no more than an eight or so foot drop from where she clung.

Carefully she braced herself between the two sides of the cave and tried to get a clearer view of what the landing area would look like. Maybe, she thought, she could get a handhold on a rock and ease herself down backwards onto the rocks she could now see directly below. She knew that to fall wouldn't kill her, but if she landed wrong, it could be fatal to the babies or cause serious injury and leave her unable to continue.

Gradually Patty made her way, angling herself toward the flattest rock surface below her. There had been a shrub growing out of the left side of the cliff right over the spot she hoped to land. Testing it with a sharp tug of her left hand, she felt reassured and grasped it with her right as well. Upon receiving her full weight, it began to give way, but it did not fully break from the cliff until she had one toe hold on the surface of the rock below.

Staggering as it broke free, she leaned into the cliff side and aside from some superficial scratches, was now safely on the ground.

Breathing a sigh of relief, she looked around in an attempt to get her bearings. She knew they must be looking for her. The babies were too important for them to just leave her for dead.

Mathias was on the cleanup crew that was sweeping the beach. Richter and Jonathan had taken off the night before after Jonathan had relocated Mr. Morgan, and Carl was left to monitor Mrs. Morgan and the rest of the lab.

He had been in shock when he first observed what appeared to be body parts scattered on the beach. Then he realized what Richter had done and it chilled him to the bone, as he had turned over the head in his hands that looked as though he were staring into a mirror and read the code.

Richter had made a prototype of him, similar to the one he had created of Alice before they created the biologically based one. He noted the synthetic skin and hair that felt so life like and noted that the gap between robot and human was smaller than what most people would care to or dare to believe.

He fingered the microchip behind the eyes and left ear. This robot would have been capable both of hearing and responding, and it would have done so in his own voice, but at Richter's command. That was the real divide between human and robot. As hard as he tried, neither Richter nor their father could ever fully dictate how he thought or felt. The idea of mind control was as old as time, but so is the basis of free will. A robot on the other hand, was devoid of free will, for it took the programming and control of a human for it to function.

Basic philosophy, Mathias thought. When he had studied it, it seemed its aim had been to deny a higher creative power such as God, but Mathias understood it to prove just the opposite. Man could never be God, because what man created, man must control. Whereas what God created was life with free will.

Richter's view was the opposite however, and he sought to create a life that was contrarily both a living human being, but under his complete control, down to the number of hairs on its head, its personality, and its intellect. The DNA experiments were Richter's way of what he believed would make him God. Mathias shuddered as he thought of it.

He was relieved when he had found no trace of Patty, but what did it mean? What did it mean for the babies she carried? He knew that if they had survived there were the means to maintain their life without Patty. Or could it be that she miraculously survived, perhaps even with minor injuries. It had happened before. He had once read about a man who fell eight floors and only sustained a broken leg. Could she be injured and hiding somewhere? He knew that she would rather die than to give birth here, and he wondered if perhaps she had survived only to allow herself to be carried away in the tide?

There was another possibility though. He knew the odds were against it, because the roof she had fallen from jutted over it, but he couldn't help but hope that somehow, she may have landed on the ledge. He knew it and its caves well. He had been an explorer and played there as a boy, entering from a cave on the other side of the island. It had been his secret place that he had never shared with his brothers. He remembered hiding on that very ledge as he listened to his father call for him from above.

He had sent the other two men back to the lab with parts of the mock him and told them he would finish up on his own. They didn't know they were looking for a human body as well, and if they had discovered her Mathias was to intervene, and they were either to be convinced she was another prototype or that she had committed suicide.

He looked out over the sea. The tide was still far enough out that he could make it around by way of the beach. It would be better that way, so that he wouldn't be seen in case he inadvertently led them to her.

Before he left, he looked up again and saw a form that could only be Suzanna Morgan sitting on the balcony. He wondered briefly who had helped her there and how long she had been there. A part of him considered going back and checking on her, but it was Patty who took priority, and he had to leave now if he was to make it to the caves ahead of the tide.

***

Shane listened as Yarnok read off the information she had received about the chopper's destination and what she had learned from Charice.

"Charice didn't know who the man was, but she did recall that Alice had shown her a photo he was in once and asked her about him," Yarnok said. "Apparently she thought her parents had hired someone to tail her. As for the chopper, it was hired in Vancouver, but is scheduled to land in Hagensborg at Bella Coola Airport."

"Hagensborg? Bella Coola? Where is that?"

"Northwest of you. In fact, if you can get to Abbotsford Air force Base in the next two hours Max has a buddy who will fly you."

"I can do that!" Shane said, as he turned onto the highway, and stepped on the accelerator. "Was there any passenger manifest? Who hired the chopper?"

"That's where it gets more interesting. It was hired under Morgan Acquisitions, and the name of the passenger is listed as Edgar Morgan."

"What?"

"Well, if nothing else, you can arrest this guy on identity theft."

"Not as long as he's in Canada I can't. Remember that little rule about jurisdiction?"

"Pardon my French, but screw jurisdiction! Not only is he traveling under an assumed identity, but he's likely a kidnapper. Shall I assume we won't see you for a few more days?"

"Probably. And put in a call to Larry Marquet at Interpol."

"Already done. I even took the liberty of faxing him the sketch."

"Well done, Yarnok. Thank you and thank Max. Was there anything else?"

"Nothing that I can give you anything solid on. You just focus on finding your wife, and we'll hold the fort here."

***

Alice got the first hit with some information on her parent's property holdings. She had been surprised to get a message from Duyi just an hour after she sent her own. The background check that he showed her listed more Morgan assets than what Alice had been aware of. Yes, she knew that her parents held international investments, but there were several private properties listed as well as business. Not only had she never seen these in the records, but she wondered why they would exist when her parents rarely went anywhere or did anything that wasn't directly related to the business.

The suite in New York was listed as leased under the business, as were several other similar properties, most of which she was aware of. The one in Hong Kong, however she was not, nor the one in Geneva. What bothered her the most though were the private property holdings in Alaska, The

Virgin Islands, The Marianas, and Washington DC. The property in the Marianas was in fact an entire small island of about three by five miles.

"Alice?" Sophie asked, popping her out of her speculations of what her parents were doing with so many properties.

"Did you find something?" Alice asked.

"Maybe, but first I need to know if Morgan has any holdings in Geneva?"

"As a matter of fact, they do. I just discovered that they even lease a suite there like the one in New York. Why? What connection did you find?"

"There's a Dr. Meschner. His name is on some of the papers in my file, and he's listed as having worked as a geneticist at a lab in Geneva, associated with one of the companies listed in the files from Mr. Amstead."

"Interesting."

"Why do I have the feeling you've found something interesting yourself?" Sophie questioned.

"Just more evidence of how little I know about the people who raised me. I ran a background check and there are properties listed that I should have been privy to when I did the books, but I never saw. One being the suite in Geneva, leased by Morgan Acquisitions, but four are listed as private properties. I can't imagine that they would maintain unused properties. There must be something going on at them. I'm going to punch in the addresses and see if I can bring up a satellite image of any of them."

***

Claire received the message back from Dr. Meschner before noon. He said that he would send a private ambulance to her that afternoon, which would take her to an airfield, from where she would be transported via a private plane and medically equipped helicopter.

She was instructed to pack nothing.

***

Patty was surprised and scared when she saw the house. She had thought that the entire Island was owned by the lab and that everybody lived in the apartments provided on site.

It was a lovely home, she thought. It was a white stucco with blue trim, reminiscent of a Greek island. It was also quite large and had a great swath of windows that faced the sea and opened onto a large, raised patio.

She saw no lights on, and she tentatively climbed the steps to the side of the patio where she could peek in through a smaller window.

For the most part it appeared deserted, but someone had to have been there recently. Everything was too clean, even down to the tile she now stood on. There were no dust covers, and as she walked around, she noted not even water spots from the sea spray, which would likely hit some of the windows at high tide.

She knew it may be dangerous, but she couldn't stay outside through another night. She was desperately hungry, and the tide was now on its way in. So, she tried the sliding door and was surprised when it slid open easily. Her heart raced as she tiptoed into the kitchen. At least if she had to make a run for it, she would do it with some nourishment.

Opening the door to the refrigerator, she found it fully stocked, and quickly grabbed a bag of bagels, and some apples, which she stuffed into her pockets. She then grabbed some water bottles and orange juice, before a sound from the floor above made her jump, and she hurried back out to the side of the patio, hoping to be able to see and access who was there before they saw her.

She was surprised at the man she saw appear from out of a wall and hurrying toward the patio area with binoculars.

Edgar Morgan had reached a radioman on a nearby trawler, and the man had agreed to send a skiff to pick him up, and then transport him back to his home island, where Edgar would be able to use a land line to call the United States.

"Mr. Morgan?" Patty ventured, as he came to the side of the patio, where she knelt by the window.

Edgar nearly had a heart attack at the sound of a voice behind him. He spun around and sighed in relief to see Patty and then the flood of worry came. If Patty was here, where was Suzanna?

"Patty? How did you get here? Where is Suzanna?"

"As far as I know she's fine. The last time I saw her she was in her bed at the lab. I fell on the way up to the roof, but landed on a ledge," she explained.

"How did you get here though? We're over three miles from the clinic."

"I found a cave, and it went all the way through to another cave just around the bend in the beach over there." She pointed. "How did you get here?"

"They tried to isolate me. I don't know their ultimate plan, but I have one that will get us both out of here. I had a radio room they didn't know about. Within the hour we should see a trawler. They agreed to send a skiff to bring me aboard and take me with them to an island where I can call via land line for help," Edgar explained, as he noted the contraband food in her hands. "There's no need to hide from me, so let's go back inside for now, I'll make us some coffee, and we can talk while we wait," he continued, as he looked through the binoculars. "I think I can see them, but it's just a dot right now." He lowered the binoculars and motioned Patty back inside.

"I'm afraid I owe you an apology for all this," Edgar said, as he located some coffee for himself and tea for Patricia. "You see this whole island, the lab, it's all mine, but what Richter is doing, well let's just say we are at odds about the intention of the research being done. The funny thing is, I didn't even realize that this lab was still active. My own lab, and I didn't even know," Edgar sighed. "How long have they kept you there Patty?"

"Too long," was all she could think to say. She was certain that by now Shane would have moved on with his life. She knew that it had been set up to look like she had left him. How could she ever explain what had really happened, much less expect him to believe her?

When Suzanna woke up, the rain had stopped, and the sun shone through the parting clouds. Under normal circumstances she would have considered it the most beautiful of days. This was her day to meet for tennis, and she wondered if anyone had missed her. Would anyone miss her? People at the office? Her charities? Had they even missed her at all? Would anyone be looking for her or Edgar? Of course, they would. She was being silly. Wasn't she? Edgar was in the office six days a week, sometimes seven. Of course, they would have had the police looking for them.

She realized in the recesses of her mind that she wasn't thinking rationally. A part of her knew that a cover story must have been arranged, but still. Then she thought about Alice and wondered where she was. Would anyone else be looking for her? They hadn't really allowed her much of a social life to be missed from, and if a plausible cover story for her and Edgar's absence had been executed, then surely Alice would be assumed in that, and no one would look for any of them. They ran a multi-million-dollar empire though she reasoned. There was no way it could go long without one of them, or could it?

How much had Albert known?

Suddenly she felt dizzy, and everything around her seemed too eerily silent as the white noise in her head became staggeringly loud. Even the gulls that seemed to be spinning overhead were silent. The sounds inside her head grew to a piercing pitch. She closed her eyes, and the cacophony grew louder. She could hear voices now, but she didn't dare open her eyes for the spinning sensation that overtook her.

As Mathias made his way around to the cave, he wondered if Patty had made it through, would she have found the house and possibly Mr. Morgan? He hoped so. He didn't even understand Richter's methods any more aside from the fact that they were horribly demented. Even Carl, he thought, was beginning to question Richter's sanity over the past days.

Richter had been present less and less, hiding away in his suite, only to come out in order to inflict punishment or make demands. He had become increasingly impatient and obsessed about receiving more samples from Geneva. He had also been secretive about the reason his absence was to be extended in Canada.

Mathias wondered briefly if he should call a conference with Jonathan and Carl? Richter had kept them so occupied lately that there had been no time when even he and Jonathan could speak privately. Did Richter suspect that Jonathan's sympathies were no longer in line with his? Did he dare include Carl, who had been a devoted puppy dog to Richter since childhood?

The rapidly encroaching tide broke Mathias revelry as it soaked his pant leg. He had better speed up if he didn't want to swim the rest of the way.

***

When Shane landed in Hagensborg he returned a missed call from Larry Marquet. Marquet had recognized the sketch as being similar to an unidentified suspect in a kidnapping case he had worked several years before where a geneticist and her then five-year-old daughter had been abducted near Geneva. The case had never been far from Larry's mind, as he had had a daughter the same age himself.

The woman had picked up her daughter from the daycare center provided by the lab where she worked, and neither had made it home. Cameras had shown a man resembling the sketch sitting for a prolonged period of time in the parking garage of the lab. At first, he had only been wanted for questioning as a potential witness, but five months later the woman had been dumped at a local hospital. She was incoherent and had undergone an abortion. The police attempt to interview her included showing her a picture of the man in question at which point she had gone into hysterics, and the interview ended.

Her physical health had been restored, but mentally she had never recovered, and her husband had no choice but to have her committed to a sanitarium. No trace of her daughter was ever found. It had been ten years now, and the father had enlisted multiple private agencies to look for his daughter with no forthcoming leads.

"So, what do you think we're looking at here Larry? This guy abducts a geneticist with her five-year-old daughter from a highly secured lab near Geneva. Then he takes my wife and now a deformed girl, working as a cleaning lady at an orphanage, who just happens to look like a sister of a missing person I'm looking for from Seattle."

"From what you're telling me though Shane, it sounds like the girl today, and your wife knew the man, and to some degree went with him freely. I mean the girl you just told us about walked out the door with him without a struggle, and your wife openly had breakfast with him and made no attempt of escape."

"I know. None of it makes any sense Larry. I was able to get a description of the car he left in from the airport here, and I'm hoping to be able to locate him, but there's not a heck of a lot I can do myself even if I do find him, except try to watch."

"Look, I've contacted our closest field office, and they're sending an agent to you. Take down this number."

Shane reached for a pen and paper from the seat beside him and jotted down the number Larry read to him.

"If you do locate this guy before the agent gets to you, I want you to notify him immediately."

"You better believe I will Larry."

"I've also sent the man's picture out to all the border patrols, so he shouldn't be able to get too far."

"Hang on a sec. Larry," Shane said, as he passed a burgundy SUV fitting the description of the one the man was seen leaving the airport in. "I may have just spotted him."

Just then a call came in from Yarnok on Shane's other line. Shane switched calls. "Tell me you have something good Yarnok? I've got Larry on the other line and the suspect's vehicle in front of me."

"I don't know if you'd call this good, but we deciphered that video clip you sent of the girl signing."

"And?"

"She was asking you for help, but not just for her. The signs she was giving mean "Help us."

"Us? Are you sure?"

"Positive."

"That means she may know where Patty is."

"Maybe, or it could be the Morgans or someone completely different."

"I know that," Shane replied, a bit more impatiently than he intended. "I have to go now."

"Wait."

"It's okay. Don't worry about it," he said, as he hung up and clicked back over to Larry.

"Are you still there Larry?"

"I'm here."

"The SUV is parked outside of a hospital in emergency parking. I'm going in."

"Got a name on the hospital?"

"Saint Xavier," Shane answered, as he entered and clicked off the phone.

At admitting Shane gave a description and asked the nurse if she had seen the man and or the woman with him. He also showed her a photo of Patricia, but she only shook her head. "You can check in the front lobby, but I'm afraid I need to ask you to leave the ER."

"How do I?"

"The second left, down the hall, elevator to level two," she said as she typed."

Shane glanced back out to where the SUV was parked. He didn't want to risk the man leaving while he was on a possible wild goose chase. They had parked in emergency parking, therefore Shane decided that emergency is most likely where they were, and his best bet was to watch the vehicle.

Going back to his rental, he looked up the phone number for the hospital and called the front lobby, once again giving a description of the man and woman with him.

"Do you have a name sir?" the nurse who answered asked?

"Have you seen them?"

"I'm afraid I can't give out random patient information based on a description. Even with a name you would have to be family."

"I'm not asking for information. I just want to know if you've seen them."

The response was a click, followed by a dial tone.

Chapter Thirty-Seven

The library was getting ready to close as Alice printed off the last of the satellite images she had pulled up of the properties listed under her family's holdings.

Duyi had also discovered and sent her information on the property in Hong Kong. It was a working genetic research lab.

"It's all starting to connect," Sophie said.

"It sure is. This makes perfect sense with the files on Mr. Amstead's computer. And it explains why they always kept such strict tabs on me. I was never a daughter to them. I was their science project," Alice answered, as she collected the printouts and tucked them in her bag.

"*We* were their science project," Sophie corrected.

"I'm sorry," Alice said, as they walked out into the frozen evening to the sounds of Christmas carols and crowds with arms full of shopping.

"They still need our help though."

"I know you're right. I'm angry at them Sophie, but I still love them. Whether they ever loved me, I don't know anymore, but I think that's one of the answers I need from them," Alice said. "We also need to find out more about Doctor Meschner and exactly what is going on at these labs. Hopefully Duyi will have more on that for us tomorrow."

"Alice?" Sophie asked as they walked. "Where are we going?"

They both stopped and looked at each other, and then at the sign pointing to the hospital.

"Is it?"

"No, It's not the same hospital I was in, but it is close to..."

"Where we were born," Alice finished.

"The only reference I saw to Dr. Meschner was connecting him to Geneva."

"He had to have been here at some time," Alice pointed out. "So, we may as well ask if anyone knows him. I don't see what it could hurt. It's only another kilometer."

Sophie took a deep breath of the frigid air. "You're right. It can't hurt to ask."

They walked the kilometer to the hospital entrance and into the lobby in silence.

"Can I help you?" asked the nurse behind the desk. "Visiting hours are over," she continued, as they approached.

"We just have a question," they said in unison, and the nurse, an owl eyed woman of around fifty stared at them.

"Yes?" asked the nurse.

"I was wondering," Sophie started, "if a doctor I heard about might work or have worked here?"

"Does this doctor have a name?" asked the nurse.

"Dr. Meschner?"

"One moment please." the nurse said as she typed something into her computer. "He's not on staff, but he is here."

"Now?" asked Sophie, startled.

"Yes, he's here as a consultant. He's scheduled to give a lecture in the morning, so if you'd like to speak with him, I can give him a message to call you, or you can go to the hotel where the lecture is being held tomorrow morning."

"Which hotel?"

"It's the Palace hotel, just over near the train station."

Sophie and Alice both stood stunned as the nurse continued.

"The lecture starts in the ballroom at 9:00 a.m. Are you genetics students?" she asked them.

"It's a field I'm interested in," Alice answered.

"Well, I believe you'll need to get a ticket to the lecture. Let me just make a call and check." The nurse dialed the phone

"Yes. Is Doctor Meschner still here? At dinner? Okay, well, do you happen to know if it's still possible to get tickets for his lecture in the morning? Yes. I have two young women here with an interest in genetics who would like to attend. You do? Let me ask them. Our lab techs have two tickets that they won't be able to use. They're $80.00 each."

"We'll take them," Alice answered.

The nurse smiled and picked up the phone again. "Yes. They would like them," she said, as she wrote down what looked like code on a note pad. "Thank you, Aaron. Goodnight," she finished and hung up the phone. "The tickets are available at the hotel concierge. This is the ticket confirmation code you need, and you should be set," she said as, she handed it to Alice.

"Thank you, Nurse Adelphi," Alice replied, looking at the nurse's badge.

"Yes. This is more than we'd hoped for. Thank you," Sophie added.

"I'm glad I could help. I wish I could go myself, but I'm on duty at noon, and the lecture goes until four. It's such a fascinating field. Good luck to you in your studies!" Nurse Adelphi said with a smile.

"Yes. Thank you!" Alice said again.

"Goodnight," Sophie added.

"Goodnight ladies," Nurse Adelphi called, as they exited.

"I can't believe this!" Sophie said once they were back outside.

"Neither can I, but ..."

***

Carl opened the door to the cabinet Richter had hastily closed when he had come in the other day, ostensibly, to discuss what should be done next with Suzanna Morgan. Carl had suspected that Richter was hiding something, but when he discovered the empty injection bottles, he knew, and it shook him to his core.

If Richter was suffering the kind of infections that the bottles suggested, then what would that mean for him? He had helped, and even subjected himself to various tests, and injections in assisting in Richter's experiments. Jonathan and Mathias had not been included, but Carl's goals were nearly as lofty as what Richter had shared in confidence with him. What Richter had not shared were any of the adverse effects that he had been suffering.

Carl grabbed one of the discarded bottles and strode down the hall to Richter's office.

Inside he punched in the code to the filing cabinet drawer on the lower left side of the desk and thumbed through the contents until he came to a folder marked subject S-1, which was the code Richter used to specify himself on the tests they ran on each other.

Then behind that file, he noted one marked S-2, which would be himself. It was only half the thickness of Richter's own test file, yet it was twice the thickness of the one Carl kept in his own private files.

As he flipped through the pages of S-2 he knew. He was no different than anyone else in Richter's eyes. He was just another Guinea pig. Richter had lied to him, falsifying the test results, but here he looked at both the original side by side with the falsified results he had been given. For the first time in his life he felt, rather than admiration for Richter, an undefined rage.

He had stood by Richter, protected his secrets from their own brothers, because Richter had told him that he suspected both Jonathan and Mathias to be against them.

Carl had always found Mathias weak, just as Richter had, but now he realized that Mathias rebellion against Richter was in fact his strength.

***

Jack felt lost. Even Nick, as worried as he was for Sophie, didn't fully understand how helpless Jack felt. Not only was he worried about both Sophie and Alice, but in a matter of weeks, his dad would be homeless, and everything they had worked for would belong to the bank. Jack would need to pull back from his skating to find regular work for himself, and some way to continue paying for his mother's care as well as find a larger place where both he and Ben could live.

He had spent the afternoon talking with Nick, who suspected that the O'Hares knew more about Sophie's origins than they let on. The thought had crossed Jack's mind as well, but he could fathom no reason for them to lie, other than what his own had been, to protect Sophie.

Afterwards Jack had gone out to take care of the sheep, and some basic maintenance on the farm, while his dad had sat by his mother's side at the care center. Now it was Jack's turn. He had promised his dad not to leave her, pleading with Ben to go home and rest so that he wouldn't wind up in a hospital too.

It was nine 9:00 p.m. as Jack sat holding his mother's hand. He had started to ramble on. He knew it wasn't the most encouraging topic to talk to her about, but right now he needed to talk to his mom, whether she responded or not. He started telling her about the suspicions they had of the type of research Sophie and Alice were a product of, and what the scope of it might be, when he felt a gentle squeeze of his mother's hand.

Startled, he looked at her. "Mom?"

She squeezed his hand again, and he reached to push the call button.

"No," came the muffled whisper, as he leaned over her, and

he stopped short.

"Mom?"

"I know Jack."

"I'll get a nurse."

"No," Anne whispered, as she tried to open her eyes. "Need to tell you…Sophie…"

Jack saw her eyelids flutter as she strained to look at him.

"Let me get the nurse."

"No. No nurse. No doctor. Please no," Anne managed as she squeezed Jack's hand again.

Jack felt torn. He didn't understand, but after months his mother was actually speaking to him, and so he squeezed her hand back, looked at the monitors, which all appeared to show steady vitals and said, "Okay mom. No nurses or doctors right now. Just us."

"Water?" Anne asked. Her throat felt parched.

Jack raised the back of the bed and applied a damp cloth to his mother's lips.

Anne sucked in the moisture, feeling the cool trickle ease her throat as she struggled against the weariness of her body to open her eyes. She looked at Jack and saw that he looked as exhausted as she felt. Their eyes met, and they smiled at each other as a tear rolled down Jack's cheek.

"Don't cry. I'm here Jack."

"Mom," Jack said, as he pulled her to him. "We missed you." His body shuddered with emotion. "I love you mom."

"I love you too Jack. I need to sleep a little now. Please promise you won't tell. I just need to rest, then I'll tell you," Anne said, as she squeezed Jack's hand again, and let her eyes close, as he lowered her back onto the pillows.

"Tell me what mom?"

"About Sophie."

"Mom?"

"Sleep," Anne whispered.

Jack watched her breathing, slow and steady as she slept and wondered, what did she know?

Chapter Thirty-Eight

Albert was scared. He knew when he got the message from reception that he had not made as clean a getaway as he had hoped.

The message was a request for him to go to a café near the train station, where he would meet a contact, and pick up a vital package. It then gave precise instructions for him to pass the package immediately on to another undisclosed party.

Soren was surprised by the request. Instead of the usual delivery system for the samples, he was to deliver them to a café in one of the busiest sections of Geneva. A faxed photo of the man who was to pick them up had been slipped under the door of his office along with a request for an unusually large amount of an anti-rejection serum.

The fact that the request came in a fax, which was then hand delivered, made it all that much clearer that this was a covert operation, and that whoever was running it did not want to be traced. Even the fax numbers on the page had been cut off, with only the time stamp remaining. It had come in at 4:00 a.m. This in itself told him only that there was a likelihood that it had come from another time zone.

Normally Soren would have gone to talk to Trudie, his section supervisor, but she had already left a message on his voice mail. She knew about the delivery.

Soren's conscience had been screaming at him ever since he discovered the files on the project. What was he supposed to do? Expose it? He didn't have enough tangible evidence. He needed to know who was behind it first.

It was two days before the vacation time he had requested for the holidays was to begin. He had promised Magdeline that he would call and confirm the reservation for her parents, who were coming in from Milan and staying for the birth of their first grandchildren. He got on well with them and knew she'd be well cared for if he were away for a few days. He also knew that they might not get along so well anymore if he did what he was thinking of.

Once he was away from the secured area where his calls could be traced and recorded, he would call the travel agency, and request information on flights to the Marianas. Then he would call Magdeline to tell her he was on his way into Geneva, and not to take the train home, as he would pick her up, take her to a nice dinner, and try to find a way to explain why he had to do what he was planning.

He reasoned that since the Marianas had always been the final delivery destination in the past, that the research being done must be nearby. He hoped he was making the right decision as he went to retrieve the samples from the cooler and sign out a company car equipped with another cooler that would preserve the integrity of the samples for the drive into the city.

Integrity, Soren mused was an interesting concept, especially considering the sources of these particular samples.

***

Claire was more than ready when the helicopter finally arrived at Saint Xavier hospital. She had been forced to wait in a plane on the tarmac of a private airfield in Juneau without her pain meds for over three hours due to high winds and low visibility from the falling snow. She was beyond exhausted, and the only thought that kept her going was the hope that she could somehow save the lives of her family.

***

Shane had waited all day in his rental car. He had eaten nothing since his breakfast early that morning, and he was about ready to call Larry again, when the call came in that an agent by the name of Philip Katz would be there to join him in ten minutes time.

Katz had the look of a seventeen-year-old high school kid, and Shane had a hard time believing that he could be a field agent for Interpol. Katz however had made a smart move that caused Shane to give the kid the benefit of the doubt. He had arrived with pizza, cinnamon sticks and drinks, including a thermos of coffee.

Shane pointed out the SUV that he had followed to this point and brought Katz as up to date as he could, being careful to not divulge too much of his personal stake in this.

It was just past 8:00 PM. when they saw the lights from the chopper as it landed.

"That's the most activity I've seen here all day," Shane commented.

"Are you sure they're in there?" Katz ventured.

"I'm not sure of anything, but I don't know where else they could be," Shane stated, as he downed some coffee. "Like I said, it's been dead here all day. I have a view of the only drives in or out, and the only people who have left are doctors and nurses who I saw well enough to know they weren't him. The only other traffic has been arrivals. Two ambulances and a few staff. Look, I don't want to be rude, but do you mind if I ask you..."

"How old I am?"

"Well?"

"Don't worry. I get that all the time. I'm twenty-five, and I've been working for Interpol for four years. I grew up on a military base in Germany, and I'm fluent in German, English,

French, Spanish, and Arabic. I can also speak some Italian. I have a degree in physics and computer science. Aside from the basic defense and surveillance tactics I'm also trained in decoding and ..."

"Okay, okay. Thanks for the bio. I'll trust you're qualified. What do you make of that?" Shane asked, as he pointed to the two ambulances whose lights had just activated. "It looks to me like they're getting ready to go somewhere."

"I'll go take a closer look. I'll use channel three," Katz said, tossing a miniature radio transmitter to Shane and jumping out before Shane could protest.

***

Edgar poured himself another cup of coffee and some tea for Patty. They had been talking for two hours now, yet when Edgar looked out towards the dot that he assumed was the trawler he had made contact with, he noted no discernable movement.

"Perhaps they anchored, and we just can't see the skiff?" Patty asked hopefully.

"They'd be too far out. No. Either they were farther away than they thought, or they changed their minds," Edgar said, as he stared blankly out the window.

Just then they heard a whistle from outside, and Patricia's heart jolted. "It can't be."

"What? What is it, Patricia?"

"That's the signal Mathias would sometimes use to let me know it was him coming and not..." Patty trailed off as she stared out at the figure who now stood at the window.

He tried the door, but Edgar had locked it.

"Patty? Edgar?" Mathias called. "Please let me in."

"Don't. It can't be him."

"Whichever one of them it is, we need to have a little chat,"

Edgar replied, as he went to the door.

"It could be a trap!" Patty's hands began to shake, as Edgar opened the door.

"Patty. Thank God!" Mathias said, as he entered, but Edgar blocked him from going to her.

"Who are you?"

"I'm Mathias."

"Mathias is dead," Patty said. "He fell last night with me."

"It wasn't me Patty. I swear," Mathias said. "I discovered that Richter would be waiting and didn't come."

"Then who was it?"

"Richter programmed a clone to trick you."

"A clone?"

"One of the projects Richter is working on is the ability to make clones that are half human, built from our DNA, but half synthetic, and programed with computerized brains."

Patty stared in disbelief.

"It's true Patricia," Edgar cut in. "What he's saying about Richter creating clones is true. I know, because he showed me one of Alice, and I couldn't even tell the difference from my own daughter."

"That explains what I thought I saw this morning then. They *were* picking up body parts."

"Yes."

"What are we supposed to do?" Patty asked. She looked to her swollen belly as the babies inside kicked, and she looked from Mathias to Edgar."

"You wouldn't happen to know anything about that fishing trawler offshore there? Would you Mathias?" Edgar ventured.

"Let me take a look," Mathias said, motioning to the binoculars.

Edgar unblocked his way, and Patty watched him cautiously.

"A clone wouldn't know our whistle," Mathias said, as he

retrieved the binoculars from the counter beside her.

"Oh Mathias!" Patty sobbed and fell into his arms. "I'm so scared. I want my life back!"

"I know," he soothed, and kissed her forehead. "Now let me take a look at this trawler you're talking about."

They walked outside together. Mathias, with far superior vision to Edgar, zoned in on the vessel in question and sighed. "It's owned by the Tungshing Corporation. Ring any bells?" he asked Edgar.

"Yes. Morgan Acquisitions bought them out about twenty years ago. They ship cargo between Asia and the United States."

"And?"

"And one of my business partners, maintained a portion of the company under a third-party corporation that allowed them to continue doing business as Tungshing and supplying...supplying this," Edgar sighed.

"Exactly. If they're making a delivery, they'll send their helicopter to the lab with it."

"Wait," Edgar stopped Mathias. "I know it's a larger trawler, but you expect me to believe they have a helicopter hiding out there?"

"It's a mini-copter in the cargo hold. The deck opens and voila! All the rigging is collapsible, giving plenty of room for a landing pad. That being said, they may stay anchored out until our chopper returns to pick it up. It's rare that anyone aside from the labs own two choppers is allowed to land."

"Two choppers?" Patty asked.

"Yes. There is an emergency backup in case something happens while the main helicopter is away. It's not as simple as what you're thinking though."

"Why not? Why can't we just take the second chopper and escape?"

"For one thing, it only accommodates four passengers."

"That's perfect! Me, you and the Morgans!"

"No. Like I said, it's not that simple," Mathias continued. "The smaller chopper doesn't have enough fuel to go beyond the airfield on the next island, and Richter has people there."

"Richter's not here though, and for all intents and purposes, you're the elder brother and senior over him. Surely, they'd listen to you. Hell, would they even be able to tell you apart?" Edgar argued.

"How is it that you were willing to hijack a helicopter last night with Richter here and not now with him gone?" Patricia questioned.

"For exactly that reason. With Richter here we would have been safer as Jonathan could help contain his reaction. If we leave now, he will be notified, and he'd have access to more resources than you can imagine. We'd be in even more danger, and so would everyone left here, who Richter would blame. The network that Richter has is beyond anything that he would dare to share with me, and over the last five or so years he's grown more and more secretive about his goals. I believe that he has projects going on outside that even Carl and Jonathan know nothing of."

"He's right," came a voice that caused them all to turn.

"Suzanna!" Edgar exclaimed, as he ran to the side of a wheelchair where she sat, unconscious.

"She's fine," Carl reassured. I just gave her a tranquilizer for the trip over. "It's good to see you look alright too," he said, looking Patricia over, as she backed away to stand behind the kitchen counter where she figured, she'd at least have access to a knife should she need it. "I'm glad to see you here too Mathias. We need to talk brother."

***

Katz radioed Shane as he watched the girl he had described being hurried into the ambulance by the man matching the photo Marquet had sent. The man then entered the back of the second ambulance with a woman on a stretcher. Katz would follow separately in his car, in case the ambulances separated. He would stay with the man while Shane would follow the girl.

***

Alice woke up in a cold sweat from the nightmare. In her dream the man had chased her through Seattle, and then through the streets of Quebec, and just when she thought she had escaped him, he was in front of her. She turned and he was behind her. No matter which direction she ran, he was there.

Alice got up and got a cold bottle of water from the mini bar and sipped it while she considered the dream. He'd been watching her for years. She assumed he was a private detective her parents had asked to watch her. If that were true though, why had they never confronted her? She had asked herself this question a million times but had no answer. Now she did. She was certain that as much as her parents had kept tabs on her that it was someone else who was having her watched, and it had to be connected to what she was and to the people who had kidnapped her parents.

She sipped the water, as she considered, and noted the rapid eye movement that indicated Sophie's own intense dream.

She was going to stay with the doctor again. They were celebrating her third birthday and there were other children. She was excited because there were no other children at the hospital. The man stood behind her, with his hands on her shoulders as the other children sang happy birthday. There were five of them, but Sophie could only make out two, a little boy of about five years and another little girl with red curls. She could also hear a baby fussing somewhere in the background.

After the singing, they all decided to play hide and seek. They had just started to count when there was a knock at the door. A man with a beard and an angry look on his face pushed his way in. Sophie had run to hide in the coat closet. She could hear the breathing of someone else in the closet with her and reached out her hand to feel the curls of another girl. They held each other's hands as the man tromped through the house, shouting something Sophie couldn't understand.

She peeked through the tiny keyhole of the closet door and saw the man's face. His gray eyes squinted and angry. She moved further back into the closet, pulling the other girl with her. She could hear the man's steps getting closer. The doorknob turned.

Sophie sat bolt upright, and Alice ran to her side.

"It was just a dream Sophie. Look at me," Alice coaxed, as Sophie's breathing began to calm. "It was just a dream."

"No. It was more than that."

"What was it about?"

Sophie got up and walked over to get a bottle of water of her own. "It was my third birthday. Remember the other little girl I thought I remembered?"

"Yes?"

"We were playing hide and seek, and this man showed up. He was angry, but I hid before he could see me. I went into a coat closet and the other girl was already hiding in there. The man was yelling, and then he came to the closet and turned the knob..."

"And?"

"And that's when I woke up. It wasn't a dream though. It was a memory. I'm sure of it."

"I had a dream too. Only mine was a nightmare, but in a way, it was also a memory."

"What was it about?"

"A man who was following me in Seattle. I had always thought he was someone my parents had hired, but now I think it's someone linked with who we are and whoever kidnapped my parents."

"What did he look like?" Sophie asked, recalling the man from her dream.

"Tall, blond, about our age."

"Definitely not the same man from my dream then."

"What did the man in your dream look like?"

"He was middle aged, with a beard, and scary eyes, balding, and he wore a suit with some kind of badge on it. I just remembered that, but I don't know what it said. His voice was deep and threatening. The doctor I was staying with was afraid of him. I think he may be the one who killed him."

"I didn't know that you knew he was dead?"

"I don't, but why else would I have never been able to find his name? All I remember was calling him Doctor T. He was clean shaven. I remember him shaving. He had brown eyes, thick brown hair, he smiled a lot, and he used to read books to me in funny accents. I don't really remember the shape of his face though. He seemed young for a doctor, and I only remember him coming to the hospital when he picked me up. I used to pretend that he was really my dad. I tried to call him that once. It's the only time I remember him yelling at me, but then he apologized, and said that I should wait until I had a real mom and dad to call that. Then I did, and this is the most I've remembered about Doctor T since. I can't help but think he must be dead though. It's the only thing that makes sense."

"Or maybe it's just easier for you to believe he's dead over the idea that he didn't adopt you himself? What about the other little girl from your dream? If she's one of us, did she live with him sometimes too?"

"I don't know. I don't have any other memory of her. You did though."

"If she's the same girl. We don't know how many of us there could be. In fact, I think that may be a good question to pose at tomorrows lecture, should our Doctor Meschner happen to bring up the subject of DNA in fertility treatments."

***

Albert had waited and watched from the train depot as the car marked only with the labs insignia on the side arrived, and Soren headed to a table at the cafe. His palms were sweating, and he knew if he messed this up his life was on the line. He needed to make the contact at precisely 11:01 by the station clock. Then he was to board the train at 11:09, give the package to a man in compartment 8B, and disembark the train before it left the station at 11:15. He had set the timers on his watch for each event, and he now strode forward to the table where Soren waited.

Soren had spotted Albert, who was going under the alias of Malcolm Davenport, as soon as he stepped into the street. He was hard to miss and looked like he was better suited to a magazine cover than an undercover drop off.

Soren stood and greeted him in an attempt of casual cordiality. The man's tension was tangible though, and when Soren asked if he would like to join him in a coffee, he only pointed to his watch, reached for the case and thanked him in American accented English. Soren waited for the man to enter the station, left enough on the table to cover his bill and followed.

He did not spot the man again until he saw him exiting a train, empty handed, ten minutes later, just as it departed.

Soren checked the board and saw that the train's destination was Paris. He was in luck too. It was an express, so no one was scheduled to get off along the way. It would also allow him plenty of time to get the car back and catch a flight, that would hopefully allow him to meet the train. Unfortunately, it meant that he would have to come up with a way to explain to Magdeline, granted an impromptu trip to Paris would be easier to explain than the Marianas.

Chapter Thirty-Nine

"I was hoping we might call a summit so to speak," Carl said. "I'd like to speak first alone with Mathias and..."

"No Carl. They have as much right if not more than me to know the truth. It's time we put the pretense aside, and get real baby brother, that is if you're capable of being real. Do you even know?"

"Fair enough," Carl continued. "First you should know that Richter isn't as in control as you may all think. When you bowed out of continuing the research Mr. Morgan, Dr. Meschner or dad, as he used to like us to call him, continued it."

"I got that much," Edgar replied. "That was why he was so adamant about keeping tabs on Alice."

"Exactly," Carl answered. "I think you should also know that he planned everything, except that is, Dr. Imberk's stroke. He used to call it a stroke of luck."

"I never realized just how sick he is."

"Yes, and you may assume that I am as well. You may even be right, after all I have more of his DNA than any of my brothers plus some even less appealing," Carl continued.

"Why are you telling us this?" Edgar asked.

"Maybe because I have some of your DNA too, or maybe because I'd like to live on. I'd like to see that utopia that Richter claims will come of this. Maybe I even want to take over from him when he dies, because I think he is, dying that is."

"What are you talking about?" Mathias asked.

"Richter has been taking additional DNA injections and not responding well. The foreign bodies are overwhelming even his enhanced immune system, and he's been taking more and more anti-rejection drugs along with stem cell injections every day. He thinks if he can just get the right combination, that he'll overcome it and become superhuman."

"That's what the two of you have been up to, and you've been taking in additional DNA as well?"

"Yes, as well as stem cell transplants. I didn't really know exactly what I'd been taking until today though. I trusted Richter, and then I discovered that he'd been adjusting the test results he gave me."

"Are you sick too?" Mathias asked.

"Not like Richter. Not yet anyway. I haven't had nearly as many of what he calls enhancement injections."

"So, let's cut to the chase Carl. Are you here to join with and help us or only because you're afraid for yourself? Who is this about? Do you give a damn about anyone beside yourself? Be honest. You weren't helping Richter to help him."

"We all wanted the same thing! Don't you remember? We all wanted what he wanted!"

"We didn't all want it for the same reasons though or at the expense of innocent lives!" Mathias retorted, as he looked to Patty.

"You think she's innocent! Do you know who she is?"

"She's our sister! You can't blame her for that!"

"What is he talking about Patricia?" Edgar asked.

"I didn't know. I..."

"She didn't know anything until she came here," Mathias interjected. "You know that," he said, turning to Carl.

"Are you saying that Meschner is her father?" Edgar asked.

"No and yes," Mathias replied. "Patricia was conceived the old-fashioned way by Meschner's younger half-brother and his wife. The brother was a missionary doctor, and he trusted his brother to care for his wife and unborn child while he was away. Instead, he used her as a test subject, and injected his own DNA into the fetus. The match was close enough that Patricia showed no obvious adverse effects, and only her mother needed to be on anti-rejection medication. It didn't work for her mother though and she died due to an intense infection shortly after Patricia's birth. Her father hid Patricia in a convent under the care of some nuns he had worked with."

"He was also Meschner's assistant!" Carl added.

"She's a victim Carl. Can't you see that? We all are!" Mathias continued. "Meschner thinks of her as his own daughter. She's the closest genetic child he has and that's why we've kept trying to, well..."

"Breed me," Patricia finished for him.

"Where is Meschner now?" Edgar cut in, asking Carl and heading off his reply to Mathias.

"Right now, he's with his favorite son in Quebec City, Canada. He runs a lab and even lectures out of a university there sometimes."

"And Jonathan? Where is he in all this now?"

"He left last minute with Richter. Doctor Meschner, AKA dad, called last night with an errand for him, and that's all I know," Carl answered.

"Mathias?"

"As far as I know he's telling the truth."

"Exactly how widespread has this project gone?" Edgar asked. "I know Meschner was conducting experiments before we met, and his test results were why he was brought on as a partner. What we didn't know was anything about any of you, and you're all older than Alice."

"You mean how many living specimens does dear ole' dad have running around the planet? Not a clue. I'm not sure he knows himself. He has as many labs as Morgan had properties he could work under. Do you recall the locations of all your properties Mr. Morgan?" Carl asked.

"Dear God. God help us all, and forgive me if it's possible," Edgar sighed, as he collapsed into a chair and stared at the portrait of Alice, whose painted in smile seemed to have vanished as she stared back at him. "This is all my fault," he finished, as he looked to where Suzanna had been laid on the couch beside him.

***

Katz followed closest to the ambulances, while Shane fell a good mile back just in case they might recognize him or his rental car. They had been on the same highway for over half an hour when the ambulance carrying the girl exited.

Katz radioed the exit to Shane, who accelerated, determined not to lose them. The road off of the exit was rural, and it was only by the grace of a nearly full moon that he was able to spot the Ambulance, which had turned off all of its lights. Shane followed suit, praying that he had not already been spotted. Then he changed his mind and switched to his brights as he saw the shadow of a cargo plane descending. By its lights, Shane spotted a runway in the distance. He sped up, soon passing the ambulance, and honking loudly as he went around it. Following a hunch, he continued speeding past the entry of the airstrip until he spotted a driveway, which he ducked into. Then he turned his lights off again and turned the car back around to face the airstrip, where his nose was telling him the ambulance would rendezvous with the plane.

He waited ten minutes, knowing that there were no other turn offs, and when the ambulance had still not passed, he made his way back toward the airfield, pulling his car to a stop just outside the gate and radioing Katz.

The ambulance had turned its lights back on and sat near the end of the landing field, as Shane took his binoculars out of the glove box for a closer look.

Katz radioed his position as within two miles of Shane, and it was a minute later that the second ambulance passed across the airfield from an entrance on the other side and parked next to the first, as Shane and Katz both watched from their opposite posts.

The older woman emerged on foot from the ambulance with the support of a medic as the younger woman ran as best she could towards her. Shane watched as they embraced in what appeared to be some kind of strange reunion. Then the man, who and been standing back watching, came and assisted them into the waiting cargo plane.

The radio beeped, and Shane's phone rang at the same time with a call from Selma. Shane would have to call her back. Right now, he had to focus here and on not losing his only lead to Patty. Shane listened as Katz told him they had an itinerary for the plane that showed it routed to Geneva.

Katz made a reservation for them on a commercial liner, while Shane dialed Selma and kept an eye on the subjects.

"Thank God, Shane! You won't believe what I found on Alice Morgan's private iPad. We need to find her and fast!"

"Whoa. Selma, slow down. What are you talking about?"

"I'm talking about a girl who may know a whole lot more about what's going on than we could have imagined."

"What are you saying?"

"I'm saying that I don't know if she's in danger, but from what I've read, she may become a danger!"

***

Alice looked at the Bible beside her bed. Sophie had managed to go back to sleep, but all Alice could do was think about what she had read.

Every time she closed her eyes she saw the man's face, and just like every time she had seen him, she began to feel at war within herself. It was as if he had some kind of power over her. She had thought the feelings stemmed from the guilt of sneaking around behind her parent's backs, but it was more than that, and the passage she had just read reminded her of those feelings. She had been tempted, tempted to do things that every fiber of her being screamed were wrong, and a part of her was feeling that temptation again. Could she resist it as Jesus had in the book of Luke, or would her doubt cause her to finally give in to it?

She'd discussed the subject several times with Sophie about their humanness. Sophie had been able to more or less come to peace with it. She believed God had given her a spirit that made her who she was and that was what made her human, regardless of her DNA or anything else.

Even though she had agreed, Alice herself hadn't fully come to that point. She still questioned if she believed the reality of God, much less if his spirit lived inside of her. Her prayer had been answered, she remembered smiling, as she touched the blemishes on her chin, but what if that had just been due to a difference in the medication?

She had felt so tired the last couple of days, but as these temptations once again flooded her mind, she felt a surge of energy, a strange power that scared her.

She tried to think of Jack. She didn't want to hurt him. She didn't want to hurt anyone, but something within her wanted to control them in the same way her parents had tried to control her. She wanted power, just as Satan had tempted Jesus with, in verse six. She was beginning to be afraid of herself again in a way she hadn't felt since the last time she had seen the man watching her. She thought back to that night on the ferry. She'd laughed about it before, but it was the power she'd felt at her escape that she'd forgotten. Now the memories returned of the need to run, not to escape him so much as herself. She had spent the rest of that night dancing at a club, trying to eliminate the pent-up tension she couldn't explain. He wanted power too, she thought, as she dressed hurriedly. Unsure why, she grabbed the Bible, put it in her purse and left Sophie sleeping, as she went downstairs to the lobby.

***

Jack hadn't realized that he'd fallen asleep until the nightmare woke him. All he could remember was Alice's face and wanting to protect her from herself. He rubbed his eyes, and looked at his mother, who appeared to still be sleeping peacefully. His neck ached where it had bent to lean against the chair as he'd dozed, and he massaged it as he stood, and went to the restroom.

After splashing water on his face, he went into the hall to get a cup of coffee from the vending machine and was surprised to see the elder Doctor Tom Marshall.

He considered telling him about his mother, but she had been adamant about no doctors. He would talk to Tom later he decided as he went back to sit with his mother. He wanted to be certain he was there when or if, he had to consider, she woke up again. He prayed she would and soon, before the nurses made their rounds and his father came back. She had wanted to tell him something, obviously something important about Sophie. He wondered for an instant if she had heard him talking and was imagining something based on the crazy story he had confided in her. How could it be anything else? He reasoned, but then again, what if it were?

Nick came over to the O'Hare's early to have breakfast with them and let them know that Sophie had called him once again. What he decided not to tell them was that she had called because Alice had disappeared.

Sophie had woken at 6:00 to the sound of the hotel room door closing, and when she hadn't been able to locate Alice by seven, she had been in such a panic that she had called, and he had convinced her to tell him where they were. Nick managed to book a flight leaving at 10:00 that morning. Sophie promised to call again just before the seminar at 9:00, and if Alice was still missing, Nick would join her at the hotel around noon.

***

Sophie was filled with an ominous sensation. There had been something different about Alice when they talked after waking from their respective dreams, but Sophie had been too caught up in her memory to put her finger on it. She had fallen back to sleep trying to remember more of the pieces that she prayed might lead them to answers.

At first, she assumed that Alice, not wanting to wake her had just gone down to maybe get a newspaper and would be back, or at least call the room about meeting for breakfast. She asked the waitresses if they had seen her, but they had not arrived until 6:30, and no one saw a woman fitting Alice's description.

Alice had spotted him the moment that she walked into the lobby. Her nightmare had followed her, and for an instant returned her gaze with a mock smile. Had he recognized her? She ducked into the ladies' room and took stock of her appearance. She looked different, but was it different enough to fool a man who had followed and observed her for years?

When she had gone back through the lobby he was gone. She wrapped her coat around her and stepped outside. Falling snow nipped at her cheeks, as she began to walk. She didn't know where she was walking, only that she had to get away. She couldn't risk being with Sophie right now, not with these feelings tearing at her like some evil demon who whispered in her ear. It was like she was in one of those movies where the person has a demon on one shoulder and an angel on the other, except she wished her angel would start speaking up.

She stopped at a coffee shop. She felt overwhelmingly famished and ordered two egg and ham bagels with cream cheese, and a large coffee. She tried to sit and read the paper as she ate, but it was as though she had to move. She couldn't stop moving her legs. This was different from the feeling she'd had in the room and at the dance club. The last time she had felt this way was back in college as she had watched all of the students, who were years older than her, stream past her across the campus. She remembered feeling lost in a wave that was about to crush her, and she had run at breakneck speed to her class.

She wanted to run now. She closed her eyes and tried to breathe deeply as she chewed her breakfast bagel. She had just begun to gain some control back when he spoke.

"Alice?"

It had been a question, but she had turned, and once again their eyes had met. She wanted to run worse than ever, but there was nowhere to run.

***

Selma had gone on and on about entries she had found in Alice's iPad. She had described them as hidden blogs. She said that there appeared to be almost two different people writing, and each was hidden behind its own layer of encryption, which had been difficult even for Selma to penetrate.

Some of the entries Selma described sounded the opposite of the composed Alice that people had come to know. The opposite of everything else discovered about her so far. Some of the entries had even been violent and Selma was sending them to a psychologist for further assessment, but they had been enough to scare her, and that wasn't an easy thing to do.

Shane had put Yarnok into the lead because of her former acquaintance with Alice and Asher would deal with all the external questioning and whatever else Yarnok may need help on. He knew Dave would rail for a moment, but they were all good friends in the end. Shane didn't know any other detectives who worked as well together as they did, and he hung up satisfied that they were making progress. He was determined to hang on to that progress too. It didn't matter that Katz had booked them tickets to Geneva, Shane wasn't about to risk losing sight of his lead now.

After Shane was certain everyone had boarded, rather than waiting and going to meet up with Katz to head for the airport, Shane made a beeline for the cargo plane. The rear cargo gate was still down, and he managed to sneak aboard just before a final crate was loaded and the gate closed.

As the engines revved, Shane suddenly recalled horror stories about stowaways freezing to death in cargo holds, but it was too late to reassess his options now.

Shane did freeze at a sound from behind him. He turned cautiously in the direction of the noise. It was coming from a covered crate. As Shane lifted the cover he nearly went into cardiac arrest, as a set of two eyes glared at him, and the occupant shrieked or maybe it had been Shane who shrieked. He wasn't sure, but when his breathing finally returned to normal, and no one from above came down to investigate, he smiled.

At least he knew he wouldn't freeze to death or suffocate for lack of oxygen. If they had chimpanzees, and God knew what else in here, at least it was climate controlled and the air would be breathable. Exhausted, Shane lay back in a space between some crates on the side and allowed his eyes to close as the plane ascended into the night.

Chapter Forty

It was just past seven when Anne awoke.

"Jack," she whispered.

"Yes mom?" Jack asked, as he leaned in closer to her.

"Dr. Marshall, Tom's dad, knows about Sophie."

"What do you mean Mom?"

"I found your research on Sophie and went to him. He knew all about it. That's why they came here. To keep an eye on her."

"I don't understand. You took what I found to Dr. Marshall?"

"Yes. I'm sorry. I only wanted to help."

"It's okay Mom, but what do you mean he knew and was here to keep an eye on her? He's hardly ever here. What connection would he have with Sophie?"

"He was part of the research. He tried to get out of it. He's the doctor who cared for Sophie when she was born. He tried to hide her. She wasn't supposed to live. They found her though."

"Who are they?"

"They tried to kill me to keep me quiet. Ran me off the road. I need some water."

Jack got a cup of water and a straw to take to his mother as he tried to grasp what she was telling him.

Anne took a few sips and continued.

"Sophie isn't the only one Jack, and the O'Hare's know ..." Anne stopped and closed her eyes.

"Know what?"

Anne squeezed Jack's hand.

Just then the door to the room opened and Jack turned to see the senior Dr. Marshall.

"Good morning Jack."

"Doctor Marshall."

"Is everything okay Jack? Has there been a change?"

"No, no change. I'm just surprised to see you here."

"Well, I know I'm not her official doctor, but I was just coming off a shift at the hospital and thought I'd swing by and check on her."

"Has there been a change?" Ben asked, as he entered the room and looked from Anne, to Jack, to Dr. Marshall.

"No. Jack says there's no change yet, Ben. Like I told Jack, I just got off at the hospital and thought I'd swing by. I'll leave you all alone now. It's been a long night, and I'm back to work at 3:00," Dr. Marshall said with a nod to them all, as he exited the room.

That's when Jack's phone rang. "I'll take this outside," Jack said and went into the hall. He didn't answer his phone but watched Dr. Marshall go to the exit and followed.

Jack watched as Dr. Marshall got into his Jeep, before Jack went to his own car. He had assumed that the doctor was staying with his son, only instead of turning down the lane that led to Tom's house, the jeep entered the highway, and a half hour later Jack found himself pulling into the airport parking garage.

"What the hell is going on?" he asked himself as he watched Dr. Marshall enter and get into the line for departures.

Jack grabbed a newspaper and leaned against a wall next to a life size Santa Clause ornament and pretended to read.

After the doctor had passed through the ticket line and headed toward the gates, Jack made his way into the same line. There were three destinations listed for that particular ticket line, Amsterdam, London and Quebec, and Jack's bet was on Quebec.

Jack knew he couldn't afford it, hell he couldn't afford the parking right now, but when he got to the front of the line he asked for a ticket to Quebec.

"I'm afraid this flight is full Mr.?"

"Wilson. Jack Wilson."

"We don't have any availability until...until after Christmas, I'm afraid, except if you would like to fly first class. We have a flight available tomorrow or you can always go standby, but honestly, if you're really in a pinch I'd try a different carrier that operates more flights in Canada. We mostly fly to Europe," the desk agent said helpfully. "Maybe Air Canada. They're just one terminal down."

"Thank you," Jack said and headed to the next terminal. Going to a self-help kiosk, he checked the schedules and then remembered that Nick had tried to call him. He opened his phone and saw three more missed calls, all from Nick, and he called him back."

Discovering that Alice had gone missing was the last thing that Jack wanted to hear but knowing that she and Sophie were both in Quebec, made him all the more certain that he needed to get there somehow too.

Jack told Nick about his mom waking up and what she had said to him. "I don't know what she meant about the O'Hare's, but they know something, and I'm betting Tom might too."

"Maybe I should just be direct and ask them?" Nick suggested.

"Not yet. Someone tried to kill my mom because she knew too much, and Nick, you can't let them know she's awake."

"Okay. So, since you're already at the airport and it's Alice that's missing, I think you should take my ticket. I'll stay here, call to have the name change made, and keep an eye on everyone."

"Keep a close eye on my dad. Will you?"

"Sure."

"He was with my mom when I left. I'm not sure what she might tell him or how he might react, especially if she tells him the accident wasn't an accident."

"You've got it. Sophie is supposed to call me again around nine. I'd better go change the ticket for you, and then I'll call you after I hear from her."

***

Mr. Amstead was worried. He had tried to contact Alice after his ordeal only to discover that not just her, but her parents as well, had gone missing. He didn't know anything else that he could do, so he took the backup thumb drive with the files, and after calling to be sure it would reach the appropriate person, overnighted it to Seattle.

***

Sophie was sitting in the lobby, watching the door as she sipped her third latte, hoping that Alice would reappear before the lecture. It was 8:40 when she saw him enter. He was older, but she'd know those eyes anywhere. The angry eyes of the man in her dream.

She didn't realize until she followed him down the hall to the room where the lecture was to be, that he was Dr. Meschner himself. She stared at the poster on the easel outside of the room.

Sophie tried to shake off her fear as she returned to the lobby. She sat, watching the door, hope against hope as she finished her coffee and went to the bank of phones to make the promised call to Nick. She couldn't wait to see him.

She had been disappointed as well as glad that Jack was the one coming now. She had not wanted Nick to tell him, but under the circumstances had to agree that it was probably for the best. Alice would need Jack.

Nick wanted to tell her everything but didn't dare. He couldn't bear to put her in anymore danger, much less for her to think that her parents had been any part of this. There was one thing he had to tell her though."

"Sophie."

"Yes Nick?"

"Be careful and..."

"I will."

"I love you, Sophie."

"I love you too," she whispered back, hung up the phone, and made her way back down the hall to the lecture.

Richter and Alice were still in the café. He had wanted her to leave with him, but she had refused. They had sat in silence as she pretended to read the newspaper. She was still going crazy inside. A part of her wanted to knock him out and make a run for it and another part of her wanted to go with him. She had to take control of this anxiety and the opposing forces within her. She needed to stay someplace public. After four cups of coffee though, she also needed to use the restroom. When a woman at a table next to her excused herself to do the same, Alice took the chance to excuse herself to Richter and follow.

"Women, huh?" the other woman's companion had turned and said to Richter before he could try and follow. "They always seem to go in pairs. What's with that?"

"I'm sure I wouldn't know," Richter replied with a polite nod, as he tried to keep an eye on the restroom through the growing crowd.

Alice surveyed the restroom, but the only window, wasn't even large enough to put her head through, much less her entire body. Her only chance would be to make a run for it. The nightmare flashed through her mind again, and she hurried, not wanting to find him waiting by the door. She exited with two other women. Richter was still at the table, where the other man was attempting to engage him in conversation. He stood as he spotted Alice, and she ran.

It took Richter a while to maneuver through the crowd, and before he could reach the door, a man from behind the counter stopped him.

"Excuse me sir," the man said. "Your girlfriend seems to have left without paying her bill. You wouldn't be doing the same thing now would you?"

Richter yanked out a twenty-dollar bill and handed it to the man, then dashed out the door searching in the direction he had seen Alice take. Damn! He thought. She'd had too long to get ahead of him.

Alice ran faster and longer than she ever had before, dodging people and even cars as she hurried down, and across busy streets. She heard a clock chiming and turned toward it where a church stood. The large clock was just above the entrance, and it read 9:00 O'clock. She knew Sophie must be worried by now, but she didn't dare go back to the hotel. To the left of the church was a high bridge that spanned an icy waterway. Alice thought momentarily about jumping and putting them all out of their misery, and then she saw Jack's face in her mind and ran up the stairs into the church instead.

Alice stood for a while in the narthex, as she listened to a choir practicing. There were a couple of other people sitting in the sanctuary listening, and after steadying her breathing she decided to slip into a pew near the back and listen as well. They were singing "What Child Is This".

***

Soren had barely made his flight to Paris. He couldn't very well explain what he was really up to, and even though Trudie had no problem with him leaving early for his vacation, she had wanted him to go back to the vault for yet another sample before doing so.

That alone had wasted over half an hour, then once he got there the throng of holiday travelers and only two out of eight lines open, apparently because airport staff was allowed holiday vacation as well, meant he had made it to his gate just as they announced the last call.

He was just now getting out of a Taxi at the Gare du Nord train station. He had no idea what the man who now carried the samples looked like, but he did know that he would have to be carrying a cooler for them.

Soren checked the boards and went to the platform where the train was due to arrive. He would have a short wait yet and stopped to get a sandwich, hot tea, and newspaper at a kiosk before making himself comfortable on a nearby bench.

***

Jonathan hoped he was making the right decision. He knew that Richter would not be pleased that he had brought them together, and Dad would probably be even less so. That was Jonathan's problem. Just as Richter had accused, he had a heart. He felt sympathy for the deformed woman, yet child, who sat strapped in on the plane beside him. She didn't know that he wasn't Richter, and that he meant her no harm, and had no plans to perform more tests on her.

She had calmed and then cried as she was reunited with her birth mother.

That was another story. Claire, he knew had likely only agreed to take part in this research again because she thought she could save her sister. In fact, that was the first thing she had asked him. "Where are Suzanna and Edgar?" She had already known that they were on the island, but that was also the only facility she had known of. When he had told her they were taking her to Geneva she had been outraged at what she felt was yet another deception. Having Rosie with her was the only thing that had calmed her, and that was the reason Jonathan would give when questioned, as to why she was brought as well.

***

Suzanna Morgan stirred on the sofa, and Edgar went to her, taking her hand in his.

The so-called summit seemed to be at an impasse. The only thing they seemed to agree on was that Richter needed to be reined in, and they had all retired for the evening.

"Edgar?" Suzanna asked. "Where are we?"

"They've brought us both to the house. Both Mathias and Carl are here as well as Patricia."

"Carl?"

"He's another of Richter and Mathias's brothers, and yes, he looks just like them too."

"How many of them are there?" Suzanna asked, as she tried to sit. Edgar helped her and propped her leg on some cushions on the coffee table.

"As far as I know there are four."

"You said Mathias is here? I saw him fall Edgar. He fell with Patty, and how, how did she survive?" Suzanna questioned.

Edgar spent the next hour explaining how and why they had all come to be there, what he had learned about the further experiments that were being conducted, and the other labs that Meschner had set up and used under the cover of the Morgan Enterprises name. These were the parts of companies that Morgan Acquisitions had retained and transferred into Morgan Enterprises. While the majority shares were owned by the Morgans, they were run by others, including Meschner. And

Edgar had unfortunately paid them little heed.

Edgar and Suzanna sat and watched the sun come up together, discussing what they would do and say to her if they were ever reunited with Alice.

Patty was the first one up to join them. The babies wouldn't let her sleep any longer without being fed, she had said, as she made them all omelets, and toast, and put the kettle on to boil water for tea, as well as coffee for everyone else.

"Just wait until they're actually born," Suzanna had said, and they had smiled at each other.

Shortly later they heard the raised voices of Mathias and Carl as they argued. When the brothers returned to the living room though they seemed to have come to terms.

"Since I can't argue that Mathias is my elder brother, I will allow him to share with you the agreement that we have come to," Carl said, as he went to fix himself a coffee.

"I hope you'll forgive me if I eat something first," Mathias said, as he joined Carl by the coffee and fixed himself a plate of breakfast. "My compliments to the chef," he said, as he bit into the omelet.

"Thank you," Patty replied.

The tension in the room was thicker than the marine layer that obscured even the end of the porch just outside.

"First, I want you to know that doing this puts us, as well as many others at risk," Mathias began...

Chapter Forty-One

Shane awoke as the plane touched down and hurried to hide, as they rolled to a stop. He wished he knew what lay outside the plane. Who would be there watching? Which way should he go? Where were they going, and how would he follow? Shane uttered a silent prayer as the cargo door began to open.

Three men entered and began offloading the crates. When they arrived at the chimpanzee, they all had to work together.

"I guess the tranquilizers wore off," said one of the men, as the chimp began to rattle around in the cage.

"Dr. Meschner only allows mild sedatives. He never was tranqued," replied another.

"Seriously?"

"Yep. Don't worry though. We'll jack him up onto a cart and wheel him out."

Shane took his chance, dropped down onto the tarmac, and ducked behind the wheel well. He looked around and saw no one. Then he noted an ambulance driving down the tarmac. He also noted that the nearest building was a good two hundred feet away and flew a Canadian flag.

He waited and watched, taking down the plate number of the ambulance as the girl and the woman, he guessed to be her mother, were loaded into it. The driver then walked over to the terminal as the man Shane didn't want to lose, jumped into the driver's seat and drove away.

Shane looked around. The men were focused on offloading the plane into an eighteen-wheeler. He quickly noted its license plate, and seeing no one else, made a beeline for the terminal.

“Where did you come from?” asked the woman behind a desk, as he entered.

“I came in on the cargo plane that just landed, only to find out I needed to book my own car,” Shane replied in all honesty.

“Your passport please?” she asked looking at him suspiciously, as she held out her hand.

Shane reached into his jacket pocket and retrieved the requested document.

She scanned it with eyes like a hawk, stamped it and directed him to another building where he could request a rental car.

As he approached the other building, Shane saw the ambulance driver get into a pale blue Nissan. The way the car was angled, he couldn’t see the plates, but he doubted the man knew anything anyway.

Inside he was told that there were no cars available.

“But what about all of the cars I see sitting out there?” Shane asked.

“They’re already reserved.”

“All of them?” Shane queried.

“Yes sir. All of them,” the man confirmed, as Shane looked around the empty lobby, and his nose began to itch.

“Where else can I go to rent a car?”

“Here,” the man said, as he handed a list of rental companies to Shane.

Shane took the list and exited the building. He didn’t like all of the tingling sensations brewing in his nose, and he called for a taxi as he made his way across a parking area, and to the main street, where a sign told him that he was at an import transit station.

The taxi was going to take at least half an hour, and Shane rubbed his hands together, and stamped his feet in an effort to stay warm. The airfield had been cleared, but all along the road were piles of snow several feet high. The icy winds blowing across them seemed to pass straight through Shane.

His phone vibrated with a number he didn't recognize.

"Hello?"

"What in hell do you think you're doing? Where are you?" came Katz voice. "The director will kill me if anything happens to you!"

"Calm down. I'm fine. A little cold but..."

"Calm down?" Katz answered, more than a little irritated. "Where are you?"

Shane read off the name on the sign. "It's not Geneva. Where are you?"

"The airport. Look, I board in ten minutes for Geneva, and it looks like you're somewhere near Quebec City, Canada. I don't suppose you have them in sight?"

"Unfortunately, no. They all took off in an ambulance, but I have the plate," Shane said, as he read it off to Katz.

"I'll call you back in two minutes."

As Shane hung up, he heard the roar of engines and turned to see the plane he had come in on taking off. He also saw the truck the cargo had been loaded onto coming up to the gate where he stood. Jumping up and down, and waving his hands, he caught the driver's attention.

The driver rolled down his window as he stopped before the road. "You alright?" he asked.

"Not really. My car broke down, and they don't have any rentals available," he said, pointing back to the terminal. "I tried to get a taxi, but..." Shane shrugged his shoulders.

"Hop on in."

"Thank you!" Shane said, and made his way around to the passenger side. "You have no idea how much I appreciate this!" he continued, as he hopped inside of the invitingly warm cab, and closed the door.

"If I left you to wait for a taxi out here, I'd have your death on my conscience. Where'd you break down at?"

"Back down that way," Shane pointed in the opposite direction of the trucks heading. "I called for a tow, but they told me..."

"It'll be a couple hours at least, I'm sure. We've been pretty pummeled with snow and high winds. So where can I drop you? Do you have a hotel?"

"Hotel?"

"Well, you don't sound like a local."

"I'm not. I just hadn't planned on staying the night, but it looks like I'll have to," Shane replied, as his phone vibrated and he answered it.

"Yes. I'm okay. I've got a ride. What's the address?"

Katz read off the address for the private hospital the ambulance was registered to, and informed Shane that he was still heading to Geneva to follow up on a connection that had been found there to the Morgans. Shane should phone the director as soon as possible to connect with an agent in Quebec.

"Okay. Thanks. Bye," Shane finished and hung up.

"Everything okay?" the driver asked.

"Yes. It was just my insurance. Are you familiar with De Roan Ave?"

"I am indeed. It actually runs parallel to where I'm headed. This whole shipment is going to a private university research center. I've got live chimps back there. My daughters would throw a fit if they knew," he said with a smile, and shake of his head.

"Why's that?"

"My oldest is big into animal rights, and my youngest, well she's three and can't get enough of the monkeys at the zoo."

"Sounds like a nice family," Shane said, as Patty's smiling

face filled his mind.

"I like them. Do you have any family?"

"Not yet. My wife couldn't conceive. We're looking at adoption though."

"Well, you might just be interested in the research the lab is doing into genetics and new fertility treatments. I don't understand it at all, but from what I've heard they've been quite successful."

"I think I'll do just that. It'll be a while before I can get a car anyway. I don't suppose you know anyone I could talk to?"

"Me. No, I just overhear things, but I imagine any of the students could help you."

"You know I'm really thankful I met you, uhm...?"

"Ralph. Ralph Le'Bonte. And you are?"

"Shane. Shane McDougal."

"Well, Shane. I believe that everything happens for a reason, even cars breaking down. Do you mind if I ask, where is your wife?"

"She's researching adoption, and I was just up here researching a book. I'm a writer."

"Anything I may have read?"

"Not yet. This is actually my first book. I used to be a detective."

"I bet the wife will feel safer having children with a writer. I love detective shows though. I even thought about getting my Private Detective license at one time, but my wife wouldn't have it. 'No way!' she told me."

"You make a good point Ralph."

***

Mathias handed Carl, who couldn't seem to stop yawning, another coffee, as he began to lay out the details of the plan.

He went over all of the people at the facility, their

background and participation in what projects as far as he knew it. Many of the staff were far from innocents. Some had served time in prison for either other illegal research projects, espionage, or counterfeiting, and others had joined before they were caught at the above activities and viewed the lab as safe hiding.

It was a perfect win win situation. There was no fear that they would expose the research, lest they themselves be exposed.

The other people involved were outside of the Island, not just workers at other facilities, but the children and adoptive parents of those children who, like Alice, had been engineered.

Carl had just gotten up to get another coffee, when his legs gave out from under him, and he collapsed unconscious to the living room floor.

"Perfect timing," Mathias said, as he went to Carl, and Edgar helped as he was moved to a chair. "It will be much easier this way," Mathias explained.

"Will he be okay?" Mrs. Morgan asked.

"He'll be fine. I dosed him with the same drug that was given to Patricia and to you."

"Where did you get it?" Patty asked.

"He had brought some with him to use on you. I'll have to get more from the lab though or he'll come around too soon. Carl being unconscious will give us the reason we need to get another chopper authorized to land out here without the suspicions of our loyal staff. Our best bet will be to fly into Guam. From there you'll be able to make whatever contacts you need to."

***

Richter stumbled through the snow and crowds of Christmas shoppers. The Carols, which seemed to come from everywhere were making his head throb. He needed an injection desperately. He couldn't allow himself to pass out. He had to find Alice. Why in hell had they allowed her bio-tracker to be disabled? Slumping onto a bench looking over the river, Richter pulled the plunger from his coat and injected himself in the back of the neck. He sat for a while, waiting for the dizziness to subside.

Alice was feeling a bit dizzy herself after all the running and anxiety. Sitting in the pew, listening to carols, made her wish that she could curl up and go back to sleep. Her eyes felt suddenly heavy.

She had just begun to doze off when she was awakened by the sound of applauds from others in the sanctuary, as the choir ended with an extended A...me...n... Alice stood and joined everyone else in the applauds. Then a man, apparently the choir director, stood up and invited everyone in both English and French to join them for refreshments in the hall next door.

Alice continued to follow everybody else, as they moved into a brightly decorated hall that had tables filled with crafts, food and drink as well as a Christmas tree in the center, which reached nearly to the top of the vaulted ceiling, where a shining star seemed to beam down as it caught the light reflecting through the skylight.

"Hello. I am Ellen," a woman said in thickly accented English, as she held out her hand in greeting. "I have not seen you here before. Are you new to our city?"

"Hello. I was just admiring your tree. I'm Alice. I'm just visiting Quebec. I was out for a walk when I heard the singing and stopped in. I'm sorry. This is probably just for members." Alice turned to exit.

"Wait. No, not at all. You are very welcome here. Come, if

you have a minute, and join me in some refreshment. We have coffee, tea, cider, and hot cocoa, and you must try the angel food cake. The minister's wife makes it, and it is divine!" Ellen said, guiding Alice along to a nearby table filled with goodies. "Where is it that you are visiting from Alice?"

"I'm from Seattle."

"And what brings you to our fine city."

"I'm visiting with my sister. She's at a lecture right now," Alice added, hoping that Sophie had indeed gone ahead to the lecture without her and that she wasn't out looking for her. The last thing she needed was for the man to spot them together.

"Oh, how nice. I was in Seattle once," Ellen continued chatting on, and Alice found herself begin to relax. The anxiety faded as she became more and more certain that she had lost him. The problem was the tiny part inside of her that still wanted to find him. He terrified her. Made her terrified of herself, but the pull or was it an attraction? was undeniable. No! The only man she was attracted to was Jack, so what was it about this man? What was the connection that she felt to him?

It was nearly noon when Ellen excused herself to help with cleanup. She had invited Alice to lunch, but Alice said that she had plans to meet up with her sister for lunch. "It was nice meeting you Ellen. Thank you for the welcome and the company."

"Oh. Any time. Please feel free to come back with Sophie. You can join us for our concert Thursday evening or for caroling. We leave from here every evening at seven," Ellen said with a smile.

"Thank you, Ellen. Oh! Do you happen to know if there's a bus to the mall from the stop in front?"

"Yes, you can either take the number two bus from directly in front of the church or there is a holiday shopper express that leaves from the corner by the river. I think it runs every twenty minutes."

"Thank you so much," Alice said, "and Merry Christmas!"

"Merry Christmas!" Ellen waved, as Alice turned to leave.

Once back outside, Alice was overcome with a familiar foreboding. She looked around, synched her coat snugly around her, and pulled a homemade hat that she had bought inside down over her ears, hoping that it would provide at least some disguise, should the man happen to be nearby.

Alice raced over to the river as she saw the bus approach and arrived just in time to board. The shopping mall had been the one place she could think of that would provide enough of a crowd, and she doubted highly that whoever he was would expect her to be shopping. Taking a seat by the window, she turned her phone back on to send Sophie a text. There were several missed calls and texts from an obviously worried Sophie, and Alice didn't really know how to reply, so she wrote simply. "Be careful Sophie. He's here."

Jack landed in Quebec just before noon and managed to get onto a shuttle for the hotel, where he had agreed to meet Sophie during the lunch break in the lecture.

Sophie herself had taken copious notes, as she continued to reassure herself that there was no way he could recognize her. Their eyes had met at one point, and her heart rate accelerated, but she noted that he seemed to make eye contact with others as well, and she forced herself to stay calm, as she pushed her fear away.

Sophie's phone vibrated, and she looked to see a message from Jack that he was on his way. Then she also saw the message from Alice. A flood of relief washed over her and then confusion. Did Alice know Dr. Meschner was the man from her dream? She had described him, and it was possible that Alice had seen the poster, but Sophie's description of the man in her dream could have fit any number of men. No, Alice was talking about the man from her own nightmare. The dreams had been premonitions for both of them.

Sophie typed her reply. "They are both here. Where are you?" She didn't expect a reply, but she was certain that they understood each other. She now understood why she had felt so unusually worried for Alice. Their connection was strong. She could feel that Alice was not in eminent danger, yet she still sensed pending danger for them both. A part of her now wished she had not called Nick. No matter how much he and Jack wanted to protect them, she felt more and more that it was her and Alice that needed to protect them.

Sophie replied to Jack, as she walked into the hotel restaurant to let him know that she had heard from Alice and where she would be when he arrived.

Twenty minutes later Jack joined her at a table in the back corner.

Sophie showed him the message. She tried to explain about their dreams and who Dr. Meschner was. She also shared her notes from the lecture. That's when Jack decided to share with her about Dr. Marshall.

"I need to go look for her. Where do you think she might go?"

"I have no idea Jack, but please don't leave. I'll know if something's wrong, just like I did that day in Central Park. Please trust me on this. We should stay together. Besides, if they're all connected then doesn't it stand to reason that we should stick close to Meschner? They're bound to meet up at some point, and I don't want to be alone with them when they do."

"You're right as usual Soph. I'm just so worried about Alice. Why would she have left your room alone in the first place?"

"I don't know. She's an adult though Jack. We both are.

Maybe she just woke up early."

"So, what am I supposed to do while you're in the lecture with Meschner? Sit here and twiddle my thumbs? And if Dr. Marshall shows up, I can just ask him to join me for coffee?" Jack replied, unable to keep the frustration out of his voice.

"Of course not. Like I said, we stay together. You'll use Alice's ticket and join me in the lecture. I think we should sit separately though. If Dr. Marshall shows up, I don't think he'll recognize me unless I'm with you."

"And if he sees you, then Meschner may realize who you are?"

"Exactly. Jack?"

"Yes?"

"There's something else that was odd. I saw Dr. Marshall in your mom's room the other day, and I could have sworn he was crying."

"My mom did say that he wanted out. Maybe he really did. After all, he did save your life."

***

Nick had gone to visit Anne and check on Ben at the care center. Ben mentioned nothing about any response from his wife, but there was an aura about him that showed renewed strength. Maybe it was just hope. Either way, Nick was relieved. He had gone with Ben to help with some of the snow shoveling and other maintenance that normally Jack would have done, and then he headed back over to the O'Hare's.

When they weren't home, he headed back into town to his own apartment and began looking through the files again. Something was nagging at the back of his mind ever since Jack told him what his mother had said about them knowing about Sophie. They had been afraid to call the police as well, but why?

Nick had a class at three. He considered cancelling, but then decided it might be just what he needed to clear his head. On his way to the rink, he saw the O'Hare's car parked in the back lot of the church. It was still there after his class more than an hour later.

Nick made his way up the front steps to the church, but when he tried to enter, he found the door was locked tight. The only other car in the lot was one he hadn't recognized. He walked back around and took a closer look at the other car. It was a rental. He then wove his way around to a rear entrance. That door was locked too, but he could hear voices, angry voices coming from inside. He wished he could make out what was being said. He thought that he recognized at least one of the voices as Mr. O'Hare.

On a whim Nick typed Mr. O'Hare's name into his smart phone and hit search. About a million O'Hare's popped up, most from Ireland. He revised his search to Canada and then narrowed it down by age range, which still left him with about fifty. He scanned down the list until he reached one that was listed as a graduate from a college in Quebec.

***

Shane didn't know what hit him, quite literally. He had spent over an hour at the hospital making an unsuccessful sweep to look for the ambulance or any of its occupants. He hadn't eaten all day and was just exiting an adjacent café, when he ran directly into the man, whose chest felt like steel. Coffee was running down Shane's coat, as he met the man's gaze.

"Are you alright? I'm so sorry. I was hurrying and not watching where I was going," Jonathan apologized. "Please let me buy you a new drink and pay for any dry cleaning."

Shane stared at the man, dumbstruck. A part of his brain said to punch his lights out, another said to just cuff him, but he did neither.

"Are you alright?" Jonathan asked again.

"Yes. Fine," Shane managed.

"Come, let me buy you a new drink," Jonathan said, clapping his hand on Shane's back and guiding him back inside.

Shane felt as though he had entered the twilight zone. The man not only genuinely seemed to not know who Shane was, he also struck Shane as being genuinely nice. His nose hairs weren't even dancing.

"I'm Jonathan Morgan," he said, extending his hand to Shane.

"Shane," Shane answered, as he returned the handshake.

"So, what can I get you Shane? It looks like your sandwich got a little soggy as well. What was it?"

"Ham, but you really don't need to."

"It's the least I can do. I don't suppose you'd care to join me? Two ham sandwiches, two coffees and a large bottle of mineral water, "Jonathan said to the cashier. "If you get some mineral water on that right away, it may not stain," Jonathan continued, turning back to Shane.

"Yes, thank you," Shane managed. Thank you was the last thing he expected to be saying to a man who had abducted his wife and led him on a crazy chase across Canada less than two weeks before Christmas. And now Shane found himself following the man to a table for a late lunch. What the hell was happening? Surely, he had to know who Shane was. If he didn't though, then this might be the perfect opportunity.

"Here," Jonathan said, as he handed the mineral water and some napkins to Shane.

"Thank you," Shane found himself saying again. "So, Jonathan, do you work at the college?"

"No. My father does sometimes though. I just decided to make an impromptu stop to meet up with him on my way to Geneva."

"Your father? Professor Morgan?"

"No. Actually Morgan is my adopted name," Jonathan said, trying to cover his tracks. He rarely ran into anyone new on these trips, much less engaged with them in conversation, and he mentally slapped himself for his carelessness. He was tired though, and Morgan was the name he'd been using for two days now. "My father is Professor Meschner. He teaches an occasional class at the college. He's in town this weekend for research and a lecture at a hotel downtown. We'll be flying out tomorrow for Geneva."

"What is your father a professor of?" Shane asked.

"He specializes in genetics and reproduction."

"That sounds interesting and you?"

"I guess you could say I'm his student, but tell me Mr.?"

"McDougal, but call me Shane," Shane replied, as he watched for a reaction. A brief shadow seemed to cross the man's face, but then disappeared, as he smiled and continued.

"So, Shane, what is it you're doing here? Christmas shopping perhaps? There's some lovely shops just down from here before the mall," Jonathan continued.

"Actually, I'm looking for my wife," Shane said, deciding to be direct, whether he had the power to arrest him or not. "I don't suppose you've seen her?" Shane asked, as he pulled out a photo of Patty.

Chapter Forty-Two

Alice saw him from the restaurant window as he seemed to stumble down the street below.

The cold, combined with the stress was having an increased adverse effect on Richter's immune system. He had to force himself to focus. He had to find her again. If only he had not been so compromised, he would have sensed that she was the one now watching him.

"This means that once the cell is isolated it cannot only be regenerated, but replicated, and those replications can be extracted and improved upon through the addition of DNA transplants, which may eventually be grown to replicate entire organs that can serve as replacements for the DNA donor. This being said, the implications for the preservation of life are limitless. It has already been shown that stem cells injected into mice can produce viable ovum. Imagine how this research can help restore not just the sick, the injured and even the elderly, but can actually help create families!" Dr. Meschner concluded to a room filled with applauds.

"Sounds like a regular saint," Jack whispered, as he caught up with Sophie, and they walked to the lobby for the last ten minute break before the final Q&A segment.

"Jack?"

"What is it?"

"Nothing. I don't know. I just suddenly felt a little overwhelmed. I don't know if I can go back in there and ask these questions," she said, as she handed Jack a page from her notebook. "Would you ask them?"

"Sure Soph. Are you sure you'll be okay?"

"I'll be fine, but I think I'd rather wait out here."

"Sophie?"

"Really Jack. I'm fine, besides if Dr. Marshall does decide to show up to meet Meschner here after, I can spot him and let you know. I'll wait right back there at the same table I met you at for lunch. He won't see me, but I'll see him."

"What if Meschner goes out a back door?"

"Stay with him and call me. Look, you'd better get back. I'll be right there," she said turning toward the restaurant.

"Okay," Jack said and headed back in. As he sat down, he looked at the questions that Sophie had written and took in a deep breath. The questions were quite blunt and to the point, questioning the ethics and questioning how such science could be controlled. She even asked outright if some of the ideas didn't resemble experiments conducted by Nazis also in the name of improving on humanity. It was a fine line that Jack wasn't sure if it would be wise to try and walk. He had some questions of his own though, and to start with he would stick to those.

As it turned out, each person was only allowed to ask a maximum of two consecutive questions. The first question that Jack asked was about controlling the rejection of foreign cells, to which the reply had been that because the cells were injected with the host DNA in isolation, they would then cease to be foreign.

"You had another question young man?"

"Yes. I'd like to know if there isn't in some way a risk that with the potential to create an improved person from their own cells, that the original person could in effect be replaced?"

Dr. Meschner smiled. "I do believe young man, that you've read one too many science fiction novels. We're not talking about replacing personalities, but DNA to help grow stronger, healthier bodies."

"But doesn't DNA contribute to personality?" Jack asked.

"I'm sorry, but you've had your two questions. Next question?" Meschner asked. "Yes. The young lady in the fourth row."

"Well, I was going to ask something else, but I'd really like to hear the answer to the question the gentleman tried to pose."

Meschner was momentarily taken aback before proceeding. "The answer is yes and no. While it is true that the DNA that make up our physical characteristics influence our personalities, it is no more than a small part, and it takes years of external life experience to create a fully formed person."

Jack sat quietly listening to the other questions, but he knew that having to answer his question had rattled the professor. He realized that it had been wise for Sophie not to be here, as she would have been less likely to let it go and may have become confrontational with a second question of her own. Jack must remember to thank the woman for asking the question on his behalf.

Jonathan had stared at Patricia's picture for nearly a minute, trying to find a response before he simply said. "She's alright."

Shane could hardly control himself from vaulting across the table at him. "Where is she? Tell me where my wife is!" he demanded under his breath.

"At the Morgan's property in the Marianas. You've got the wrong man though. It wasn't me who took her."

"Really? Then why is it your description that I was given as being seen with her after she disappeared?"

"It was my brother."

Shane sat back as he noticed other patrons beginning to look their way. He tried to analyze the truthfulness of Jonathan's expression. It was the lack of nasal vibration that settled him on believing Jonathan's story.

"When did you last see Patty? When did you last see my wife?"

"Two days ago."

"And the Morgan family?"

"Mr. and Mrs. Morgan are there as well and no, they didn't know that Patricia was there."

"It's their property. Explain."

"You're a detective? Correct Mr. McDougal? In Seattle?"

"Correct."

"You have no jurisdiction here, and technically I don't have to tell you anything, but I will, on one condition."

"And just what would that be?"

"I want protection."

"If you didn't take them yourself and cooperate in getting them home safely, then I think that can be arranged."

"I appreciate that, but I meant now. I need protection from my brother or should I say my brothers, and my father. Believe me when I say they won't appreciate my thwarting their plans, and they have plenty of people who would gladly come after me on their behalf."

"I want to hear more of what you have to say first. For instance, why? Why was Patty taken?"

"Richter, my brother, promised he could help her have a baby."

"And he didn't think I should take part in that?"

"She went with him willingly, and she is pregnant. Are you sure you want to know more?"

"Are you telling me that bastard raped my wife?"

"No. My brother may be a lot of things, but he's not a rapist. To be honest, I fully suspect that he's impotent. Your wife is pregnant through a new form of invitro."

"Patty never would have agreed to have another man's

baby."

"You're right. That isn't what she agreed to. She had no idea what Richter had in mind when she went with him."

"Tell me about the other two women."

Jonathan cocked a questioning brow.

"The two you traveled here with in the ambulance."

"I must say you impress me Detective."

"Who are they?"

"One is Mrs. Morgan's sister, and the other would be Alice Morgan's sister."

"What?"

"If you're confused now, just wait until you meet my brothers."

"Triplets?"

"No."

"Where is Alice Morgan, and where are your brothers?"

"I'm afraid I'm as stumped as you on the first one. Alice is more adept at hiding than Richter gave her credit for. As for my brothers, Richter, who is the one you really want to be talking with, is here in Quebec somewhere. In fact, I expected him to be here by now."

Shane's phone had been vibrating on and off for several minutes. "Don't move. I need to get this," Shane said, as he answered a call from Selma.

"Don't worry. I consider myself under your protection now. I'll be needing it after what I've told you."

"What is it, Selma?"

"I'm not sure how to explain this, except to say that according to the tests we ran for DNA from Alice's apartment and her parent's home, Alice Morgan can't just be the Morgan's."

"What does that mean?"

"It means that according to her DNA, she is related to them, but not closely."

"Adopted from a family member?"

"I don't know. Shane, I've never seen DNA like this before in my life. The tests were re-run five times. Remember how I said her blogs were like different people?"

"Yeah?"

"So is her DNA. It's messed up somehow. That must be why she was on that strange anti-rejection cocktail."

"And?"

"And you received an overnighted thumb drive from Mr. Amstead, the Morgan's associate that went missing in New York. I'm analyzing it now, but I think this is something you need to look at. How is everything going there?"

"That's a long story, but I think I'm finally making progress."

"That's great! Anything on Patty?"

"Yes, but I'll have to go into that later, right now I need you to call Larry and give him this address. Use his mobile number, it's in my address book in the left top drawer of my desk. Okay, tell him it's urgent and if possible, to send at least two. Got it?"

"Got it. Are you okay?"

"More than."

"Okay, I'm on it, and I'll try to get those files forwarded to you tonight."

"Thanks Selma. I don't know what we'd do without you" Shane said as he hung up.

"Selma?" Jonathan asked.

"Forensics specialist and no. Not that it's any of your business, but there's nothing romantic between us. I love my wife, and she had damned well better be okay, and home safe for Christmas or you, your brothers, your father, and whoever else, won't be celebrating at the New Year."

Alice watched from behind a sign, as Richter gave himself another injection. He had waited a couple of minutes and then seemed revived and began moving more quickly towards what appeared to be a hospital.

She watched as he stopped and looked in the window of a café, and the look on his face terrified her as he spun around. He all but ran the rest of the way past the ambulance dock and beyond the hospital to the neighboring college.

She almost lost him, but he had stopped to look for a key and she followed him as far as the office with Dr. Meschner's name on the plate beside the door.

***

Soren watched as the passengers disembarked. Fortunately, there was only one cooler that came off the train, but it left Soren uncertain, as it was carried by a woman, accompanied by a man and two young girls, who appeared to be her husband and daughters.

He sat for a minute more, keeping one eye on the train and another on the family, but when he heard the porter state that the cars were all cleared, he hurried to catch up with the family.

It didn't make any sense, he thought as he managed to get into a cab and asked the driver to follow the one in front of them. When the other taxi stopped, he asked his driver to pull over a half block behind. The driver gave Soren an odd look over his shoulder, as he sat watching while only the woman, the girls, and the cooler got out of the cab.

"Let me guess," asked the driver. "You're a private eye, and either the man or the woman from that cab is having an affair? Or maybe both? With the children though? Not that I'm one to judge. So, who are you going to follow?"

"The cooler," Soren said, as he paid his fare.

"What?"

"Long story. Merry Christmas!" he said, giving the man an

extra ten euro note as he stepped out into the frigid night air.

As he followed them down the crowded street, he guessed the girls to both be between nine and thirteen. Both were slender, with delicate facial features, and had long wavy auburn hair. He noted that they looked nothing like their mother. The woman was not fat, but she was of a more sturdy, broad shouldered build with black hair.

A few blocks down they stopped at a café, where they met with another man. All exchanged hugs and kisses, then walked to a side street where the man ushered them into his car.

Soren looked around for a taxi, but on a cold night with thousands of people out enjoying their holidays, there were none. He didn't know that it would help, but he took down the make, model, and plate of the car.

He felt like a failure as he ordered an espresso to go and continued down the street. The Bed and Breakfast he had booked, he knew was only a few streets over, and as he walked, he thought more and more about what he had read. The woman and children must be part of it. Could the children even be a product of the experiments? That would explain why they looked nothing like their parents.

Soren had been so deep in thought that he had passed his accommodations. It was his nose and his grumbling stomach that made him look up at the bistro. It was the man he saw inside though that made him enter. It was the same man who had gotten off the train with the woman and girls. And he was with another man, who struck Soren as vaguely familiar.

It was after 10:30, but he had already rang the Bed and Breakfast to tell them he would be arriving late, and they assured him that they had a twenty-four hour desk.

When Soren entered the bistro, he was guided to a table directly in front of the men. Using his mobile phone to record, he listened as he pretended to look over the menu. He had eaten here before and already knew his order, so it was only a brief interruption when the waiter arrived to take it.

It was the man's voice that Soren recognized first. Yes, he was sure of it. He had been a speaker at a conference Soren had gone to last year in Quebec, Canada.

On a normal night, Larry Marquet would have been at home, in bed with his wife when he got the call from Seattle, but tonight he had decided to sleep at the office and dig through that old file again. Not that he expected to find anything new, but he wanted it all fresh in his mind again in case Shane should find anything. So, he was thrilled when Selma's call came in. He immediately got on the phone to the field office in Quebec. Next, he called to book his own flight to Quebec, called his wife, grabbed his go bag, and headed to the airport.

Chapter Forty-Three

Carl was still unconscious when Mathias, with Edgar as copilot, landed the helicopter in Guam. Mathias stayed with Carl, while the others disembarked. The helicopter would refuel, and they would return to the island. It was really the only way. Carl would be safer contained on the island. Mathias would be in complete control with Jonathan and Richter away. He would continue to sedate Carl as needed and go through all of Richter and Carl's files, talk with the lab technicians, gather evidence, and bring this madness to a halt.

Only Edgar, who he had managed to talk with privately, while Patty was in conversation with Suzanna, knew about the plan, and he had promised to keep Patty with them until they were safely back in Seattle.

Mathias knew that Patty would be angry, but she'd understand later, and it was safer, safer for them all if he and Carl were not with them.

***

Charice was beside herself when she heard the Morgan's voices on the phone. At first, she had thought it was a dream, but after pinching herself until it hurt, she realized, much to her relief that it really was them. They talked for over an hour.

Charice would make the flight arrangements for the three of them from her end, as they had no money or credit cards with them. She would also have to fax over copies of photo I.D.'s for them.

After they had agreed to all of the arrangements, Charice went to the office, where she already had copies of the I.D.'s on her computer for just such events as a stolen or lost passport occurring on a business trip. She faxed these to the first charter company that she found in Guam that could get them on a flight home later that day.

Edgar had insisted that she not notify the police, but that they should go together to meet with the detectives after their arrival.

Charice had been too relieved to argue. Edgar, Suzanna and Alice were all safe and coming home.

Edgar had allowed Charice to believe Alice was the third person. He wished that it were true, but he couldn't think about that now. Fortunately, Patty had her passport with her, and since they were not technically crossing any foreign borders, and were flying via private charter, they should all be home in a matter of hours.

***

Nick nearly froze as he watched and waited for the O'Hares to leave the church. He watched, as they along with another man, whom he did not recognize, got into their respective vehicles. He snapped a couple of photos and took note of both license plates and tried to follow at an inconspicuous distance, as a light snow began to fall.

When he saw them turn off towards the airport, he thought he knew, and he called Jack to let him know.

***

Jack listened to Nick and waited for the photo he had sent to download as he walked through the crowds of shoppers on the city sidewalks, with Sophie close to his side.

Jack had learned where Meschner kept an office from the woman who had asked his question for him. It turned out that she had gone to a lecture he gave several years prior while she was at college. The college was the same one which Nick's search had listed Sophie's dad as attending, and that they were now just blocks away from.

"That's not possible," Sophie protested. "Da had all his education in Ireland. I've seen the certificates."

"Look, Soph, I know. I've seen them too, but you can't deny this would be quite a coincidence," Jack said, as he showed her the search result on his own phone."

Sophie stopped.

"Sophie," Jack said stopping beside her, and putting a comforting arm around her shoulders. She shrugged him off. "I'm sorry Soph. I wanted to protect you from this whole thing. I..."

"I know Jack. I asked for this. I'm the one who had to know the truth. I know! Okay? It's just that I had finally realized when I met Alice, that I was lucky to have been adopted. I thought that I had parents I could trust, but now I find out they aren't any better."

"We don't really know anything yet Soph. Let's not jump to conclusions."

"What if it's because of them that your mother was almost killed?"

"That's not your fault. None of this is your or Alice's fault."

Sophie looked at him with a stare that if it hadn't already been ten below, would have frozen him. Then she turned away and continued to walk toward the address they had been given. Jack practically had to jog to keep up, and he felt bad as he bumped into several shoppers, trying to keep up, while Sophie seemed to weave effortlessly through the crowd.

Meschner had received the call from Richter just as he was waiting for a car from the hotel. He had gone first to the lab to get the medical supplies he would need, and then headed to meet Richter at the office he used when in town. There were two other doctors who used the office as well, but Meschner had no concerns. Dr. Nadier was a devoted follower and the other? Well, he had his doubts. He knew Dr. Jordan was soft. Too much like his pathetic brother, but he was rarely here. Besides, Meschner intended to have everything and everyone back in order soon.

He stopped for a moment to observe the woman who seemed to be watching his office. Taking out his phone, he zoomed in on her face. She had changed her hair, but he'd know those features anywhere, and he could hardly believe his luck. She had come to him. Perhaps it wouldn't be too late for Richter.

He was just reaching for her when she spun around. He grabbed for her arm. Damn! He'd forgotten how strong they could be! He hated to do it, but he pulled a taser from his pocket and gave her a zap, which was enough to gain control of her long enough to drag her into the office.

Richter didn't stand. He was feeling too weak, but he smiled broadly as they entered.

"Merry Christmas son," Meschner managed, as he pushed Alice into a chair facing Richter across the desk.

Sophie had just reached the covered path to Meschner's office and watched as he forced Alice inside with him. She turned and waved at Jack to hurry.

"What is it?"

"Meschner has Alice."

"What?" Jack asked, already heading to the door. He took one look through the narrow window and ducked back, heading over to Sophie.

***

Jonathan's phone was ringing.

"You going to answer that?" Shane asked.

"No. Actually, I don't think that I will," he said, pushing the phone to Shane. "It's either Richter or our father. So, how long before your agents arrive?"

Shane stared at the phone, which had stopped ringing and back up at Jonathon. "Any minute now."

"Good. Maybe you can take us all at one time. That call was from my father's office. At least one of them is just next door," Jonathan said, as he leaned back with a smile.

Shane couldn't quite get a grasp on this man in front of him. He was calm in an almost eerie way as if this were all just part of a game.

Jonathan looked up as the two men approached.

"Detective McDougal?" asked one. "I'm inspector L'Coure," he said as he flashed a badge, while the other kept an eye on Jonathan. "And this is Rene'," he continued, pointing to the man beside him.

"Yes," Shane said rising, and pulling out his own badge. "I'm glad you're here. According to him," he motioned to Jonathan, "it's his brother who may be just next door, that we really want. Keep a close eye on him though," Shane told them, as he headed for the door.

"What the hell!" L'Coure said, as he looked from his partner to Shane, who was already to the door.

"I think you'd better go with him," Jonathan said, as he stood. "It's office 1123, just down the outside corridor to the right."

L'Coure stared up at Jonathan, who now standing, dwarfed his five seven frame.

"I've waited here willingly, and I'll go now willingly. There's no need for a scene," Jonathan continued, as he looked at the cuffs the other agent had out. "I can't say the same for my brother."

"Follow McDougal Rene', and call for back up."

Richter took one of the fresh injections Meschner had brought for him, followed by a dose of some liquid, which he had no sooner drank down than he started retching back up.

"What in hell is wrong with you?" Meschner snapped at Richter. "I guess I was wrong about you. You're too weak. Maybe I should just take her for myself. Do you like older men Alice?"

Alice was weak from the injection he'd given her, but she still managed to spit in his face.

"Do you know where you get that gene from Alice? The feisty one. The one that insights your rage. The one you've somehow managed to repress for all these years. Would you like to know who all of your parents are Alice?"

Her vision was getting fuzzy, her head sank, and Meschner brought a wheelchair around, lifted her into it, and took her out a door to an inside corridor.

Jack tried the handle, but the door was locked. Meschner turned at the sound, and Jack ducked back.

"He went right. I'm going around," Jack said. "I can't let him take her. Stay here," he told Sophie.

"In your dreams!" Sophie said, as she followed Jack.

When Shane arrived at the office, he could see nothing at first. The only light, being what filtered in from the hall. He could hear moaning though. He tried the door, but it was locked tight. That's when the other agent arrived.

"There's someone in there. Listen."

"I have this," Rene' said, as he took a tool from his belt. Ten seconds later they were in.

Shane stared at the man, who could have been a twin of

Jonathan. He was on the floor, laying in a puddle of his own vomit, and seemed delirious. Sweat was beaded on his forehead.

Rene' was already on the phone to a medic.

"He'd better recover."

Rene' looked at Shane. "I just hope he's not contagious. He smells like death."

A minute later, a medical crew from the hospital next door showed up with a stretcher.

"Keep a close eye on him. We need him alive for questioning," Shane said, as they loaded Richter onto the stretcher.

"What are these?" Rene' asked, as he discovered the bag with injection pens and vials under the desk where it had fallen with Richter.

"Follow us next door with it," one of the medics said. "Let's move!" he told the other.

"If his heart keeps racing like it is, it'll explode," said the other, as they hurried him out.

Rene' looked at Shane and handed him the Bag. "Are you okay to take this and head to the hospital with them?"

"On my way. You head back and go with L'Coure."

"You're sure you're alright detective? If you don't mind my saying, you don't look so good," Rene' said, as they reached the road.

"I'm fine. Call Marquet and update him. Tell him I'll call him when I find out more."

Rene' headed back to the café, where Jonathan was sitting with L'Coure much as he had been with Shane earlier. Both rose as he entered. L'Coure took one arm and Rene' the other as they guided Jonathan through the crowd and to an awaiting unmarked car.

Jack didn't see Meschner or Alice anywhere. It was Sophie who spotted them through an air vent that led to the lower level of a parking garage.

"There they are!" Sophie whispered, as she pointed.

"How do we get down there though?" Jack asked, as he ran around the other side of the structure. The only thing he saw was an elevator. Pushing the down button about a hundred times, he motioned for Sophie, who was still watching through the vent as Meschner attempted to load Alice into a van.

Alice could feel that rage boiling up inside of her like she had never felt before. She knew that he thought she was out, but she had never really fully lost consciousness. So as soon as he attempted to move her to the van, she had reached up and bitten him on the earlobe. Meschner screamed in agony, as he pushed her to the ground. His earlobe tearing away.

The elevator dinged, Meschner jumped into the van, and the driver took off skidding up the exit ramp. Alice spat out the earlobe and stood just as the elevator door opened.

"Alice," Jack sighed in relief, as he started toward her.

"Stop! Stay there!" she said.

"Alice?"

"You shouldn't be here Jack."

"Alice?" Sophie asked.

"Sophie, I'm sorry, but I need you to leave with Jack."

"I'm not going anywhere," Jack said, as he moved closer to her. "I love you, Alice."

"No! You can't. You don't know me."

"What are you talking about?" asked Sophie, as she moved closer.

"I said stop! I meant you too Sophie!"

"But Alice?"

Jack took a step closer, and she ran. Jack and Sophie both

took off after her, but something had been loosed and she ran so fast that she felt she wasn't even able to catch up with herself. She had no conscious idea of where she was going, yet her every movement was intentional.

Jack and Sophie lost sight of her as they reached the emergency entrance to the hospital, and Jack recognized the man being wheeled in on the gurney. "That's the other man from the office," Jack said, as he ran to the entrance, Sophie close behind him.

"Sorry," said a guard. "Emergencies only. You'll have to go around to the front."

"Did another woman come through here? She looks like me, only with different hair," Sophie asked.

"Like I said, emergencies only."

"Damn! What is going on with her Sophie?"

"I think she's trying to protect us."

"We're already part of this though. I don't..."

"There's something different about her Jack. I could feel it, but I don't understand it either. There is something about that man too. I need to see him."

"What?"

"I don't know, but he's somehow connected to us, to Alice and me," Sophie said, as she headed around to the main entrance of the hospital.

"We need to find Alice. I don't care what she thinks. We're safer together. We can work this out together."

"Jack!" Sophie said, stopping and spinning to face him. "I think that Alice proved in the garage that she can take care of herself. I'm worried about her too, but not for her physical safety. I can't explain it, but there's something deeper going on here. Something more personal," Sophie said, as she entered the front lobby of the hospital.

"What am I supposed to do Sophie?"

"Pray Jack. Pray hard for both of us, and right now, I need you to leave me alone too. Please," she said with a penetrating look, and then she went to the nurse's station to enquire about the man who had just been brought into emergency.

Jack stood for a moment, unsure. He didn't want to leave Sophie alone, but he knew her well enough to know not to push her. Looking at the directory, he noted the location of the chapel and headed toward it.

Shane entered the lobby from emergency just as Sophie was talking with the nurse.

"Do you know him?" Shane asked.

Startled Sophie turned to face Shane.

"Alice?" Shane asked, as he took in her facial features.

"Who are you?" she asked.

"It's okay," Shane said, as he opened his badge. "You are Alice Morgan. Aren't you? We've met before at one of your mother's charity events."

"I think we need to talk detective."

"I couldn't agree more," Shane said, as he motioned her to sit with him at a nearby couch. "Can I buy you a coffee?" he asked, nodding to a kiosk in the corner.

"Okay." Sophie wasn't sure how to proceed with this, but she hoped to get as much information as possible from him before saying much herself. "I'll take a plain medium Latte."

Keeping one eye on her, Shane gave their orders to the barista. As he waited, he wondered where to start. He was concerned by what Selma had told him, yet his nose was calm, and he sensed no danger or hostility from her.

"What do you know about that man?" Sophie asked, before Shane had a chance to ask her the same. "What's wrong with him?"

"How do you know him?" Shane asked as he sat and handed her drink to her.

Alice opened the Bible Sophie had given her. She had never felt so many conflicting emotions. Fear, both that the man would live and that he would die. Love, hate, anger, pity, all welled up alongside the fear to create a turmoil that made her feel she would burst. She felt fragmented and unknowable even to herself. "Who am I?" she sobbed, looking up at the altar of the chapel where a life-size Jesus hung from the cross.

Jack hadn't dared go in. He didn't want to risk her pushing him away and running again, so he simply stood by the door and watched her through the window in it.

Claire looked up as Meschner entered the plane. His ear had a bloodied mesh bandage taped to it.

"Where are they? What did you do with my sister and my babies? You..."

"Now, now," said Meschner as he put a hand over her mouth. "Is that any way to talk to the only man who can save your pathetic life?"

Claire managed to bite one of his fingers, and he yanked his hand away.

"Shit! Like mother like daughter!"

She glared up at him.

"Yes, it was one of your poor babies that did this to me," he said pointing to his ear. "I guess it just proves my point though. The evil does triumph. Just the one additional gene, stimulated just enough." Meschner started laughing uncontrollably. "It's perfect! Of course, your precious Rosie isn't able bodied enough, but the others are, and they'll make great little breeders for my army."

"You're psychotic."

"Maybe. Many great men are."

"My Rosie never hurt anyone, and Alice..."

"Oh? Alice, the one near perfect specimen. She's the one who did this. She bit it clean off, and it hurts like the devil. As for precious Rosie, consider it my Christmas gift for what you're about to help me with. She's sleeping right in there," he said pointing to another cabin. "I don't know how you can stand to look at her, but a mothers love is blind I guess."

"You don't know what love is. You're a monster!" Claire spat.

"A monster? Really Claire. I've developed techniques for life. Would a monster do that? Would a monster help make families or cure the incurable? No Claire. I think that puts me closer to a god. I can even control good and evil to an extent, and yet I recognize free will. I'm sounding more and more like a god all the time. Wouldn't you agree now?"

Chapter Forty-Four

Thomas Marshall knew that this was his only option. He had come to Quebec to confront his half-brother once and for all. This had to stop, and he had to be the one to face his fears and take a stand. He had considered confronting him during the lecture but feared what he might do to Sophie.

Everywhere he had turned, Sophie had been there too. She'd managed to find one of her sisters. He smiled. He was happy for that, but he also knew that the truth would be exposed now, and there was no escaping his part in it. He thought about the others and wondered if they were still alive. Then he thought about Patricia. She was as much his as Tom was, no matter how that maniac had tried to claim her as his own. He knew that after everything came to light that Tom would probably hate him. His career and reputation would be destroyed. There'd be no more mission trips, but there would also be no more running or hiding. He was tired and far too many people had been hurt. His only prayer was that he could somehow prevent Patty from ever finding out about him. She had thought him dead for years, and that's what he wanted her to continue to think. At least he would have one child who might still love him, or at least his memory.

He had followed his brother to the airfield after spotting him leaving the parking garage in the van. The plane had just started to taxi when he accelerated and jumped the median to drive across the tarmac, honking. The plane wasn't slowing down, so he parked directly in its path.

Following the directions that Jonathan had given them,

L'Coure and Rene' raced as fast as they dared down the icy road toward the private airfield. They arrived just in time to see the front wheel graze the vehicle that had tried to block its path and ascend into the night sky.

After taking his statement, the agent that had questioned Jonathan left him waiting in the interrogation room. When he returned, an alarm was blaring, and Jonathan had disappeared.

"How the hell?" he asked entering the room and staring at the broken glass and dislodged bars of the window.

***

Marquet got the call from L'Coure just as his taxi pulled up to the airport terminal.

The first suspect, Jonathan had somehow escaped after giving a statement pointing to his brother Richter and their father, Dr. Meschner as the true culprits.

Richter, according to the hospital, was now suffering from massive organ failure. Without a miracle there was no way he'd survive the night, and Meschner had managed to leave on a private jet headed for Geneva.

"Were you able to get an ETA?" Marquet asked.

"6:33 AM."

"Okay. Give this number to McDougal and tell him to update agent Katz. He's already in Geneva and familiar with the case. I'm on my way to you, and that bastard had better not die until I get a chance at him!"

"You sound like McDougal."

"If you knew the case, you'd feel the same. He's the prime suspect in the kidnapping of a mother and her five-year-old daughter. The mother showed up five months later. She'd had an abortion, but her husband swears she wasn't pregnant when she disappeared, and the little girl was never found. She's still a mess. Had to be institutionalized for her own safety."

"And how was McDougal involved?"

"The same man was seen with his wife before she disappeared."

"Shit! No wonder!"

***

Patty had been angry at Mathias, but her mind was far more distracted with thoughts of Shane. How could she ever explain to him, she wondered, as the babies kicked. Why had she left with him? She had truly trusted Richter at first. Why? She should have been smarter than that. It terrified her to think that they shared the same genes and the explanation for it had terrified her even more.

What if Shane had moved on? A part of her hoped that he had. He'd be better off without her. Even if he still loved her, she couldn't expect him to ever accept the babies. Not only were they not his, they were... Well, she'd have to wait and see. For her it didn't matter. She was still their mother, and she had to protect them. Maybe she could go back to the convent?

Eventually she had fallen asleep, exhausted. When she finally awoke, it was to a view of the Space Needle far below, as they gradually descended through the clouds. It was an unusually sunny day for December in Seattle. The rooftops were smattered with a thin layer of snow as they glided over Burien and onto a runway at Sea-Tac.

***

"Are you the ones waiting for information on the man we brought in from next door?" A young doctor, whose name badge read Dr. Korin, asked Shane and Sophie, as he entered the hospital lobby.

"Yes," Shane answered.

"Are you family?"

"A detective," Shane answered. "Please tell me he hasn't died yet. I need to pick his brain about some missing persons."

The young doctor looked taken aback at Shane's tone. "Well detective, his brain is about the only thing not losing function. We're doing what we can to flush his system, but his kidneys are gone, and his liver might as well be. The only good news is that his heart seems to be stabilizing. He has intestinal hemorrhaging, and the only way you'll ever get to pick his brain is if we can find a blood donor in the next hour or less, so that we can go in. This guy has the weirdest blood work up I've ever seen. We don't know if it's an infection or what, but we can't even verify a blood type."

"Shit! The only relatives I know of just made their escape to Geneva!"

"What?" asked the doctor.

"Excuse me," Sophie spoke up. "I might..."

Shane turned to stare at her.

"I may be his sister."

"Might be?" asked the doctor.

"What? Alice?"

"My name is Sophie Mr. McDougal, and I was adopted. I can't explain now, but I think we have to at least try. Don't we doctor?"

"Come with me Miss?"

"O'Hare."

Sophie hurried along behind the doctor as Shane stared dumbfounded and then followed after them. As they entered the ICU though the doctor gave Shane a stern look and forbid his entry. Shane would have ignored this had it not been for the burley guard nearby and his lack of jurisdictional authority.

Shane was surprised when he was met by a man in the hallway, as he headed back toward the lobby.

Jack had seen a glimpse of Sophie, as she hurried down the hall behind the doctor. He had watched as Shane was turned away and waited for him.

"Excuse me. Sir?"

"Yes?"

"My cousin, the girl you were following down the hall, what's going on?"

"Your cousin? What would her name be?" Shane asked, as he pulled out his badge.

"Seattle? You're here because of the Morgans?"

"And you are?" Shane asked.

"Jack. Jack Wilson," he said, offering his hand to Shane.

"Okay Jack. Maybe you can clear up a few things for me. I spent the last twenty minutes in the lobby with a woman I believed to be Alice Morgan, only to have her tell me her name is Sophie, and that she may be the sister of the man we have in custody in ICU."

"Sister?"

"Funny. She didn't seem too sure either. So, let's you and I have a chat so I can at least figure out who's who. I'm getting tired of feeling like the underdog on my own case," Shane said pointing toward the chapel. "It'll be private in there."

"Actually, there's someone in there."

"Well then, the lobby it is. Coffee?" Shane asked pointing to a vending machine. "They just closed the espresso bar in the lobby, and I don't know about you, but ..." Shane continued, as he fed change into the machine.

"Sure. Thanks. Black is fine." Jack's nerves felt as if they were on their last end. He was more scared for Alice and now Sophie than ever. In all honesty, coffee was probably the last thing he needed, but he took it and followed Shane into the lobby.

Alice was jarred from her meditation on what she was

reading by an image of blood. Her eyes shot open and up to the crucifix above and then darted around the chapel. Even though the room appeared empty, she had an overwhelming sensation that she was not alone. She tried to stand up and leave but was overcome by dizziness. She touched the spot behind her ear and nearly passed out from the pain. It was inflamed again and hot to the touch. She was hot she realized suddenly, just like with the fever she had had before. Then she realized she had not taken her pill that day.

Here she was at a hospital, feeling helpless with the image of Jesus staring down on her, and she was angry as the tears streamed down her face. "What? What am I? What am I supposed to do?"

The Bible Sophie had given her had fallen and lay open to Colossians chapter one beside her. She picked it up to try and read some more, but the tears wouldn't let her. She tried to stand. She suddenly wanted to run away again. Instead, she fell, hitting her head hard against a chair.

The sound of her falling caught a passing nurse's attention and minutes later she was hurried into the emergency room.

"What happened to her? No wait!" said Dr. Nadier, who was in charge of the ER. Looking at Alice, he pulled back a curtain to where Sophie was resting. "Put her right there," he said, pointing to the bed next to Sophie.

Sophie was faint from having given as much blood as they'd allow, but when she saw Alice, she tried to sit up. "Alice?" she started to ask, as a nurse gently pushed her back down.

"Twins?" asked doctor Korin.

"Apparently," Dr. Nadier replied.

"Your sister's burning up," Dr. Korin said to Sophie.

"Behind her ear," Sophie answered.

"What?"

"I'll get this," said Dr. Nadier. "You go check on the man."

Sophie watched as Dr. Korin left, and the nurse went to check on whoever was in the next cubicle. Dr. Nadier took Alice's temperature, pulled back her hair and examined the swelling. He then checked to make sure no one else was watching, as he went to a bag that was labeled evidence. The officer left to guard the man and evidence had gone to take a phone call, and the doctor wasted no time at all in taking two vials. He turned and caught Sophie's gaze. "You need to rest," he said, as he took another vial from a cabinet, filled a needle, and went to Sophie.

She tried to sit up again. "Who are you?"

He managed to grab her arm. She tried to struggle as he jabbed the syringe into her already sore arm into the exact spot where they had drawn her blood.

"Don't worry. It won't even leave a mark."

Next, he turned and injected Alice with the two other drugs. He then called the nurse back and hurried Alice into the operating room adjacent to where Richter was.

A half hour later he had removed one of her kidneys. "Not to worry, we'll replace it later," he said to the unconscious Alice, as he sewed up the incision. He called an orderly then to watch her vitals while he delivered the kidney to the surgical staff next door.

When he returned, he made about a centimeter incision behind Alice's ear and removed a small black disk. "That was old technology my dear," he said. "Shaun," he said to the orderly. "This woman has a visual laceration, and I need my nurse to stay with the other patient, but we have to try and save her sight, so I need you to go to Meschner's office next door and bring the box in the second cabinet from his desk on the third shelf up. Can you do that Shaun?"

"Wasn't it blocked off as a crime scene Dr. Nadier?"

"That may be, but this is an emergency, and what I need has

nothing to do with their case."

"Well..." Shaun stuttered.

"Should I let this innocent young woman go blind?"

"No sir. I'll be right back."

Shane and Jack had been talking for two hours when the surgeon who had worked on Richter, Dr. Cidik came out to tell them that everyone was in recovery, and if he was lucky, Shane would be able to question Richter in the morning along with the local agents. For now, they should go back to their hotel and try to get some sleep.

"What about Sophie? She only gave blood," Jack asked.

"Her vitals are fine, but she appears to be exhausted. I think it's probably best if you just leave her to sleep, and the other one will need to stay a few days."

"Other one?"

"Her sister."

"What's happened to Alice?" Jack asked in alarm.

"Let me check," Dr. Cidik said. "I was in surgery with the man when she came in."

"For what?"

"So, they're both here? Everyone together. Now that sounds like a nice change for me," Shane sighed. "I'll be needing to question them all."

"And you should be able to. You'll just have to wait until the morning. It looks like the sister was brought in with a high fever, concussion, and an optical laceration. I'm sorry, that's all the information I have."

"Can I see her?" Jack asked.

"In the morning."

Just then Shane's phone went off again. He had ignored her first calls, wanting to stay focused on what was right here in front of him, but he seemed to be at a standstill now. "Don't go anywhere," he said to Jack, as he answered the call.

"Hey Lidia...What? Book a flight for me and call me back. I'm on my way to the airport!" Shane said, hardly able to grasp what she had told him. "I have to go! Shane pushed the same number he had gotten for a taxi service earlier that morning and ordered a cab. Then he called L'Coure back and told him about Jack and Patty. "Where are you staying Mr. Wilson?" he asked Jack.

"I'm not going anywhere until I know Sophie and Alice are both safe."

"He says he'll be here, and I believe him. Call Marquet, tell him everything I told you, and that I'll call him as soon as I land in Seattle."

***

At his bed and breakfast Soren listened to everything he had recorded on his phone of the conversation. He had also managed to snap a couple of covert photos. They were fuzzy, but recognizable. The man he had recognized from Quebec was headed back there on a red eye. He had told the other man that the woman had done her job well, and she could count on treatment for the girls. What did it all mean?

Soren felt as though he had hit a dead end. As he considered the connection to the Marianas again, he knew he couldn't just pick up and go. He couldn't leave Magdeline this close to the birth.

Getting on his laptop, he first looked up the names of the speakers from the convention he had been at the year before. He was in luck there at least. Each one had a photograph next to their name. The man at the restaurant had been a Dr. Caleb Jordan.

***

Mr. O'Hare sent his wife home and boarded the plane with the other man. They would have to act fast if the deal was going to work. What he hated most was knowing that he'd never see his family again. It was the only way though. The only way to keep them safe was basically to sell his soul.

***

Dr. Marshall had gone to a hotel after his near miss with the plane. He didn't know what he should do. Maybe he should just go back as planned to one of the remote villages where he had been able to help so many. Then he thought about Anne and Ben. He had to confess to what he knew.

In the morning, he picked up the phone and dialed his son. "I have to tell you something important Tom," he started, but was cut off by Tom's own excitement that Anne was awake.

"Has she said what happened?" he asked and was told that he hadn't heard any details yet. "Tom, listen son. I know this won't make sense, but please tell Anne and Ben and Jack that I'm sorry. I love you and I want you to know that I didn't believe in what he was doing. I tried to, I did save as many as I could. I just need you to know that. I love you son," he finished and hung up unable to say more. Taking some hotel stationary from a desk in his room, he wrote to Tom what he could not speak. He wrote a letter to Sophie as well. When he had finished, he put them in a hotel envelope, posted them in the lobby and paid for two more nights.

The air was filled with Christmas carols as he made his way through the crowds of shoppers and students. He wasn't sure why or what he hoped to find, but he made his way to his brother's office. There were a couple of police just outside and he followed behind them, listening as they made their way over to the hospital.

***

Phillip Katz was ready and waiting at the airstrip in Geneva, and Meschner was in cuffs before he was even out of his seat. An ambulance was there as well for Claire and Rosie, who were taken to a local hospital. Meschner soon followed them as he claimed he was in agony from his injured ear, which had begun bleeding profusely.

***

Jack had just left Sophie and Alice who were both still, to the doctor's lack of understanding, unconscious. Their vitals and reflexes were normal however, so they would wait before further testing.

As he entered the lobby he saw through the windows, two police officers walking toward the entrance, and following close behind was Dr. Marshall. Jack could hardly believe it. Their eyes met briefly through the glass.

***

Nick had spent the night on edge. They had all known that this was much larger than just Alice and Sophie, but after hearing about Jack's encounter with Detective McDougal, he was relieved to hear that though Dr. Meschner and his colleagues were under investigation for kidnapping, they did not seem to have knowledge yet of the experiments they had performed. Jack and Nick agreed to the importance of protecting Alice and Sophie however they could from the physical probing that would result if the truth of their conception were to be known. He was looking through the files again that Jack had found and trying to separate out just enough evidence to give the authorities without including anything that may be tied back to Alice or Sophie, when there was a knock on his door. He was surprised to see Tom there.

Tom looked like he'd been run over by a truck. Nick had

always liked Tom, but with the possibility of his father's involvement, he was leery of the visit. It had to be ten below outside though, so he opened the door, and offered Tom a cup of coffee as he tucked away the files.

"Cream and sugar?" Nick asked, trying to sound casual.

"Please." Tom stirred the coffee silently. "I just received a very concerning phone call from my father. I have no idea what he was talking about or even where he is, but he mentioned Jack and his parents. Jack wasn't home or answering his phone, so I ... I don't know... I'm scared Nick. He sounded really upset and then the phone went dead. Dad missed his shift at the hospital, but the police can't do anything at this point, and you're the only other person I thought might know something? You're Jack's best friend and... Do you know anything?"

"What did he say when he called?"

"He said that he loved me, and that he wanted me to tell Jack and his parents that he was sorry, and that he didn't agree with what was being done, and that he tried to save as many as he could. Then he repeated that he loved me and hung up. I'm really worried!"

"How much do you know about your fathers work?"

"What?"

"What do you know about Sophie's medical history?"

"Excuse me?" Tom asked, standing.

"It's connected." Nick wasn't sure where he was going with this, but he had just thought of something and wanted to verify his suspicions. "You knew how to treat her infection in New York, yet you're only a few years older than her, so you must have gotten the records from her previous doctor which was your father?"

"Dad was in the mission fields most of the time. You know that."

"Were you with him?"

"Sometimes and sometimes when he went somewhere he thought was too dangerous, he left me with my grandparents. My mom's parents. She died when I was young so they, but..."

"Who was Sophie's doctor?"

"I don't remember his name, someone from the hospital in Halifax, I think. What does this have to do with my dad though?"

"You don't know anything?"

"No! You clearly do though!"

"I only know that your dad knew what was going on," Nick said, as he walked to a cupboard, removed the file and brought it over. "He knew about this," he said, laying the folder in front of Tom. "I don't know what his part was in it, but he knew about it."

"What the hell is this? Where did this come from?" Tom asked, as he opened to one of the photos, and a look of horror covered his face.

"Does the name Meschner mean anything to you?"

Tom sat silent as he thought back. "I used to have an uncle Meschner, my dad's half-brother. He was a scientist somewhere in Europe, but I think he's dead. Why?"

"So that's how they're connected!"

"Who?"

Nick turned on the television and replayed the news from earlier that morning. "Your uncle was arrested this morning. This file is at least partly his work. Your dad knew about it. This is what he was trying to tell you about."

"Dear God in heaven. Surely dad didn't participate in this. He couldn't have," Tom said, as he stared at another one of the photos of a severely deformed fetus. "This is insanity!"

"Agreed."

"I have to find him. Confront him with this."

"He's in Quebec."

"How do you know that?"

"Because Jack followed him there right after his mother told him."

"How could Jack have talked to Anne? She just came around last night. How?"

"She started coming around before, but she was scared. She was scared of your father finding out, because she was going to expose him, expose this. She had been to see your dad when the accident, if that's what you want to call it, happened."

"Now you're trying to say my dad is responsible for Anne's accident?"

"No. I'm saying that her finding out about this, and that someone, not necessarily your dad, was behind it. At least from what she told Jack, that's the theory, but maybe you should ask her."

"I need to find my dad!" Tom said, grabbing the file and striding toward the door.

"Whoa! That stays here!" Nick said, as he wrenched the file from Tom's hands. Then he made a final decision and tossed it into the fireplace.

"What are you doing?"

"I think this has already caused enough harm," Nick said, as he blocked Tom from pulling it out. "Look Tom, I've known you for years. I want to believe you and to believe that your dad is sorry for whatever part he had in this. I really do. So, let's work together. I'll call Jack. If he sees it's me, he'll answer. I think you need to tell him about your dads call. I have to go over to the farm for Ben. You can come with me. We'll put Jack on speaker and see what we can figure out. Okay?"

Tom followed Nick to his car, got in and waited as Nick turned the heat on, and dialed Jack as the windows defrosted.

***

The two officers continued through the lobby and back to ICU. Dr. Marshall wasn't sure what to do. He knew he had to face Jack.

It was then that Jack's phone rang, and he answered it.

"Listen Nick, you'll never believe who just showed up," he said as Dr. Marshall entered... Well, that's quite a coincidence. Uhuh...put him on." Jack extended the phone toward Dr. Marshall. "This is actually for you, but I sure would like to listen in, so let's go have a seat," Jack said, pointing to a group of chairs in the corner away from the now busy espresso bar.

"Dr. Jordan?" Sophie asked, as she looked up groggily into the face of her old pediatrician. "What are you doing here?"

"Your parents called me as soon as they found out you were here and asked me to check on you."

"My parents? Where are they?"

"They're sorry, but they weren't able to get a flight. Everything is booked, but I'm here, and I'm sure you're going to be just fine and back home in no time. It seems you had an adverse reaction to some medication."

"Medication, but all I did was give blood."

"You gave blood?"

"Yes. She gave blood," L'Coure said, as he entered through from emergency and showed his ID. "She saved a life. A life I'm about to question, but I'd like to speak with her first if I may Dr.?"

"Dr. Jordan. I'm her doctor from Halifax. I was here, and her parents asked me to check on her," he continued, noting L'Coure's look of confusion.

"And her?" L'Coure questioned, as he looked at Alice.

"Sophie was adopted. I only found out about her sister today. You'll have to ask at the nurse's station who her doctor is."

"I'll do that, but first, if you don't mind?"

"I'll be right outside," Dr. Jordan said.

"Who are you?" Sophie asked.

"Detective L'Coure." he said, holding his badge out again for her to see.

"I was drugged last night detective and so was Alice, by another doctor. We're not safe here. He did something. He took Alice away and did something," Sophie said, trying to sit up and look at Alice.

"Whoa. You just stay put. What did they do to her?" L'Coure asked, as he picked up a chart off the end of Alice's bed "According to this she suffered a corneal abrasion from a fall."

"He did something to her. I know he did detective," Sophie said, as she swung her legs over the side of the bed. He caught her, as she tried to stand. "What did he give us?" Sophie asked, blinking hard to try and stabilize the room, as L'Coure helped her to sit on the side of the bed.

"Can you describe this other doctor, Sophie?"

"I think so."

"Okay. I'll send in one of the officers to take your statement and description. What I came in here to find out though is what you might know about the suspect, and to thank you for keeping him alive for us. I was told you're his sister?"

"I'm afraid I don't actually know him detective. Like Dr. Jordan said. I was adopted. I only recently discovered I had siblings."

"And how did you discover this? "

"I met Alice by coincidence when we were both in New York. It was kind of obvious."

"And your brother?"

"Alice recognized him," was all she could think to say. Richter had fit the description of the man in Alice's dream to a 'T'. The only other link had been Meschner, and Sophie didn't want herself or Alice linked to him. If they found out what he had done, they might discover what she and Alice were. She didn't know if they had linked Richter to Meschner other than as an accomplice, she prayed not.

Jack and Dr. Marshall, after talking with Nick and Tom and hearing of Meschner's arrest had agreed. Though angry with the deception, Jack had gained an understanding of Meschner's reach and of why Dr. Marshall had done what he had. They also all agreed on the importance of protecting Sophie and Alice, and would therefore limit their statements.

They knew that just because he was behind bars, it didn't mean that anyone was safe yet. There were countless others involved in the research, however with both Meschner and Richter out of the picture, they prayed that the most horrific part of the project had been cut off, and that only the original intended good might continue on.

Then Jack asked about the O'Hares and what they knew.

"Mr. O'Hare had been a student here in Quebec when my... I don't want to call him my brother, was on staff. We studied together, and after I discovered what Meschner was up to I confided some of my concerns to him. I tried not to tell him anything that could have been a danger, but I can't swear to what he may have found out on his own. I did what I could to protect Sophie. I couldn't keep her myself, and I knew the O'Hares would be good parents to her."

"So, you're the doctor she lived her first years with?"

"Yes, and I would prefer it if she didn't know that. After this is over, I think it's best for everyone if I go back to Africa or the Amazon as I had originally planned, and you don't see me again."

"What about Tom?"

"I think by now he's used to me not being around, and if you can find it in your heart to not..."

"To not bring your name into my mom's accident? I'm afraid what she tells my dad is up to her, but I agree that this is better if it doesn't go any farther. For Sophie and Alice's sakes, we don't need any more questions."

"She will be okay, Jack, and I want to cover all of your expenses. It's the least I can do. Just let me know the amount."

Jack just looked at him for a long minute before holding his hand out. They shook. Jack wrote something on a piece of paper he took from a nearby desk and handed it to Dr. Marshall.

"Consider it done."

Marquet was relieved to find that the suspect had survived the night and went directly to the hospital to meet with L'Coure. Unfortunately, the suspect was still unconscious, as was Alice Morgan.

Sophie was shown photos of the medical staff, but she recognized none of them as the doctor who had drugged her and Alice. She was then released and asked to accompany the other officers along with Jack as well as Doctor Marshall to the station to make a formal statement and meet with a sketch artist. An extra guard would be left with Alice.

L'Coure and Marquet followed. Marquet also wanted to review the statement from Jonathan and see for himself the bars he had miraculously escaped through.

After giving their statements Dr. Marshall returned to his hotel. Tom had insisted on flying in that evening, and he looked forward to what may be the last dinner he would ever share with his son.

Chapter Forty-five

Sophie and Jack along with L'Coure and Marquet returned to the hospital only to be told that both Richter and Alice were being transported via helicopter to another hospital, some twenty miles away. The chopper had just taken off.

"On whose authority?" Marquet spat at the young intern who gave them the news. "Where are the guards?"

"Dr. Nadier signed the release. He said it was urgent. The other hospital is better equipped, and he said that he had been told to do everything in his power to keep the man alive. The guards went too, I think," the intern stammered.

"Why was the woman taken?"

"Something to do with her blood workup, I think. I don't really know."

"I don't suppose you know who this man is?" L'Coure asked, flashing the sketch.

"That's Dr. Nadier."

"Okay. L'Coure, let's head out. Do you two want to ride along?" he asked Jack and Sophie.

"You better believe we're coming!" Sophie said, as they all raced back to the car they'd arrived in, and L'Coure put the siren on.

Marquet looked through the file on the hospital personal they had showed Sophie earlier, only to discover that Nadier 's photo had been replaced by that of a woman. He forwarded her photo to headquarters to see if they could pull up anything on her identity.

***

Back in Seattle, Asher met Shane at the airport and escorted him to the hospital where Patty was being checked over.

He had gone over it a million times in his head, but he still didn't know what he would say to her.

Yarnok had left the Morgan's at their home under guard and come to meet them at the hospital. She had spoken with Patricia, who had asked that Lidia meet with Shane before he was let in to see her.

"She's scared Shane," Lidia said, as she pulled Shane aside on his arrival.

"Of me? Why Lidia? What did they do to her?"

"She's pregnant."

"I know."

"You do?"

"The brother of...I'll explain it all later. Where is she?"

"Follow me."

Patty was watching the screen of the ultrasound machine when Shane opened the door. She looked up, their eyes met, and then both looked at the ultrasound.

"They both look healthy," the tech said, "You must be the father?" she asked innocently, as Patty stared at the screen trying not to cry.

"Yes," Shane said, as he went to Patty. "Yes," he repeated, as he took her hand, and she looked at him, searching his face.

***

The explosion could be seen for miles as the ambulance chopper plunged into the St. Lawrence River.

The call came through on L'Coure's radio just as they had slowed in the traffic jam of onlookers.

There was no need to tell them. They had all heard and seen the same thing.

"Go! We have to go there now!" Jack shouted, looked around

at the jammed freeway, jumped from the car and started running in the direction of the crash.

Marquet went after him as L'Coure turned to Sophie. "I'm sorry," was all he could say, as he looked at her ashen face. She looked like a mannequin only her eyes gave her away as the tears overflowed.

Seattle: Christmas Eve Morning

The church overflowed with people for Alice's memorial. Edgar and Suzanna looked out at the faces, most of which they had never seen before. They sat to the side in front, between two plain clothed detectives. If Sophie or Jack wanted to talk to them, they would have to choose to do so themselves.

There were no words though as Sophie met their gaze and turned away. She still couldn't believe Alice was really gone. She could still feel her, but she had heard the explosion herself, seen the pictures of the wreckage and all the bodies had been accounted for. She was also mourning the loss of the man she considered to be her real father. Mr. O'Hare had not left so much as a note, but had simply vanished. Mrs. O'Hare said that he had met another woman and decided it was time to leave and embrace his new life. Sophie knew her mother was lying, but had no idea why, and when Sophie left for the memorial, Mrs. O'Hare went to visit with her sister in France.

Nick had wanted to come with Sophie to Seattle, but she had not wanted him to, and Jack asked him to keep an eye on his father and mother, who was now back home.

Shane and Patricia sat in the front row across from Jack and Sophie along with Selma, Dave, Lidia, Charice and Max.

Shane could hardly believe that in two short months he would be the father of twin boys. The past days back with Patty had been some of the most awkward, yet happy, he had ever had. He looked forward to putting this all behind them.

Patty on the other hand knew too much to believe that it could ever all be behind them. No one who knew had brought to light the full extent of the project behind everything that had happened. The authorities only knew of the labs in the Marianas, Geneva and Quebec. There had been no other arrests though, and by the time detectives reached the compound on the island, every trace had vanished. Patty knew they were out there somewhere, but she prayed that Mathias had done as he promised and put an end to the research. She also prayed hard that the twins could somehow be normal, and meeting Sophie had given her hope for that possibility.

She thought about the night Shane had brought her home. He had had someone put up a tree and they had spent the next day decorating it together, and every day she had woken to see a new package beneath it. She hugged his arm, and he kissed her forehead as the service commenced.

Geneva: Christmas Day

Magdeline had arrived at the hospital just past midnight and labor was slow. She had heard that Dr. Meschner was also a patient. She knew of his arrest and subsequent stroke after hearing of his son's death, but this was the man who had done the research that gave her the ability to walk. Although he was technically under arrest, as a doctor herself, she had gained special permission to visit him.

"He's in pretty bad condition. We're surprised he's survived this long," the doctor told her. "He probably won't even realize you're there."

"That's alright. I just want to thank him. "

"Thank him?" asked a guard, who Marquet had stationed outside Meschner's room.

"Yes. I was born paralyzed from the waist down and dealing with other degenerative issues. His research is why we're here," she said rubbing her abdomen, "and even able to walk today."

The guard opened the door to her, and she walked in.

He was staring out the window. She went around to the other side of his bed so that he needn't move to see her. "Dr. Meschner? My name is Magdeline. I also am a doctor studying genetic cures."

His pale blue eyes slowly looked up toward her face with its emerald gaze and seemed to widen.

Magdeline smiled. "I wanted to thank you for..."

"No." came the muffled whisper.

"Dr. Meschner?" She moved closer to him.

His eyes linked with hers and the heart monitor flat lined.

" REVIVAL"

Chapter One

Switzerland: December 21st 2018

Jonathan ran his fingers through his, now black, buzz cut hair. He thanked the barber, tipped him twenty francs, and made his way up the street to a sporting goods store. In the dressing room, he barely recognized himself. The carefully applied mustache and brown contacts had made his new look complete.

He hadn't wanted to do it. It would have been nice to live a normal life, but he knew too well that normal was something he could never be. None of them could. He also knew he had to protect himself. Regardless of how good Mr. McDougle or any of the others may have been at their jobs, he would have been dead by now if he hadn't left and nobody would have even realized it was murder. All it would take was a phone call. He knew there was a trigger hidden within him. Like a self-destruct button. In reality we all have triggers that can cause self-destructive actions, but most of us also have warning signs and a chance to get a grip, so to speak. Jonathan knew that if he were found he wouldn't have that chance. He knew too much to be left alive. Even if they didn't cause him to kill himself, they would turn him, and he would lose himself, much like Richter had been lost.

For a moment he wondered about Carl and Mathias. Granted

they had slightly different DNA, and he didn't know the complete DNA log for them. He did for himself though and aside from Meschner as a father, it was what he had learned about his birth mother that scared him the most.

***

She couldn't seem to stop shivering, and her eyelids were heavy. She had to open her eyes, to wake up. She tried to think. Her last memory had been of blood, a crucifix and a Bible, but where had she been? She couldn't remember. She just knew she was somewhere else now and it smelled terrible, like dead fish. She could hear someone else breathing shallowly nearby. She forced her eyes to open. Only a thin beam of light came through a nearby window in a door, but she could see now that the walls were indeed hung with dead fish. A freezer? She also saw the source of the other breathing. He lay not three feet away on a hospital bed, under some kind of plastic tented enclosure, and there were tubes going in and coming out of him in every direction. He looked familiar but her head was so foggy she could not place him. In fact, she realized, she wasn't sure who she was either.

Voices came from the other side of the door. They came closer, and she closed her eyes against the flood of light that came as they opened the door.

She lay as still as possible, willing herself to stop shivering and listen.

"I say as soon as she's conscious, we give her a test ride!"

"Be my guest, but I value my life! Can you imagine what would happen if he found out?"

"Look at him! He can't do a bloody thing and the old man is dead! We have enough money. I don't even know what the hell we're doing freezen our asses off in the middle of nowhere! I say we leave him, take her and head to the Caribbean."

"And how do you propose to get there Einstein? They're not stupid. There's a reason they dropped us out here in the middle of nowhere. My guess is it's a good twenty miles to even get to a road, so no thanks. She's pretty, but not worth it. Besides, Fritz said they'd be back in the morning."

She used all her will not to flinch as a finger traced the contour of her face. She could smell the alcohol on his breath, mingling with the scent of dead fish. She had a sudden urge to knock him out and make run for it. The way her adrenaline was building, she was sure that she could take them both and run fifty miles if she had to. That's when the realization hit that her hands were bound. Were her feet bound as well? She couldn't tell without trying to move them, which she didn't dare until the men were gone.

"At least let me give her the next injection Frankie. A boy's gotta have some fun and it's been way too long since I've seen...."

"Sober up, Eric!" Frankie warned, as he went to the man. "You remember what happened to Clause?"

That seemed to get Eric's attention, and he turned away from her.

"Okay. His vitals look good," Frankie said. "Let's get out of this deep freeze! I'll play you a round of five card stud. Winner gets to inject the princess there."

After the door closed, she opened her eyes again. The grogginess had lifted, though she still didn't know who or where she was, but she was determined she wasn't staying. Testing her feet, she could feel they were unbound. Pulling herself into a sitting position, she noted that she was zipped into a thermal sleeping bag on what appeared to be a hospital bed. Quietly she used her feet to pull the bag down her body and lowered it gently to the floor. Then she looked around for something she could use to help free her hands. The rope wasn't thick. Looking at the hooks that the fish hung on, she made her way to one which protruded at just the right level and used it to tear at the rope until it was so shredded that it broke easily when she twisted her wrists. Then she disconnected the hook to use as a weapon, climbed back onto the bed, into the sleeping bag, and waited.

Made in the USA
Columbia, SC
11 March 2022